GAR\

JOURNEY TO 2125

ONE CENTURY,

ONE FAMILY,

RISING TO CHALLENGES

Chiliagon Press
Napa, California

Chiliagon Press

1370 Trancas Street #710
Napa, California 94558
www.chiliagonpress.com

Published 2024

Publisher's Cataloging-in-Publication Data

Names: Bengier, Gary F. (Gary Francis), 1955—, author.
Title: Journey to 2125: One century, one family, rising to challenges / Gary F. Bengier.
Description: Napa, CA: Chiliagon Press, 2024.
Identifiers: LCCN: 2024912846 | ISBN 978-1-64886-114-7 (paperback) ISBN: 978-1-64886-112-3 (ebook)
Subjects: LCSH Artificial intelligence--Fiction. | Robots--Fiction. | Family--Fiction. | Science fiction. | BISAC FICTION / Science Fiction / Action & Adventure. | FICTION / Literary
Classification: LCC PS3602.E468 J68 2024 | DDC 813.6—dc23

First Edition
10 9 8 7 6 5 4 3 2 1

Of the many challenges ahead this century,
a few matter.
Focus on and overcome those few,
and you, yours, and the world
will survive, and perhaps even thrive.

Contents

The ebook edition contains links to the glossary for the first appearance of many technologies (and complementary links to return to the previous spot in the novel). For the print version, please rely on the twentieth-century technique of flipping to the back pages.

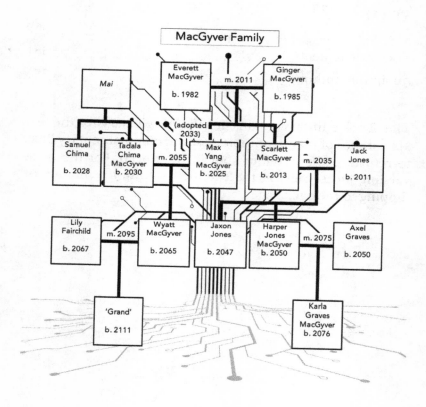

MacGyver Family

Mai

Everett MacGyver b. 1982

m. 2011

Ginger MacGyver b. 1985

(adopted 2033)

Samuel Chima b. 2028

Tadala Chima MacGyver b. 2030

m. 2055

Max Yang MacGyver b. 2025

Scarlett MacGyver b. 2013

m. 2035

Jack Jones b. 2011

Lily Fairchild b. 2067

m. 2095

Wyatt MacGyver b. 2065

Jaxon Jones b. 2047

Harper Jones MacGyver b. 2050

m. 2075

Axel Graves b. 2050

'Grand' b. 2111

Karla Graves MacGyver b. 2076

1

MAX YANG MACGYVER—2033 (TAIWAN), PRESENT, 2125 (CALIFORNIA)

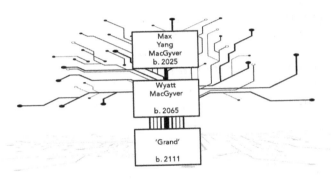

It begins with a splash, then rushing down the unknown river of life, each unique as Heraclitus said, around and through each oxbow and rapids, no doubt ending at an astonishing waterfall.

That visceral memory still wakes me after all these years—a recurring nightmare of bone-chilling cold water. Salt in my mouth and the burn in my eyes. The big man behind me pushes me up and I dog-paddle toward the white ship with the big red cross. People surround me in the water, crying, swimming. My life vest is too big, the straps loose, and the big man lifts me when a swell splashes over. I am tired, and my arms are heavy. I swallow seawater with each wave. Some people are sinking, and their heads disappear.

He hollers at me in Mandarin, his hard face close to mine. "Help me help you. Swim!"

We reach the ship, and he boosts me up to the thick, hanging rope net, and I grab hold and pull myself out of the cold water. It's like the playground bars, and I climb to the top.

I sit shivering on the deck next to the big man as a nice woman in white dries me with a towel and wraps me with a blanket. He tousles my hair, then he looks at me, and tears come from his eyes. I can tell he is thinking of someone else. His muscled hand is not too rough, though I still flinch when he reaches out. I lose track of the big man, and when the ship fills with so many people from the water like me, I don't see him again until days later.

The nice woman points me to a doorway to descend into the ship, but I duck to the side and stay by the railing to watch everyone else come up the net. I'm short, and it is noisy and crowded, so I can hide by the rail. The tiny boat is now empty. It drifts away from the ship.

Before we all jumped off the boat to get to the ship, a jet had roared overhead. Everyone screamed, and many had prayed. But the ship was near, and people on its deck watched, and nothing bad happened.

Now the boat's sail flaps in the wind, and it bobs sideways as the ship's engines vibrate the deck, and our big ship turns away.

The fishing boat grows smaller behind us, and the jet returns. It flies low over the little boat. Fire shoots from the jet, there is a huge explosion, and the boat is gone. I watch the pile of drifting wood where it had been. The jet streaks away. My heart beats in my chest like a drum. The nice woman in the white dress is back, and she takes me inside the ship.

"How old were you when this happened?"

I am brought back to 2125. To my grandson. To my story. "I was eight when we were rescued by the Americans."

He sits at the table eating eggs and bacon. He has a full head of black hair, as much as I ever had, but his is curly. Do his cheekbones resemble mine? He has an oval face with an attractive chin like so many in our family. Sadly, I see few signs of his grandmother in him, except for a softness around his mouth and fullness to his lips. His arms are tanned and muscular, more than I'd expect for a fourteen-year-old boy, like he spends time outdoors doing heavy labor.

"And the big man? Who was he?" His eyes are alive for the first time since he arrived near sunrise. Some of the trapped expression he wore then has disappeared. I'll tell him stories for a while and let him decide when to tell me his story.

"Someone who kismet placed on that fishing boat, and then swam for safety, like me. I know he was separated from his family because he was alone. I reminded him of someone close. I last saw him at the refugee center but never learned his name. Afterward, I never saw him again."

"He saved your life. If it weren't for him, I wouldn't be here." A shadow passes across his face. Good. My story has become personal to him.

"We make choices that affect other people, sometimes in profound ways. Sometimes they notice, but often they never know."

The allbook is on the end table. It feels solid. Books—such an old technology, and the antithesis of most of our tech, which now passes by voice and blinks through our AIs. I call up an old 2D photo to help me remember.

"Momma Ginger must have snapped this one a few months later in Berkeley."

Grandson looks at it with interest. "You were a cute kid."

"Yes. It didn't hurt my chances." I had an angelic face, looking hopefully toward the camera in the photo, dark brown eyes framed by straight hair, pure unwrinkled skin. I sat on a playground swing. As if through a distant mirror, I see the boy separated from me by a century minus eight years.

"Is that an earliest mem'ry?"

"No. Of course, I remember my birth mother and father. I recall details of growing up in Keelung City outside Taipei. I was their only child. We'd go to the night market, with colorful stalls and people milling around and the smell of food. Mama loved the crab soup. Baba—my dad—liked the stinky tofu." Like a sprite floating in the air, the pungent aroma is in my nose.

"What were your parents like?"

"Baba was tall and a bit gruff. He was a research chemist and spent long hours at work. I have this memory, sitting in the kitchen, of him making me memorize the periodic table of elements, however unsuccessfully."

Grandson snickers at this. Perhaps he relates as a young boy.

"Baba had a job with a global company and used English there, so we spoke both Mandarin and English at home. I've lost most of my Mandarin. Mama taught school, so she was home early every day. I remember her tucking me into bed."

Her voice comes softly to me, singing the lullaby:

Jīntiān wǒmen chéngzhǎng zài yángguāng xià,
Míngtiān wǒmen qù chuàngzào qī cǎi shìjiè.

Today we grow under the sunlight,
Tomorrow we will create a colorful world.

There she is again, standing next to Baba, both dim ghosts, their faces not sharp like the allbook photo of me. I have no photos of them since I brought nothing with me, and everything was lost in the rubble.

Was the memory of Mama from that last morning when they sent me off to school? It could be, because she looks worried, as they were for weeks before the attack. Everyone held their breaths, waiting, but life went on as before. My class took a field trip to the museum downtown.

Recollection of the day comes back sharp, ahead of his questions, and my heart is beating hard again. We are walking back when the bombs start to fall. The noise hurts my ears. Everyone runs like a spooked herd of animals, and I am by myself and running. I see the ocean, and two fishermen pull people onto the boat at the pier.

He crunches on the bacon. His eyes are curious now. "How did you land in a boat alone?"

"The Chinese were bombing the town. I was afraid of the explosions and ran away from my school friends. I jumped on a fishing boat."

"That's terrifying." Grandson reaches for the photo again and studies it. "So young. Pa never told me this story. Besides getting wet and cold, it sounds like that experience didn't traumatize you too much. You were lucky to find the boat and lucky the American ship picked you up."

The rest of the story comes brutally to mind. The part when the big man saved me, shoving me off the boat and into the water. It's the same then as now, that in times of acute distress most worry first about survival; humanity and our fellow men are a distant abstraction. A very few big men and women don't forget everyone else.

The man puts an adult-sized life vest on me. There are not enough vests to go around. I paddle beside him, the life vest hanging loose.

"Too big for him anyway," yells the other man in the water as he tries to steal my vest.

My head goes under, my mouth full of salt water. I can't breathe. I'm drowning. Then my head is up, and there's air again. The big man hits the other man on the head and wrestles with him, both shouting. The smaller man fights desperately, pulling me under water when he pulls on the vest. More salt water.

The big man holds him down until he stops struggling. "It was never yours. It belongs to the kid," he says then to no one.

The smaller man's limp hand disappears under a wave. The big man tightens the vest straps on me and begins towing me away from the boat. Everyone else swimming pretends not to see anything.

"Yes, lucky."

"Pa told me I was part Chinese and part other things, read from my DNA. He and Ma never mentioned details."

"The details are missing because your mother leads a simple life without modern science. Your Pa followed her."

My grandson pursues his and my roots. "What was your original family name?"

"My name was Max Yang. Max, because Western first names were already popular then. But I left Yang behind. At age eight, I became Max MacGyver. With no regrets." It's been my name for so long, and I'm proud of it. It's who I made myself.

I look him in the eye now over my eggs and smile. "It's good to see you. My only Grand. Do you mind if I call you that? It's grand to have a grandson."

His dark brown eyes stare back. "I'm not so sure what could be grand 'bout me. But you can call me that. Though I'm proud to be called a MacGyver. Pa said to never be ashamed of your name."

"That's a fact." However, he doesn't know how some people resented that association. He'll learn about that history in due time.

"Shall I call you Grandpa?"

"Let's go with Grandfather. Then we'll both be grand." I prefer to leave that 'Pa' in the Piney Woods, or in whatever century that it belongs. I like the grand and proper. So one should live one's life.

The robot comes from the kitchen with a tray of drinks. Robert's oval head swivels toward Grand, the eyebrows raised in inquiry mode. "Coffee, tea, cappuccino, or salakorange juice, young sir?"

Grand seems confused, and I help him out. "Salakorange juice is from a bioengineered fruit, popular these days."

"Salakorange juice, please. And a glass of water."

Grand finishes breakfast before anything to drink arrives. He likely hasn't eaten since before stepping on the train. Robert sets down Grand's two drinks and then serves me my usual cappuccino. I begin to eat the eggs and toast on my plate. Robert moves to stand at attention near the wall. Grand tastes the juice. His eyes light up with surprise, and he sips again.

How sheltered is his life there, deep in the woods in East Texas? And why does he choose to leave now? "Did you come here to wish me a happy birthday? That was last month."

"I heard that you turned one hundred, but no, that ain't the reason. But happy birthday, Grandfather."

I learned to fish a long time ago in Yosemite, and now I dangle a line to find what he is hungry for, and to put together what he knows. "So, why the sudden mysterious message? I didn't know that you had my contact ID."

"I'm pretty good at figurin' out 'lectronic stuff. I got it from Pa's contacts."

The robot's lenses move back and forth between us. Robert is recording all this.

Grand cradles the juice glass and bites his lip. Was he going to tell me anything? I eat the eggs and wait.

"It was disheartenin' living there. I had some ideas about how to make life a bit easier, but they wouldn't listen. Not much patience with any new idea. I didn't like everyone telling me what to do. Everyone was repeatin' the same things that the Commune leadership said."

"So you got fed up, and decided to leave?"

Grand's face hardens. The trapped expression returns. "I couldn't take it anymore."

"Understandable. Well, glad to have you here."

It has been too many years since Grand and his father, Wyatt, last visited. How did I allow that to happen in the family? The hurricane that pummeled the Commune kept them busy with cleanup. That was followed a year later by the fire, and further rebuilding. They weren't encouraging visitors.

But the real reason was because Lily, Grand's mother, wanted to forget the real world, to keep him a child, to shield him from the truth. Still, I should have pushed more to see him, and his appearance today makes for both joy and regret. "It seems you had no trouble traveling here."

"I stole a com unit to message you first. Thanks for sending the money, pass, and train ticket. I put 'em in the com unit. A big robot stopped me at the Commune's south gate, but it let me by when I showed the pass. I got to the train station on foot, a good hike. I figured out how to hop on the right train. It was a long trip. And the robot here met me with the autocar at the station."

"Very enterprising."

At the word "stole," Robert's lenses flick back and forth again, and a metal eyebrow rises toward me. "Sir, perhaps the boy's parents should be informed of his whereabouts?"

"The young man is fourteen. I can decide when to tell them. There're no reasons under the law to report anything, correct?" I don't disguise a glare. Robert has been more presumptuous since the latest software update. But the robot nods yes and stands against the wall.

Grand leans closer at the bot's question, making his rumpled clothes and dirty face obvious. He traveled all night, no doubt with only catnaps on the train.

"Grand, I'm sure you'd like to shower and change into clean clothes. Then we can talk more. I'll sit here and enjoy my cappuccino." He smiles gratefully, and Robert leads him to the guest suite and bathroom.

The robot returns.

"Robert, did the new clothing we ordered for Grand arrive? It looks like we guessed his size about right."

"Sir, the drone will deliver them in seven minutes. I will go outside now to await the landing."

"Thank you, Robert." I look out the window and sip. Robert walks into view outside, and soon a delivery drone is visible against the blue sky, its black shape gliding like a raven. It approaches and settles on the lawn.

The ocean sparkles in the distance, too far away to hear. It will be a good day for a stroll. While we walk, I need to figure out what he wants to do next. But first, I must learn what he already knows. Given all that has happened these last years, maybe they've kept him more in the dark than I imagined possible.

Now that he is here, the task feels paralyzing. Once I discover how much of the family story he's missing, I'll have to disclose some parts. I've long contemplated this conversation, both wishing for and dreading it.

My hand quivers around my cup. There's a bitterness in my throat, not from my drink but rising from my very soul—an angst from holding these secrets inside. What should I share? What dark secrets should be left buried for his own good?

We'll start the story from the beginning. I'll call it a hundred-year story. The story of the MacGyver family.

2

'GRAND'—PRESENT, 2125 (CALIFORNIA)

The shower feels warm against my skin, but I get a chill thinking about Grandfather's story, swimming for his life. He was younger than me. I'm having a hard time being away from home for only the second time, but I reckon hard times is relative. No one threatened to kill me yet, though that big robot at the Commune didn't look friendly. Ma said never to trust 'em.

Another chill goes through me, recollectin' the robot that appeared out of the gloom like some animal ready to attack. I couldn't run because its head was shining a bright light in my eyes. I raised my hand, even though it was shakin' so bad, showed it the pass flashing on the com, and held my breath.

"Young sir," said the voice, all deep and rumbly, "you may go," and it moved out of my way. And then I *did* run, before it changed its mind.

The bathroom door opens, and the robot Robert barges in. "Your new clothing, young sir."

I feel naked, 'cause I am naked, and 'cause there's almost no one in the Piney Woods to spy on you skinny-dipping in the river except the drones. It doesn't bat an eye at me and just leaves the stack of folded clothes. Seems this Robert is programmed the same way as that one at the Commune, which was too dumb to think that the com unit was stolen.

The towel feels good. Fluffy material is not the only soft thing in this new place. Natural stone covers the bathroom, smooth and shiny. I peek into the bedroom. It's beautiful too. Huge with a big bed, soft light streaming through the windows, and the ocean in the distance. Grandfather has a nice house, all to his self.

The Commune houses are tiny, and we make the furniture ourselves in the wood shop. Rocky would stand there and tell me to be careful with the saw whenever I made anything. He always hung by my side like a cautious little brother.

I got to be leader, and he followed behind, out into the forest until he got scared and said we had to stop. We'd hide in the tall grass above the lake and wait for deer to come by to drink. He'd make a noise, and they'd run off, and he'd look at me sheepish and sorry. I taught him later not to make any sound so we could watch all the animals living there. Rocky found allbook articles about how to track animals, and we practiced and learned about all of 'em.

Rocky came to the door every day, asking for me. Ma was not too sweet on him, but Pa defended him. One time Ma and Pa got into it right in front of me. I shrank into the kitchen chair and heard every word.

Pa said I needed friends, and there weren't many kids there. He said Rocky was essential for my education because home schooling only goes so far.

"But he's learning that accent. Another insidious oppression for me."

Pa said, like it's an explanation, "It's the local dialect in the Piney Woods." Then Ma clenched her hands and stormed off, while Pa rolled his eyes at me and shrugged his shoulders. I feel sorry for Pa at times like that when Ma gets distraught and into her head.

Hardly anyone visits the Commune; just drones unloading supplies on the landing pad. I was happy enough going off into the forest every day without the adults saying much. I'd tote my allbook and we'd go to the creek, and I'd read to Rocky and we'd talk about the stories. I like tellin' tales.

My chest feels tight, and I'm sorry I didn't say goodbye to Rocky when I left, but it's best because he couldn't have come with me. It's hard leaving your best friend.

I always thought that when you got older, everything would make sense. But it's the opposite. Ma is more jumpy, looking at me with her face anxious, like she's afraid to lose me. Pa used to give advice, knowing all sorts of things about the forest and life, but lately he mostly worries about Ma. Now without Rocky too, I'm alone in the world, without their voices to tell me anything.

The jeans fit nice and comfortable. There's a new blue shirt that fits too. I comb my hair. I'm dressed and now can find Grandfather.

He can tell me about the family, and I can figure out why Ma and Pa decided to join the Commune. That's what I got to find out. Then, I can decide what to do next.

Grandfather is sitting and drinking his special coffee. I've never had one, and it might be an interestin' experience. "I'll try one of those too."

Grandfather nods to the robot, who returns to the kitchen to fetch me one. "You don't mind spending the day with me?"

"No. That'd be fine. I haven't thought too far ahead."

"We can walk around the property a bit later. I need to keep the body moving. Or else."

Grandfather's words shake me, but he has a wry grin sayin' it, so he's joking. I see him in full, how ancient he is. He's tall, but he stoops over, his gray hair combed neatly across his brow. There wasn't gray hair like his around the Commune. Ma and Pa use some sort of medicine to keep their hair regular, but Grandfather doesn't seem to care. He's gruff to the robot, but he looks at me with big kind eyes surrounded by deep wrinkles, making them look farther away like he's seen a lot.

The bot returns with my cappuccino. I take a little sip. It's more bitter than I expected, but it might perk me up. "What happened next, after being rescued?"

"I know now that it was a hospital ship. Those were the only American ships that came close to Taiwan during the invasion, and they carried away many thousands of refugees."

"Is that why the Chinese jet didn't attack?"

"Yes. It would have been a war crime for that Chinese plane to attack the fishing boat filled with civilians or the hospital ship. I was lucky to find both."

"That's how you came to America."

He nodded. "A refugee arriving in California. I don't remember much about the crossing except that the boat was crowded, and it was rolling during some high seas. I got sick. I think we went to Okinawa, and then they put me on an airplane to California, to a refugee center in Berkeley. That is where I met Momma Ginger. Ginger MacGyver."

The drink rolls creamy on my tongue. "So, this is how you and all of us became MacGyvers. No one's ever told me before."

An expression comes over Grandfather's face, like he's been aching to tell someone these last years. "Since you have the day, relax, and I'll tell you the story of our family."

3

Ginger MacGyver—2033 (California)

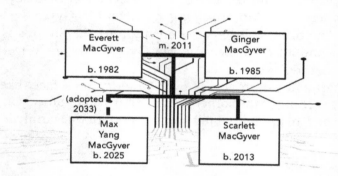

Ginger walked down the hill toward Telegraph Avenue in Berkeley. She always strode with purpose, though her head was miles away, envisioning the refugees crowding the sanctuary offices. It would be a full day's work to register information from the throngs of people, followed by a frantic search for sufficient housing. The immediate effect of the war in Taiwan was this first wave of displaced souls washing the US shores. Northern California was a favored destination, and her employer, Unity Bridge Services, was just one of the nonprofit organizations managing triage processes amid the latest humanitarian crisis.

Cars moved on the street. The ubiquitous self-driving vehicles glided empty and ghostlike, their rooftop sensors swirling, mimicking some signs of life. She reached the corner to cross and paused when a fire truck's lights flashed nearby until it turned the other direction. The siren's piercing wail dropped an octave and broke the silence of the street. The pedestrian walk sign changed to the familiar walking man. Another fire vehicle followed the first.

A small boy wobbled a little when he left the curb to pedal his bike into the crosswalk from the opposite side. The strobing light on the handlebars caught her eye.

They met mid-street when the self-driving car waiting second in line jerked into the left lane and accelerated. She saw it sideways, bearing down. Adrenaline pumped through her veins.

Ginger grabbed the boy, wrenched him backward off the bike, and, with two giant steps, jumped toward the curb. Though he was lightweight, pain shot through her shoulder, and it hurt even more when they tumbled together. The car's brakes screeched in her ears. It had halted halfway into the pedestrian way, just where she and the boy had been. Had the self-driving car become confused by the bike's light? She stood and picked the boy up from the pavement.

The boy seemed to be annoyed with *her*. She didn't think he'd even noticed how close the car had come to running them over. The car smoothly returned to the right lane and drove away when the light changed.

His eyes widened. "It would've hit us."

The vehicle disappeared down the street, leaving the scene of its near-crime.

"Be careful. You can't always trust those self-driving vehicles." Or the programmers who write the code and the inscrutable AIs at the heart of so many systems.

She patted the boy on his head and watched him pedal away. Her mind went to Scarlett—off to college in New Hampshire now two years ago, so not actually little anymore—but she sent a prayer for her safety. She rubbed her shoulder and felt hyper-vigilant for the rest of her walk to the office.

The refugee center was jam-packed, even worse than she'd feared. People lined the walls. The elderly sat on the few chairs, some people stood, and many squatted on the floor. Meager belongings were piled near each family. The inadequate number of staff collected information and attempted to identify housing and services. Two colleagues who spoke Taiwanese and Mandarin worked the counter. Other staff members spread out around the room. Ginger took a desk and chair in an empty corner, motioned for refugees to line up, then got to work. First was a woman holding a baby. When the woman said, *"lí-hó,"* Ginger tapped the AI HASP on her lapel, so it would translate the Taiwanese into English. Her colleague Debbie, looking flustered, nodded in appreciation from across the room as each line of refugees already seemed more manageable. The near-accident invaded her thoughts a few times, but she put it from her mind. She had her reputation to uphold as the calm one in the office.

Ginger processed her line and then turned to those who sat along the walls. She moved from one huddled refugee to another, responding to their concerns and hoping to erase the apprehension on every face. Her AI HASP switched effortlessly between English, Mandarin, and Taiwanese without delay between each spoken sentence and the audio translation. There was almost no advantage to learning a language, she thought. The translation software broke verbal barriers, and she forgot that her AI HASP was even being used.

She came to a big, stocky man sitting on the floor with a beautiful small boy beside him. "What is your name? Please tell me your story. I'm here to help you find what you need."

Her HASP translated the man's answer, helpfully storing the surname because she immediately forgot it. "I am here alone. I know no one here in America. I have nowhere to go."

She raised her eyebrows. "And the boy?"

"He's a stranger. I helped him leave the boat that we escaped on before the Chinese sank it."

She knelt next to the boy. He had dark hair, almost black, an angelic face, and looked about eight. His brown eyes revealed a warm soul. Her heart missed a beat, thinking again of her Scarlett. "Can you tell me if any of your family came with you?"

He didn't need the translation software. His English had a slight accent but was clear. "My Mama and Baba didn't come. I was with my school class when the planes came. I don't know what happened to them all." A tear slid down his cheek.

"Could you use a hug?" He wrapped his arms around her at the invitation, and Ginger gave him a squeeze in return before gently wiping his face with her finger. "Don't you worry. We'll take care of you. We'll try the best we can to find your parents."

The big man nodded and said "thank you" in English, but he said nothing to signal the boy should stay with him. She checked them into the system separately.

The day proceeded in a blur. Half the refugees they'd seen were placed in acceptable housing. The rest were taken to a nearby school gymnasium, where they organized a makeshift soup kitchen and found sleeping bags for the exhausted, frightened people. They settled into marked spaces on the floor.

Ginger sought out the small boy in the gym before she left and tucked him into his sleeping bag. "Everything will be okay. I'll see you tomorrow."

He looked tired but not fearful. He was resilient—a good sign for his recovery from something so traumatic.

The staff slumped into chairs in the rear lounge as the sun settled on the hills outside the office window.

Debbie sat across from her, exhaustion lining her face. "What a day. And there'll be more of the same tomorrow."

"War sucks." Ginger reclined in the comfy chair for a few minutes, massaging her shoulder. "How lucky we are to have homes; to have family." She sighed deeply as she pulled herself to standing, overcome with a quiet sense of security as she made her way home to her husband.

Everett sat at the kitchen table. His big hands dwarfed the enormous sandwich he wolfed down. His arms and broad shoulders hinted at some Scottish ancestor who might have tossed the caber. His hair was windblown above strong eyebrows and a thin, well-trimmed beard. Her handsome engineer.

"Sorry. I couldn't wait any longer."

She barely made out the words he said around his mouthful of ham and cheese. Half of a loaf of bread past its prime—he'd made it three days ago—lay on the counter.

He baked bread to unwind, and Ginger liked to watch as his hands worked the dough. That breadmaking diversion was one of their few escapes from the unease that permeated every conversation. The shots fired on one side of the globe circled round, and no one knew who they might find or what might happen next.

He stood and pulled her into his embrace with a kiss. She flinched when he squeezed her, and he pulled back. "What's wrong?"

"Sore shoulder. A self-driving car nearly hit me in the crosswalk. And it almost hit a little boy next to me. I hurt my shoulder jumping out of the way." She didn't mention grabbing the boy.

"I'm glad you're not just giving me the cold shoulder," he said with a wink. "Are you hurt?"

"I'm fine."

"Did you report the car? That rarely happens, but it's important that they fix glitches in the AI's training data."

"No. I don't have time to fix annoying machines."

"But remember that plane crash a month ago, blamed on the autopilot? Some companies are pushing technology too fast. It's irritating and sometimes deadly. We should do the right thing."

"You're always worrying about *everyone*."

His gaze revealed that he'd caught the emphasis on the last word. Ginger had known him so long, she could visualize the gears turning in his head.

Everett's expression changed to concern. "There was a real risk of being run over? You were so flippant. I missed that." He gave her a deep but gentle hug, avoiding her shoulder.

"I'm fine, and stopped thinking about it right away because of work. We had a building overflowing with refugees. We don't have enough rooms to house them. So many of the cases are heartbreaking. Especially the children." She thought about the boy with the angelic face and hoped he would be able to find rest, even in the gym, among strangers.

"Everyone loses in this war." He finished the last bite of his sandwich. "And why now? To humor an old man on his birthday."

"And for what gain? They didn't even save the chip factories." She brushed back her auburn hair with both hands. While Everett focused on military strategy, she preferred economics and politics. Every major electronics company had ordered all the chip-making photomasks stored in Taiwan to be destroyed. The rest of the chip manufacturing equipment was probably damaged in revenge for the invasion. Western companies no doubt had copies of the masks in the US but would need months to restart factories. Global electronics production had collapsed, stock markets had nosedived, and took with it their retirement investments. It was an odd time to worry about their savings, and Ginger pushed the thought away with some guilt.

Everett worked the espresso machine. "I would have waited for you for dinner, but I'll be on a plane tonight for Tokyo. The company decided we need a core team closer to Taiwan to do what we can. It's imperative that we shut down the test reactor without any leaks. We can't risk a release of radioactivity or any bad press about fission power plants."

She used the rest of the bread to make herself a sandwich and sat across the table eating as he drank his espresso.

"You're sure you'll be safe in Japan?" She waited for his logical response, which often dispelled her worries.

He scratched his beard. "I presume so. As safe as here. China was strategic when they launched the Taiwan invasion. The announcement that they wouldn't attack the US or anyone else beyond Taiwan, and were only recovering their rightful rebel territory, put the ball into our court."

Ginger thought back to her political science minor classes. "The US will look like the aggressor if we jump in."

"Exactly. It's a gutsy bet that the US won't start a nuclear war. China has the conventional military force to fight at their doorstep. The naval blockade, except for the passage of humanitarian aid, dares the US to try to resupply the Taiwanese military."

"That move reminds me of Kennedy's naval blockade during the Cuban missile crisis."

He sipped the espresso, leaning in the chair. "But there is some treaty. How far are we obligated to help Taiwan?"

She had looked this up when the war began. "The Taiwan Relations Act says we'll provide Taiwan 'with arms of a defensive character' and that we'll 'maintain the capacity to resist force' from mainland China. It doesn't say we'd ever send troops."

He finished his coffee. "A good thing, too. The US mainland is six thousand miles away, and there's not enough equipment stockpiled in the western Pacific to stop them. If our ships approached, we'd be sitting ducks for their missiles and drone swarms. We don't have a strategic response, except for a direct attack on China."

She tapped her fingers nervously on the table. "Could it still come to nuclear war? Could it hit here?"

"If someone miscalculates. It's a fear gnawing at my gut. But neither side wants that."

"And short of nuclear war, you think China will win?" She cared less about the military strategy, though she knew Everett was deeply interested in the subject.

"China has been preparing this invasion for a decade. The Taiwanese have already lost any chance of reversing the landings with conventional weapons." She prepared for what she knew would be a well-thought out analysis. "China's opening cyberattack took down communications, command, and control. Then their hypersonic missiles destroyed Taiwan's air force in the first few days. China's army lost a hundred thousand with the amphibious landings but still got ashore. Now, they've secured beachheads and are overrunning the island. Taiwanese resistance is already weakening."

"And the rumor that Marines are fighting?" There was no escaping from the news feeds reporting both facts and speculation.

He furrowed his brow. "No doubt our littoral Marine forces that were pre-positioned in Guam landed in Taiwan and are there fighting. China is not discussing that for strategic political reasons, and neither is the administration. That's part of why I think both sides are still rational, avoiding nuclear war. There simply are not enough American conventional forces to swing the outcome now."

Ginger finished her sandwich and wiped the crumbs from the table. "I know we hoped they feared the downside—global economic isolation—shown by the Russian experience in Ukraine."

Everett nodded in agreement. "But the aging leadership saw their chance slipping away."

"Why reunification with Taiwan became so important to them is a psychological mystery. But we see crazy things happen all over the world." Ginger sat close to him and held his hand, the touch reminding her that she'd be alone for a few days for the first time since this surreal war began. "How much longer do you expect it will last?"

"I'd give it a month or three. The weapons today are terrifyingly lethal, and China can now resupply easily. The Taiwanese will fight, but they'll still be rooted out of their underground bunkers and mountain hideaways. There might be a million people who die from this war. But I don't see it ending another way. China will control the island."

She squeezed his hand. "Be very careful. It isn't logical, but I worry about you being closer to the fighting."

Everett glanced at his watch. "I need to pack and go. It'll be a tough week. For you too. I'll call whenever I have a break." He stood, lovingly wrapped her in his arms, and kissed her. Then, he was gone to pack and she heard clothes being shoveled into a suitcase. He kissed her again before he headed for the airport.

4

"Let's begin bringing all the reactor modules off-line."

"Roger that." Chih-hao, their manager in Taiwan, waved from the display, his yellow hard hat bobbing. An engineer bent over a computer behind him.

Everett sat next to Tom, his business partner and the leader of the team who had traveled from Berkeley to Japan. The other two engineers on the company's Japan team, Kenzo and Himari, huddled with them around the screen, remotely watching their crew in Taiwan at the nuclear power plant test site. Though Tokyo was two thousand kilometers away from the war there, he viscerally felt their danger.

Chih-hao leaned into the control center panel and turned a switch. "Bringing down module number one. The reactor pressure is nominal."

Kenzo frowned. "We could have shut this reactor down remotely. It's fail-safe in any case. But it's a good idea to permanently put it to sleep."

Tom nodded. "Agreed. And putting this test reactor in Taiwan wasn't the smartest corporate decision."

Everett glanced at the team to see that most seemed to agree.

"We push the mission forward wherever there's a good chance," Himari said in defense of the choice. "Since the island-wide blackouts, there's been public concern about running out of electricity. That finally changed the conversation in Taiwan about fission energy."

Himari was voicing the company line. It was a dumb decision, and now they were paying for it. Everett gave her a half-smile to be polite. But he was sure his face told her he didn't buy it.

She cut her gaze away from him and sighed. "The fact that Taiwan Power Company approached us explains why we're there. But, yes, Taiwan was a politically dicey location."

The Tokyo engineers watched the data feeds, checking the shutdown procedures.

"Powering down module number two."

The broadcast came through so cleanly, it felt to Everett like Chih-hao was in the same room. All was going smoothly.

A large explosion rang through the broadcast feed. The second Taiwan engineer involuntarily ducked.

"What was that?" Kenzo wiped his forehead and stared into the screen in front of him.

An alarm sounded in the background. Chih-hao checked his panel and then turned a switch to quell it. "The Chinese have been lobbing shells at the perimeter on and off for a few hours. They're getting closer after landing just twenty kilometers away."

"Then let's finish it." Tom's voice was determined.

Chih-hao nodded. "Shutting down module number three."

They all watched the temperature readings drop.

"The invaders probably won't repeat what happened at the Southern Taiwan Science Park." Chih-hao glanced up from his screen and then back again. "Chinese shelling convinced the TSMC staff to destroy all the gigafab lithography machines and chip masks. Now the Chinese can't make the military chips they need."

"I heard Keelung City was bombed," Tom said.

Chih-hao nodded. "The port is now rubble. That was the headquarters of Taiwan's third naval district, half an hour from Taipei. Now, we can't ship resupplies into the country through there."

"That's a big city." Everett thought about military tactics, the attackers denying ports on the eastern side of the island for resupply. Then he envisioned people lying in pieces scattered among crumbled buildings and shuddered.

Himari swallowed hard, and her lip trembled.

"Four hundred thousand people. There are terrible casualties reported." Chih-hao rubbed his eye.

"So many children." Himari looked a little ill.

The associate behind Chih-hao whispered in his ear. Chih-hao studied his panel. "We're having a problem with one of the control rods. The software just needs a reset."

Chih-hao and the second engineer hunkered over the panel and tapped onto a keyboard. Everett adjusted his PAWN, and a private message from Tom appeared.

How much of a problem?

He pinched his fingers together under the table, bringing up his checklist and troubleshooting lists. *Manageable. They can solve it*, he sent back in a private message.

Tom gave him a tiny nod. They'd allow the Taiwan engineers to solve the problem alone. With no calls for help from them, Tom muted the channel through which they'd been talking to the Taiwan team, and the Tokyo team was free to discuss the war again.

"This fight has far more AIs and robots than the Russian–Ukraine war ten years ago," Kenzo said. "*Shinu hodo.* Fast-moving machines killing at a distance. Those Chinese drone swarms scare me to death."

"I was surprised by the autonomous subs they used to control the Taiwan strait." Tom leaned on the console. "They sank all the Taiwanese ships, protected the beachhead, and put a half million men ashore."

"And women," Himari said.

"Yes, and women. Like the pilots flying the J-11B, giving China air superiority," Everett added. "They continue to land equipment and troops without much opposition."

Kenzo clutched the table. "It looks hopeless to me. And now some Taiwanese politicians are calling for a truce, even while their country is occupied! I know there was a sizable minority who didn't mind uniting with the mainland. Now that so many have died, the Taiwanese realize they've lost, and they don't have their hearts in this remaining fight. But they'll hate their overlords, as we all would."

Another explosion echoed through the screen. Tom unmuted the channel. "As soon as we're finished, you two hightail yourself to safety." His words sounded like an order.

"*Hǎo de*. Will do." Chih-hao nodded. "We'll blend in with the rest of the people here and leave quietly. We've solved the control rod problem. Module 3 is done. Now we're adding the neutron absorber, boron, to the primary coolant. Not much longer, and we'll have these reactors sleeping. There's no danger of radiation leaks—the underground concrete pool housing the reactor modules is bulletproof."

Chih-hao turned to review the checklists. Everett admired his coolness under fire. They all believed in the mission. Nuclear energy had been set back for far too many decades to let it happen again.

The engineers continued the work for another half an hour. At last, Chih-hao gave a thumbs-up, and his fellow engineer high-fived him. Tom thanked the two in Taiwan and begged them to find shelter where they could. The broadcast feed faded. Everett and the Tokyo team were alone in their office war room.

Kenzo pulled a bottle of sake from his desk with four glasses. His hand shook while he poured. "Here's to their safety."

Everyone quietly raised a glass and drank.

Kenzo cleared his throat. "It's macabre to celebrate in the middle of such a war, but at least we're doing something to save the planet."

"Here's to protecting Mother Earth," Himari said.

Everett wondered if she was the most passionate of all of them about the company mission.

Himari swirled the remaining liquid in her glass after she drank. "Why do people conflate nuclear power with nuclear war? It's like confusing hydropower and hurricanes."

Tom sighed over his glass. "I wish I had more faith in the average ability to think logically. People hear the word 'nuclear,' and they go crazy. Just a knee-jerk emotional reaction."

Everett jumped in. "We're doing our part to prevent an accident that conflates the two again. But the choice of words gets in the way of understanding."

Kenzo took a long swig. "We need some word to replace nuclear. Atomic fission produces clean energy the world can run on. Without electricity, we have no modern civilization. Anyone who's experienced a long power outage knows this. We need it to replace the coal that's killing the atmosphere. Only fission can save us."

"Ah, a Penn State grad and Nittany Lion too." Everett tapped Kenzo's glass.

As the level of sake in the bottle dropped, the engineers discussed the merits of the modular reactors they'd invested years in developing. Though the Taiwan deployment had ended in failure, it was one of a dozen underway. All was not lost. After the day's tension, Everett felt himself relax. Kenzo found two more bottles of sake and opened them. The conversation inevitably turned back to war.

"Do you think there's still a risk of this turning into a nuclear confrontation between China and the US?" The thought was lodged in Everett's mind.

"There's always the chance. It's an existential risk on a couple of levels," Himari said. "There are plenty of nuclear missiles to destroy us all. Russia still hangs on to too many, desperate, as it fades from geopolitical relevance. But now China has over a thousand, and dozens would sneak through to vaporize US cities."

"That's my fear," Everett said.

Himari nodded with his encouragement. "If that were to happen, the US and China would spend decades rebuilding and then not have the money and time to fight climate change, a second existential risk. Humanity would lose that battle." She shivered and looked at Everett. "In either case, we're toast."

Their worries were identical. He returned a forlorn smile. "There's a tendency to downplay momentous long-term risks while prioritizing immediate threats. I worry that the fear over China replacing the US economically and militarily could make some trigger happy. Politicians are guilty of letting emotions guide policy rather than logic."

Tom raised his glass. "Let's drink to American politicians playing this game without hubris." He finished half of it in one swig.

Kenzo had at last loosened up, and he shuffled back to his desk for another two bottles of sake. As he opened them, Tom caught Everett's eye and raised one eyebrow. They had discussed the common Japanese business etiquette of the corporate drinking parties known as *nomikai*, and to be polite, both held their glasses to be refilled.

Kenzo downed his sake. "China has missed the chance to be top tiger. The country's demographics are headed downhill with a shrinking population. Now they've become a global pariah. Their economy will be fractured for a decade. They'll follow the sorry path of Russia a decade ago."

Himari seemed lost in her glass, which she finished with a large gulp.

The conversation came to a natural end when the bottles sat empty. It had been a long day, and they parted with Tom shaking everyone's hand. They were headed home the next day.

Everett waved goodnight and walked out of the office. Darkness shrouded the streets, with small groups of revelers wandering home. He crossed to the business hotel where they all stayed, while the others stumbled after him.

He got off the elevator at his floor just as another elevator door opened. Himari exited it and followed him down the hallway, stopping at his door.

"Do you really think there's a chance of nuclear war?"

He looked back at Himari to answer. They were alone in the corridor. She stood close to him, her eyes sad, drunk, and imploring. He considered her closely for the first time. She looked more heavily racked by the current events than he had noticed earlier.

"Maybe the worst danger has passed. If politicians stay as logical as engineers, it should work out okay."

She stood lopsided against the doorframe. What was that look she gave him? Fear? Remembrance? "*Shitemorote*. It scares me so much." She buried her face in his chest.

Everett held her shoulder to gently put some space between them. "I understand your distress. All of us are worried, but your country has already lived through a nuclear disaster, so you must especially feel it."

She wiped her cheek. "As a little girl, I remember that our school took a trip to visit the Genbaku Dome in Hiroshima Peace Memorial Park. The photos of the children there cannot be forgotten."

Everett nodded sympathetically, confirmed in his guess that a memory had undone her. He was glad she didn't personally associate him, an American, with the deed.

"I think it'll work out. Perhaps it's best to head back to your family as soon as you can. We're done with everything we need to do for the project, so you can take some time off."

Himari lurched back a step. She looked at the floor and nodded. "You're right. It's been so stressful." She was frozen in place for several seconds. "I can catch a late train and visit my parents outside Tokyo."

He lowered his gaze with a bow. "Thank you for your kindness here, and please take care of yourself."

Himari made a dainty bow and rushed to the elevator. The door closed, and she was gone.

Everett sighed. If her fear caused her to seek a comforting hug, it was best to let her family deliver it. So many had forgotten the horrors of nuclear war, but in Japan, they lived with the trauma of the aftermath and had not forgotten.

He washed his face with cool water and looked in the mirror. He felt more sober than the sake should have allowed.

On the desk was a holo-display. It was morning in Berkeley. He found a Wi-Fi link to the display with his PAWN and connected. Soon Ginger's face filled the screen in 3D. It felt comforting to see her, so close and real, as if he could reach out and touch her.

"Honey, it's all good now. We shut down the test reactor in Taiwan so it can't cause a problem. My flight will bring me back home on your tomorrow."

The concern melted from her eyes. "I'll be so glad to have you back with me," she said. "I love you."

"I love you too, honey."

They talked for several minutes about her day and his, and then he signed off. He sat at the window seat and looked down onto the streets streaming with vehicles below him. Greater Tokyo stretched in a blanket of lights as far as he could see. His thoughts turned from Ginger to the scene outside. Thirty-six million people crammed into the pulsing city, alive with as many stories of love, heartbreak, forgiveness, and hope. Each homeland is built over centuries, a cradle of a particular part of human culture and history, not to be repeated, priceless to preserve. Thinking that, he was sad again for all the loss in Taiwan. And then worried for the world.

What might happen if some soulless politicians started a nuclear war? If the US and China began lobbing nuclear missiles at each other, how might allies avoid the same fate? Wouldn't it be logical to also destroy every postapocalyptic enemy? How probable would it be that the first spark might be extinguished before the modern world lay in ruins? That included this city. It included his own Northern California home. A cold sweat bathed his face. That existential threat was real tonight.

With it was paired a second existential threat that Himari had articulated; the money spent to rebuild from a grand-scale nuclear war would not leave sufficient resources to fight climate change. Two threats to humanity, and one of them immediate that could sharpen the other executioner's ax. He sat staring out the window.

At last, he broke from his depressive reverie. There were immediate problems to deal with, and they had solved at least one today. Everett turned out the light.

The sun was up when Everett came through the door of their Berkeley home. Ginger stood at the stove, bent over a pan of frying eggs. She wore a happy smile, and he kissed her long and hugged her tight for several minutes.

"Back from saving the world?" Her comment sounded only half in jest.

"It was a successful trip. And no one has blown us up yet."

Out of the corner of his eye, he spied a little boy sitting quietly. The boy stared at them with an inquisitive and angelic expression. He looked to be Asian, maybe Taiwanese or Chinese.

"And who is our guest?" He was already almost sure of the answer.

Ginger flipped the eggs and slid them onto the boy's plate. She faced Everett. "Remember I mentioned that many of the refugees couldn't find temporary housing? Max here was one. He spent two days living on the floor of Berkeley High School's gym. No rooms became available. I felt we could provide him a home for a few days." Her look was questioning, but her lip was firm in the way that he knew meant she'd already made the decision for them both.

"He's temporarily staying with us?"

She nodded. A slow nod.

He sat down, looking at the kid across the table. "I could use some of those eggs too."

Ginger gave him another hug. She turned to the stove and broke three more eggs open.

"Do you know much about his family? Where in Taiwan is he from?"

"The refugees we processed that day were on a ship coming from the northeast coast," she said.

"The northeast coast? It wasn't Keelung City?"

"Yes, that's exactly where. We found out from interviewing the adult refugees in the group."

"Then his parents are probably dead. The Chinese leveled the city."

"My Mama and Baba are dead?" Max dropped his fork, and his face contorted in agony.

Everett's throat tightened at the horror, at himself. "My God. You speak English."

5

Max MacGyver—Present, 2125

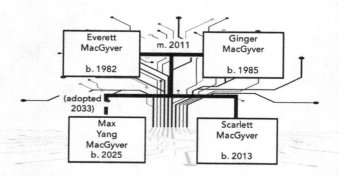

"The Chinese bombed Keelung City, and your birth parents died in the air raids?"

My story and the caffeine bring an alertness to Grand's face. The word "died" pricks my heart anew.

"Momma Ginger kept trying to find any information about them while I lived in their daughter's old bedroom." So long ago, and yet the memories of those first months without them are fresh. There was a hole in my heart that only slowly healed. I doubt that anyone gets over losing their parents.

Grand sips the salakorange juice. We're going to have to buy a lot more of that while he visits.

I finish my cappuccino. "Maybe Momma was confused about what she hoped to hear. It was a painful time for me, not knowing but dreading the worst. I clung to her, and she clung back. Sadly, a couple months later, after the war ended, Dad's guess proved to be correct."

"And they adopted you?"

"Yes. Scarlett, their daughter and only child, had left for college two years before. I think Momma Ginger wasn't ready to stop being a mother."

"And Everett?"

"I guess he came around to the idea when he saw how Momma loved me and truly became my father. And I adored him. He was easy to admire—serious, principled. Always kind to me. He often guided me with a thoughtful word at the right time."

I feel the sudden urge to move, and Grand also fidgets in his chair. "Let's make some bread, hey? We'll use it on sandwiches for lunch."

His eyes brighten with the idea. I lead him into the kitchen, where the dough has been rising since last evening. Robert moves from his position against the wall to follow us. "Robert, did you preheat the oven?"

"Yes, sir, to 200 degrees Celsius, as you requested."

I lift the risen dough from the warming drawer and lay it on the counter. We punch down the loaf to release air bubbles, and he finishes the shaping and sets it in the oven. "Robert, please monitor it and remove it when it's done in about thirty minutes."

"Yes, sir."

"Now, let's prepare the dough for tomorrow's loaf."

Grand eagerly pours out flour. He likes to work with his hands and to learn, like so many in our family. I show him how to mix the yeast with warm water and a pinch of sugar to activate it. Robert retrieves the mixing bowl. We stand around the counter, my leg aching a wee bit this morning. Grand wants to knead the flour, salt, water, and starter. His large hands are in the bowl, and I give a few instructions, but he quickly masters the process.

"What happened to Taiwan after the fighting began?" My stare at Grand may be too surprised because he adds, "My history ain't very good. The Commune school didn't favor the subject."

"Perhaps you've seen a porcupine in the woods?"

He nods.

"Then this will make sense. Taiwan's 'porcupine strategy' failed because they started too late to build defenses and didn't have enough 'quills' to prevent an attack. They lost the war far faster than they expected, albeit with heavy casualties on both sides. The invasion scarred the Taiwanese psyche, and even now they're not 'united in spirit' as China had supposed they would be."

I nod approval of the stickiness of Grand's loaf of dough and show him how to grease a bowl. He puts the loaf into the warming drawer to rise for tomorrow.

"So, at least we avoided nuclear war."

His comment shows he's been listening closely, finding key points. I'm impressed.

"Exactly. Widescale nuclear war with multiple cities destroyed by the leading nuclear powers—the US, China, Russia—would have been an existential risk for humanity. That was the first great challenge of the past century we navigated successfully." I can't prevent the smile on my face, a mix of relief and happiness that people his age don't have to understand that danger. "It was followed by serious nuclear arms reductions, moving toward the goal of zero nukes."

Grand frowns. "But your country was lost. Did the US stay the top military power, even though China took Taiwan?"

"The US coexisted militarily with China. A country can win through alliances too, which can be a better strategy than throwing your weight around. It seems that no one takes kindly to being invaded."

Grand laughs. "Were there other wars after that one?"

"There were—especially the Climate Wars much later. But the other good news, the great achievement, is that the very idea of war between sovereign states to acquire land began to disappear. Since ancient ages, humankind has engaged in war. Now there have been fewer wars. Maybe the better angels of our nature have come forward."

"And what happened to China?"

I feel his question press my memory, and I reach back a long time to the first half of the last century. I give myself some time to think by peeking at the baking loaf through the glass window, though I know Robert will monitor it without error. The crust is already browning nicely.

The history comes back to me, like hiking a familiar trail. In any decade, some countries are rising, some falling, some in slow arcs, and some off a cliff when their leaders make catastrophic decisions. The rise of Nigeria, Indonesia, and Türkiye were slow arcs. There's a string of cataclysmic examples—Hitler and Napoleon invading Russia, Japan attacking the US at Pearl Harbor, countries slipping into WWI, the Peloponnesian War and Athens' destruction. One secret to countries that succeed in the long run is, through luck or wisdom, to avoid the worst decisions.

I pour Grand another cup of juice. "China was foolhardy too, like Russia in Ukraine, and global sanctions hobbled their economy. China and the US competed for global leadership. China won in economics but lost its opportunity to be a moral leader of the world—not that it aspired to that. Dictatorships can't lead the world ideologically because repression thwarts creative and critical thinking."

"Everyone wants to be top dog."

"Yes, and China has the largest economy in the world today. India is hot on its heels, and the US is third."

Grand raises his eyebrows. "I didn't know that."

"It's important to study economics. China grew theirs through the simple math of a large population. Dictatorship allows them to be efficient, if not free, and their standard of living remains high. China ceded being the workshop for the world to India and Africa around midcentury, and it turned inward, focused on its own market. Demographic trends worked against it then, as their population has been shrinking for the past century."

Grand wipes the flour from his hands. "So, the US is kinda tied with China's military power, and there ain't so many wars. We're behind on the economy, but that's mostly 'cause they have more people. Then the US is still the favorite."

I check his expression and realize once again that he knows little about the world outside the Piney Woods of Texas. He's more isolated than I could imagine, missing all the US politics too. It's time to break it to him.

"If we'd come together as a nation under exceptional leadership, we might have remained the respected leader of the global community. Unfortunately, the US isn't the favorite dog economically, politically, or morally. We lost the economic lead to China, and then US borrowing weakened the dollar. That's why we have credit$ as our currency today. And the European Union took moral leadership when the Levels Acts went into law, about when you were born."

His eyes betray his surprise. "There's a lot I don't know."

"Not to worry. You'll learn much of that in high school. I can see from your breadmaking that you're a quick study."

"That's something I learned at the Commune. Everyone is expected to pull their own weight. You need to pitch in and get the job done."

"We MacGyvers believe in that."

Grand frowns like he's uncomfortable with the subject. "You mentioned they had a daughter, Scarlett? I always wished I had a sister."

"In most Global North countries, families have one or two children. Until I came along, Scarlett was an only child too." My lip hurts when I bite it. "My only sister. Both of us surprised by sudden siblings."

Robert removes the baked loaf of bread from the oven, and the aroma wafts over us.

"What was Scarlett like?"

Grand has the look of someone who has discovered a treasure map, with coordinates leading to something long buried. I'm clearly the map.

"She was twenty when I arrived in California. I met her a month later when she came back from New Hampshire, where she was in college. She had red hair like Momma Ginger, and freckles across her nose. I remember how she hugged me when we first met, glad to have a sibling."

I can't relay the family history, getting to his parents Lily and Wyatt, until he knows about Scarlett and her husband, Jack Jones, one of the technology proponents who transformed everything this past century. But first things first. We are all swept along in this story.

6

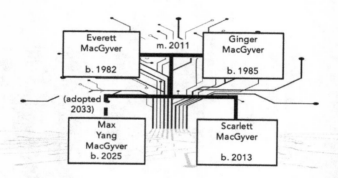

The plane touched down at SFO, and Scarlett reflexively squeezed Jack's hand. She warmed to his touch as she always did.

He flashed his trademark dazzling smile. "Worried about something, sport?"

Scarlett's lip quirked upward, and she brushed her hair back into place. "I was thinking about how my parents will react to having you here."

She doubted they would approve of her becoming attached to someone in her second year of college. Now it seemed like a mistake not to mention he was coming when she texted her mom.

"Not to worry. We can sell this. Wait until they see us together." Jack leaned back comfortably in his seat.

He didn't lack assurance, and she couldn't deny she'd succumbed to that charm.

The plane coasted into the gate. Scarlett unfastened her seat belt. Her hand grazed her slim belly, reminding her of her mother's admonition when she started college to watch her weight. The "freshman fifteen" was a thing in her parents' generation, but it showed how out of touch they were. In a college like Dartmouth, where social competition was hidden under a thin veneer, everyone used weight-control medications, and nearly everyone was slim. Scarlett personally believed there was no way a guy like Jack would have looked at her otherwise. Somehow, she'd won the heart of one of the most handsome and confident men on campus, which she considered her greatest social victory.

He retrieved his tennis racket from the overhead bin and flicked it at her as they exited the plane, eliciting the anticipated smile. His confidence quieted her anxiety; another reason she'd fallen for him. They picked up their luggage and walked out of the terminal. Scarlett gave a two-word command to the personal intelligent digital assistant on her HASP, which she'd named Zelda.

In an instant, PIDA Zelda ordered transport home. *Your Uber is arriving in one minute, and you will be home in thirty-five minutes.*

The car headed north through San Francisco in light traffic. As they crossed the Bay Bridge to Berkeley, the giant port cranes loomed like Star Wars' attack robots waiting to pounce out of the gathering dark. It was unclear whether a fight was ahead. Scarlett's thoughts raced as she turned over in her mind how to break the news to her mother about her summer internship.

You need to chill. Zelda's programmed hipster nonchalance in her earbud didn't help.

Her watch, which monitored her vitals through a sensor, emitted a steady alarm that indicated elevated blood pressure. She turned the warning off and took deep breaths.

She squeezed Jack's hand again. "We'll stay two nights at my house, and then I've got flights booked to Sydney for Wednesday morning."

"I can avoid annoying your parents for that long." Jack winked at her.

"Remember, we're telling them you're going to be in Australia to talk about corporate possibilities after graduation through your friend Alistair. Best not to mention the Australian tennis money tournaments until you break into the pros."

Scarlett couldn't yet tell if Jack's career aspirations were realistic, though he swung a racket beautifully. And he did light up when talking about the prize money. But she didn't think her mom and dad would approve of her following him on a lark, so it was better to explain the choice for career reasons, though she had no career in mind other than to keep Jack.

"Don't worry. I can sell anything."

The Uber wound its way up Claremont Avenue into the hills above Berkeley and stopped in front of her home. She wondered what Jack thought about it. It was enormous by most standards, and only acquired when she was in high school, but it was her mother's dream Tudor-style house, and she'd grown used to it. The car deposited them and departed.

As they walked up the path through the perfectly mani-cured yard, Jack wore his radiant smile. "I can't wait to meet your parents."

The door opened, and Scarlett was enveloped in her mother's arms. Jack held the suitcases and his racket a step behind her.

"You didn't say anyone else was coming." A worried look crossed her mother's face as she took Jack's hand. Her dad eyed Jack a moment, and she took a deep breath.

"Mom, Dad, this is my boyfriend, Jack. Jack, my mom Ginger, and my dad Everett."

"Nice to meet you, Jack," said her dad, and they shook hands. Her mom opened the door wider, and they all filed into the living room.

A small boy sat on the corner sofa. Her mom touched his shoulder. "This is Max. He's staying with us a while. He's from Keelung City in Taiwan."

Max's gaze went straight to Scarlett's T-shirt. She'd got it at a rally on campus to show support for the underdog nation. The white sun emblem from the Taiwanese flag blazed across the front.

"Surprises all around." She tilted her head to one side, and he gave her a beautiful smile in return, almost as warm as Jack's. "Welcome, Max."

"Nice to meet you, Scarlett. I hope you don't mind my staying in your bedroom."

She understood his English easily. He was cute, like a doll with a perfectly sculpted face, and easy to like. Just like Jack. She pulled him onto her lap with a hug. He hugged her back.

"Max has moved to the spare bedroom for tonight, though," Ginger said. "Everything in your room is the same as when you last left."

Scarlett thought it sounded a bit defensive, and she wondered about that.

Everett took charge as he usually did, smoothing over everyone's social uncertainties. He offered to open a bottle of wine after making sure that Jack was over twenty-one. Twenty-two, to be exact. It was revealed that he would be a fifth-year senior at Dartmouth in the fall, to her annoyance. The cabernet was poured, and Scarlett, permitted to drink wine since their trips to Europe, downed a large swig. Everett wanted to know about Jack's career plans and, with Scarlett's encouragement, he talked about his most recent decision on majors.

"There's still a lot of money to be made in AI," Jack said. "My favorite business professor recommended I go into sales. It's mostly business-to-business and leads to closing big deals when you move up."

Everett stroked his beard. "The field certainly has been strong this last decade. Now everyone has a digital assistant. So many jobs have disappeared in customer service, in creative fields like Hollywood, and in professional fields like law and medicine. I'm wondering though whether it's time for another 'AI winter' with the technology's limits showing. The tech people talk about 'Artificial General Intelligence,' but I'm not sure it's a kind of intelligence that will replace us yet."

"I've discussed that in my classes too. No one seems to know. There's still room to sell the product benefits."

"Let's hope the global economy begins to recover in a year. It's going to take time for chip factories outside Taiwan to increase production," Everett said.

Scarlett knew that her dad had been in Japan working on something for Taiwan, but only because her mom had texted her when he left. It must be top of mind for him, but she didn't really know the details.

"Job opportunities right now are dead. This next year at Dartmouth for Jack isn't wasted time." Scarlett hoped that would set the stage to reveal their summer plans.

Ginger announced that dinner was ready—they had expected Scarlett earlier—and they carried their wine glasses to the dining room table. Everett pulled up an extra chair for Jack while Ginger arranged an extra place setting. She served the main dish, and they passed around the vegetables. Scarlett noticed her mom took a very small portion of the chicken, and everything else, and her face flushed.

Scarlett speared a brussels sprout and caught Max's eye. "You've gone through so many challenges this last month. You're brave." She tilted her head toward her mom. "You must be swamped, too, handling the newcomers."

"It's like a wave hit us, and it's a struggle to find housing for everyone. But it's being worked out."

On hearing the word "wave," Max's face turned somber.

"Are you alone?" Jack asked Max. "Where are your parents?"

Now he seemed ready to cry. "I don't know." His voice was very quiet. "They might be dead."

"We're still trying to extract information from Taiwan, and the situation is confusing," Ginger said.

"Satellite images?" Jack asked.

Everett nodded, not elaborating, his gaze on the table.

Scarlett squeezed Max's shoulder. "Then there's still a chance they'll be calling you."

The dinner conversation turned to her sophomore year, now ended. After meeting Jack a semester ago, she'd become less communicative, telling them she was fitting into the university well and had plenty of friends. The truth was that Jack filled most of her thoughts and time. But she chatted about a couple of interesting classes and her roommate. There was no reason to mention she'd spent scant time in her room these last months.

"I'm so glad the year was happy for you. But you haven't said anything about how you'll spend the summer." Ginger sipped her water.

Scarlett gathered herself to answer and took a deep breath. "I'm taking an internship at a nonprofit this summer. The kind of thing that you do, Mom. It's in Sydney."

Jack jumped in. "A fraternity buddy of mine suggested the opportunity. Oh, and I'll be there too. His uncle is in a tech company that may have something for me."

"You'll both be in Sydney." Everett leaned back and crossed his arms. "I see." He eyed Jack closely then turned to Scarlett. "What is the nonprofit?"

Scarlett found her voice. "It's TerraGuard Alliance, involved with environmental activism, which is perfect because I'm thinking of, like, majoring in sustainability. The environmental science degree at Dartmouth requires half their courses in the science departments." The last was a nod to her dad's harping on science all these years.

"That might be a promising career." Ginger glanced at Everett. "Lord knows, we need to do so much to save the environment, with the weather changing for the worse every year. But we thought you'd be back here for summer. We've missed you." Ginger took a large sip of her wine.

"I've heard of that nonprofit." Her dad was not smiling. "They've got a reputation for publicity stunts. And they don't believe that fission power is part of the formula to fight climate change."

She'd heard these arguments before from her father, which weren't supported by many of her eco friends. It was frustrating that he was bringing it all up yet again. "Well, nuclear power is prohibited in Australia. Maybe we can avoid nuclear by using solar and wind energy to save the planet."

Everett gripped his wineglass tightly. "We can't avoid it because the math doesn't pencil out. Unless fission energy is a significant electricity source, the world can't both eliminate burning fossil fuels and keep the lights on."

Scarlett hated that he always went back to math, her weakest subject. She felt her palms sweating. "Dad, you're too involved to notice the downsides. Like the safety issues."

"The current generation of fission plants is very safe, putting those concerns behind us." Everett pushed his plate away. "They don't have risks like those back in the time of Chernobyl. They use passive shutoff, which means no person needs to do anything. They turn off automatically. You should study the designs and science. Fission energy is the most impactful thing we can do to dramatically slow climate change."

Ginger nervously watched them bicker, her gaze going between Everett and Scarlett.

Scarlett threw her hands into the air. "You know everyone is afraid of the word nuclear."

"If you do pursue the sustainability major, I'm glad there are science courses in the program. The fears are emotional and not in line with the current reality. There's still an illogical association of the word 'nuclear' with just bombs."

Jack watched them while he lounged back in his chair.

She tried to calm herself. "That's just how I feel—afraid." She knew her last salvo was weak.

Everett finished his wine in a defiant gulp. "Blind emotion gets in the way of meeting this existential threat in time for your grandchildren. Without fission power in the equation, we won't solve the climate problem in time. That is what you should be afraid of."

"Where is Sydney?"

The adults all looked at Max, glad for the question.

"It's south of Taiwan, which is very roughly a third of the way around the Earth, west of here," Everett said.

Max squinted his eyes. "And one-third plus two-thirds is three-thirds."

Everett's face lit up at the teaching moment. "Where would you be if you went another two-thirds around?"

"Another two-thirds? It's all the way around. I'd be back home here." Max grinned.

"Very roughly. But your visualization is good," Everett said.

Ginger clapped her hands. "Yes, home. Pretty good math for an eight-year-old!"

———————◆———————

Her dad had retired for the night. Jack carried the suitcases into her bedroom as she'd directed, and she was glad her parents hadn't questioned her boldness.

Her mom, looking worried, cornered Scarlett in the kitchen as she drank a glass of water before bed. "I can see you're attached to Jack. He seems like a nice, handsome guy. But is this relationship moving too fast? Heading off to Sydney without even discussing it with us. It's a big surprise."

Jack was attractive, and given her own choices, her mom had no reasonable objection on that score. "The internship is a good opportunity. And I've been with Jack for several months now. You've always wanted me to make my own decisions." Scarlett's frustration, sparked by the argument with her father earlier, came back with too much ease. She could feel her tone rising, and she forced the volume down.

Her mother defaulted to logic. "I care about your happiness. We've encouraged you not to make snap decisions. You know you tend to do that. These important life choices need both heart and head so you don't regret them later. I worry that you're plunging in too fast."

It was not an argument Scarlett would win, even with herself. Deciding was a weakness for her, as was fighting against the current of her emotions. Now she felt nothing beyond the gravity of Jack, lying achingly close in her bedroom. Ready to be done with the conversation, she said the one thing that couldn't be debated. "I love you, Mom. Goodnight."

7

JACK JONES—2033 (CALIFORNIA)

The elegant mansion was familiar on his second visit, but it still impressed him. Jack sat on a sofa in Scarlett's Berkeley home, opposite her father. A Christmas tree decorated one corner of the living room. A magnificent fireplace crackled with heat, and the view through the leaded glass windows included a backyard swimming pool, now covered against the December chill.

Theirs was a palatial home unlike any he had known. Everett had clearly done well in his profession. He was one of the founders of an energy startup company, which an on-line search showed had gone public five years earlier. They could afford to send their daughter to Dartmouth and no doubt had a stash of investments. That checked one of his requirement boxes.

They were talking about Max, who sat between Everett and Ginger. The kid held Ginger's hand.

"We completed the adoption process in time for Thanksgiving," she said.

"What a great Thanksgiving. It's nice the legal stuff is behind you," Jack said. "Scarlett, you have a cute brother. We're sorry we couldn't be here. We promised my mother we'd spend Thanksgiving with her."

The adoption details were familiar to him because Ginger had been texting with Scarlett, sharing her anxiety about the process. After China had taken the island, casualty information was slow to be released and only provided when Western nations threatened war-crime charges. Ginger received the terse message in October, on official letterhead, in Chinese and English. It confirmed the death of Max's parents in Keelung City. With Jack listening in the background beside Scarlett, Ginger shared on a video call that he was officially an orphan with no living relatives.

Scarlett crossed the room to give Max a hug. "Okay, little brother, you can keep my room." Jack was at her side, and he tousled Max's hair.

Ginger blinked. "That's been a temporary plan."

Jack touched Scarlett's arm as she tensed, looking to broach the topic. Despite her doubts, he knew he could sell this.

"Jack and I have an announcement too. We got engaged over Thanksgiving." She uncovered her hand and the ring that she'd been hiding. It wasn't a big diamond, and Jack needed a loan from her for it, but Scarlett proudly showed it off. Max reached to admire her ring, turning her finger to watch it sparkle.

After a stunned silence, everyone talked at once. Ginger asked about the wedding plans.

"Not until I graduate, in well over a year," Scarlett reassured her.

Everett asked about where they planned to live.

"That depends on where Jack finds a job."

"I'm so happy that your daughter agreed to take my hand." Jack delivered the well-practiced line to his future father-in-law. "We're a good team together."

"We know next to nothing about your family, Jack. Where do you plan to have the wedding?" Ginger seemed to struggle to hold the changed world in her head.

"I'm afraid I don't have many relatives left. Just a few in New Hampshire."

"Don't you feel a bit young for such an important step as marriage?" Ginger seemed to struggle not to raise her voice to her daughter.

"I'll be twenty-two when we marry; not much younger than you were." To Jack's ear, Scarlett sounded defensive—not the way to sell the deal.

"And in between, I'll still be at Dartmouth too, since I'll enroll in graduate-level tech sales coursework. That year will better prepare me for the business world," Jack said.

Meanwhile, he'd warned Scarlett not to mention anything about his Sydney experience. His attempt to break into the pro tennis circuit in Australia had been a bust. He'd been naïve. His tennis game was not at pro caliber. Still, it was painful to give up the fantasy of making effortless millions like the top players seemed to do.

The following month spent with Alistair's uncle hadn't led to further interest from the company, so it wasn't much to brag about; just a shred of tech company experience. Of course, a Dartmouth degree carried weight. He still thought he could parlay that minor job, along with a few computer science courses, into a tech sales position.

"Are you considering living in Sydney afterward?" Everett was onto the next step after a wedding.

Jack shrugged, feeling he might now spin the Sydney experience positively. "The summer job didn't turn into an offer after graduation. Sydney's not a place we plan to settle."

"Well, we're happy that you'll finish your undergraduate education." Everett's gaze was on his daughter. "Jobs are changing at a head-spinning pace and, without a degree, you could be left out in the cold."

"I promise to finish." Her lip quivered as she looked to him for confidence, and Jack knew he could sell her on everything he wanted.

◆

He sipped the glass of port that Everett had handed him half an hour ago. They'd talked in his study, with the older man asking careful questions and Jack parrying them. The interview tested his sales skills, but Everett rubbed his beard throughout, and at the end shook his hand. Then, Ginger and Everett huddled with Scarlett in the living room, and the intermittent buzz of conversation floated into the study. He left it to her to get them comfortable with their plans.

Life was looking up. In the past semester, he'd finished the last nagging requirements to snag a coveted Ivy League degree. He'd use the sixth year to take tech courses and wait for Scarlett to graduate. Better to have luck and cunning than talent alone. It was lucky he got into Dartmouth as the last of the legacy entries before the university suspended the program, and lucky he qualified for low-income grants to afford the tuition.

His great-grandfather had the cunning during Prohibition, which led to newfound money. A large donation by him opened Dartmouth doors to his son and great-grandson, creating an uneven legacy of graduates. That luck skipped his father. It had been only a temporary rise in the family's fortunes. Everyone, especially his useless father, had pissed away the money.

Luck and cunning were the keys to success. He'd joined the fraternity with cunning and a smile, looking for wealthy brothers to be best friends. Greek life on campus offered the surest social scene, superior to the campus alternative of Collis After Dark, and the girls were easy to attract to their frat parties. It had all been fun for years. But now it was time to move on.

Scarlett's animated face appeared as she turned toward the study, still talking with her mother. She was pretty enough, rich enough, and willing to overlook his small dalliances. Just two months ago, she'd ignored the obvious, believing his lies about Rachael. Well, he was drunk that night, and he couldn't resist her. He'd been hungry for something all his life, and he knew he was no good at denying himself what he craved. Now he wanted to focus on another hunger—on making the kind of money his great-grandfather had made.

Max watched him from the hallway corner. He beckoned, and Max moved to stand at the study doorway. "Hey, buddy, come on in and keep me company. Everyone else is busy." Max hovered beside his chair. "Little guy, I remember from our last visit that you're good at math already. Stick with it. You'll make money someday in tech."

"I like math," Max said.

"What else do you like?"

"I like movies too. I like to listen to them talk."

Jack imagined the kid improving his English; the studious type. "Have you watched the new pirate movie? It has the best pirate since Jack Sparrow, and they use the latest AI-driven CGI for the pirate-ship battles."

Max squinted his face in a question. "What's a pirate?"

Jack lit up in childlike excitement. "A pirate is a buccaneer who sinks ships and takes all the gold. There's lots of swashbuckling adventure. Now, that's the life, being a pirate."

Max shivered. "Sinking ships? No...I never want to be a pirate."

"Ah, it's the pirate's life for me," he said liltingly, mimicking the cliché line from an old Disney movie song. Max vigorously shook his head. Jack laughed as the boy backed away and ran from the room.

Scarlett rose from the sofa and stood at the study door. "It's time to go."

In response to Ginger's protests for them to stay, Scarlett said, "It's easier for you and less crowded, and the hotel isn't expensive. Besides, we have an early plane back tomorrow." There were the usual hugs and waves. They walked through the brisk evening to the rental car parked at the corner.

As they pulled away, Jack's teeth flashed brilliantly at her. "On to our big adventure."

8

The smell of cooling bread reminds me of yeast and green apples. Grandfather's story about his sister Scarlett and new brother-in-law Jack has made him stand a bit straighter, forgetting whatever ailment he has, which could just be old age.

Grandfather sees me sniffing. "Already enjoying my bread recipe?"

"I can't wait to taste it. Is it a family secret?" Ma doesn't bake bread so good.

"There are many family secrets, though this is the least of them. Your being here already tells me you haven't heard many."

He's got me there. I have a feeling like sweeping the tall grass out of the way and suddenly seeing a herd of deer, them as surprised as me before they spring away.

"I'd like someone to tell me the family secrets. You're startin' with your sister because she has a role in it?"

Grandfather leans on the counter. "Every person in a family has a role. Everyone is interconnected."

I nod. "Everyone at the Commune needs to pitch in to help. Otherwise, work doesn't get done."

"Your actions affect everyone else, whatever you decide. And a non-decision is a decision. My sister's choices affected her kids, and their decisions affected your parents, Wyatt and Lily. Let me tell you how those connections touched each other." He looks me in the eye. "It was a challenging century, and our family was more than a footnote."

The look tells me that secrets are strewn about like leaves in a November windstorm. He's got my attention.

The robot is standing in the kitchen, taking it all in.

Grandfather says, "Robert, please slice the loaf for sandwiches."

The robot takes a bread knife from the drawer. After a blur of motion, the loaf is in perfect slices on the counter and still warm to the touch.

"You were close to Scarlett. She lived happily with Jack?"

"At first."

I glance at him.

"Everyone knows their view of the universe, their lived experience, and their version of the story of their family. I can tell the part that I know. I loved my sister and wished she would love me always too, but it didn't work out that way. I'm afraid jealousy, misunderstanding, and self-interest got in the way."

My chest tightens the way it does when the Commune leadership acts like I don't understand, but my heart tells me what's right. "Jealousy? But you were the refugee kid."

9

Scarlett peered through the image-stabilized binoculars at the black shape moving out into the South Pacific. When paired with her PAWN, they could zoom in to a superhuman vision level that let her pick out the details of Australia's first Virginia-class nuclear submarine. The description on her PAWN assured her that only the propulsion was nuclear, and that—so far—the sub only carried conventional missiles. The social media post alerting her to its movement half an hour before was no doubt authorized by the government, a not-so-subtle message to the Chinese that the Australians had the craft on patrol.

The angular hull glided through the blue water. Even without nuclear warheads, it was ominous, like some deep-sea predator. She shivered imagining the crew crowded inside, following orders to hunt and kill whatever enemy threatened the country. She watched the sub dive, leaving the conning tower visible for a few final moments. Then, there was just empty ocean.

She dragged her toes in the white sand one last time. The long curve of Bondi Beach lay before her, still filled by sunbathers this afternoon. A few intrepid surfers braved the combers breaking white amid turquoise water. All were oblivious of the submarine farther offshore. Scarlett breathed in the salt air, reliving Australian memories of her summer internship nearly two years before, of the wedding just over and honeymoon almost finished, experiences that had turned her world upside down.

The cool sand and submarine reminded her of that old book and her first summer here. By then, the media had revealed how close the world had come to nuclear war. China had taken Taiwan with conventional weapons, China and the US had faced off for several missed heartbeats for humanity, neither pulling the nuclear trigger, and then the ages-old clash of metal against flesh continued until Taiwan lay defeated.

The inevitable analysis frenzy ensued. The news cycle perseverated on nuclear payloads, MIRVs, missile counts, and inadequate communications among nuclear powers. The world woke up to the possibility of nuclear holocaust. Anxiety had been high among the nonprofit interns, college students who hadn't thought about this threat before. That summer in Australia, they all read *On the Beach*, an old apocalyptic book with humankind destroyed by nuclear war, and a last survivor on a beach in Melbourne. She remembered the closing scene and felt the threat in her toes.

Today, besides the appearance of the submarine, the threat was less visceral. In the intervening year and a half, she'd graduated with her degree in environmental science. The UN held multiple meetings, and there was hope for new nuclear disarmament treaties. The world had come to its senses and backtracked from that abyss.

Scarlett thought of her ongoing disagreements with her dad. At first, the old book seemed to lend weight to her anti-nuclear energy ideas. She took science classes so she might better argue her convictions. But digging into the nuances, she realized the distinction between nuclear weapons and fission power, and that the issues were more complicated than she'd imagined. She wondered if Dad could be right that fission power was necessary to fight climate change. Scarlett pushed the thought away. Nuclear war was too worrying to even consider nuclear power. All things nuclear frightened her.

She turned to happier thoughts. From her beach vantage, she could see the frontage road, Campbell Parade, and the venue where she and Jack had been married. It had been an intimate event with her parents, Jack's mother, four friends from her summer internship, and a dozen friends who'd splurged on the airline tickets for their destination wedding.

Their guests left within days, and they were alone. Jack's frat brother, Alistair, had lent them his family's vacation house at Darling Point for their honeymoon. They had time to swim, sunbathe, and sightsee. They'd ventured along the coastal areas of New South Wales and Victoria, with a trip to Melbourne.

Jack suggested continuing beyond, to the Twelve Apostles standing like their namesakes, facing the cold Antarctic waters. "Better relax while we can," he'd said.

And they had, enjoying an idyllic, warm Australian autumn. It was an odd feeling, given her penchant for not making decisions, to find that her gut decision to marry Jack had resulted in the event itself. The past month together had made her comfortable with the new role. Now it was time to say goodbye to Australia.

Scarlett brushed the sand from her feet, put on her sneakers, and used her PIDA Zelda to call a ride. The self-driving vehicle pulled up in minutes then rolled up the hill past Cooper Park and down Ocean Street to their borrowed home.

Jack lay on the sofa, the setting sun's rays in the window behind him. His sparkling eyes greeted her, and there was a springiness in his manner when he jumped to his feet.

"Sport, are you ready to turn the world upside down?" It was a variation of their joke about being Down Under, their summer and the honeymoon both out of the normal.

"It's been upside down since you arrived." She kissed him hard on the lips.

"Okay, some news first." He held her tightly. "I've landed a great AI sales job."

"Wonderful! Finally, they recognize your talents. I'm so happy for you." She hugged him.

Jack had been searching for months after the global recession had left unemployment soaring. She knew he'd been disappointed when his tennis game didn't measure up and that career option had closed. Jack muddled through since that summer, only regaining his joie de vivre in the month leading up to the wedding.

"And the other good news is, we'll be moving to New York City." His eyes gleamed.

Her heart thumped. "Not back to California?"

"It's not like your father is going to support us in the lifestyle to which we aspire." He said it with an edge.

Did Jack ever expect that? Her gaze met his, revealing a fire she wasn't familiar with.

"You take the best job you can find. This one pays very well and has a fast track. I need to sell hard, and that I can do."

"We'll live in New York City itself?"

"Right in the action. I'll be on the road for a while to start. But you can figure out how to settle down there. We're going places, sport."

He folded her in his arms. Scarlett didn't need to make any decisions. Her career could be decided later. She was happy Jack had found something that lit his smile and that it was now directed at her. She would let it carry her along.

10

"I will be your new best friend. What is your name? Can you play a game with me?" The petite robot raised its cartoon eyebrows and wagged its left hand.

Jack winked at it. He smiled more broadly when the robot locked onto his eyes and appeared to be engaged. The prototype wasn't bad. It moved without jerkiness, and its expressions matched the speech. Most importantly, the facial components—large round lenses, cute nose, and a mouth that could form a wry expression—left a cuddly impression that should be appealing to kids.

He checked his PAWN for the test list and ran through questions for the robot, leaving himself notes on weak responses.

His PAWN buzzed with a message from Scarlett.

I'll be there in ten minutes. I borrowed my friend's little girl to help you test.

Jack replied, then picked up his coffee and waited, studying his creation. This might be his ticket—a way out of a rut, a path to big money.

The robot offered a road forward, beyond AI and into a growing related field. He thought back to his first sales job in AI at the end of the deep learning wave. Those AIs had automated millions of jobs, making billions for company founders and investors. He hadn't been among them. His first AI employer had a poorly designed product, and even his skills couldn't cover up the flaws. He'd missed the AI products making money on celebrity rip-offs. Now, deep fakes were illegal. Next, he tried selling into the education market, where learning-personalized AIs were disrupting the classroom, revamping teachers' roles. But the large AI companies controlled that business segment.

During the few times he and Scarlett had visited her parents in California, he and Everett had debated the end of the AI wave. True, he'd warned Jack about being too bullish on the AI field. What was his joke? Some old saying about "winter is coming." His father-in-law always said it with a glint in his eye. The joke, and the advice, hadn't landed. Now he had to acknowledge the insight, though maybe the debate ended in a tie. The technology had been transformative, but AGI had not yet arrived in a meaningful way.

AI was now the base technology for related fields. The tech giants offered assistants used by everyone. He was intrigued by the idea of employing the same technology for children's toys. Parents paid so much to get their kids off their hands.

Jack finished his coffee. He looked around the office, into the empty warehouse and beyond. Maybe someday he could fill a production line there.

The door opened, and Scarlett walked in with a young girl. She had bouncy blonde curls and an air of confidence for one so young.

"This is Victoria. She's five. Her mother works with me at the nonprofit and let me take her to play here this afternoon."

Victoria looked at Jack, but her gaze quickly moved to the robot.

"Victoria, meet Ada. She might be your new friend." He shepherded Victoria to sit next to the robot. "Ada, please meet Victoria," he said.

The robot rolled its lenses to focus on the girl. "It's so nice to meet you. Would you like to be my friend?"

Jack set the video recording of the interaction and watched the robot talk with Victoria for several minutes. He stood at a distance next to Scarlett, giving the child space to interact naturally.

"It was a bit of a schlep here." Scarlett kept her voice low.

"White Plains was the closest place to the city that I could afford space."

Her tenor changed. "But the drive gave us time to talk. Victoria is very sweet." Scarlett had a motherly expression on her face.

"Don't get any ideas."

She frowned. "Well, maybe some time."

It was best to cut off the idea now. "Forget about it. You can't take time off for child raising. We need you to keep working so we have enough money to live on. I've got everything in this idea." He didn't smile now. "I'm making it big. Give me a halfway-okay product, and I can sell it. A robot company is the ticket."

"Oww oww oww! Ada hit me." Victoria clutched her hand.

Scarlett found some tissues to wrap around Victoria's hand, where a cut welled up red.

"She swung her hand and hit me. It hurts. I don't like her." Victoria sniffled and wiped her eyes with her free hand.

"Damn kids." Jack made a note about adding safety protocols to the robot's motion files. When Victoria stopped sniffling, he knelt beside her. "What did you like about Ada?"

"Besides that, how was the theater, Mrs. Lincoln?" Scarlett said under her breath.

Jack turned to glare. "You don't appreciate how hard it is."

11

"You have arrived." The door of the AV unlocked, Everett exited, and his PAWN buzzed with payment confirmation.

The car drove away from his front gate. The dead golden grass of summer covered the Berkeley Hills. He took a deep breath, glad to be home. The hills reminded him that he missed the outdoors, having been cooped up inside the control room of the latest project, a fission plant in Argentina. It was a successful commissioning and meant there was, at last, some momentum for modular fission power units. His mission accomplished, he'd have some time to relax this summer before the next project.

Ginger had pinged his PIDA, promising to be home soon to cook his favorite meal tonight. Everett opened the front door and glanced into the empty living room while hanging his coat on the hook, and headed down the hallway. Max's door was open. He paused and watched him move in the HDSET. Max flicked his hands, twirled his fingers, and moved his body in a dance. War game or some futuristic fantasy? Everett couldn't tell.

Textbooks and the allbook reader covered the desk. A bookcase held a few paperback readers from when he'd arrived seven years ago and cubbies contained games and old toys, including a Captain America action figure. The VR games and HDSET held this generation's current interest.

Max was now just a couple inches shorter than himself— no longer a boy. Did a bit of peach fuzz darken his face? Everett made a mental note to teach him how to shave.

He was fifteen now. Max wouldn't grace their home for many more years. Life seemed to speed past. He'd been home as much as work allowed for Max's soccer games, and he'd encouraged his mathematics, but Everett wondered if he'd juggled the conflicting time demands well enough. Two energy projects had kept him away for months on end the last year, and that thought left him with a lump in his throat.

Max turned in his direction and removed the HDSET. Had he made a sound?

"Hi, Dad." Max's face revealed a moment's discomfort at the interruption, and then he relaxed. "Welcome home."

"Some new game release?"

Max shrugged. "There's always a new one. This one takes place on Earth after nuclear war, and the sea level has risen ten meters. You need to fight off the mutants and find food to survive."

Everett collapsed into the beanbag chair, glad for the weight off his legs, and considered how to respond. "There are many dystopian tropes, and some businesses make a profit by playing on our fears that the world is falling apart."

"But isn't it?" Max asked the question without irony. "At least in the game, you can pretend to fight back."

Everett reached for the Captain America figure tucked in the corner cubby. It was well used years ago. He held it up. "They don't call them action figures for nothing."

Max laughed at the joke. "Avengers, assemble!"

"You can fight back in the real world too. That's what I try to do every day—something useful to fight climate change."

"But can it make a difference?"

Everett set the figure back on the shelf and straightened its head to look upward. "I can hope it does. So much is non-linear in a complex world. But isn't that better than living in an alternative world?" He gestured at the HDSET. "Or to just exist in the world? Isn't it best to try to create the world you want to live in?"

Max made a small frown. "I don't know what else to do now, except what I'm doing."

"That's fine. Summers are for taking time off. I know you're doing a good job at Maybeck High, with fine grades last year."

Everett saw past the vestiges of the bookish kid to the young man he now faced, his hair thick above his forehead. Maybe he should focus less on encouraging the studiousness that Max naturally had and instead on developing new skills. He remembered his teenage trips to the Lair of the Bear, weeks each summer spent hiking in the Sierra. He'd tried to spur the same outdoor interests with Scarlett, but she hadn't enjoyed the trips. Work had intruded, and he hadn't invited Max into the mountains. It was time to try again.

"Hey, I'm thinking about something different and fun. Doesn't your summer session end soon? How about taking a break from studying and tech? If I can score a slot in the Yosemite lottery, are you interested in a backpacking trip? The high country should be open soon."

His face brightened, but hesitation immediately followed. "Sure, Dad, but I don't know much about the woods."

"No worries. You'll pick up the basics fast."

◆

Everett parked the car in Tuolumne Meadows and stowed his PAWN in the glove box, symbolically leaving his tech connections behind. He filled his lungs with mountain air. "A few days spent in the Yosemite high country will remind you of your primal soul."

Max stared up at the surrounding granite peaks with an awed expression. He seemed excited by the trail leading off into the wilderness and flexed his arms in anticipation.

They filled water bottles, shouldered packs, and Max walked easily beside him as they started up Lyell Canyon. Everett planned the first day introduction to backpacking for Max to be amply rigorous, with a bit under two thousand feet of elevation gain to their campsite. The trail wandered alongside the Lyell Fork of the Tuolumne River, still flowing midsummer through alpine meadow flanked by red fir and lodgepole pine, with western juniper adorning the rocky fringes. A light breeze carrying the aroma of pine whistled down from Donahue Pass.

Everett stepped nimbly over a fallen log barring the trail. "A tenderfoot hiking rule is to step over logs instead of on them. You can't tell when one might break under your foot and turn an ankle." Max followed his example. He wore the same contemplative expression that Everett had noticed when he was intent on a math problem, now absorbing new lessons.

They hiked through the morning at an easy pace. Everett called a halt for lunch and took sandwiches from his pack, which they ate next to the river where it rushed noisily at a rocky turn. Afterward, he showed Max how to operate the filter and watched him hunch on a rock to fill their water containers. Deer grazed by the riverbank then leaped away at a sound.

The trees thinned out as they climbed in elevation, still a gentle uphill trek. By afternoon, they'd turned out of the canyon and pushed on into steeper terrain to Evelyn Lake.

Everett stopped for a drink from his water bottle. "Tired?"

"My shoulders aren't used to this pack, but it isn't so bad."

"If we continue to Bernice Lake, we can camp two nights in one place."

"How's the fishing there?"

"Better than here, I suspect, since it's farther off the main trail."

Max gave a thumbs-up. "Then let's go."

They slogged on for another two hours and approached the tree line to wind past Vogelsang Lake and High Sierra Camp, which was closed that year for refurbishment, and then crossed rugged landscape up the spur trail to Bernice Lake.

The lake rested in a rocky bowl, and bare granite rose around the deep blue water. Everett suggested a campsite next to a couple of pines. He let Max puzzle over setting up the tents while he refilled the water bottles from the lake, working the filter pump. On his return, the two tents were neatly aligned on level ground.

"Good job with the instructions."

Max grinned. "Just like Legos."

Everett pulled two steaks from his pack. "Normally, dinner is dehydrated food, but since it's a short trip, the extra weight wasn't too much to haul. We can spoil ourselves tonight." He showed Max how to operate the propane stove to boil water for the freeze-dried veggies, and he soon had the steaks sizzling in the pan. They lounged outside the tents, eating the hearty dinner and washing it down with cool mountain water.

He patted his contented stomach. The sun dipped below the horizon, and alpenglow spread across the peaks, the reds in contrast to the blue water. Max studied the sunset, serious and thoughtful. The mountains elicited many reactions from people, and he wondered what Max was considering. Everett rested against a log to enjoy the moment together.

"Dad, you wake up every day and go to work. Do you think you make a difference?"

Everett recollected it as the same question from the beginning of the summer. "I have to believe I do."

"But can you really do anything? In my physics class, the teacher talked about deterministic equations. Isn't it all determined, anyway?"

"Well, that is a heavy metaphysical statement. You were discussing determinism philosophy in a science class?"

Max nodded.

He collected his thoughts. "Some of the physics equations are deterministic. But there is much that is nonlinear, like what's found in nature, out here." He waved his hand toward Vogelsang Peak, with the last pink radiance dimming. "The Uncertainty Principle is at the heart of quantum physics. The philosophers may quibble, but I don't buy the arguments for determinism."

"And free will?"

"Any fool can see that we have free will. At every moment, we can decide to do something different. Any argument to the contrary can be just a lame excuse for inaction."

Max's face was lit by the glow of his backpacker's lantern. "I've been thinking about what I might do after high school. The world seems too complicated to plan for anything."

"Yes, the world is more challenging than ever before. I won't pretend to give you advice that can foresee the future. It's complex, and no one can predict what will happen this century."

He rubbed his neck. "So Dad, no advice?"

"Start with what you might be good at, and what you might enjoy doing, and think about what might be of benefit to more than yourself. I'd like to believe humanity is heading somewhere grand, not petty." Everett's expression softened. "Don't worry. You'll have time in college to find something to be passionate about."

"Okay, but that doesn't help with planning now."

Everett chuckled. "You're a planner, like me. Well, my advice is to plan three scenarios. Plan a best case about what you might do next. Then plan a worst case. That might uncover surprises; what the world will throw at you. Third, plan a most likely case, assuming everything won't work out but we'll somehow muddle through. Then, just recognize that the world will always surprise us, so learn to be resilient and deal with whatever comes."

"So do something useful. And roll with the punches."

"That sums it up." Everett patted his arm and picked up his lantern. "Time for bed."

"Thanks. Night, Dad."

———————◆———————

Everett was surprised that they had Bernice Lake to themselves both days. The first morning, Max baited the fishing poles for casting at sunrise and caught two brown trout to his one. They grilled them for brunch. The weather remained clear and warm during the day. Max wanted to explore, so they day-hiked to Gallison Lake. They carried their fishing poles and spent an hour casting without result, but Max was uncomplaining. He had adapted to camping and seemed to enjoy the outdoors. The day ended with a chill over the mountains as soon as sunset kissed the peaks, and Everett fell asleep to the rumble of the waterfall on the far side of the lake. They woke with the rustling of alpine trees above them.

"Time to break camp and head down Lewis Creek to Echo Valley," Everett said.

"I'll take down the tents." Max scurried about the task, appearing confident with his new knowledge.

Everett showed him how to check the bare campsite for any evidence of their visit, leaving the wilderness pristine. When Max finished cleaning up, Everett playfully punched his arm in approval, and soon after sunrise, they shouldered their packs, said goodbye to the blue lake rimmed by granite peaks, and headed down the trail.

Delicate dew lay upon the white mountain heather, and the bright pink Sierra beardtongue along the trail brushed its wetness onto Everett's hiking pants. He took the lead, following the narrow trail over rough granite and then through short grass, where the trees grew closer to the trail. A broken log had fallen across the trail. Everett stepped over it quickly and placed his foot on the other side.

He felt the fangs clawing at his calf muscle, the pain sudden, at the same instant that the rattle filled his ears and the snake writhed under his heel. The rattlesnake held on, and Everett cursed and stumbled. The snake wriggled from underfoot, still holding on, then its jaws released his aching calf. It slithered a few feet away and rattled again.

"Dad!" Max was at his side. The snake slunk into the underbrush.

"Damn. He got me good." Everett's calf muscle sported two red fang marks and felt like he'd slammed it in a trap.

"He was six feet long." Max stared at the grass where the rattlesnake had disappeared. "Let me help you sit down."

Everett gripped his arm and hobbled the few steps to a large log, sat, and leaned back against a ponderosa pine. "A Western Diamondback rattlesnake. I'm surprised to find him up here so high, but it's warmer than it used to be."

He tried to calm his respiration. His leg was lower than his heart, and he tried to move as little as possible.

"Dad, you need help. Right away." Max's anguished gaze met his.

With the growing misery came the remembrance of his PAWN left behind. When he'd rambled these high-country trails years before, there had been spotty cell coverage, and it hadn't seemed necessary. Now, whether that had changed was moot.

"You're right. The only effective treatment is antivenom. And even Yosemite Medical Clinic way down in the valley likely doesn't have it."

Everett recalled the previous night's lecture about planning. He wondered if the irony added to his discomfort. He tried for some levity. "I guess there's an exception to every rule. Including the one about stepping over every log on the trail."

"Where's the closest ranger station?" Max was all business.

"That's at Merced Lake High Sierra Camp. Not too many miles." He motioned to his pack, now on the ground.

Max found the paper map. "We're here," Max said, and Everett agreed.

Everett thought about the rugged trail and the hours to traverse it. His leg throbbed. "I think it best for you to bring help back to me as soon as you can. I'll sit here."

"You'll need antivenom soon. In hours, right?" From his expression, Max was making worried calculations.

"Within four hours is best, I think."

Max studied the landscape in all directions. "Planning," he muttered. "I'll need a medevac helicopter to get back to you in time."

Max walked a hundred yards to a flat patch of bare granite away from the trees. He dragged branches and logs into a large X. He was soon back at Everett's side, his expression anxious and determined. He handed Everett a full water bottle and hooked one to his belt for himself.

"Dad, I'll be back as soon as I can. Stay still."

"Will do, boss." Everett winced through the pain.

Max loped off down the trail.

The mountain was silent, except for the occasional gust of wind blowing mournfully through the trees. Everett studied the growing bruise around the bite marks. He refreshed his memory about snakebite treatment besides antivenom. Fumbling in his pack, he found a pen, circled the bruised area, and labeled it with the time. He lay back, counting to remain calm, and watched the swelling increase. An hour later, he drew another circle around the expanded swelling and marked the time. His calf felt scalding hot.

The tingling spread up his leg, and he imagined the black fluid moving through tissue. He circled the larger area of swelling and labeled it again to keep himself occupied with something useful. Everett was sweating, and a wave of nausea made his head swim. He sipped the water. His ears buzzed.

The buzzing resolved into a rumble and grew louder. A helicopter swooped low to circle the hillside and settled onto the granite. Dust rose around him as the aircraft cut its engine. Max and the pilot ran toward him. Relief washed over him from seeing both Max, determination lining his face, and the pilot lugging a medical bag. Blonde curls poked from beneath her helmet.

She checked his pulse and bent over his leg. "Good to note the times and progression. Not a moment to lose." She pulled a vial from her bag and filled a syringe. "We need to push the serum intravenously. Let's get this started."

Everett smiled crookedly at Max. He must have passed out for a few minutes because, the next he knew, he floated in the clouds under a thumping helicopter blade while Max held his hand.

Everett woke in a hospital bed. Tubes protruded from his body, and screens blinked overhead. His leg ached. His hand was warm, and Ginger squeezed his fingers. Her face bore the marks of recent crying, but she gazed into his eyes with relief. Max moved from the corner to sit next to the bed and took his other hand.

Everett grinned at them through the pain. "Max, I hadn't expected your first backpacking trip to be so memorable. You saved me out there. Thank you, son."

A tear dripped down her cheek, but she smiled. "Max, you did us proud. I love you."

12

"But jealousy just ain't right. You were the refugee kid." Grand repeats his comment from before I filled in details about growing up in California. It warms me to find a concern for justice deep in his genes.

I wipe the stray bits of flour and bread dough from my hands and relax into the cushy chair in the corner of the kitchen. Grand has stirred up old memories with his questions, turning back the pages of a book I haven't opened for years.

"Scarlett's jealousy developed over time. It's in the nature of siblings to have some. Maybe it's because I'm the adopted son, and Scarlett had the idea that the genetic relationship should be given precedence. Every family's history is complex."

"What happened to Scarlett that turned it sour?"

"I don't think she was ever as happy as she expected. She married Jack after graduation. He got a job selling AI in New York City, and they moved to Brooklyn Heights, then Manhattan. He focused on making money, and they delayed having kids. Eventually, there was a son, Jaxon. And a daughter, Harper, came along."

"Your sister was across the country, and you were in California?" Grand's question comforts me that he's at least learned some geography.

"Yes. It was difficult for Scarlett to come back to Berkeley because Jack didn't prioritize family. I had Momma Ginger and Dad to myself by default."

"Had the world calmed down by then?"

It took a moment to remember the feel of the world during those decades in the first half of the century. "Politics grew a bit calmer. Tech made the world spin ever faster. The AI wave transformed many jobs, but people were able to find newly created jobs, some of which were things we'd never thought to do before. The feared AI apocalypse never materialized, at least not then. There was more wealth per person because of increasing efficiency."

Grand stands with his hands in his pockets. "Were people happier?"

"In the main, they were. Poverty fell around the world. Health improved because of biotechnology. Technology transformed employment, but many escaped drudgery and did more interesting things. Hey, humanity survived, and even thrived." I don't want to paint a picture of all gloom about those years. Despite our worries about climate change, on a personal level, there were many good times.

Grand's eyes brighten. "After a tough start, then you had a normal life growin' up."

"Yes. I grew up in that comfortable suburban house with Momma Ginger and Dad until college. After Elmwood Academy and Maybeck High School, I went on to Penn State for a mechanical engineering degree focused on nuclear energy. I followed Dad's footsteps."

With the question, the images flood back. Everything was new and different. New kids, new friends. The ache of missing Mama and Baba. But Momma Ginger and Dad were there with me. Riding to high school on my bicycle. Cute Emma in the eleventh grade and making out with her on Grizzly Peak Vista. My nerdy friends in computer and math classes. Then heading off to university for my degree in energy engineering. Keg parties at Penn State. Meeting my roommate, lifelong friend, and future colleague, Buzz Henderson. ME classes in the Hallowell Building, where I studied fission engineering. My favorite professor, Dr. Zander Flocke, firing us all up, and afterward, hanging out with engineering buddies, talking about saving the world. Did we save the world?

13

Buzz Henderson—2046 (Pennsylvania)

Buzz sat in the third row to get a clear view as Dr. Zander Flocke, a special visitor to the class, moved to the lectern. He walked with a limp, rumored to be the result of an engineering accident from his days in the field. His upper body was still muscled like he kept himself in shape, but otherwise he looked old, with thinning gray hair and a clipped beard.

Buzz had heard stories from graduate engineering students at Penn State about this talk, which Flocke had given for years, and he waited expectantly. Half the class planned to continue into the field of fission energy after graduation, including himself. Max MacGyver, his roommate, sat on his right, 3D screen open.

Flocke connected his PAWN to launch his presentation, and the luminescent panels covering the classroom walls blazed with light. Buzz opened his PAWN so he could access the augmented reality features. The 3D projectors left him feeling that he was inside a gleaming modern power plant facility. Projected behind Flocke was a long chart, the year 2015 on one end, the year 2045 on the other, overlaying an ominous reddish maelstrom.

Flocke looked down at tattered notes. His PAWN rested on his nose like glasses from the last century. He surveyed the room.

"Let me tell you today why you're here. You're here to save the world." Buzz clenched his hand, waiting for the next words.

"Since we are engineers, and scientists, we value facts. Let's review the facts of how we, as a species, got ourselves into this dire predicament. Many of you are familiar with these arguments. But much of the public, sadly, is still not. I'll give you my version of the concise points. Then, critique it. Learn the counterarguments; learn why they're weak. If you find this line of reasoning compelling, then help spread the word."

Flocke clutched the podium. "I've been making this argument for nearly forty years. Perhaps you'll be successful. But either way, know that time has run out."

Buzz poked his roommate, and Max gave him a slightly annoyed look at the distraction. Max had said his father graduated from Penn State, too, many years ago. Buzz wondered whether he might have heard a similar lecture.

Flocke flicked his laser pointer, and two articles appeared on the large 3D side wall. "You've no doubt reviewed the course materials, beginning with studies published in *Nature* in 2015, by McGlade and Elkins, and in 2009, by Meinshausen et al. We will understand the portrait of global fossil fuel use at a strategic level. From there, the conclusions are clear." Flocke came out from behind the podium and put his hand on it. He was quite comfortable with this lecture.

"First, to definitions. We'll not discuss the roughly 11,000 gigatons of carbon <u>resources</u> estimated to be in the ground, because the models show that if we extract those, then it's the end of the world." Heads nodded.

"We'll focus on the subset, <u>reserves</u>—oil, gas, coal—that can be profitably extracted with today's known technologies. In 2015, reserves were about 3,000 gigatons. In the *Nature* studies, the authors calculated that if more than about 1,000 gigatons were burned from 2016 through the year 2050, then it would be unlikely that global temperature rise could be held below 2 degrees Celsius." He looked directly at Buzz, who had been tapping a rhythm on his thigh. "Even a 2-degree Celsius increase means that bad things happen to humans and the environment."

Flocke frowned. "I didn't overlook the fact that in 2015 the Paris Agreement called for nations to target stopping at a maximum temperature rise off baseline of 1.5 degrees Celsius. That showed itself to be a wish and a prayer."

Flocke paused to measure his audience. "But let's review how we've done in the following thirty years. To remember the big picture, to stay at about 2 degrees Celsius from baseline, humanity had a 1,000 gigaton maximum budget, 3,000 gigatons in reserves, and so must leave 2,000 gigatons in the ground."

Max took careful notes with his PAWN and display. His roommate was really sigma, hard-working and always prepared. He got things done and helped keep Buzz organized for the exams. Buzz kept Max from being a hermit. They already made a good team, partly because they just did things differently.

"So, how did we do?"

Flocke flicked his pointer at the 3D display behind the podium, and the chart came to life with a timeline of temperatures rising as fossil fuel use barely decreased year-over-year and the carbon budget declined. The chart and a clock counted off the past thirty years. "In the first decade after 2015, the world burned roughly 350 gigatons of carbon. That's between 35 and 40 gigatons each year.

"In the second decade after 2015, from 2026 through 2035, another 350 gigatons were burned, reaching a total of about 700 gigatons against the budget. In that decade, the global community put some teeth into targets for each country. Another positive was a dramatic increase in renewables, particularly solar and wind. These gains were offset by the simple fact that the world had added people, especially in less-developed countries, where people obviously seek an improved quality of life, which comes with energy use."

Flocke paced between the aisles, his body agitated and his limp even more pronounced. "Now to the third decade, from 2036 through 2045, to last year. Many developed countries are carbon negative through the use of costly carbon sequestration technologies. Carbon use has declined every year. But still not enough. To round out the thirty years, in the last decade, the world has burned another 300 gigatons of carbon. We've used up the entire budget. Five years too early. We cannot hold the temperature rise to under 2 degrees Celsius by 2100." On the display, the energy budget counter shrank to zero. Flocke's eyes were sorrowful. His audience was silent.

"Where do we stand today, in 2046? We are still burning between 20 and 30 gigatons of carbon each year."

Flocke shook his head in despair then continued. "Electricity demand will be four times as much in 2050 compared to 2015, even as transportation and heating transitioned away from oil and coal. The global population will grow by two billion. Critically, less-developed countries want the same energy as the Global North. In 2015, developed countries, such as the US, used as much as a hundred times the per capita energy as the poorest. There's a minimum electricity budget needed to maintain a modern, civilized existence, even if it is a fifth of US per capita use then. People in the Global South want air conditioning, good housing, transportation, and food security."

"Hella more renewables," Buzz mumbled.

Flocke looked up, caught by the flippant remark. "Unfortunately, renewables have not completely replaced fossil fuels. Why? The list of non-fossil fuel alternatives is short—solar energy, wind energy, hydro, and fission energy. Solar and wind have grown dramatically over the past twenty years, taking over large areas of land. We've begun to deal with maintenance issues, which increase the cost per kilowatt beyond what was envisioned. Hydro is an excellent sustainable energy source. However, the best sites for hydro have been developed, and new sites entail ecological tradeoffs. And energy storage, in the form of batteries and pumped storage, gives some flexibility to managing time-of-day use, but with a high energy loss cost."

Flocke had sweated through his shirt in his fervor, and wet circles appeared under his armpits. His voice rose as he finished the argument, waving two fingers in the air. "Now to the critical ideas, which are twofold. First, of those renewables, solar only works during the day. Wind varies by time of day and season, so it makes load balancing difficult and can require large grid investments to move electricity to where it's needed. Only hydro and fission energy work around the clock to balance demand loads. Hydro is only a significant part of the energy equation in some geographies. Where hydro isn't, only fission power can easily balance demand loads." There was a rumble of agreement throughout the room.

"The second key idea is that, globally, we face a tragedy of the commons. Carbon in the atmosphere impacts everyone. It's not enough for developed countries to be carbon negative. The Global North needs to offer renewable energy alternatives to everyone because, otherwise, less-developed countries can't create energy systems with balanced loads. We must give those countries fission energy."

Dr. Flocke studied his audience. "Let's hear some objections and other opinions. The floor is open." His gaze darted to Buzz, still caught by his sarcastic remark.

Buzz was saved by Max, whose hand shot up. "Haven't carbon credits and cap-and-trade been effective?"

"Very good," Flocke said. "The EU was early to try such systems, and others followed. Those systems set limits on emissions and inject incentives for market innovation. The good news is that they have directed efforts toward cost-effective ways to reduce emissions. That's in the positive column."

Flocke tapped his pointer on the podium. "But there's a negative column. It's proven difficult to monitor and enforce compliance. There's been abuse of these systems as companies find loopholes. It's been hard to keep the carbon prices on the markets stable. In summary, the systems require large bureaucracies. They've been effective in the Global North, but much less so in the Global South, where there has been that high growth in energy demand. These systems haven't kept the world within the carbon budget. And the world needs more non-carbon power."

A student in the back row shook her head. "Can't governments do more to stop the use of fossil fuels?"

Zander Flocke adjusted his PAWN further up the bridge of his nose. "Governments have the authority to tax fossil fuels. They can ban them outright. To date, taxation has been somewhat successful. Bans have been tried, but profits accrue to cheaters. Lamentably, many of the fossil fuel source countries are willing to abet the cheaters. There will be pressure on both sides, supply and demand, to use the stranded resources. Remember, the 2015 report tallied about 11,000 gigatons, and exploration has continued since then. It's difficult to keep that resource stranded in Pandora's box."

A student in the corner chimed in. "Why has it taken so long to develop fission energy? It seems obvious. We're two decades behind in ramping up fission power plants in the global energy system."

"Nonscientific environmental worries," Buzz said sotto voce. "Unreasonable fears will cost us an extra meter of sea level rise this century."

Flocke gave a slight nod in Buzz's direction. "Public opinion turned against atomic energy because of Chernobyl, Fukushima, and a few other accidents. Opponents led PR campaigns based on fear. Utilities lost the will to take on the risk of building plants, and politicians failed to explain the true risks versus the benefits in the fight against climate change. For three decades now, major climate change studies have included huge fission energy development in mitigation plans but also failed to highlight them as required investments. There's timidity all around."

"But fission technology is so much safer now," a student in the back called out. "Current modular, passive safety designs are completely different from the first generation."

"Someday, we'll have fusion power," said another student. "But commercial plants are still decades away."

This time, Buzz couldn't restrain himself and joined the discussion aloud. "Engineering is damn hard. Anyone who said to wait, that fusion power was around the corner, never understood the practical problems of fail-safe plasma containment, heat management, materials durability, and reliability. Wishing for fusion has been a big mistake."

"Both true." Zander Flocke clasped his hands together in angst. Buzz thought he might suddenly fall to his knees. His voice dropped near a whisper. "When I was a kid, we were still watching the old Star Trek shows, where in a couple of centuries from now, they imagined we'd be exploring planets around other stars. But now we know there aren't any 'Class M' planets close enough for humankind to personally explore in a thousand years." His hands appeared to cup some precious object. "The best planet we'll have is right here. Climate change is a clear existential risk that will eventually make Earth unlivable if we don't stop it. It's in our hands."

Flocke stood to full height and raised a hand in the air, as if blessing the class. His voice rose to a thunderous conclusion. "We have the technology. We must spread it around the globe. We must develop it for all parts of the world. We don't have any time left." Flocke flicked his pointer toward the wall display, and giant letters appeared to spell out, "Only fission can save us."

Flocke turned to the class. "Now, go out and save the world."

14

Save the world. Save the world. The words echo inside me.

"Grandfather, you mumbled something."

I am caught with my memories spilling out. "I was remembering my best friend Buzz and the years we worked together to build renewable energy plants around the world. It was the only way to fight climate change, to save the planet. The second great challenge that humanity faced this last century. My life's work."

The memories bluster past like the wind. They push at my mainsail, my wife, my balancing force, Grand's grandmother, Tadala. Her caring soul, always thinking of others, was part of why she was so good at her work. And she was so good for me. My soulmate, we loved and lived and worked together, wing on wing.

I hesitate a moment and try to keep the story on track.

"Climate change brought about increasingly dangerous storms that threatened the lives of people we hold dear."

Grand stares blankly at me. He hasn't made the connection and doesn't know the story of his grandmother.

"Let's go into the living room, and I'll show you a hurricane. A cyclone, as they call it in Africa."

Grand follows me, and Robert shuffles behind us to the great room. Two solid walls rise to the cathedral ceiling, a height of two stories, with large windows on the third side. I still like the way I designed this room.

"Robert, please pull up the saved news vid summary from the 2050 Malawi cyclone."

"Yes, sir." Robert's forehead shades to green, and the twin walls fill with light. Palm trees sway violently in the wind.

"Here, wear this." I hand Grand the second HDSET from the table to complete the 3D effect. We both put them on.

"Yesterday, Cyclone Kanga grew over the Indian Ocean into a severe tropical cyclone, bringing winds of 300 kilometers per hour," a newscaster intones. "It headed west to clip the tip of Madagascar before slamming into Mozambique and Malawi. Casualties in Malawi are particularly high, as the cyclone stalled over the country. The storm dumped massive quantities of rain. Hillsides have collapsed. The government is having difficulty reaching outlying villages. First reports are that three hundred thousand people have died. As many as four million are homeless."

With the HDSET on, the cyclone surrounds me again. Trees fly like arrows through the air. Goats roll down a hillside. A river overflows its banks, submerging small houses, and one is torn from its foundation. It tips sideways into the muddy churn. The video cuts to families wandering among broken houses, scavenging to save belongings. The vid frames a baby girl sitting on a log in a muddy field, tears glistening on her cheeks. My heart falters.

Grand watches until the video ends and rips off the HDSET. He looks shaken, as if he's never experienced a modern immersive. I too catch my breath but more from the memories it induced. The cyclone footage created a swirl of emotions within me—flashes again of Tadala and her brother Samuel. The screens fade to normal wall color.

I grab my walking stick from its spot leaning against my favorite chair by the fireplace. I had filled the built-in flask with wine before Grand arrived this morning.

"Robert, please pack our lunches and follow us." I take Grand's arm. "Let's walk now, first down to the ocean, then to see my vineyard. If you want to know something about hurricanes, then you should have known your Great Uncle Sam. He and his sister, your grandmother Tadala, were hit by a bad one—the one you just watched. I'll tell you about meeting your grandmother and great-uncle while trying to save the world."

15

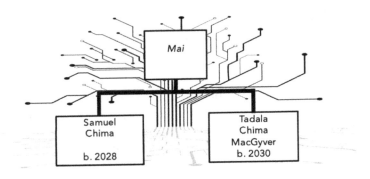

The sun was up an hour, and Samuel slipped into the kitchen for a bowl of *nsima*. He could tell already that they faced another hot day in Thyolo. These past three years, Malawi had suffered through yet another drought. Drought and rain; extremes seemed to be the rule now. Tadala smiled at him as she stirred the maize flour and ladled the hot porridge into his bowl.

"Thank you, *atate*." It's nice to have a little sister with a kind heart. And one willing to fix your breakfast.

"Let's not disturb Mum. It's her one day off, and she deserves to sleep late." At her words, he lifted his chair instead of pulling it out so it didn't scrape against the rough floor.

"*Mai* always works too much, and the tea plantation takes advantage of it." Samuel had grown up using the Chichewa word, but Tadala switched to the English for "mother" when she embraced the global language.

Tadala filled her bowl, sat beside him, and changed the topic. "You're almost finished with your degree." There was pride in her voice.

The IT courses at Malawi University had been a grind, but as a big brother, he was setting an example. "One more semester. Now I'm looking out for a decent job."

Her face edged with unease. "Do you think I'll be able to start classes by the new year?"

Samuel touched her hand. "We said we'd help each other. I'll find the money somehow." She was two years his junior. Just twenty, but forced to wait to begin college because they didn't have the resources to cover tuition. It was his promise to fund her education once he graduated and found a job. Tadala was even better at her classes than he was.

"And I won't let you down, *m'chimwene wamkulu.*"

He liked it when she called him big brother. But her open smile made him feel the weight not only of helping her but also of protecting his sister. She was too beautiful for her own good. Malawi was not as modern as he wished and not as protective of women's rights as many countries.

A college degree was the sole road out of their district town. The modern world beckoned from the smartphones they held in their pockets, advertising riches and an easier life. But finding the time and resources to complete an education were just the first barriers in Malawi, and most there only knew those wonders of the outside world through their screens.

Samuel finished the nsima. "I think it'll be a pleasant day," he said. "I can feel it in my bones."

"I like your confidence, but better drink some water. I expect it to be hot. That approaching storm might push humidity ahead of it." His sister was usually on top of the news and admittedly better at predicting what would happen next.

Samuel inspected his phone. Indeed, the storm off the coast had changed direction since last night. "You're right. The weather AI says it's heading toward Mozambique and expected to come ashore and turn up the coast. We'll see high winds and rain by tomorrow. Better let Mai know."

Tadala nodded as she cleared the plates. "I'll keep an eye on Mum."

Drawing from the kitchen water purifier, distributed gratis by the UN, Samuel drank two glasses and then filled his liter bottle. He left in silence and walked the two kilometers down the dusty road toward the college for his morning class.

Placid mountains graced the horizon, and the rising sun flooded light into ravines that led to the rolling savanna below. Tea plantations had covered the hillsides like neat green gardens when he was a kid, but now the land was brown and uneven. Never a leading tea producer, Malawi plantation investments had fallen behind other countries, and there wasn't the money to supplement failing rainfall with irrigation. Samuel had seen videos of the automated tea harvesting robots in China and Türkiye. He wondered if Mai would be part of the last generation of tea workers in Malawi. It was a tough, hot job, carrying the large woven basket on her back, and Samuel thought the plantation's disappearance wasn't such a bad outcome, even if finding other employment was a constant struggle.

Haze shimmered in the air. Sweat poured off his forehead, and he felt his breath catch from the effort of breathing in humidity. His heat watch listed the wet-bulb globe temperature and his internal body temperature, both in orange. Also distributed by the UN's World Health Organization, the watch was scant help and instead served as an anxious reminder of their peril. These gifts from the Global North were small consolations for the toll of climate change. His internal temperature had reached 38 degrees Celsius. It was time to slow down. When it hit 38.5, heat exhaustion was a risk.

Most people living in the huts there worked on the farms, the disappearing tea and tobacco plantations, and the paprika fields that yielded additional cash to their owners. For most, jobs were hit or miss, and earning a living required juggling multiple jobs. Samuel saw no future in farming. He studied architectural drafting, wishing to someday build something tall and beautiful.

As he approached the college, squat simple houses like his own made of fired bricks and mortar lined the winding street, many with new metal roofs. A few bicycles and motor scooters bumped past. People sat outside their doors, ready to begin work while nurturing a forlorn hope to lower their body temperature.

He turned a corner onto a narrower street and continued toward two men hunched in a doorway smoking a joint. One looked up.

"Man, want a drag? It's Malawi Gold." His eyes were cloudy and friendly.

"Thanks, *bwenzi*. Nah, I'm goin' someplace. No time."

"You can go some high places with us," the other man said.

"Oh, I'm goin' high places." Samuel kept his tone friendly.

The two men laughed and waved him off. Samuel strolled past them and turned onto the main road. At another hut, an old woman shelled a bowl of cow peas. Her hands wore calluses, like those on Mai's hands, from working in the tea plantations.

The old and the young, with different ideas about the need to work, with similar doubts about the future. When life was harsh and unpredictable, it was unfair to judge how people lived their lives. His smartphone vibrated in his pocket, and he checked the screen.

The woman squinted up at him. "Witchcraft," she murmured.

Samuel tried to keep in his chuckle. "Nah, *amai*. It's a weather AI telling me about the storm coming." He studied the track on his smartphone and, despite the heat, he felt a shiver down his spine. He darkened his tone in warning. "It's heading for us here. You should be careful."

Looking frightened, the woman whispered, "Chiuta. Chiuta brings the clouds, the rain, and lightning."

"I'm not talking about the old Tumbuka ways. This is modern science. Better prepare for a monsoon."

"Where go the old ways? Everything changes too fast."

Samuel opened his water bottle, took a long drink, and then shared it with the woman. "Some change is good. Don't you remember when we had malaria in Africa not so long ago? You were young, I'm sure. Now, they've used gene drives in mosquitoes to wipe it out. HIV, AIDS, and TB have vaccines. Modern science. That's the cure."

"And much change is bad. Chiuta comes now to teach us."

It wasn't an easy argument to counter—good and bad. But he prayed she would prepare for the storm, for whatever reason moved her.

The main college buildings were ahead on the road. He had time for his one class, and then he must race home to protect their windows against the wind. He ducked into the classroom just as the bell rang. Except for student interaction, the classes were a partial waste of time. Personal AI technology had revolutionized education around the world. His AI instructor, an app calibrated to his learning style and pace and synchronized with his prior knowledge, was twice as fast at teaching the course material. But the instructors needed the jobs, especially in Malawi where professional positions were scarce. He attended all the in-person classes, if only to show support for the instructors.

"Today's subject is ultra-white paint. Consider it for all building design. The paint doesn't look different to the eye than any white paint, yet it reflects 98 percent of the sun's heat," the instructor said. "There are grants available from the UN that make this an inexpensive feature to lower energy costs and cut solar heating. Buildings don't heat up as much, so air-conditioning systems are cheaper." The professor paused to show examples on the display behind the podium, and gave a technical description, talking of barium sulfate and paint composition.

Samuel's smartphone buzzed. The weather AI was blazing red. The storm had been upgraded to an intense cyclone. Higher forecasted winds were pushing it farther west, over Malawi instead of turning north through Mozambique. Several students also scrutinized their smartphones.

The instructor looked puzzled until a student said, "The storm is movin' in. More importan' things to worry about right now than paint."

The instructor reluctantly nodded and dismissed the class. Samuel headed back home, only pausing for a moment as he walked by the old woman's house, hoping she'd taken his warning to heart and would take cover.

When he arrived in front of his house, Tadala was already outside fixing plywood over the windows with Mai holding the boards. She finished driving a nail, and said with conviction, "It's going to be bad."

"Where did you get the money for the wood?" Samuel picked up the next piece on the pile.

She put down the hammer. "The UN handed out cash through their app an hour ago, the same way they sometimes hand out grants." She showed him the app and pointed to the storm grant. "This money went to towns in the eye of the storm. That's how I know it will hit us hard."

Samuel took over holding the wood. "Mai, just relax and drink some water. It's too hot for you." He was struck by how frail she looked. She wasn't much younger than the woman he'd passed on the way to class.

After Mai got them all cups of water, Samuel filled jugs and brought them to the center room, where Tadala had piled canned food and torches. They moved their most valuable possessions into the room and covered everything with plastic tarps. He surveyed their work.

Tadala left to visit the elder neighbors to ensure they were prepared too, and Samuel peered through the doorway. Out of the stillness, a cooler breeze stirred the fronds of a nearby palm, as if in anticipation of a threat approaching.

When Tadala returned, she cooked *mpasa* with potatoes and filled their plates. The sun disappeared behind the distant hills as they finished the meal.

It wasn't long before the wind picked up and rain lashed the porch. Samuel and Tadala sat on either side of Mai and watched news reports on the TV. Mozambique had evacuated coastal areas, and Malawi also ordered evacuations to shelters for everyone near rivers and streams. The closest to them was the Shire River, some distance to the west.

Tadala was busy on her smartphone. "The orders for Thyolo are to shelter in place." She frowned. "They say to stay at home because the only shelter building is full."

His mother trembled as if reliving a nightmare.

"Mai, we'll be prepared to weather this storm." Samuel gave her a hug.

Tadala hugged her from the other side and met his gaze. They must stay positive. Rain rattled on the metal roof like machine-gun fire. The wind screamed under the threshold of the front door. Lights flickered before they went out, and the TV went black. He examined his smartphone. There was no signal.

"I suppose it's time to pretend to sleep." He dragged two mattresses from their beds onto the floor by the sofa and encouraged Mai to lie down.

The three huddled in the dark. Mai covered her ears against the wind's wail and rocked back and forth, whispering prayers to ancient gods, Christian saints, and any unknown power that might protect them.

The downpour thrummed all night. They never slept. Samuel's watch eventually showed it to be morning, but it was gray outside, and the wind still howled. Impatient and curious, he peeked out the front door but was pushed back. The wind almost tore the door out of his hand. Rivulets of dirty water sluiced down the road. He glanced up at the surrounding hillsides. Water coursed off ravines, where water never flowed. No one was outside. He shut the door with force.

In the dim light from two torches, Tadala fixed a cold breakfast, and they ate in silence. Electricity had not come back on. Samuel studied his smartphone again to find the battery reduced to one-quarter. There was still no signal.

"Time to try the pay satellite." He toggled the app for paid satellite access, which at last connected.

News feeds opened, and he read the latest forecasts. The cyclone had stalled over Malawi, and flooding had occurred throughout the country. The endless cloudburst drumming on the roof kept time with his rising heartbeat as he read.

It wasn't good to alarm Mai and Tadala, but he couldn't deceive them, either. "It's bad, and there's no word on how long this will last."

Mai sat between them slumped at the table, her face twisted with old memories. "I was younger than you, Tadala, when Cyclone Freddy came through. It drenched us then too."

"Mai, don't trouble yourself. This storm can't be as bad as that. Anyway, we're all together, and we love you," he said.

Tadala touched Mai's shoulder. "We love you."

A loud sound filled his ears, a groaning, growling, squealing, rising in pitch, and the wall of the house bulged. The groan rose into a shriek, like a thousand hyenas attacking. Suddenly, the attacker was visible in the light of the torch he pointed at the wall, a black water gushing through fissures opening between falling bricks. The wall buckled and collapsed onto his leg, and pain shot through his entire body. The raging torrent tore the torch from his hand. Samuel's last thought was of how cool the water felt rising on his face before darkness enveloped him.

16

Buzz Henderson—2050 (Malawi)

"Our damn luck to try doing this in the middle of a cyclone." Buzz sat at the console, his yellow hard hat tossed beside him. He wondered how he'd gotten into this situation so quickly after graduating. The wind hammered rain against the window.

Max looked up from his fixation on the gauges, all showing green. "It *is* our luck. Two newly minted engineers like us, and we made it happen."

He and Max had joined the fission energy company together. They offered small modular reactors, already a well-tested technology. Their first major project was a power plant in Malawi in east central Africa. It had taken many months of work to complete the plant. That effort was followed by months of plant commissioning, including system commissioning and testing, performance and reliability testing, final inspection, and certification.

Buzz wrinkled his nose. "Max, you've been kicking your own butt *and* mine to get everything running perfectly. And you're right. We did it. This plant is safe and ready for operation."

"But now what?" That intensity in Max's eyes meant he was solving a nasty problem. "We're the only US engineers here from the company. No one else can decide when to start it up."

"This cyclone showing up in October—the wrong damn season—shows exactly why we need these plants to fight climate change." Buzz was all in on however Max wanted to handle this fight, which was part of why the two had stuck together.

"They know that here already," Max said. "The drought strangled outflows from Lake Malawi. Without being able to depend on the Shire River, there's limited electricity from the hydro generating stations."

They watched news reports on the control room displays, and rain sheeted off the windows. They were now operating outside normal corporate rules. No instructions had arrived—or would arrive—from headquarters in California.

The lights pulsed for a moment, then the emergency electricity switched over.

"Shit. Was that a test? I think this country needs a reliable fission power plant." Buzz had never been able to bite his jokes back, even in situations like this. But it seemed to push Max to a decision.

"Let's check in with MERA. I'd like to know how the national grid is faring."

Buzz nodded and opened a call to the appointed representative. The face of Limbani Phiri filled the 3D screen. The Malawi Energy Regulatory Authority logo hovered below.

"Hello, Limbani," Max said. "We've been following the storm news. I'm sure you have your hands full, but I think we can help."

Limbani's big face was haggard, a man missing sleep. "It's worse than the reports. Yesterday, Kanga blew the roof off the Kammwamba plant. It's in bad shape. There's extensive damage, and no one is sure how long to repair it, if ever."

With effort, Buzz tried to keep his face sorrowful. Both hated the Kammwamba Thermal Power Station. It was their reason for being there; to replace another dirty coal-fired power plant.

"Commissioned in 2030, right?" Buzz nodded in commiseration. "It's a shame." Buzz didn't think it was a shame at all. "But our fission plant easily replaces those 300 megawatts."

Limbani rubbed his temples. "We need electricity. We're struggling to keep the grid online. We lost our hydro plants when the Shire River flash flood shut them down. Silt and debris clogged the intakes. That's my morning headache."

Max jumped in. "We have the modular fission energy plant ready to go online a month earlier than scheduled. It's passed all environmental and safety certifications. We've tested everything and have no issues. We are fully operational."

Hope crossed Limbani's face. "Everything's tested? And the storm hasn't affected you?"

"Solid construction here," Buzz said. "Damn well-built to withstand a cyclone. Performing as designed."

"Are you authorized to start it up?"

Max wore the face of a general going to battle. "I'm authorized to turn it on when I judge it ready. It's ready. Get your team in place. Today."

The bent man stood taller, like a weight had been lifted. "Let's do it."

"Holy shit. We're the main plant for the entire country." Buzz thumped Max on the shoulder. "I hope to hell we've put one more coal power plant to sleep permanently."

"That's the game. Maybe giving the power stations away will let the transition occur."

Buzz nodded at the comment. This fission plant fit the description as a gift because all the financing was from USAID, the US EXIM Bank, the World Bank, and European Development Bank. The debt would probably be offset with Global North carbon credits.

"Yep, we need a big carrot to convince Malawi not to import those billion tons of coal Tanzania has in the ground." Buzz toyed with his hard hat.

The deluge slackened, so Buzz volunteered to check the exterior of the plant, leaving Max in the control room. A young Malawian engineer joined him to inspect the intermediate piping sending heat to the energy island.

"These modular designs are simple compared with coal-fired plants," the Malawian engineer said.

"And cleaner. No dirt and coal dust, no giant boilers, no scrubbers, and no piles of coal."

The man shook his head vigorously. "I grew up near the Kammwamba plant. It's choking. The smoke makes people sick."

They circled back to the reactor island, passing two inspection teams. The reactor itself was underground. There were puddles of water everywhere, but the cyclone had done no damage.

When he returned, Max was watching a current news reel he'd opened on the control room display.

He waved Buzz over. "Kammwamba is in worse condition than Limbani thought. Look at this footage."

They pointed at details, attuned to the engineering issues. The drone flew over the main building, where part of the roof had been torn away, exposing a damaged boiler. It hovered low over smoke still rising from the coal tipple and conveyor, now open to the sky, with twisted metal lying about.

"It looks to me like there was a spark in the conveyor tunnel, and the damn thing blew up," Buzz said.

"I'd rather see a planned decommissioning of these old smokers."

Buzz snorted. "Hell, I'll take it any way it comes."

Rainwater slapped against the windows. But lights glistened here and there on the hillsides, proof that electricity was restored in the immediate area at least. Several other engineers were in the control room, and all systems operated normally. It was a huge step forward. With the grid connection made and layers of fail-safe systems in place, running a fission plant was now like watching a sleeping baby.

"I'd like to see how bad the damage is outside," Max said.

Buzz turned to the next most seasoned engineer to ask if she could take charge of supervising the team.

"Sure, I've got it covered." Her eyes danced.

Buzz and Max took the Land Rover. They stayed in low gear as they surveyed the soaked asphalt road, dodging torn pavement and navigating flooded sections, where new streams washed down off the hills. Muddy water was everywhere. Sirens wailed in the distance from emergency vehicles. Malawi Defense Force trucks drove past on patrol. Fractured houses lay sideways off their foundations.

Topping a hill, the scale of devastation shocked the eye. Bloated cattle filled a ravine. Entire hillsides had given way, and rubble had tumbled to the bottom. It was impossible to guess how many people might lie within the wreckage. A few emergency workers scrambled among the ruins with cadaver dogs.

"Damn." Buzz averted his gaze from a team discovering the lifeless body of an elderly man and slapped the steering wheel.

"I never imagined anything like this." Max looked shaken.

The past several months in Malawi had shown Buzz a lovely people, friendly and kind; "the warm heart of Africa." He felt his chest ache seeing the destruction caused by the cyclone, the misery and loss etched on the faces of the survivors. He couldn't think of what he could do, besides leaping into the mud with the people wandering aimlessly, in symbolic empathy. Sadly, no one had yet gestured to them for help. His view from the vehicle felt like cheap voyeurism. He glanced at Max, who bore a similar stunned expression.

Unable to pull themselves from the horror, they drove up through the edge of the Michiru Mountain Conservation Area. The road was washed out in places and nearly impassable. On the other side, the tea plantations that had been choked by drought just days before were flooded. Trees lay ripped up by their roots, exposing the ugliness underground. The district town of Thyolo was ahead. Mud churned from the red soil-covered streets that must have held houses, but now only piles of debris remained.

"Are you thinking what I am?" Max asked. "The power plant is functioning well. We need to do something to help."

"Do you know where administrative buildings might be? Is there a hospital?"

Max strained to see out the windshield. "Thyolo District Hospital is up on the east side." The lights were on in that section of the broken town. Buzz pulled the Land Rover up to the hospital, snaking through cars and scooters parked haphazardly outside.

"Let's check to see if there's anything we can do to help."

Buzz was doubtful, but he pulled the vehicle to a stop, and they both climbed out. Rain soaked Buzz's slicker instantly as he ran beside Max to the entrance, the hard hat giving meager protection.

Inside, nurses scurried among injured people in a crowded waiting room with stretchers lining the corridor. Max walked several steps ahead.

A doctor looked up from assisting a patient. Glancing at their badges and hard hats, he lit up graciously. "Thank God the power is back on. Are you here with an update? Will it stay on now? We've got every operating room working."

A face appeared behind the doctor, eyes bright and animated. The young nurse came forward and took Max's hand.

Buzz was glad he was a few steps behind, because from the arc light appearing on both faces, the electricity he witnessed between the two might have killed him.

She held Max's hand for a long time without him pulling away, as if already familiar with his touch. "You gave us the electricity back? Thank you with all my heart."

His friend stood unmoving, shocked into silence. The doctor waited for a response.

"We'll do everything in our power to keep the electricity on," Buzz said. Somebody had to break the spell.

17

TADALA CHIMA—2050 (MALAWI)

Mud and water surged through the broken wall, and the house cracked at its corners. Mum suddenly wasn't there. Tadala felt for Samuel's arm and reflexively grabbed. She pinwheeled, holding to him with every bit of her strength as a vortex of turbid water pulled her down. Samuel was her anchor to survive, her reason to navigate her way free of the torrents. The house dissolved, and the door hit her before it washed past.

They swirled in red mud and water until she pulled Samuel free. Tadala spit muddy water and, holding him with one arm, swam sidestroke with him out to the edge of the maelstrom. He was heavy, unmoving. She hauled him several meters up the bank so they wouldn't be sucked down in the torrent.

Samuel seemed lifeless. She rolled him over, pounded him on his back, and muddy water trickled from the corner of his mouth. She wiped the grime and pressed her face against his. His weak breath tickled her cheek. She cradled him and watched the mucky avalanche carry parts of houses down the hillside.

Tears mixed with the rain on her face. Mum was gone. No one could survive the mud after going under. She was so tired.

Samuel's leg was bloody under his grimy pants, injured from when the wall had fallen on it. Tadala couldn't wake him, but he was still alive. She had to get him to medical care. The hospital was on the other side of town. The upper road was a hundred meters away. With her barefoot heels digging into the muddy hillside, in pulls of a few meters each, she dragged him up the hill and laid him by the road. Half the houses there had slid off their foundations.

A pickup truck owned by their rich neighbor, who'd left the day before to visit family in Blantyre, sat crooked on the road in the mud. In a flash, Tadala was inside his house looking for keys and internally promising that she'd return them once Samuel was safe. She found them in a desk hidden in the back.

Samuel was a deadweight to lift, and she struggled to hoist his inert body into the truck's bed, then closed the lift door. Rain pelted the windshield and, as she tried not to get stuck on the half-destroyed road, she wondered how all of Malawi was not yet an ocean.

A few ambulances emptied patients at the hospital emergency entrance. At least it was not yet overwhelmed. A generator droned in the parking lot, maintaining emergency lights. She parked the truck and ran inside for help. People filled the gurneys lining the entry, and nurses scurried between them.

"My brother." Tadala's voice cracked as she bellowed into the room, the dry mud still stuck in her throat. "He needs help. He's bleeding."

An orderly grabbed a gurney and followed her to the truck. Together, they loaded Samuel onto it and brought him inside. The orderly ran to a doctor, who rushed back.

"I'm Dr. Tembo," he said. He cut Samuel's trousers above the knee to expose his crushed leg and stanched the blood oozing over the gurney. "Take his blood pressure, STAT."

They bandaged him, and the orderly swabbed Samuel's face. A nurse checked his blood pressure and heart rate.

His eyelids fluttered, and he groaned. His breaths were shallow and strained.

The doctor turned him onto his side and exposed deep lacerations on his ribs, rectangular outlines of the bricks from the falling wall. "How long has he been bleeding?"

"I'd say a half hour since the wall fell on him."

"We'll stabilize him. We've too many casualties right now to do more. But his leg is badly hurt, and he might have internal injuries. I can't tell how serious it is without x-rays and surgery." Dr. Tembo's gaze met hers. "There are already patients with worse injuries ahead of him. We'll do what we can."

The doctor and a nurse immobilized Samuel's leg with a splint wrap. Dr. Tembo hurried off when a siren announced another ambulance.

"There's an open bed available, and he looks like he needs it," the orderly said.

They pushed Samuel into a room with another patient. The orderly helped Tadala swab the mud from him then hung a drip of painkiller and sedative over his bed.

"You need to change those clothes too," the orderly said.

She gratefully took the scrubs he handed her and went down the hall to shower.

She returned to her brother's side within minutes. The anesthetic had begun to work. His face had relaxed, and he was awake.

He searched her face. "Mai didn't make it, did she?"

She shook her head.

"Was it fast?"

"Gone before she knew it. It's just us now."

They held hands and cried, drops of suffering in the sea.

As Samuel slept, Tadala sat at his bedside and watched the frenetic activity in the hallway. Injured people continued to be wheeled into the hospital.

Feeling useless, she walked to the doorway and stopped a doctor rushing by. "Is there something I can do to help?"

"Follow me." Soon, Tadala worked alongside the nurses, cleaning mud off patients, bandaging wounds, and assisting as doctors sewed up serious injuries. She spent the rest of the day helping with emergency care and checking on Samuel. Sitting for a few minutes to eat a sandwich with two others, she felt indistinguishable from the hospital staff.

The generator's drone stopped, and the lights went out. "We're out of petrol," someone said.

A surgeon came out of an operating room, his gloved hands held in the air. "Find some torches. It's too dark in there to continue."

It was late afternoon, and the light through the hospital windows dimmed. But more vehicles jammed into the parking lot. Gurneys lined the corridors.

Tadala had heard the word "triage" from the doctors. Now she saw that the worst patients had been left on gurneys in one corridor, and no one was caring for them. The reality that they'd been abandoned to die dawned on her. She shuddered to consider making such a decision.

She checked again on her brother. Sweat beaded on his feverish forehead. Tadala measured his blood pressure with the handheld AI. Low and dropping. She found Dr. Tembo finishing with a patient and escorted him to Samuel's room.

As they walked, he said, "You've never done any nursing before?"

She shook her head.

"You're good at this. And not squeamish about the unpleasantness that comes with the job."

She shrugged. "I want to be useful. There's so much need here; it would be wrong not to pitch in."

The doctor examined Samuel, focusing on his injured side.

She couldn't wait for an answer. "What can we do?"

"We need to operate to find the internal injuries. But there isn't enough light until the electricity comes back on. Keep him company and wait." Dr. Tembo tried to hide his concern, but his face betrayed him.

———————————◆———————————

Tadala woke with a start. She was slumped over Samuel's bed in the hospital room. Had the other patient made a noise? Perspiration still covered Samuel's face. Then she noticed—the electricity was back on.

"Lights! Open the operating rooms," someone shouted from the hallway.

Dr. Tembo came into the room and checked Samuel's vital signs with the handheld monitor. "Move him to the surgery pre-op holding area."

They wheeled him away, and Tadala was left in the empty room. With Samuel's life at risk, and the image of Mum disappearing below that relentless, muddy floodwater seared in her brain, she felt all alone in the world. Her chest heaved in unstable breaths, and Tadala finally cried—releasing the day's emotions as quickly as Chiuta's pounding rain had come down on Thyolo.

* * *

"How is Samuel?"

The doctor's face couldn't hide relief. "He's stable. We repaired internal injuries, including a hemothorax."

"Wha—"

"Blood around the lungs."

Tadala nodded.

"The blood loss might have killed him without surgery. The antibiotics are controlling infection. I expect him to regain consciousness soon."

She let out her breath in relief. "He'll be okay?"

"His prognosis is positive, except for his knee joint and lower leg, which are not good. Reconstructive surgery is beyond our capability here. A more advanced hospital is needed for that." Dr. Tembo lowered his voice and added the bad news. "He'll need such surgery to walk normally again."

"That doesn't sound okay."

The doctor looked at the ceiling as if searching for an answer and then back at her. "I have a medical school colleague in Bordeaux who does that surgery. But you know the difficulty of getting your hands on a visa to Europe, and I have no idea how we might transport Samuel there, given the troubles that Cyclone Kanga has unleashed on Malawi."

They discussed Samuel's recovery care. The doctor patted her arm, and he was gone. Tadala stayed with Samuel until morning when his fever broke and he opened his eyes. She fed him small bites for breakfast.

The storm was expected to slacken later that day. Patients still streamed through the emergency doors, and a temporary morgue was set up in the side parking lot. Grim stories from throughout Malawi came from the staff and her news feed, and her thoughts seemed to only make everything worse.

She was in the hallway when Dr. Tembo passed her. He pointed to the entrance. "It looks like one of the men in charge of restoring power service has arrived—the big Chinese man over there. Lucky for Samuel the power came back on when it did."

Her gaze followed his pointing finger to a tall man wearing a yellow hard hat. He had a large build, softened by a sweet face and thick eyebrows. He looked bewildered, like he was unsure who he had come to visit. But the confusion was mixed with kindness in his expression. Her heart swelled.

Tadala reached out a hand. "You gave us the power back? Thank you with all my heart."

As their hands met, an electricity ran through her, as if his touch restored her spirit.

◆

In the morning, Dr. Tembo found Tadala to relay the video conference conversation with his surgeon colleague in Bordeaux. They agreed that, without reconstructive surgery, Samuel would not regain full use of his leg.

"Medicine has fewer barriers among doctors than among politicians. If only we could find a way to get your brother to France. I wish I had an answer to that problem, but I have none at the moment."

Her morning saw another visitor. The yellow hard hat on the tall man was unmistakable.

"I said yesterday I'd come back to check on things here. The power grid is stable and in good hands, so I thought I might come back early."

Tadala glanced at his large hands, remembering their warmth and the fondness she had felt when she'd held them. "I don't think I thanked you enough yesterday. When you came in, the doctor pointed to you and said, 'That big Chinese man turned the power on.' It was just in time to operate on my brother, and that surgery saved him. I'm grateful."

He was thoughtful, and there was a hint of a recollection on his face. "Saved by the big...man...I can relate. But I'm American now. And not much to do with China." His gaze met hers. "I felt your pain when you mentioned losing your mother."

Her chest tightened. "The wall collapsed on Samuel. Our house was swept away. Mum was lost then. I held on to my brother and got him out of the water." At the mention of Mum, her heart felt heavy. "Now, I have no one else except Samuel. Malawi is just a sad place."

Max touched her hand. She turned it over in his, and it felt natural.

"I also came to see how your brother is doing. Is he improving?" The concern in his eyes was genuine.

"He's doing well, considering his injuries. Would you like to meet him?"

They walked down the long corridor, and their gazes met briefly at the door before they entered Samuel's hospital room. He sat in bed eating a bowl of nsima.

She introduced them and relayed Dr. Tembo's assessment, including the need for further surgery in an advanced hospital.

Samuel gulped nervously. "Without the painkiller in this tube, I wonder how much my leg would hurt. It's numb now, like I don't have a leg."

Max straightened, speaking with inspiring confidence. "The issue is getting Samuel to France? Maybe I can help.

My mother knows about international relief organizations—about refugees and how the laws work. How to gain asylum." He blushed. "Well, I also know a thing or two about refugees."

———————————◆———————————

It all happened so quickly, starting with Max and Tadala finding Dr. Tembo. Max asked questions and searched for solutions in a swirl of planning.

Soon, Tadala and Max were seated upstairs in Dr. Tembo's office. With his help, Max made the connection, and faces filled the display. Max introduced everyone all around.

Max's parents were seated in a pleasant room, the windows dark behind them. A reminder of their time zone far away.

"Nice to meet you, Doctor, and Tadala," Everett said. "Max, I understand you put the Malawi fission plant in service."

"Just in time."

"I'm proud of you. Saving the planet."

"Saving more than Mother Earth," Tadala added.

"Thanks for saying that."

Tadala's heart warmed with the thought that his comment included both his father and her.

Max turned the conversation to treatment for Samuel. It was easy to admire how determined Max was to accomplish the problems set before him. His mother took notes as he talked, asking precise questions and asking the doctor to describe the medical necessity for Samuel's care, followed by questions for Tadala.

Ginger offered the most promising suggestion to address transport. "The France-based organization, *Médecins Sans Frontières,* Doctors Without Borders, must already be helping cyclone victims. It's possible that Samuel may qualify to be included."

The group was problem-solving, and Tadala's spirits rose. She enjoyed taking action. And she was struck by the closeness between Max and his parents.

Dr. Tembo sighed. "The Western countries have tightened immigration laws significantly over the past decades. There's still the visa issue."

"But emergencies, especially those caused by climate change, offer the chance for exceptions. We can explore several sources to see if the emergency of the cyclone may create a way to obtain a special visa. Humanitarian medical treatment in such catastrophes is a special category exemption."

Tadala didn't want to ask for too much, but her heart thumped. "Just for Samuel?"

"For you, too, Tadala. You are Samuel's only living relative and the person who must be entrusted with power of attorney over his medical health."

"I will go anywhere to protect my *m'chimwene wamkulu.*"

------------- ◆ -------------

For the few hours she slept each day, Tadala stayed in a cramped room in the hospital commandeered for her by the staff. She had nowhere else to go, there was far more work than could be handled, and patient care distracted her from thinking about Samuel's injury and the loss of Mum. Because she never left, it was always easy for Max to find her.

His eyes glowed with excitement. "We have a breakthrough. My mother found a flight taking cyclone medical patients to France, organized by *Médecins Sans Frontières.* She's confirmed two spots can be made available. There's a process to apply for a medical exception, and Samuel—and you—can be issued one-month visas to France."

"When? Are there any requirements?"

"If Dr. Tembo certifies that it's necessary to proceed with the operation before Samuel's leg worsens, which is the truth, then you can leave tomorrow. You need proof of a financial sponsor. That's a formality, as France wants to protect against financial burdens on its social services."

Tadala stepped back. "Where will I find a sponsor?"

Max grinned at her. "That's me."

Her heart leaped. "But why?"

"Because you remind me so much of myself. In the same situation, a refugee without family or any ties to a country. I want to help."

Tadala hugged him, gratitude filling her. "Thank you for everything you're doing, for Samuel and me."

◆

Tadala stared out the window of the chartered jet as it circled Bordeaux Airport. Verdant fields and vineyards glistened in the sun below, reminding her of the tea plantations surrounding Thyolo before the years of drought and the cyclone. But it wasn't the aroma of tea that accompanied the flight; it was the smell of the hospital. The faint metallic tang of blood, a slightly sweet odor of medications, and the warm organic smell of bodies permeated the plane. Tadala was unperturbed by it. A dozen cyclone victims suffering a variety of injuries were strapped to gurneys. Two doctors and three nurses attended to them. Samuel lay in the back, sedated, and didn't stir, even when the plane landed.

Multiple ambulances waited at the gate, along with a customs agent who checked visas.

"You're cleared to travel directly to Dr. Durand at L'hôpital Saint-André," he said to Tadala. "Place your visa in a secure location so it can't be lost and you always have access to it. Serious consequences can result from not having the visa."

Tadala thanked him and uploaded the encrypted visa to her cloud account alongside her passport and other identification documents. It was impossible to travel anywhere without them.

Ambulances left for separate destinations with their new patients. She waited while two medical personnel carried Samuel from the aircraft and wondered at the absence of a smartphone in the hand of the customs agent. And everyone else.

Tadala had seen these newer communication devices, the HASP and PAWN, on social media, but they were too expensive for the average Malawian. Lightweight, almost invisible, and easy to forget that the person you're talking to was wearing a PAWN, it had replaced smartphones in the Global North.

The medic turned to her, and she felt momentarily confused. "Don't you need to scan my ID or visa?"

He glanced at her smartphone. "Ah." He shook his head. "The customs agent sent that to me already. And my PAWN matched your face, so you and Monsieur Samuel Chima are clear for transport to the hospital." He tapped his PAWN. "It adds quick access to the net. Some people even add corneal inserts. But I don't trust that the technology won't change, so I use the contact lens connection."

The ambulance team loaded her brother, allowed Tadala to sit at a window, and navigated the wide boulevards of Bordeaux while she marveled at the sights. Her heart beat with excitement, and it felt like a grand adventure.

Imposing white limestone buildings marked every thoroughfare, speaking of wealth beyond any in Malawi. Cafés lined side streets filled with people lingering over lunch. Cars, all electric vehicles, moved methodically. She glimpsed many self-driving cars maneuvering in traffic. Peering at one at a stoplight next to the ambulance, she was surprised that the vehicle had no front seats, a detail she hadn't seen on social media. In the large rear compartment, two people lounged on sofas, engaged in conversation and oblivious to the proceedings outside.

Besides the autonomous vehicles, she was struck by the density of drones filling the air. They flitted overhead, hovered before entering the delivery entrances of buildings, and moved in sweeping patterns like Cape Glossy Starlings in Malawi, lacking only their iridescent colors. She feared for the local birds against these metallic competitors for the sky.

The ambulance turned onto Rue Jean Burguet, and they passed a sign that read *Service des Urgences*. The hospital loomed in front of them. Some signs need no translation.

A serious woman stood at the door, pushing blond hair behind her ear. "Tadala, I'm Dr. Durand. Happy to meet you."

She stopped to inspect Samuel and directed the ambulance team where to transfer him. Then, she led Tadala to her office. Dr. Durand sat in a swivel chair next to her, where they could both look out the window into the hospital courtyard. It was encircled by the hospital wings, which enclosed a well-manicured lawn and a gigantic fountain tossing water in colorful sprays all the way up to the height of her office. In contrast to the cyclone's flood, this water was clear and controlled. France felt a world removed from Malawi.

The doctor spoke with a French accent. "Dr. Tembo forwarded Samuel's medical records. He's going through confirmatory procedures here, including full MRI, in preparation for the surgical robot to perform the operation via MRI-fusion surgery. Of course, all such delicate surgery is performed by surgical machines."

The worry that Tadala felt for Samuel must have appeared on her face because Dr. Durand's tone softened. "I've overseen hundreds of cases like your brother's, and he has a good chance of regaining the full use of his leg."

Tadala and the doctor discussed the details of the surgery, which was scheduled for the following day. With taps on her computer, she transferred the authorization forms, which appeared on Tadala's smartphone for signature, and the formalities were completed.

Dr. Durand studied her, a finger resting against her cheek. "Dr. Tembo mentioned that you pitched right in to assist after the cyclone hit."

"I helped in Thyolo's hospital. There were many serious injuries." With Dr. Durand's urging, she described the injuries she'd helped treat.

"You've compressed much experience into a short time. And you seem to have the stomach for the *sanglant* parts of the profession. If you don't mind more blood, you're welcome to watch the surgery."

The conversation energized Tadala. She found medicine interesting. Dr. Durand blinked, and Tadala realized her PAWN must have buzzed with another obligation. But the doctor remained unhurried.

"We also have arranged an apartment for you to use during the four weeks that your visa is authorized."

Her thoughts about joining Dr. Durand and Dr. Tembo's field were brought up short by the reminder that her time in France had an expiration date. "And after that?"

Dr. Durand shrugged. "*L'avenir est inconnaissable.*" A second later, Tadala's earbud whispered the translation of, "We take one day at a time," confirming the meaning she'd suspected.

The operating room was framed by two displays through the large window. One showed the robot surgeon's arms cutting tissue around Samuel's knee, and the other was a view from the nanobot pillcam inside an artery. Dr. Durand had been overseeing from the operating room but now came to stand beside her.

"The surgery is proceeding well, with no unforeseen issues."

"You can repair everything?"

"Materials science has made amazing advances in the past decades. New biomaterials will replace the affected joints, and I expect your brother will walk without even a limp."

At the words, Tadala took a deep breath, releasing the worry she'd held for Samuel since he was injured, and she thanked the surgeon.

She returned her gaze to the moving robot fingers enlarged on the screen as they tucked back layers of tissue. Her only experience with surgery was during the past week, watching surgeons with bloody hands operating in the old fashion.

"Do you ever do surgery without the AI robot?"

The doctor folded her arms across her chest. "Not for years. Of course, I learned the techniques in medical school. But surgical robots have better precision than human hands can achieve."

"Does that leave you feeling less in charge?"

Dr. Durand glanced again at the screen. "My job is focused strategically on the entire procedure, which entails understanding the general objectives and the implementation details."

"Still, your job depends on the AIs, on the machines." Tadala wondered whether the medical professionals led or followed the machines.

Dr. Durand waved casually toward the operation. "Our job is to orchestrate the robots, to assess whether they are performing what we want done, and to look for potential errors. The machines are still not good at those steps."

"Are all medical jobs dominated by robots?"

"Medicine is still patient-focused. We need good nurses, and hands-on care hasn't been replaced by machines. We all need human encouragement and touch when we're healing." Dr. Durand smiled. "It is a stable profession if you're considering it for yourself."

Tadala remembered the French. "*L'avenir est inconnaissable.*"

The doctor laughed. "You have a good memory. We can't know the future. We can only live it as it happens."

"I don't know what I can possibly do after Samuel is released and our visas expire. These jobs in the Global North countries are different from what we can find in Malawi."

"Since I studied medicine two decades ago, so many jobs disappeared or were replaced by new kinds of jobs, in all professions. AI changed everything. Middle-level jobs have disappeared, replaced by AIs. Higher-level jobs require understanding how to manage our technology." Dr. Durand touched her arm. "The jobs delivering personal care also survived, though changed. Nursing is one of those."

The surgical robot beeped, and its arms retracted, while green numbers filled the left screen.

The doctor scanned the figures. "The surgery was successful. I anticipate a normal recovery, and Samuel should be ready for release after the second phase of his treatment."

Tadala didn't hide her surprise. "What second phase?"

"Perhaps you're unfamiliar with the treatment protocols here. I suppose you haven't seen them in Malawi? After the surgery to repair bones and certain tissues, the next phase uses synthetic biology. We've withdrawn a sample of Samuel's cells and, designing with BioBricks, we've engineered materials that will rebuild his muscles and connective tissue. Just like a baby in utero, these tissues will regrow, and should nicely match, almost as good as new."

"I don't think synthetic biology is used in Malawi." The concept sounded like witchcraft to her.

Dr. Durand leaned in and seemed happy to be teaching. "Beginning with *M. Labiratorium*, used as a chassis for synthetic life, bioscientists have programmed all sorts of organic devices to reengineer human health. If you were to become a nurse, you might learn all about these techniques and help bring them to Malawi."

Tadala now saw the reason for the doctor's helpfulness, which was admirable. She sighed. While Mum was alive, she had always thought she would live in Malawi despite the allure of the Global North, so visible through social media. She hadn't dreamed to *japa*, even though the idea of running away from the home country was common now throughout Africa. The gulf between the wealthy north and the poor south left her sad.

"How long will this treatment phase last?"

Dr. Durand seemed to read her mood and took her hand. "Three weeks. That's the reason your visas last a month. Maybe take some time to enjoy yourself in our city."

━━━━━━━━━◆━━━━━━━━━

Tadala liked wandering the streets of Bordeaux, discovering neighborhoods of beautiful old architecture, all alive with a buzzing cosmopolitan crowd. Tourists and locals filled Rue Saint-Catherine, and she marveled at the amount of time people had.

People in Malawi moved slowly because of the heat but with a steadfastness, with no other choice than to eke out a living.

At night, a fall breeze cooled Bordeaux, and Tadala loved seeing the Place de la Bourse aglow, and the lights dancing on the Miroir d'eau.

Rich enough to merge the modern with classic beauty, Bordeaux seemed a century ahead of anything in Malawi. She wandered to the station, the Gare de Bordeaux-Saint-Jean, and watched the newest maglev trains whisk passengers away to Paris. Police patrolled the streets, some eyeing her as she walked by, but no one accosted her.

Beyond the tourist center, Tadala found neighborhoods that resembled Malawi, though with most people from West Africa. From the poorer apartments, the lilting rhythms of African beats softly colored the air and reminded her of home. After a few days, she encountered areas where people shrank into the shadows as she approached until they saw her clearly, and she guessed that they were illegally in France.

Further down at the street corner stood a Tabac shop, with *Inès Martin, propriétaire* written on the door. The Tabac sign was surprising because it no longer sold tobacco. It had been banned in France and much of Europe, and global demand had declined, which was why the tobacco plantations had disappeared from Malawi. She entered to better read the news headline blinking on a screen behind the counter.

"*La Chine frappe un site militaire nord-coréen.*"

China attacking North Korea? Tadala opened her smartphone news app to read the details.

The shopkeeper behind the counter, a Frenchwoman of middle age with intelligent eyes, must have read her worried expression. "They say China attacked a North Korean command center where military and political leaders were gathered. At last, the leadership was beyond crazy, and too many Korean refugees crossed the border to escape."

She shivered. "What are the Americans doing about it?"

"So far, nothing. North Korea has been a rogue state for decades. China is the only country that could deal with it, since Korea depends on them for economic survival. It seems the Chinese will cause regime change."

Seeing Tadala shiver, the woman put out her hand, and they introduced themselves.

Tadala found Inès to be knowledgeable about world affairs. She thought back to her own geography lessons, trying to picture the situation.

The risk of war upset her. "And what about the South Koreans? I expect they'd want reunification with fellow Koreans, just like Germany was eventually reunited."

Inès tapped the counter to emphasize a thought. "Beware of false analogies. Taiwan was not like Ukraine, and North Korea is not today like East Germany was. The North Koreans have more in common with the Chinese. Both have spent long years living under dictatorships."

Tadala's next question was interrupted when the owner glanced at a disturbance outside the shop. Police had swarmed the street, and they were stopping people.

"I trust you have a visa," Inès said, as a police officer entered.

"I do," Tadala said. The police officer sternly eyed her. "I have a visa." She opened her smartphone app and produced it.

The officer stared at it closely, then at her, and she realized that he was verifying the encrypted code with his PAWN. He nodded and left the shop. Tadala wiped the sweat that beaded her brow.

She and Inès watched as the police rounded up several people. They were loaded into vans and carted away. One man struggled with two policewomen, shouting *"Mais je parle français!"* He, too, was hauled away. Tadala wondered at the comment; her smartphone translation app made speaking French irrelevant.

"Whenever anything surprising happens in the world, the authorities get nervous. Illegal immigration is an intractable problem for all Europe." Inès pursed her lips. "Liberty, Equality, Fraternity. We still say it. We used to believe the main mark of being French was to speak the French language natively. We need immigrants to do many jobs because our

French population is shrinking. But not all agree that the country should be open to immigration."

Tadala felt lucky to have the visa. "Why do some disagree?"

Inès sucked in her breath and shrugged. "People fear change. With climate change, refugees try to pour in. There are political pressures to keep them out. Draconian technology is used to guard borders. There are *beaucoup* drones and AI surveillance. Now Spain, France, Italy, and Greece have a joint squadron of unmanned coast guard ships that intercept all boats smuggling refugees into Europe."

Tadala studied the woman closely. Inès had empathy for the immigrants, like herself, who wished to live in a better climate in a country like France. Yet Tadala could not detect in her classically European appearance any non-native heritage.

She chose her ambiguous answer carefully. "There are many people who find this country so attractive."

Inès shrugged and sighed. "There are two and a half billion people in Africa. That's a billion added over the last thirty years. A billion would migrate to Europe in a heartbeat if they thought they could stay."

Tadala nodded in sympathy. "What to do?"

"Indeed. We're caught between Scylla and Charybdis. We'd like to believe we still hold our equality and fraternity as sacrosanct. But populist and nationalist leaders use fear of cultural dilution to gain power. And these *poseur* dictators challenge democracy. We're forced to make choices against our values. As much as it breaks my heart, we can't accept everyone freely into our country and maintain our democracy."

Tadala felt her chest heave. "I won't forget your humanity to honestly share that insight with me."

The street had cleared of pedestrians and police, so she thanked Inès for her friendliness and walked home. Passing a bakery, the aroma of fresh bread left her feeling the hint of something wonderful yet out of reach. Her visa had saved her from deportation, but it expired in a few days. She and Samuel would be sent back to Malawi, where nothing remained for her—no family, no home, no prospects. Tadala climbed the steps to her temporary apartment and closed the door against a dark, divided world.

Tadala was glad to see Samuel out of his hospital bed, tottering clumsily on new crutches. "Thank you, *atate*. You saved me. You are the strong one." He hugged her while standing on one leg.

"My *m'chimwene wamkulu*, I'll always be here."

He rested while she sat on the edge of his bed. They talked about the muscle reconstruction and his recovering strength. Her smartphone buzzed. Dr. Durand requested that she meet in her office.

"I'll be back soon." Tadala patted his arm and left.

The doctor sat at her office desk and smiled broadly when Tadala entered. "You've visited Samuel? He's healing well because he is young."

"I did visit him. He's beginning to resemble his old self."

"I expect his limp will go away. His injuries were extensive, but the synthetic biology reconstruction worked very well. There's no futbol in his future, if that was his game, but he otherwise should recover full mobility."

"Doctor, we both thank you."

"Of course. We inserted a chipset under the skin on his left hip to monitor his condition continuously."

"An embedded chip?"

The doctor nodded. "You'll need to follow normal protocols with the chipset."

"What is the normal protocol?" Tadala was confused.

"He'll communicate with the chip via a PAWN." Dr. Durand paused. "Embedded chipsets have become common in the Global North."

"Thank you, Doctor," she said, now jittery about how to pay for a PAWN and all the technology Samuel might need.

Dr. Durand patted her hand. "You may be thinking about what's next. But...you should hear it from the source."

With that, she crossed to the door and whooshed it open. Max appeared framed in the doorway. A smile creased his face directed only at Tadala.

Doctor Durand gave her a small wave. "I'll leave you to discuss that." She closed the door behind her.

Max settled into the seat next to Tadala. She was warmed by the presence of the big man, like a knight in armor from a European fairy tale.

Her heart beat hard in her chest. "I'm so glad to see you here in France."

"My Malawi project is finished. Now I'm homeward bound. In the past two weeks, I've been working—with my mother's advice—to investigate possibilities, and we've found one. There is a refugee exception that allows you to come to the United States."

A flush crept over her face in anticipation, and she leaned her head for him to go on.

"The rules are a bit crazy and bureaucratic. My mother ran an AI analysis to find a path through them that meets the exception requirements for you and Samuel. It helps that you and your brother are victims of a climate change-induced event, that Samuel had life-threatening but treatable injuries, and that you now hold French visas, even though they're only temporary. Those facts place you in a special category. If you are trained or entering a university program for certain high-need professions, then you can qualify for entry."

She digested his words. "Is nursing on the list of high-need professions?"

Max looked surprised by her quick response and thumbed through a link on his PAWN. "Actually, yes, it is. And there's a program at UC Berkeley."

She couldn't suppress her exuberance at finding that stars had aligned. "Then nursing it is!"

"You're certainly decisive." He laughed deep in his belly. "That settles it. The upshot is that we can arrange US visas, if you wish. We can sponsor you, and you can come to California."

Tadala's breath caught in her throat, and she was left speechless.

His expression turned serious. "There is one more thing. There are no strings attached. You will not owe me or my family anything. It's a promise."

He was a knight, with a dreaded dragon retreating from his lance. She could only hug Max as tears ran down her cheeks.

18

SAMUEL CHIMA—2050 (CALIFORNIA)

It was only the second time he'd been on an airplane, and he wasn't conscious during the first trip. Now, Samuel was very much awake. His leg ached from flying for eight hours. He recalled the talk with the two men smoking Malawi Gold the day of the cyclone and his prediction about being up high some time. Then, he'd hoped his future held an architecture career with tall buildings, but now the window revealed he'd never been so high.

The conversation between Tadala and Max was going strong. Several hours ago, Max had been describing life in California, and Tadala peppered him with questions. Max explained his own beginnings as a refugee. The topic transitioned to gaining admission to a nursing program in California, which was a necessity for both their visas to be extended beyond a year.

Driven by Tadala's endless curiosity, Max then explained his job building fission energy plants. The Malawi facility was his first project. Now, they discussed the Chinese attack on North Korea. Samuel found the change in tone amusing as they'd advanced from tentative conversation to energetic repartee. Tadala was clearly enjoying herself.

Max rubbed his eyes. "The situation in North Korea has been an unstable anomaly. Isolated dictatorships with failing economies can't survive forever. Information spreads around the globe, so eventually everyone learns how well-off other people are in comparison."

"When we heard the news, the police were rounding up people in Bordeaux in a blink. I was so glad I had the French visa."

"The attack didn't make the Chinese popular. I was stopped twice in France."

Samuel joined their discussion. "Will the attack set back your work on power plants?"

"Global political instability often does, but the attack hasn't led to wider war. North Korea had few friends and a despised dictatorship."

Samuel hoped Max was right, that war was contained. But from the plane window, it seemed he was hanging above a world in flux, waiting for the next catastrophe.

A recorded arrival announcement was made, and the airplane prepared for landing.

"About time." Samuel stretched his throbbing leg. It had felt like a long flight. "I guess they go as fast as they can."

"Why *can't* they go faster?" Tadala asked.

"The planes could be designed to go faster, but there are costs," Max said. "These commercial aircraft fly at about Mach 0.85. Above the speed of sound, there are aerodynamic challenges, such as shock waves and higher skin temperature. Flying supersonic burns a ton more fuel because drag is proportional to the square of velocity."

"More fuel burned," Tadala said. "I guess flying faster does additional harm to the environment."

Max nodded. "Some environmentalists want to limit air travel in general."

With the cyclone in mind, Samuel found the argument compelling.

The plane banked and descended over San Francisco. Upon landing, they joined the stream of passengers walking to US Customs and Border Protection. Samuel hobbled on his crutches, making them the last in line. Max found a customs agent and explained their special situation. They were escorted to a small office. Half an hour was required to produce and validate the visas and record Tadala's and Samuel's biometric information.

The customs inspector, a solemn redheaded woman, at last closed her display. "Welcome to the United States. Do you wish to get a biometric ID tile for positive identity authentication? It may save you time in the future."

"These are standard in the US, replacing passwords. You can only acquire one through some government agencies." Max unbuttoned the top button of his shirt and pointed to a tiny depression where his own ID tile had been inserted under the skin on his chest. "It's not a requirement if you have privacy concerns, but it does speed up authentication for all sorts of day-to-day activities. It's also another immigration enforcement protocol."

"Sure, if Americans have them, we'll get them." Tadala answered for both of them.

At the instant, he realized that he wanted to leave Malawi permanently and live in the US, though he recognized the risks to secure permanent residency. Clearly, Tadala had crossed that Rubicon too.

The customs inspector sent a message from her PAWN. A nurse arrived and ushered them into a side room, where they would insert the biometric ID tiles containing a computer chip. Samuel found the procedure only mildly uncomfortable, and a thin line denoted the incision.

"Just use a dab of antibiotic on the cut, and it'll heal without a mark," the nurse said.

His ID tile was then authenticated by the customs inspector. "Do you go by Samuel, or Sam?" she asked, uploading the encrypted ID code to her machine.

He looked at Max. "Does 'Sam' sound American?"

Max shrugged but with his cheeks dimpling.

"Then please call me Sam."

They found their luggage and exited the airport. Max tapped his PAWN to order a self-driving taxi. They piled in and headed north through the fog.

"San Francisco seems to be foggy later in the year than when I first arrived here," Max said. "That's because the Central Valley stays hotter longer, and the fog is drawn in."

The delicious cold tickled Sam's spine. "I'll take the fog."

Rounding a curve, the city came into view. Lights covered the hills and a mass of skyscrapers in the central downtown.

Max pointed to several landmarks, including the old Coit Tower, nearly hidden behind two modern mega-towers.

"The City has recovered from the Northern California earthquake a decade ago," Max said.

The car glided across the Bay Bridge to the rented apartment Max had arranged.

"I've taken the next few days off so I can help you get settled." Max helped them take their bags out and open the door. He waved as he walked back to the car. "I'll be back tomorrow morning."

Sam and Tadala waved and then stood grinning at each other. Sam couldn't stop hugging his *atate* to celebrate their good fortune.

———◆———

"Starting with a hair salon?" Tadala gave Max a side-eye and a grin as he ushered them inside.

"Not that there's anything wrong with your appearance," Max said with a wink. "But new clothing can follow this stop, and then you'll both be prepared for interviews. When you get into the nursing program and Sam finds a job, those will check the first box toward permanent status in the US."

Sam stared at the hairbots perched on the back of each seat in the salon. A client flipped through hairstyles on a pad. Tadala sat down in the adjoining chair, and the other woman showed her how to operate the device.

Tadala selected a style, which was projected onto her head. She tried several, admiring each in the mirror as they were overlaid on her reflection.

"How about this one?" Tadala's question was not directed at him but at Max.

"Beautiful."

She sat upright as the robot's appendage combed and snipped her hair, moving surely but carefully, adjusting whenever Tadala moved too much in the seat. In a few minutes, the hairstyling was complete. She looked pleased with the result and relieved when the robot's arm retracted.

"I'll just get a simple cut." Sam took the chair vacated by the woman next to Tadala. He selected from the men's hairstyles, and the hairbot began cutting.

"I haven't seen working robots in Malawi yet," Tadala said.

"The US has more and more every day, it seems. They work best in situations like this, where the problem is well defined," Max said. "It's been harder than they thought to develop general-purpose robots outside factory situations and for simple retail tasks like this."

Max pointed out the window at an eighteen-wheeler navigating a turn. "Autonomous trucks are the poster child example. Everyone thought long-haul trucking would be easier to automate since freeways are standardized. It's kind of what's known as a closed domain—there are boundaries and a limited number of variables. But trucks have tons of weight, so accidents can be very bad. There were a couple of terrible accidents with school buses that ended up slowing deployment."

Tadala's eyes widened. "Kids were *killed?*"

"Yes. And many people were injured. The argument was that fewer people in total are dying on the road, which is true. But the social adjustments—like litigation around the new risks—take time."

"Then you don't have truck drivers in the US?" Sam thought of all the drivers in Malawi and of how many families would be without income because of that technology.

"Very few, and just to drive the last miles in congested cities. Millions of jobs for long-haul trucking disappeared."

The differences between the US and Malawi felt overwhelming. But with Max offering guidance, it felt like Sam had an older brother. Since he'd been injured, it felt like Tadala had grown up, and he felt less of a need to be the head of the family. Sam decided he could get used to this new role.

Max led them to a store and found the clothing section. The fitting robot was another new experience. Sam stepped onto the platform and selected from a menu of pants and shirts. Each clothing item projected onto his body was met with Tadala's thumbs-up or -down, and he made several selections. Tadala followed, and it seemed to Sam that Max's opinions mattered more to her. A few of their choices were in the store inventory. The clerk brought those out and informed them the rest would be shipped the next day.

It made Sam a little uncomfortable, but Max paid for everything. "Typically, we'd buy these online, but we're in a hurry."

"What an experience," Tadala said. "Thank you."

Max smiled. "I thought you'd find US stores interesting."

At the apartment, Max gave them instructions for their upcoming interviews. Tadala had an interview with UC Berkeley's School of Health Studies to pursue an LPN degree in nursing.

Max's expression was serious. "Remember, if you're accepted into the program and finish it, you're committing to working in the field for five years."

"I can do that." She nodded vigorously. "There's a permanent resident card waiting at the end."

Max handed Sam a small package. "You'll need this."

Thanks to Max, Sam had an interview in two weeks for a federal work–study program, which would allow him to complete his undergraduate degree while working.

Sam fumbled with the wrapping. Inside was a new PAWN unit. He held it nervously, like a fragile relic from a magical land.

"Thank you."

Max rubbed his neck. "You'll need to pass a basic proficiency exam before you interview for a drafting job. I can give you some pointers for studying."

"Thanks for helping us figure out all the things we need to do to get settled," Sam said.

"Thanks for caring." Tadala's eyes shone with a glow Sam hadn't seen before.

"I try to think ahead to the next step. It's just something my dad taught me."

Max's attempt to downplay the kindness of his actions was belied by his blush and how long he held Tadala's gaze. It was like Sam wasn't even there.

"I wonder how different the material on the test is from the technical drafting classes I took in Malawi." Exams always worried Sam, and now he was facing one extremely important to his residency in the US.

"With what you told me about the coursework, you'll be fine. That's where the PAWN comes in." Max took the device from him.

Sam had been fiddling with it all morning. It marginally resembled his smartphone with its AI instruction app. "I've figured out some basics, like how to connect to the net and some apps." He hated to admit how confused he was. "Now to use it to prepare for the test."

"I'd suggest that you set up your PIDA first. The AI will learn your personality and knowledge level, like lots of apps, and will customize its responses."

They hovered over the device. Max pointed to settings and made suggestions. "It's pretty intuitive. With a bit of practice and creative searches, you'll find the materials."

Max left him alone to study with his new learning companion.

I am your new personal intelligent digital assistant. What name would you like to give me?

It seemed like an important question. It would be a name mostly known only to himself. Male or female? Both were popular in Malawi, but Sam knew he'd prefer a soothing intonation in his ear, so he didn't change that setting. What sort of character would this be? He would be reliant on the advice, so perhaps a strong, confident avatar would be appropriate. He checked several sources on the net, and at last found an interesting African historical character. He typed in "Princess Kandake."

I am Princess Kandake. I am happy to serve you, Sam.

"Maybe it is I who will be serving you, Princess Kandake," he mumbled.

As you wish, Sam, the lilting voice said.

Two weeks later, Sam found the job placement service by following the red line outlined on a map drawn by his PIDA on his PAWN. Sam admired the undulating outline of the gleaming steel government building and thought about a future designing such structures. It sat among other buildings with organic forms and looked futuristic in contrast to the old rectangular brick buildings of Malawi. AI design and new manufacturing techniques changed everything. The architecture left him feeling both inspired and nervous about his meager drafting skills.

His interview was with a clerk on the fifth floor. The new clothes gave him some confidence as he sat across the desk, back straight and shoulders broad. The clerk reviewed his documents, which he'd beamed from his PAWN.

"Congratulations to you and your sister. These programs are tough to qualify for."

"I'm grateful for the chance to work in the US." Sam clasped his hands.

"I see you passed the drafting basic proficiency exam." The clerk looked up. "For you, five years of employment after completing your degree qualifies you for a permanent resident card. Demographics are working in your favor now."

"What do you mean?"

"AIs are stealing jobs left and right, but we still have a shortage of workers in some fields because the population is aging. So we need workers with certain skills who aren't drawing guaranteed income checks."

"Guaranteed income?"

"It's now $2,500 a month, $30,000 annually. But only citizens qualify."

He shifted in his seat, barely able to imagine how wealthy this country must be. "With that guarantee, why does anyone work?"

"That's the federal poverty level. It's expensive to live here. It's difficult to live, even with a guaranteed income. With the inflation we've seen, prices have roughly doubled in the past twenty-five years, and a Big Mac costs you twelve bucks these days."

The clerk adjusted the PAWN on his nose, seeming to show it off. "Capitalism is a ruthlessly efficient economic system, wringing out costs. The concern, though, is that if the minimum wage is set too high to protect incomes, then private companies will hire fewer workers, and jobs disappear. So the government offers an earned income credit to workers who take lower-paid positions. Then companies can afford to hire, and employees can afford to accept those jobs. Legal noncitizens qualify for earned income credits."

Sam struggled to understand the economics. "I'm glad to work. Can you tell me about jobs I qualify for?"

The clerk reviewed his college classes focused on architectural drafting then thumbed through a list of openings. He suggested a drafting job and named the salary.

Sam whistled. It was twice the guaranteed income. "I'll take it." The salary was beyond his imagination.

The clerk smirked at his eagerness. "Well, it's not well paid, given the cost of living here. So that position also comes with an earned income credit; in this case, 100 percent of the guaranteed income—the max."

Sam felt numb. He would earn three times the guaranteed income.

"Your next step is to interview with the company. The job is the standard thirty-two hours per week. The position allows you to take a class per semester to complete your degree to US standards, but that's on your own time. There isn't a future without an undergraduate degree, at the very least."

Half an hour later, Sam left the office building with a job interview scheduled for the next day. The mellow sunlight bathed his skin, and he walked with a new purpose back to the apartment, his injuries almost forgotten.

That evening, Max returned to hear about their interviews.

"I really enjoyed talking about the nursing program. It seemed positive." Tadala's confident words were betrayed by a hesitant expression.

"I have a job interview tomorrow," Sam said. He and Tadala exchanged anxious looks.

Max tilted his head. "Is something wrong?"

"It's wrong to be so lucky. Like we won the lottery when everyone else died. I don't know what I did to deserve this."

Even though they hadn't discussed it, Tadala had said exactly what Sam had been feeling. He was glad he wasn't the only one with the thought.

"Survivor's guilt." Max swallowed hard. "I know. I felt that for years after I arrived in California. I was so lucky to have Momma Ginger and Dad."

"And we lost Mai," Sam said. Tadala took his hand.

Max's face was somber, now wiping his eye. "And I lost Mama and Baba. God, I haven't thought about them for a while."

Max hummed a quiet tune then sang softly in his baritone, "Tomorrow we will create a colorful world." His voice was shaky when he spoke again. "Today it's a different world than you've ever envisioned. And tomorrow it'll be so hard for us to create that colorful world. There's a lot of work to do."

They stood in a quiet circle, holding hands, all now with tears in their eyes as they thought about those the world had left behind.

19

Grandfather leads me down the path along the cliff, taking his time while leaning on his walking stick. The story of Grandma Tadala and Great Uncle Sam spins out as we stroll, with more pauses than steps. But that's okay, because it's a gripping story. It takes time to tell the interesting details, and after being cooped up on the train, it's good to stretch my legs too. The morning eggs and bacon filled an empty stomach, and my head is clearer than when I left the Commune, even if I feel plumb tuckered.

Why didn't anyone tell me anything about our family history? I have ancestors from two continents, and the countries are as unalike as they can be. The tiny Commune school only gave me a vague idea of the geography of Taiwan and Malawi. The world has grown overnight, and there's so much more to it than the Piney Woods.

Grandfather stops at a bench looking out at the Pacific. This is my first time seeing it, besides the glimpse through the bedroom window. He points out Big Lagoon seven kilometers to the north, beyond Patrick's Point, where it hovers in coastal fog. We sit so he can rest his legs. Overhead, a skein of Canada Geese glides south, the V-shaped pattern dancing in the sunlight.

Watching the geese, he says, "They rest at the lagoon. They migrate later every year. Now, it's October."

"It's even hot here in Northern California, not just East Texas," I say.

Robert stands behind Grandfather, holding our lunches. "The global temperature has increased 2.5 degrees Celsius when compared with the standard baseline," he says.

Grandfather scowls at the robot to discourage him from speaking again, and its oval face glints with a slight pink color.

Grandfather rests on the bench, looking toward the ocean again. "Don't take the wrong conclusion from mister doom and gloom here. I'd chalk the fight against climate change as a terrific win. That's the second existential challenge we've faced. The corner has been turned. The models suggest that temperatures will only climb modestly from now on. It's manageable."

He breathes deeply as we sit. Maybe he was thinking of me when he worked to build clean electricity, but I'm thinking about what I've seen in the Piney Woods—the hurricane and fire.

"There's problems with the environment, though," I say.

Grandfather is old, but he's still sharp, and his eyes look on me kindly. "Yes, humankind started to solve the problem too slowly. We were almost too late, but now we've stabilized, although at higher temperatures than we'd wish."

At last, I feel calm. The geese remind me of the wood ducks and wild turkey flying over the Piney Woods. I kick a rock over the cliff, and it bounces down, ricocheting off a tree below.

"Life will be harder for many around the world. Much has been lost, and the effort will be costly," he says.

There have been too many new things to process—hundreds of people on the train, more than everybody at the Commune—and gobs of vehicles buzzing around when the robot brought me to Grandfather's house in the autocar. Again, the world seems much bigger and more complicated than it was only a day ago.

"We need to deal with more fires, hurricanes, and ecosystem damage. But we're adapting to our climate reality. I believe humanity can save the planet."

That room-sized display he showed me was scary. It was as real as the hurricane that came through Texas five years ago.

"That hurricane...cyclone that Grandma lived through was bad. You both lived through terrifying times before getting here."

"We were kindred spirits from the moment I met her. I liked her grit. She was never afraid." Grandfather's hands rest on his stick, and he looks me in the eye. "But now tell me about your hurricane experience."

"It was the second scariest thing I ever saw when it hit Galveston and rolled up into the Piney Woods." I tell the story quickly, about the sound of the wind howling and all of us hunkered down inside. "The storm wasn't as bad as the one Grandma lived through, but it was terrifying. I was almost nine at the time. There was a lot of rebuilding. That's one reason Ma and Pa haven't come visit you lately."

"I see." He looks at his shoes. "And the scariest experience?"

"'Into the fire,' as I heard 'em say. A year after the hurricane, the big fires burned East Texas."

"Your father and I were messaging constantly then. I was worried, especially after the pyrocumulus cloud appeared."

Grandfather clicks on his PIDA, looking up some facts. I'm envious. The Commune doesn't allow these, and they seem pretty useful.

"Pyro-tornadogenesis it's called. That one was rated an EF-3 on the Enhanced Fugita Scale. It could burn a hundred hectares in seconds."

I can still picture it, like a fire tornado hanging on the distant horizon. "Half the sky was red, even though it was far away. Ash rained down on us, and the animals ran out of the forest. Ma was petrified when the mice ran through after the deer, foxes, and skunks."

"Your father said it was a good thing that it ran up against the lake, which was wide enough to slow it down." He rubs his beard.

"The firefighters used auto-helis to drop firebots on the edge of fires. I watched them lowered out of the sky. If it weren't for that, we would've been trapped. As it was, we lost the Commune barn."

"A good use of robots, taking those risky jobs." Grandfather glances at the robot, which stands mutely. I reckon it doesn't care about its kind. "No one was hurt, I understand?"

I shook my head. "We just inhaled a lot of smoke. I helped rebuild the barn and outbuildings. That took almost two years, and I got to work alongside the men. So now I know a bit about carpentry—and barns."

I rub my hands where I have the calluses first developed from that work. I'm proud that they said they needed me. It would've been faster if they'd used bots to help, but I guess they wanted to take the credit.

"We have fires here in the Pacific Northwest too, and into Canada. They're doing a fine job of fire suppression with drone networks. But forest management is the key. That's where your dad comes in, as a forestry ranger."

"He loves the forest. I do too. I just don't like the Commune and their dumb rules."

"Now you're fourteen. You don't need to go back, unless you want to."

His words feel like a pardon.

"I don't want to go back to the Commune. But I'm not sure what to do here."

He fixes me with an intense gaze. "It's time for you to start high school. The Commune is no place for that. You need to be with other kids to develop social skills. It may be a difficult transition after spending so much time in the woods."

I'm thinking about the comfort of walking the forest paths I know well, finding where the newborn fauns hide in the loblolly pines and where the fox prey on the swamp rabbits. I know their habits. Learning the same for people would be a challenge. "Let's talk about that later."

Grandfather doesn't push the topic. "You don't have many working robots besides the firebots?"

"Folks at the Commune are expected to do their own work, so you don't see many bots. Pa said never to walk to the perimeter of the Commune's land, or I'd find plenty of 'em, and they would stop me."

Grandfather leans on his walking stick to stand, taking another look at the water. "Like this ocean rising, robots have been taking all the jobs, and somehow, we didn't think about the consequences in time. The loss of jobs, and of the self-esteem that went with them, is still one of the challenges of this century."

"Has that affected our family?"

"My brother-in-law, Jack, and his daughter Harper were very involved in pushing for the deployment of robots. And that had an impact on a lot of people."

"While you were buildin' power plants," I say.

"We took quite different paths. That's the next chapter of our family story." He turns away. "Let's go to my vineyard. We can eat lunch there." He walks past the robot that stands behind the bench. "Robert, please call an autocar to take us to the vineyard."

"Yes, sir. An autocar will arrive in eleven minutes." Robert gestures toward the road. I hurry to join Grandfather, and the robot follows us.

20

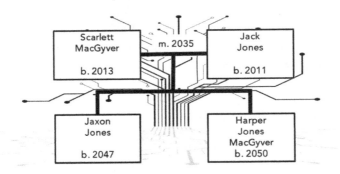

The AV exited I-287 onto North Broadway in White Plains, turned at a cross street, and approached his factory. Ahead, a sanitation truck picked up garbage. The automated lifter couldn't reach one of the trash containers because it was under a tree instead of on the street.

Jack's gaze naturally latched onto the robot that had been riding the back bumper. It dismounted, trundled to the container, and loaded it onto the lifter. The robot then remounted the bumper, and the truck continued down the road.

A near-closed domain, easy to automate. Another market he'd missed. Jack glanced again at the message from Larry that had put him in a bad mood twenty minutes ago. His ruminations about missed opportunities only fanned the flames.

The AV parked in his president's reserved spot, and Jack marched into the General RoboMechs building. As he walked down the corridor, several employees stepped to the side. Did they always do that?

On the main demonstration floor, three rows of robots stretched half the length of the building, cordoned off by low walls, like horse paddocks. Each enclosure had signs summarizing the testing underway. Robot arms moved smoothly, like dancers choreographed for a ballet. Stand-alone robots held salvers with teacups, serving tea to other robots, the backgrounds decorated like comfortable living rooms. Employees adjusted robots and tested new programs in several of the demonstration scenes. It worked well as a demo to puff capabilities for visiting customers. If only the robots worked as advertised.

Normally, he took a meandering path through the floor to eyeball every employee working to his exacting standards, but today he skipped the assembly area occupying the rear half of the factory and hurried through the demo area to his office overlooking the floor.

"Tell Larry I want a meeting with him in fifteen minutes."

His admin jumped for her holo-com.

She hadn't seemed very busy when he walked in. He made a mental note to give her more to do. He turned back before closing his door. "I'm not in today, if anybody calls."

"Yes, sir."

◆

He nursed a coffee from the espresso machine, feet propped on his desk. What was it about him that gave him such bad luck? Thirty-nine years old, fifteen years in the industry, and the big chance seemed just out of reach. He was always too late, or too early.

"Admin," he said.

The girl's voice said "yes, sir" in his ear.

"Send over all the news reports on the incident as they come in."

"Incident, sir?"

He pinched the bridge of his nose. This was why he never bothered to change the command to contact his admin to their actual names. "Do a search for General RoboMechs in the news scroll and send me everything that comes in before Larry gets here—video and print."

"Yes, sir."

The first reports were from Japan, of course, but they were followed quickly by reports from every major country as the news rolled across Europe toward the US. He'd need some time to process.

"Admin."

"Yes, sir."

"Push Larry back fifteen minutes."

"Yes, sir."

Each news outlet had done more digging into the background of the company. By the time the reporting reached the UK, it was getting personal.

Jack threw his coffee cup against the wall. "Failed toymaker?"

His first company had been a good idea, but the market had been flooded by products where toy companies had the edge. Robot friends for kids were a bust, but at least he'd been smart enough to convince Scarlett's father to lend the initial investment money. That had been one payoff from the marriage.

He'd been chasing AGI from the first job he'd had out of college. He'd switched companies to catch that tech boom. Sure, the AIs got smarter, demonstrating surprising capabilities. But so far, they'd never broken through to general intelligence, never crossed over the barrier of meaning.

Personal care robots distributed through hospital outpatient care made some progress—step-by-step advances. He'd flogged the vision until he caught Wall Street's attention, enough to take the company public in an IPO.

"Sir?"

"Yes…" He really should look up her name.

"There are quite a lot of messages for you. Would you like me to forward them?"

Reporters probably. "No. Get janitorial up here."

"Yes, sir."

Jack made another coffee and remembered the brief flush of success the first time his company's stock symbol flashed across trading screens.

The virtual cash sat in his account fleetingly, untouchable because of the underwriter's lockup. They pushed ahead against his programmers' advice, but the financial markets had their own rhythms, and they moved fast.

That product hadn't met expectations, and the stock went sideways before he could extract any money. The window always seemed to close on his hands, never letting him cash in.

Jack used his PAWN to check the current stock price. "Damn." He slammed the arm of his chair but refrained from throwing his coffee again.

"Come," he called after a hesitant knock at the door.

A woman in a blue dress pushed a cart with a garbage can and a mop bucket into the office.

"Finally, an employee who's prepared." He pointed at the mess he'd made and went back to watching a video out of Germany talking about inferior materials and insufficient regulatory procedures. At least this one wasn't blaming it all on him.

He barely registered the click of the door closing when the janitor left.

The Darwinian business-scape startups faced was to blame for his problems in this business. Big corporations had the capital to compete, and startups were trampled or acquired. With the end of Moore's Law, which had to happen eventually, chip costs per logic gate stopped dropping exponentially, and cost became a factor favoring established companies. His company had hung on by its fingernails through some major challenges. That's what they should be highlighting.

Meanwhile, huge deals for military robots had been awarded, and factories and farms were already automated. Were those robots perfect all the time? He didn't think so.

The big companies also won all the lucrative contracts for robots guarding the borders, which had effectively reduced illegal refugee crossings, and the wave of robotic space exploration—building a base on the moon and three Mars landings.

Jack finished his espresso and turned off the reports. He'd had enough; they were beginning to repeat themselves, and they didn't seem to have any more information than Larry had sent to him earlier. There was a bitter taste in his mouth that had little to do with the coffee.

Since the turn of the century, half the jobs in existence in the US had been automated, with the largest companies earning the profits. Smaller companies like his fought over the scraps.

If he gave up on this venture, what markets were left? Robots should already be in homes performing typical housekeeping tasks, but household robots were still a nascent industry. Robots that did enough to be useful cost too much.

The job losses from other automation had left plenty of low-skill people to fill personal service jobs like housekeeping and elder care in the US. An affordable general-purpose robot still eluded every robotic company.

Knowing that, Jack had pivoted to the international market for home care robots. The potential in Japan and South Korea was huge. Population had been falling dramatically, and elder care robots might demand a high price. But even the extra cash from early investors couldn't get them to the next level so the robots could perform all the functions. They still required people to look in on the patients. As Larry's message demonstrated.

There was another knock on the door.

"Come."

Larry, the company PR crisis manager, general counsel, and the CFO stood there looking grim. He took his feet off the desk and motioned them inside. They settled at the large conference table, and Jack took the commanding seat at the end.

"Tell me what happened and what we do next," he demanded.

Larry used his PAWN to load a presentation onto Jack's wall display. A video of a robot appeared holding the hand of an aged patient.

Jack waved his hand to get Larry to shut off the video. "I've seen that report already in three different languages. Move on to what really happened."

"The latest model, the PalImōto 211, allegedly caused the accident in an elderly care community in Yokohama. The model was providing personal care, with human oversight provided by the condo medical staff with video chat and weekly in-person visits. Yesterday, our model reported that the patient was not responding and notified emergency services. The patient was pronounced dead on arrival at the hospital."

"And the cause of death?"

"An overdose. Video records show the PalImōto 211 handing the patient an incorrect quantity of a prescribed medication several days in a row."

"A mix-up between two prescriptions. The patient was given the wrong pills by our robot," said the PR crisis manager.

Jack glared at Larry and then turned back to the PR manager. "What's our next step to contain this?"

"We've drafted a general apology, expected within Japanese culture, and expressed regret for the loss of a human life, with a promise that we'll conduct a full investigation."

The PR manager sent the release to Jack. He read it on his PAWN and approved it.

"What else from legal?"

"I've drafted a Form 8-K. Disclosure is required for a material event, and this certainly qualifies. The net is already awash with rumors and social commentary," said the general counsel.

"And the stock is down 30 percent. I've been fielding investor calls all morning," the CFO said.

"Yes, I know." There was silence. "Okay. You three figure out an action plan. Get the stock price out of this spiral. Larry, stay here."

The three cleared the room. Larry was silent as they left, his gaze fixed on Jack.

The door closed, and Jack's eyes blazed with uncontained fury. "It's your project. How did you let this happen? The stock will take forever to recover."

Larry's eyes widened, as if he hadn't anticipated Jack's reaction. "It was that last procedural update when we announced that the model could monitor all patient needs without human assistance. Before the change, drug monitoring was excluded. We needed additional time to fail-safe the code."

Jack vividly remembered the argument. Larry was dragging his feet, and Jack had to make the announcement about the enhanced feature set to seal a deal. Well, mistakes will be made in the race to keep up with competition.

Jack thought about the special obligations of Japanese culture alluded to by his PR manager. "You're the project VP. You own it."

That led to the other expectation. Someone had to be the scapegoat.

"Larry, you're fired. Clean out your desk."

* * *

Jack's PAWN glimmered with an incoming message, identified as Scarlett calling again. This time he took it.

Her face materialized in 3D, her hair disheveled and lines of worry around her eyes. "Oh, Jack, I don't know what to do with Jaxon."

"What are you talking about?" His gruffness came easily.

She blathered on, oblivious to his mood. "You know he started preschool last week. And already, the teachers are saying that he has trouble playing with the other kids. He doesn't talk well enough for his age. And he doesn't make eye contact with us. I'm worried about his development."

The edge in his voice hardened, and he hoped she'd actually notice. "Look, I'm up to my ass in alligators right now. Do you expect I have time to think about your stupid kid?"

She choked up. "Our kid. And he's your namesake. What the hell, Jack?"

"Well, the stupid must come from your side. Everyone on my side can talk and look people in the eye."

She stared at him.

"Look, we have a big problem here. I can't deal with this now. The stock is crashing. You should worry about having a roof over your head. Now let me get back to work." Jack ended the call.

The office was quiet, but he knew the team of three was still working down the hall. They wouldn't risk leaving before he did. He slumped in his chair and rubbed his forehead, recalling Scarlett's face fading into the ether, her dwindling beauty apparent. Fifteen years earlier, he'd counted on her to be the obedient wife, covering the tedious duties so he could crack into the big money. Instead, she just complicated his life. She must be partly to blame for the fact that he hadn't made it big. She was baggage. It was something to deal with later. Jack shoved the holo-com away and turned back to his screen to focus on saving what he could of his company.

21

SCARLETT JONES MACGYVER—2051

Scarlett ran the home test a third time to be sure she hadn't contaminated the sample of her blood drawn with the auto-lancet. The results crystallized on her screen, the same as before. The sexually transmitted disease was uncommon since most STDs had disappeared. A check with her PIDA confirmed that treatment was straightforward and that medication would clear the infection within a month with no side effects.

The disease itself was not an issue. She studied her red eyes in the bathroom mirror. Her infection could come from only one source. Jack had become distant in the past months, supposedly devoted to his company. His business trips over the last year had a new, now-obvious explanation. He was late again, and she didn't know when he'd be home.

In the bathroom medicine cabinet, the small bottle beckoned to her. She picked it up, swirled it to make the multicolored pills roll around, and then took one. There were many synpsychs available to regulate mood or adjust brain chemical balance, and many were on the banned substances list. The authorities couldn't keep up with the variations churned out by chemical compounder AIs, and many could be found in shadowy corners of the net. Scarlett wasn't sure they helped, but she kept trying them anyway.

Harper cried from the nursery. As she entered, the robot in the back corner moved forward.

"Shall I feed the baby?" Its oval face tilted toward her.

"Don't touch the baby or come within two meters of her." Jack insisted they have two robots in their apartment for appearance's sake, but that didn't mean she needed to trust them. Scarlett found a bottle, and soon the cries were replaced by sucking sounds. Harper drifted back to sleep.

She checked on Jaxon in the second bedroom. He was curled into a ball, clutching his pillow and sleeping soundly. He was already four, but his inability to communicate held him back. Scarlett had been worried enough to have Jaxon tested, and it had revealed mild cognitive impairment. The doctor assured her it wasn't serious, but Jaxon was a bit slower than typical when solving problems in unfamiliar situations.

Now she believed it had been a mistake to have two kids so close in age with all the parental responsibility falling on her. She tucked the blanket around his chin.

Scarlett sat on the living room sofa in the dim light of a single lamp, letting the pill take effect. Outside, twenty stories below, the setting sun cast shadows down the canyoned streets of Midtown Manhattan. Farther west, a dozen new towers had been built in the past decades, several topping five hundred meters. Jack had aspired to own a condo in one.

She wasn't sure what the future held for herself, or even what she wanted. Whatever teamwork she had felt with him to succeed in this tough city was gone too.

Jack walked in and locked the bolt behind him. He peered into the semi-darkness. "Waiting up for me?"

"We need to talk." Her voice quavered only a little.

He dropped his coat on the opposite sofa and sat. "What about? It's late, and I'm exhausted."

Best to get it over with. "Just this." She clicked her PAWN and sent the lab test. He looked at his PAWN when it appeared.

"It wasn't me. That leaves one possibility." She gritted her teeth and pinned him with her gaze.

"Yes...?"

His face gave him away to her. She had long ago learned his tells, and this bland expression was one he adopted while concocting a particularly ballsy lie, no doubt practiced in his sales pitches. Her mouth tightened. She kept her silence.

Jack shrugged, and his face told of a new inward concern. "A simple treatment should solve this. Now I need to tell Rachael." He stared directly at her. "I was meaning to tell you about Rachael."

Blood surged to her face. "Rachael? Not Rachael from back when we were dating?"

"Yes, that Rachael. We're back together."

His confession was followed not by contrition but by his anger. The story unfolded. He had reconnected with Rachael after Harper was born and had been seeing her since. Scarlett couldn't sort the truth, whether he or Rachael had reached out first, but it had been a full-fledged affair, and he was unrepentant. She screamed, cried, unable to express her feelings of betrayal. Jack had destroyed the last bridge between them. Their shaky marriage crumbled in front of her.

Exhausted, she lay back on the sofa. "I thought you were acting strange, maybe having a midlife crisis with the big 4-0 coming up. Instead, it's full-on disloyalty. You're leaving me with two kids, no warning, and you want a divorce?"

"Sure. It's in the open now, and it's good timing. My company isn't worth much, so alimony will be cheaper than ever. Time for a new start for me."

Fury overwhelmed her, enhanced by the pill. "Just get out!"

He picked up his coat and opened the door. "Sure. I know where to sleep. You can have the half-paid condo; that's all I've got for you. Goodbye and good luck."

The door slammed, and he was gone.

Scarlett cried softly. Ever since she'd fallen into his orbit, Jack had been the center of her life—a hot sun she couldn't break free from. She had circled him, allowed him to draw her in, locked into that gravitational embrace, with no path for herself. She hadn't expected to be flung away so suddenly. Now she was flying alone into the unknown.

22

Ginger MacGyver—2051 (California)

The call came from Scarlett, and Ginger put it on the 3D display so Everett could participate. They sat next to each other on the living room sofa. Scarlett appeared holding Harper, and Jaxon ran around behind her, playing with a toy spaceship.

"It's so nice to see the grandkids." Ginger waved, and joy surged through her when Harper flapped both hands in the air at her. "Oh, she's changing so fast."

"She started waving just this month." But Scarlett wasn't smiling. "Mom, Dad, I called to tell you Jack and I are getting a divorce."

Her mouth twitched as she finished the sentence. Then she launched into the details, words pouring out.

Ginger winced with sorrow for Scarlett, and her mind raced ahead. "Are you considering coming back to California? We so miss the chance to spend time with you, and with Harper and Jaxon. We've hardly seen them."

"Jack never wanted to take the time away from the company, so we didn't visit. And I'm sorry we didn't invite you much." Scarlett jingled a toy at Harper, a momentary distraction before she looked back, resolve lining her face. "I've been in New York a long time, though. I have a good job and friends. I'm going to keep the condo as the least consolation from this marriage. Besides, you've got your own jobs to attend to."

Everett joined the conversation. "We've enjoyed our careers. But it's not so long until we'll retire."

"Retiring? When?" Ginger saw confusion cross Scarlett's face, and she was glad it didn't seem an obvious step to her.

"In two or three years, probably," Everett said. "For the first time in decades, jobs are scarce. Now companies are trying to accommodate the next generation—that's you and Max—by forcing folks like us to leave the workforce."

Scarlett changed the topic. "How is Max? The last I heard, he was building stuff overseas."

"He's back from Africa, where he finished a fission power plant," Everett said.

"I guess that's good for the planet."

"I understand your organization endorsed fission energy as necessary to help solve the climate change crisis. Just in time for my retirement," Everett added dryly.

It was an old squabble, and not one to reignite now. Ginger jumped in. "Max met a lovely woman in Malawi. Her name is Tadala. She and her brother got immigration status and are now living here in Berkeley. She's studying to be a nurse."

"Good for Max."

Ginger detected some annoyance in the comment. "Can I at least fly out to help you with the grandkids for a week or two, to give you a hand?"

"Let me think about it. I'm sorting out stuff and need time by myself."

Ginger kept her face calm, but she thought about what she might have done differently to have not gotten to this place. They'd spent years living on the opposite coast from Scarlett, with decreasing visits and time slipping by. Scarlett had always been headstrong, making her own decisions, and she'd decided to follow Jack, blind to his faults. That stubbornness had stymied all her attempts to reason with Scarlett, and it had been a losing exercise. Still, she was a mother who couldn't protect her children from the world, and it felt like a personal failure.

"Scarlett," Everett said, "know we're here for you. Remember, you're a MacGyver. You're strong, and you can overcome this too."

Ginger passed the lamb dish to Tadala, who thanked her and continued to describe her nursing classes. Everett and Max were engaged in a technical discussion about the latest fission plant designs.

Ginger glanced out her dining room window at the setting sun on the horizon. The dinner had gone as perfectly as she'd wished, and the presence of Max and Tadala left her energized. Having them in the house made her feel younger. It had been a wise decision to adopt him eighteen years earlier—to have a family in two acts.

"I'm happy about the focus on fail-safe power plants, and how fast they're being built. We have a chance to head off the climate crisis in time. Keep on working hard, son. It's a worthwhile mission."

Ginger felt her heart surge to see the bond that had developed between them.

Tadala folded her napkin and glanced at Everett before she took a deep breath. "Thank you both again for the tremendous support you've given to Sam and me." She glanced coyly at Max. "Max has been so helpful finding a job for Sam, and I love the nursing program."

Ginger wondered if they were a couple. Max had said Tadala was a friend. He'd always been a bit of an idealist—a commonality with Everett and one reason they had swept Max into their lives without reservation. Perhaps he was oblivious to Tadala's body language, like Everett had been to hers.

Everett refilled everyone's wine glasses, and they moved to the living room to continue the conversation.

"How is Scarlett? She told me that she and Jack are splitting," Max said.

"She texts you often?" Ginger thought about how seldom she heard from her.

"Not really. Less and less since the kids were born. Just big news like this."

Everett sipped his wine. "It's not been the easiest life for her. I'm not sure how much she enjoys New York, but she said she's committed. Offsetting the difficulty with Jack, some good news is that she was offered the development officer role at her nonprofit, and she accepted. She'll be talking to potential donors."

"That sounds positive for her," Max said.

"It will be difficult while managing Jaxon and Harper by herself, but at least she'll have money to cover childcare," Ginger said.

When the thought intruded, as now, Ginger tried not to dwell on the disappointment of so little time spent with their two grandkids.

"The US is such a large country, and New York is so far away. In Malawi, families stay close. At least we did." Tadala's face suddenly turned serious to match Ginger's mood.

"Ever-smaller families living farther apart. It's a curse of the modern world," Everett said.

Tadala brightened. "Well, we just need to work hard to stay tight and hold on to those connections."

She looked at Max again, and Ginger felt increasingly close to this young woman who lit up the room with her smile. Ginger peeked at Max again to see whether he had noticed. She discerned a flicker of pride—a positive sign that warmed her more than the wine.

23

SCARLETT MACGYVER—2051 (NEW YORK)

Scarlett waved goodbye to her colleagues at the Midtown office and walked outside where the AV waited. A patch of blue sky was visible between the skyscrapers. She breathed in the early summer air. It had been a month since her divorce from Jack was final, and the seasons had changed, offering the best weather in New York.

She entered the vehicle and clicked her PAWN. The car's AI authenticated her ID tile, and the car moved into traffic and toward her condo. When she'd first arrived, there had been yellow taxis everywhere, but now human drivers were banned. All the vehicles in Manhattan were self-driving. In other boroughs, most of the remaining taxi drivers had left the profession because of competition from the three largest AV taxi services. She felt sorry for the drivers forced into other jobs, but she had to admit that the experiment on the island had worked, and traffic moved smoothly.

"You will arrive at your destination in seven minutes," the car's AI intoned.

Even though she had a nanny at home, she had PIDA Zelda check the puppycam. It was the only useful robot to result from Jack's abortive attempt to enter the robot toy market.

PIDA Zelda spoke in her ear. *Snowball followed Jaxon for seven hours, fifteen minutes today, and here is the current live vid.*

Her PAWN filled with the video, viewed from floor level, that showed Jaxon jumping on his bed.

She keyed the *SPEAK* button. "Jaxon, stop jumping on the bed."

He startled and climbed down.

She settled back in her seat and scrolled her social media feed on the PAWN. On top was a photo of Mom and Dad after dinner with Max and this new friend, Tadala. They appeared quite happy. That wasn't the emotion she felt.

It wasn't fair. Why did Max get to be the golden child? She'd been first, and he was adopted so much later, when it had seemed their family was a perfect size.

She felt her face flush and realized the irony of the thought. She thumbed through her photos, found one of Jaxon and Harper from a month ago, and posted it to the net.

Scarlett thought she'd been the do-gooder in the family, pursuing a career like her mother. Why did they not see it that way? Sure, they'd congratulated her for the promotion to development officer for TerraGuard Network. It had been the move she'd worked for all these years. The surprise promotion was a light antidote to the pain of her divorce, though it did absolutely nothing to alleviate her increasing loneliness.

Part of the problem was her long-running battle with Dad and his insistence that he was on the right side of the climate change solution. She hated to admit that he'd been right. She came around to the argument that fission energy was essential in the quest to mitigate climate change, but it was difficult work to reverse people's belief structures. She had been a prime example, and now one of her challenges as development officer was to rein in the people who saw all power companies as evil. She had to convince them to support her nonprofit financially, and those same people did not connect their own electricity use to the problem. Counting ironies today, a second was that she often found herself using her father's arguments on the day-to-day in her new role.

The AV sped across town. A maglev train hissed overhead, carrying passengers to New Jersey. Several blocks farther on, the car pulled to the curb in front of her building. She rode the elevator to her condo, and the door opened with a *swish* as she approached. The nanny looked up with a dog-tired expression. She was feeding Harper with a bottle. Jaxon jumped on the sofa—his usual wild self.

"Your groceries were delivered, and I fed the ingredients into the autocooker," the nanny said. "The nutrition plans for the kids included Jaxon's cultured cheese." She lowered her gaze. "Jaxon is a handful to keep track of."

Scarlett guessed she'd heard her voice over Snowball's puppycam connection.

"Don't I know it. I'll see you tomorrow," Scarlett said.

The nanny handed Harper to her and made for the door. Snowball, the robot dog, wagged its tail, and she reached down to pet the machine, a habit that developed just because the soft, fluffy coating felt nice to touch. That had been her design idea. It turned its head to follow Jaxon as he came into the room.

"I don't like Snowball. He tattles on me." He rubbed his eyes and pouted.

Scarlett settled the kids and readied dinner.

Jaxon slapped his spoon on the table until it rang. "More cheese," he yelled.

The meal ended with Jaxon slurping soup and Harper shoving orange slices into her mouth. In another hour, they were dressed in pajamas and settled into bed. Harper fell quickly to sleep, and Jaxon at last began to lie still as she closed his bedroom door.

She opened the bathroom cabinet and took one of the multicolored pills. As she swallowed it, she spied Jaxon standing behind her.

"Can I have some more candy too?"

"It's not candy." She clicked the cabinet lock, protected by her ID tile password.

He ran from the bathroom, lay on the living room floor, and pounded his fists against the hardwood. Scarlett thought about Jaxon's last demand and wondered at the word "more" and whether her synpsychs were candy to him. Did she forget to keep the child lock secured on the bottle? Had her nanny somehow let him get into them? It was a new worry.

"Can't you try harder to control your tantrums?" She said it but recognized the futility of the question.

She sat on the floor beside him and let the episode continue, She prayed it wasn't disturbing her downstairs neighbor again. She didn't know what to do. At last, he lay exhausted, and she picked him up, put him back in bed, and tucked the covers.

With the kids in their rooms and the building silent, Scarlett mixed a scotch and soda and plopped into her favorite seat. The hum of the city rose from the street below. She sighed, trying to sort out the jumble that was her life.

It felt like a book written by someone else. She'd tried to scratch out the chapters about Jack. She'd gotten through the divorce, gained full custody of the kids, and kept the condo. Jack had minor visitation rights, but he was only interested in seeing Harper on the rare occasion. He had no patience for Jaxon.

What were the next chapters? With her promotion, her career was on solid footing. She hoped she might find the mental strength to take care of herself. Her parents were a continent away, and she had little choice. Scarlett finished the glass.

24

Tadala MacGyver—2055 (California)

The sounds of chirping birds wafted in through the hotel window. It was the beginning of June; the rains had ended, and the weather had been hot for three weeks. Now the sun shone on Napa vineyards, the grapes full of promise for the harvest. Tadala told herself it would be a perfect day. Though she was seldom nervous, there were butterflies in her stomach.

The welcome brunch for the wedding party began downstairs in half an hour. The wedding would be in the afternoon, and few details remained.

The last year had been a whirlwind. Max had proposed to her the spring before near the Ahwahnee Hotel, with Yosemite Falls roaring in the background. The mist hadn't hidden her tears of happiness.

The timing of career and education for them intersected nicely. Max was offered a senior manager position for a new fission plant project in India beginning in July. She'd finished the last nursing classes and the clinical practicum at Stanford Medical Center and walked for graduation three weeks before. They planned some travel in Asia before she took a nursing position in the city near his job site.

The wedding planning was a lot of work on top of finishing her degree, but Ginger had volunteered to assist. She's the one who'd found this stylish hotel in Napa to accommodate their seventy guests for the ceremony and reception, not to mention tying together all the small details needed for a big event. Tadala had not planned anything like it before, and working as a team on uniting their small families brought them closer. The only family that Tadala had was

Sam, and the MacGyver family wasn't large, either, so most guests were work and school friends.

Max had been unconcerned with the wedding details as long as she was happy. He'd only asked whether she wanted any traditional Malawian elements. She wanted to follow only modern traditions, except for a dress made from traditional, colorful *chitenje* cloth.

Tadala glanced at her wedding dress in whites, blues, and golds, hanging neatly pressed in the corner. There was time to dress later. She checked her reflection in a mirror and looked again at the vintage diamond engagement ring that Max had given her nestled comfortably on her finger. The present reminded her of Max's playful humor. "No *kulobola?*" Max had joked after giving it to her, showing he had done his homework.

She laughed and playfully slapped his shoulder. "No, no bride price. I don't think that Sam, or I, need the cattle." That practice had ended in Malawi with her grandmother. Somehow Max had known that too.

Tadala took a deep breath and went to join the family for a pre-wedding brunch.

Ginger and Everett waited at the end of a long table that was nearly filled by the wedding party. There were six groomsmen—three of Max's friends, including his best man, Buzz, two of her friends from the nursing program, and Sam. Sitting across the table were her bridesmaids—four friends from her nursing program, an engineer friend of Max's, and Jessica, Buzz's fiancée, who served as her maid of honor.

Max kissed her at the door. "As beautiful as when I first saw you," he said, and his eyes danced. "Nervous?"

"No, just happy. How about you?" she whispered.

"Euphoric. It will be a wonderful day."

Their guests clamored for attention, so they joined everyone at the table.

Tadala went first to Ginger and gave her a warm hug. "Thank you so much for putting together this occasion. I couldn't have done it without you, and I never would have wanted to."

"It was fun for me, more so because I got to do it for my new daughter."

Everett beamed by her side. "It's a beautiful day for a wedding. And the weather will be hot but manageable."

She reached out to Sam and hugged him too. "My *m'chim-wene wamkulu*."

The table filled with conversation as the plates were served onto the table family style, with fruit, eggs, and other breakfast items piled high.

Scarlett entered with Jaxon, Harper, and their nanny in tow. Tadala settled everyone in the empty seats at their end of the table, with Jaxon next to Sam.

"I'm sorry to be late. We got in last night from New York, and the kids were difficult to wake up this morning." Scarlett brushed her amber hair into place, looking frazzled.

"We're so happy you could join us." Tadala said it sincerely. She had offered the matron of honor role to Scarlett, but she hadn't been sure she could be away from important meetings at her nonprofit. Tadala suspected she only made the trip at Ginger's insistence.

Tadala didn't wish for Scarlett to be left out, and she eyed the two children, who were dressed for the occasion, though Jaxon had rumpled his shirt. "If you'd like, the kids can serve as a flower girl and ringbearer at the beginning of the ceremony. We don't have anyone to do that."

"I will! I will!" Harper's sharp eyes were alive with excitement.

"Ah, sure." Scarlett gave Tadala a glance as she helped the nanny seat the children.

"It's wonderful to see you and the grands," Everett said. "We miss you all."

"It's a chore to take the kids anywhere. And you haven't stopped in New York much to visit." There was an edge in Scarlett's voice.

"Remember, we had offered to stop after our trip to Tanzania last August. And then again after Kyiv, in the fall." Ginger's tones were measured.

"Well, both were bad times, given my work."

"You've been all over the world lately," Max said to his father.

"There's so much to see, and with the current eco push to use the metaverse to travel instead, we haven't wanted to waste a minute."

"The metaverse just isn't the same." Ginger let out an exasperated sigh. "I feel so much is lost. I travel for connection to people, not just places."

Max rubbed his jaw. "I agree. I like that my job will let me travel the world. We're looking forward to this next assignment in Rajasthan."

"I'm deciding between job offers there, too, from two medical centers. Neither of us have ever been to India, so it'll be an interesting place for us to begin our marriage." Tadala squeezed his hand.

"I want mac and cheese." Jaxon's demanding scream broke the moment.

"No" Scarlett said firmly She turned back to her family with an embarrassed look. "I wish I could say otherwise, but he's usually like this. A big difference from his sister."

"Don't apologize. That's like me and my sister," Sam said. "She's always been faster than me at learning. Give him time."

As the main course arrived, Buzz raised a glass of champagne and offered a toast. "To a perfect couple. I'll save the fun stories about Max until later today, when the party really starts," he said.

They finished the meal, this preliminary to the wedding setting a cheery tone. Tadala retired with her bridesmaids, and Max with his groomsmen, to prepare for the afternoon.

———————◆———————

The rest of the day was a blur. She gathered with her bridesmaids to put on her *chitenje* gown. Guests arrived by AVs and took seats set in rows alongside the vineyard. A susurration of conversation arose in the garden.

Tadala found herself holding her breath when four musicians with classical instruments started to play. She waited at the top of a staircase that led down to the garden and vineyard. She was hidden from the guests, but she clutched her bouquet. Her head swam as a vision of her mother sprung to mind, and she suddenly wished for her now. She pushed that single unhappy thought of the day from her head and reached for her brother's arm. The weight of his support by her side comforted her.

Max waited for her at the end of the aisle. He stood proud, handsome, and confident. Her heart beat wildly with each step, the path before her littered with rose petals scattered by Jaxon and Harper. Sam tucked her hand into Max's, who squeezed it with pure happiness on his face. The officiant led a short ceremony. Max was serious as he said his vows without missing a word, and her eyes were teary as she recited hers. The newlyweds kissed to wild applause and walked back, waving at those assembled. A photo drone murmured overhead.

They moved to the pavilion next to the vineyard for cocktails and the reception. Dinner was served.

Buzz led the toasts with Jessica by his side. "Max, as always, you're ahead of me. We love you two!"

Her new father-in-law wiped his eyes while holding Ginger, a sentimental expression on his face as he made a moving toast. A deep love for Everett and Ginger welled up. They had become her new parents.

The setting sun was a dappled orange as they cut the wedding cake, and then the dance floor opened. Hours later, the musicians played the closing song as Max held her tightly. A murmur rose from the guests when a swarm of drones appeared overhead, forming patterns with multicolored lights in the sky, dancing in hearts that intertwined.

As the drones disappeared, she smiled at an approaching whirling sound, and a sleek vehicle settled onto the open field neighboring the vineyard. Its rotors stopped turning, and the chauffeur stepped out. He stood at attention like a maître d', flying scarves draped over his arm.

"A flying car?" Max's eyes were bright at the surprise.

"We should leave in style." Tadala grinned. "Mom and I figured out this little extravagance, just for fun."

"Is it eco?"

"Not very. I researched it and found the engineering is interesting. It's too noisy and power-hungry for regular use. So, they remain for the rich, not mainstream. But we'll do it for the novelty—just this once."

Max's grin matched hers. "I'll fly with you anywhere." Tadala took his hand, and they strolled to the aircraft accompanied by cheers. The chauffeur handed them the decorative scarves. Max wrapped one elegantly around her neck and kissed her as the crowd clapped.

The chauffeur motioned to the aircraft. "She's ready to carry you to your honeymoon resort. I'll keep everyone clear for safety and give you a signal. Just push the green button on the autopilot."

He helped them into the seats and stepped aside, then directed the tipsy guests back and gave Max a thumbs-up. Tadala pushed the button, the rotors turned, and in a moment, they ascended. Their wedding guests and the lights faded below as they flew into their future.

25

SCARLETT MACGYVER—2055 (CALIFORNIA)

The nanny had taken Jaxon and Harper back to her hotel room so Scarlett could at last relax. She carried a scotch and soda to the edge of the dance floor, where she found an empty table. Fumbling in her purse for the synpsychs, she downed one with a swig from her drink. The musicians played an old song she recognized as one of Jack's favorites, and she sipped again. She huddled beyond the muted lights in the darkness and watched.

Couples danced in swirls of motion to the music. Dad looked at Mom with an expression of sublime joy. It reminded her of his expression earlier that afternoon when he made the toast. His eyes shone as he described how happy he and Mom were to have Tadala join the family. Was he that happy when she married Jack? Scarlett didn't think so.

How could he give his love away so easily? To an adopted son, and now to a daughter-in-law from across the world? She didn't think it was normal, and it certainly wasn't fair.

Max had said that Tadala wanted to take his surname, becoming another MacGyver. Wasn't that an outdated anti-feminist concept? So, like Max, she had come into the family and stolen their name, which her parents seemed prodigal in confirming upon anyone.

When Harper was only one and her divorce was final, she had petitioned to reverse her middle and surname on the public records so that Harper's surname matched her own. She'd told Mom and Dad that it was to honor them, but it was really just the last stab she could think of taking at Jack.

Scarlett looked surprised at the finished drink in her hand, ordered another, and wandered around the wedding venue.

It was beautiful, but the charm didn't cast its spell on her. Her bitterness was too palpable, too all-encompassing, and it felt like she was being avoided. She saw Max and Tadala on the dance floor, now dancing next to her parents.

She rested her elbows on the tall round bar table and sipped her drink. Why was she uneasy? Her AI was good at recognizing her emotional state. After a pause, Scarlett tapped her device.

Zelda gave her the result from the biometric monitor built into her PAWN. *Your oxytocin is surging. You are likely feeling jealousy right now. Better chill.*

It was late, and she was tired, so Scarlett downed her drink and blundered back to her hotel room.

The nanny had tucked the kids into bed. She stood by the door. "They're all set. Jaxon's asleep, and Harper's close."

"Good. I'll take over. Goodnight."

The nanny waved and left for her room nearby.

The room was lit by a single nightlight. Scarlett bent over to kiss Harper on the forehead, but she'd only been pretending to sleep.

Harper opened her eyes. "Mommy, it was fun throwing the flowers. I like having an important job."

Scarlett sat on the edge of the bed. "You're smart and competitive and will have a successful professional career."

"I know." Harper's face blazed with the blind, wide-eyed, youthful confidence of a five-year-old.

Scarlett felt the blood pulse in her chest. "But promise me one thing. Whatever you do, promise you'll keep the MacGyver name. We need some real MacGyvers to carry on."

"Why would I give up my name?"

"Some people do when they get married."

"Did you?"

"No, never."

"Then I won't, either. I like my name." She said it loud enough to wake Jaxon, who rolled over in the next bed.

"I like our name too. And we'll hold on to it."

26

Buzz Henderson—2070 (Indonesia)

Max was hunched over the screen of the 3D printer, manipulating the design before he fabricated the replacement gear. Buzz left him to his work, knowing that Max would eventually conquer the broken part. He was better at parts design and better at figuring out an answer. He always persevered long after Buzz accepted defeat. Buzz busied himself with reviewing the startup procedure.

There was a knock at the door. Outside stood the plant's soon-to-be manager, Adhi Gunawan, with Dewi, his teenage daughter. The Borneo heat sizzled him in the moment the door was open.

Buzz ushered them into the control room. He tapped his PAWN to adjust the phase change materials layer in his jumpsuit, and coolness ran down his spine before he sat.

"Any problems?" Adhi smoothed his batik shirt as he sat down at the round table behind the control panels. Dewi cautiously sat next to him, gaze darting between Buzz and Max. Buzz knew about her from several visits with Adhi. He proudly gushed that she was mathematically gifted and perhaps a future engineer.

"One trivial problem—and analog, surprisingly—a broken gear in one gauge. It's not essential to the safety of plant operation, but I can fix it. I'll have the replacement part in ten minutes." Max went back to his screen.

"Trivial for you," Buzz said. He turned his attention to Dewi. "So you're still tagging along with your father to these boring power plants?" He liked to joke with the girl, who was serious on every visit. He wanted to make her laugh.

But Dewi didn't take the bait. "Oh no, I like to see the plant. We need it to keep the air conditioning running for everyone. It's an important plant for my *Bapak* to manage." She spoke with defiant confidence.

Adhi smiled at his daughter. "Nusantara is growing, so the plant comes online not a moment too soon."

"I've finished and verified the part design." Max pushed buttons, and the 3D printer whirled and sputtered. The new gear began to appear.

"Are you looking to be an engineer like your *Bapak*?" Buzz asked.

Dewi nodded, her gaze glued to the printer. "In some energy field. We need electricity from a source that doesn't ruin the environment." She dripped perspiration as she glanced out the window toward the steamy sago palms swaying in a light breeze. "Besides fission, how about space-based solar? I've been reading about that idea."

Buzz chuckled. "Hell, no. That's been science fiction for over a century now, and counting."

"That idea hasn't made much headway for practical reasons." Max's tone, as always, was gentle. "It's difficult to do maintenance for the orbital equipment. Things always break, and at the most inconvenient times. And that part of the cost equation has been the Achilles heel of the technology." He gestured toward the 3D printer clanking away.

"Sure, there's three to six times efficiency improvement by first capturing solar energy in orbit. And the vehicle launch costs have been reduced substantially." Buzz turned serious now too. "But don't forget the steps to transmit the power wirelessly to Earth, and then to transform that transmission back into electricity at a receiving station. Those require tons of infrastructure in space and on the ground. Space-based solar has been proposed to replace fission, and that's largely because of the irrational fear of the atom."

Buzz and Max had debated these alternatives endless times. The fission plant designs were well-tested over a half century, capable of being built cookie-cutter style with safety paramount. Buzz admired the passion still in Max's eyes.

This was his purpose in life. And he had convinced Buzz to join him in it long ago, cooped up in their dorm room during a heat wave.

"But solar has worked well, right? At least, on the ground, in larger plants with arrays covering deserts, and through rooftop solar, providing distributed electricity." Dewi 's argument for solar was prevalent in Indonesia.

"Damn true," Buzz conceded. "There's a large role for solar in the energy equation."

Dewi waved her hands. "Okay, how about fusion?"

Buzz felt a fondness for her interest, and he was sorry the project was done and he'd no longer have the chance to encourage her. "Fusion is looking a bit closer to commercial operation. They got ITER operational in the late 2040s."

Max chimed in. "The DEMO reactor helped prove feasibility."

"Many private companies are still experimenting," Buzz said.

"A challenge has been the high operating temperatures. Fusion operates at over 100 million degrees Celsius. Fission reactors operate under 1000 degrees Celsius." Max was now sitting next to Dewi, and Adhi stood behind, grinning at the conversation.

"Wow, that's a huge temperature difference," Dewi said.

"So, one challenge has been plasma containment, requiring new materials," Buzz said. "Fortunately, materials science advances are helping to solve those problems."

"So fusion is on the near horizon," Max said.

Dewi nodded energetically. "I understand these technologies aren't there yet, but they will be in my lifetime."

"Fission plants supply the always-on power now, especially the modular power designs like this one. But diversifying our power will also be important," Buzz said.

Max leaned forward, his elbows resting on his knees. "I'm glad you're thinking this way. Even if I don't believe space-based solar will work, and we still have work to do on fusion power, we need to always be thinking about power alternatives like this. Practical engineering dictates what technologies develop. It's good to think critically about it. You could be building it in the future."

"And to acknowledge what will likely remain science fiction," Buzz said. "Everyone thinks of dramatic advances, but technology also advances in subtle ways."

Max elaborated. "Like the decades to reengineer the microbiome in the cow's rumen—that's its largest stomach—to reduce methane production."

"Yep, no big cow farts anymore." Buzz snickered. "Or like in transportation, it was never likely we'd go straight from trains, planes, and automobiles to 'Beam me up, Scotty.'"

"Or even flying cars," Max said.

"Hey, you had that at your wedding. A memorable exit." They laughed together and explained to Dewi and Adhi.

The 3D printer chirped, and a green light blinked as the task completed. Max pulled the finished gear free. Max and Adhi worked to insert it into the broken gauge.

Dewi fidgeted in her seat. "I'm thinking about engineering school after high school and wondered if you had any advice about attending one in the US?"

Buzz frowned. "All the US programs are extremely competitive. There's been political backlash against so-called climate refugees, and there are no longer exceptions to the immigration rules. I'd hate to raise your hopes."

Adhi raised an eyebrow.

She lowered her gaze. "We lived in Jakarta before moving here. It's almost abandoned now that the water has risen. I have some friends who tried to go to the US and got deported."

Buzz stared down at his hands. "Anyone caught illegally crossing into the US is banned for life, along with their immediate families, even if they weren't involved. There is a strict criterion based on certain skills, talents, and intelligence. We disagree with the policy, but it is what it is."

"Bandung Institute of Technology and Gadjah Mada University are a couple of schools you should consider." Wiping his hands on a towel, Max had returned to the discussion to add words of encouragement. "You've got the brain for this field, and the world needs people like you in it."

She was quiet for a moment, and then she looked deeply into Buzz's eyes, hers full of determination. "Then I'll stay in Indonesia and make my country as livable as I can."

———————◆———————

With the gauge repaired, the plant startup procedure followed, and soon the turbines began their soft hum on the floor below. Outside, the sago palms hung limp in the now-bearable evening heat. They had opened the window, and the sounds of the tropics filled the air with a chorus of chattering insects and the occasional muffled grunt of an animal.

Adhi had formally taken charge of the fission plant. They were leaving the next day for home.

"I'm so looking forward to seeing you again." Max spoke with Tadala on the holo-display on the far side of the control room, while Buzz sat quietly looking out the window. He couldn't help overhearing parts of their conversation, although it faded in and out with the jungle noise in the background. Buzz caught the name "Dewi" and "We were lucky to leave when we did."

"It's good neither of us had family in Taiwan or Malawi, because today we couldn't have brought them to the US." Tadala's soft, dulcet tones carried in a lull.

They would drive back to the hotel in Nusantara and leave on the morning flight. Buzz couldn't stop thinking about Dewi, the kid who might one day become an engineer.

It was a new city in a growing country with over three hundred million people. Since he'd been born, China had lost that much population. It had been ostracized for a decade because of its conquest of Taiwan. Now, its influence was lessened, and it was ignored by countries like India and Indonesia. The world was always changing, and there were important roles for people to play everywhere. Dewi would find a place for herself and make a difference.

27

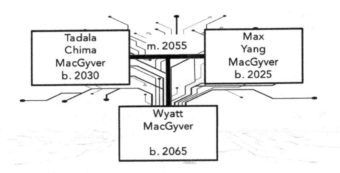

The autocar arrives just as we reach the road after climbing the path from the ocean. I take my time climbing into the vehicle, with Grand beside me and Robert in the backward-facing seat. The robot's forehead glows green, so I know he has given the coordinates. We set off, and my view of the Pacific disappears. We follow the frontage road and turn south onto Highway 101. The autocar heads to the cutoff road, through the coastal redwoods that have still survived, and toward the vineyard nestled against the coastal hills.

"Did you marry right after Grandma came to California?"

"Not until she finished her nursing degree in 2055. We were best friends for several years—really since she arrived in the US. I didn't want her to feel beholden to me because I helped her settle here."

"I don't think somebody would marry somebody just because they helped them move," he says.

"I had an overstated sense of propriety. Grandma Tadala let me know I was old-fashioned and she really loved me.

I felt like the luckiest man alive. We were very much in love. I still am."

"Then you had my Pa?"

"Wyatt was born ten years later. Your grandmother worked as a nurse for several years before and then part-time when Wyatt was a toddler." There is a warm feeling in my chest when I think about bouncing Wyatt on my knee. Tadala and I loved our little family.

"When I was overseas building fission plants, she worked in nearby cities, usually in private clinics. We saw a lot of countries back in the day when people still traveled."

"They say travel isn't eco. That's the reason the Commune people say we stay put."

"Long-distance airplanes do still burn carbon. People travel less for ethical reasons and because the taxes make it expensive. Most people travel virtually, on the net. There's something lost, though. Like a depth of human connection to understand how people live."

Grand makes a face. "I've never done net travel either. No net connections in the Commune. We're cut off, just hunker-in' down in the woods."

I have no comment as we ride along the country road to my vineyard.

"You lost Grandma ten years ago, when I was four. I hardly remember being four. But I do remember seein' her on one of my trips outside the Commune. Just Pa and me. It was one of the times I 'member seein' you, and then you were sad."

I don't want to think about it long—losing Tadala and the infrequent chances to see Grand growing up. "She was past middle age but just eighty-five. And unlucky. Most of the old frightening diseases—cancers, heart disease, stroke, organ diseases—have treatments. But she was brought down by a complex disease. There are many complex diseases, and she just happened to have one."

"What is a complex disease?"

I don't meet his gaze. We've cured many things, but some things we can't fix. He'll learn that later. "A complex disease is caused by a combination of genetic, environmental, and lifestyle issues. These diseases are hard to sort out, and it's difficult to assemble good data for AI research. That's why there aren't cures yet."

"A lot of diseases must have cures, though. Nobody gets sick at the Commune."

My smile returns as I recall the successes of this past century, particularly relevant to me. "Advances in bioscience and medical technology have dramatically extended human lifespan. Without obesity, high blood pressure, heart disease, and diabetes, the average life expectancy in the US has risen from about seventy-seven years to nearly ninety." I can see Grand doing mental math when he looks at me, and I chuckle. "Of course, a few of us are lucky to beat even those odds."

The autocar stops. Grand helps me to the bench next to the vineyard, and we face the rows blanketing the hillside. I like to sit here in the different seasons and watch the vineyard change. The stoic vines wrapped in winter slowly awaken with spring rains and gathering sun and send out green shoots. Then bud break leads to blossoms when I manage the irrigation to build the protective canopy of leaves over the green bunches of fruit. I decrease the irrigation to stress the vines just a bit during the dry summer, and that encourages them to concentrate on ripening perfect clusters. They pass through veraison as the berries turn a deep purple, like they are now, ready for harvest. And when the vines have done their work, like a signal was given, the oranges of autumn paint the vineyard. In all the seasons, this is my favorite spot to watch the sunset.

I wish I could have shared it with Tadala.

Robert passes the container with sandwiches. With a soft *whir,* he opens the water jug and pours two glasses.

Grand bites into his sandwich. "Wow, this is great bread."

"And you helped make it."

It's early for lunch, but I guessed right that he'd have a good appetite after missing a meal yesterday. Below us, the robopickers move between rows. The arms snake out to each side, and ripe berries flow into the holding bin.

He gestures at the equipment. "It's harvest time?"

"Just this month. The machines pass through every day, collecting the grapes at prime ripeness."

I know each step, refined since taking over the vineyard. The wine is improving too. Not that I'll be around when it hits its prime to drink. As we eat, I explain the process to him, and between mouthfuls, he asks questions about the machinery.

"Is there much farmwork for people to do on a vineyard like this?"

I presume from his question that Grand has farmed, as it's one of the tasks at the Commune. "There's hardly any. The AIs have stolen the fun out of grape growing."

Several years ago, Robert gave me the most efficient planting alternatives. I accidentally glance at the robot, and it takes that as permission to enter the conversation.

"The c29 rootstock was optimized for soil and climate variables and was expected to yield an additional 17 percent of quality grapes."

"Thank you, Robert."

Someday, the robot might recognize irony and that the inflection I used means "shut up." I wave Robert away, and the robot gives us a bit more distance.

"How long have you owned the vineyard?"

"After Grandma passed away, I decided to move here on the coast, bought the vineyard, and remodeled the house. There wasn't anything to hold me in Berkeley anymore."

I unscrew the top from my walking stick and pour about a hundred milliliters of wine into the empty water glass. At my age, I have no reason to worry about the effects.

He eyes my glass.

"Want a sip?"

"I've never tasted wine before. But sure."

As I pour a bit into Grand's glass, Robert's forehead glows orange. "Sir, I understand that it is illegal for anyone under age twenty-one to drink wine, including this one, which contains 14.3 percent alcohol by volume."

"Well, I think we can safely ignore that this time."

The robot blinks twice then is silent. I think about what that means in the software.

Grand leans back on the bench and licks his lips. "I'm trying to imagine Pa as a little kid. Tell me more about what he was like growing up."

"It was a normal, typical life. The country and the world were optimistic about the future. I'll tell you just a couple stories." Like an earthquake once reawakened an old spring, his questions have restarted the flow of these pleasant memories when Wyatt was small. I'm certain now that it's a story outside his experience, but it will help him understand what once was and what can be possible again.

28

TADALA MACGYVER—2070 (CALIFORNIA)

Wyatt walked beside her, examining the maple leaf he had pulled a block ago. Tadala had an urge to hurry the boy. She knew Max treasured these chances for their family to spend time together, and she didn't want to be late. Now she glanced more closely at the leaf, and it reminded her of Malawi and the tea plantations gracing the hillsides. That reminded her of Mum, gone now twenty years. Tadala involuntarily shivered.

She thought of the slow days of her home country and how the heat prevented her from hurrying to anything. Immigrating to the US had been a culture shock, with everything so technologically advanced, and the pace seemed to speed up every year. Tadala slowed a touch and held Wyatt's hand while she took deep breaths to calm herself. She focused her attention entirely on Wyatt to savor this quiet moment spent with him. Now five, he had become an interesting conversationalist capable of engaging her thoughts away from the difficult parts of her past.

Wyatt twirled the leaf by the stem. "This is the petiole."

"Where did you learn that word?"

"I saw it on my HDSET. It lists all the parts of a leaf. Remember, Mommy, you said I could look at anything with science." Wyatt continued to examine the leaf, and she took his other hand as they crossed the street so he didn't trip on the curbs.

"Yes, you can. We need science to live in today's world. Good job."

Wyatt had begun reading at a first-grade level by studying all the pictures of plants, then learned the names with the AI trainer.

"Did you know that now there are a dozen astronauts at the base on Mars? They must be brave scientists to make the journey." Space science had been a fleeting passion for Tadala, though there had been no chance of a career before nursing offered her the opportunity to leave Malawi.

"Do they have trees there?"

"No trees at all."

"Do they have music?"

"No, they don't have music in space because space doesn't have air. But you can listen to music in the crew's habitats. The moon base is growing, too, and they need scientists to care for the biosphere garden. I guess there are trees in the garden. There are a hundred astronauts there."

"Then I don't want to go. I like music and a big forest with lots of trees."

She let space science drop. There were plenty of choices for him if he kept his interest in learning. They went through the college gate, walked down the main pedestrian way, and approached the quad with the medical science building on one corner, where she found most of the classes she was taking now.

Tadala used her PAWN to call Max. His avatar danced in front of her eyes, and she smiled back. He'd be there in a few minutes. She closed the app and sat on a bench. Wyatt walked around all the benches in the vicinity, counting the screws. Several students lay on the grass in the opposite field, talking in small groups. Drones buzzed overhead, making deliveries to the cafeteria on the other corner.

Max strolled into the quad and swooped the boy into his arms. "Wyatt!" he cooed in his baritone.

With one parent holding each hand, they walked back through the gate and into the bordering town. They passed cafés and specialty shops serving most customers via drone, though they saw the occasional window shopper strolling by.

They reached a favorite lunch restaurant. It wasn't epicurean but served solid fare and had large booths where it was easy to sit with a child and have privacy to talk.

A robot approached the table and took their orders. "Thank you, sir and miss. We will prepare your delicious meal, and I will return in five minutes."

Max discreetly pointed to the logo emblazoned on the robot's frontispiece before it turned. When it left, he said, "PalImōto 517. Jack owns that company."

"I know. They started testing here last week."

"There's another class of jobs on the way to being eliminated."

Tadala met his gaze. "My medical degree will keep me ahead of the automation going on."

"I'm so happy we'll have a doctor in the family just in a couple of years."

Tadala was warmed by the pride in his voice. "Thank you for being so supportive."

"Of course, I support you. Personalized medicine is such a great choice. It's exciting that we can now tailor medical treatment based on individual genetic profiles." Max laced his fingers in hers. "We make a good team."

"I'm sorry I can't travel with you as much on your projects."

"We both have careers. We can manage this until you finish your residency."

The robot returned with a tray. It moved plates onto the table. Wyatt reached for his orange juice just as the robot's hand touched it. The cup wobbled then tipped over on the tray. Max saved half of it, but the rest ran off the tray onto the robot.

The robot looked down at the empty tray, task complete, and turned away toward the kitchen, oblivious to the liquid dribbling onto the floor from its leg.

Tadala stifled a laugh. "There's still hope on the job front."

As they finished lunch, Wyatt pulled the leaf from his pocket and explained the parts to Max, who gave him his full attention.

After a while, Max checked his PAWN. "My flight out leaves tonight at seven. This time for the power project in Argentina."

Wyatt frowned. "Is Daddy going away?"

"Just for two weeks," Tadala said. "I'll take good care of you while he's gone."

"Why are you going away again?" Wyatt slurped the remainder of his orange juice and squinted up at Max.

"Mommy and Daddy do important work. Sometimes we need to be away, but we would always rather be with you."

"I want to do important work, too, with trees."

"That's a good plan. Study the science, and you can do anything."

29

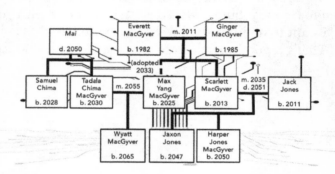

Buzz sat at the picnic table with a beer in one hand and Jessica beside him. Their two children, Oskar and Emmie, rambled under the trees. Emmie searched for insects, and her older brother avoided them. Off on the horizon toward Lewis Cove, a hovercraft approached.

The island operators, a husband-and-wife team, worked the pit for the traditional New England clambake. Down on the sand, the husband peeked under the edge of the covering tarp, and a curl of steam rose. The man gave Buzz a thumbs-up.

The host walked to their table. "We'll begin serving in half an hour."

"Perfect timing. Thanks," Buzz said. He sipped his beer.

"A perfect temperature too," Jessica said. "My PIDA says twenty-eight degrees."

Buzz skipped his PIDA and did the mental math, figuring that was eighty-two degrees Fahrenheit. He had spent so much time internationally working with Max that he thought in both temperature scales. It was a low temperature for the Fourth of July in Maine these days, and the breeze off the water was refreshing.

The hovercraft set down on the asphalt pad twenty meters away, and Max led his family toward Buzz and the waiting tables.

Buzz gave Max a bear hug. "Great to see you, buddy. Welcome to Cabbage Island."

"Thanks again for the invitation. I haven't spent much time in Maine. This place is beautiful."

"The family secret. We used to come here for clambakes when I was a kid. That connection helped snag the holiday reservation." Though the traditional association was his only claim, Buzz felt like a prince welcoming friends to his lands.

"Who doesn't love family traditions?" Jessica hugged Tadala.

Oskar and Emmie had run up when the aircraft arrived and found Wyatt as he came down the ramp. The three kids played together often, and they were already deep in conversation.

"Please stay within sight," Jessica said.

Buzz set a surveillance circle around the three kids with his PIDA so he wouldn't need to think about it again.

Tadala and Jessica made the introductions. Buzz had met Max's parents, Everett and Ginger, on several occasions, but he only recalled meeting Max's sister Scarlett once before. Tadala's brother Sam rounded out the party.

"Beer, anyone?" Buzz handed out the cold recyclable containers, along with organic drinks and lemonade for the kids.

They stood around talking in the warm summer air. Seagulls squawked along the shore. Jessica was describing the little island. He was happy she'd fallen in love with it during their summer excursions over the past few years.

The island operator removed the tarp covering the pit. Aromas of seafood, herbs and butter, seaweed, and salt water arose with the steam. They gathered around to watch the layers of food being removed. Out came the corn, followed by potatoes and then steaming clams. They filled plates and found seats together at the long table.

"What are you up to, Sam?" Buzz asked.

"Still architectural drafting. There's a cool building we're designing off Commonwealth in Boston. I'm close by this summer, so thanks for letting Max invite me to tag along."

"We're delighted you could join us," Jessica said. "And you too, Scarlett."

"It wasn't so far for me either. I'm still in New York City, in Midtown." She paused, as if searching for an explanation. "Too bad that Jaxon couldn't come. He just finished college and is looking for a job."

Buzz nodded, remembering that Max said his nephew was struggling to finish a two-year degree. Looking around the table, it occurred to Buzz that the best-educated person there was Tadala, near to becoming a doctor. He and Max might have gone back for more education, but they were having too much fun building energy plants around the world.

Everett raised his beer in a toast. "To Buzz and Jessica. Thank you for a wonderful holiday invitation." They eagerly clanked their beers and began on the food. Buzz enjoyed the familiar salty, mineral edge to the fare. The flavors brought memories of his childhood back to the surface—like the time he got sick after eating so many potatoes.

"We all have so much to celebrate. We should share it," Tadala said. "I remember being sworn in for my citizenship, so I'm just proud to be here. Sam and I have gotten quite comfortable as Americans, and Max and I have a nice family." She looked lovingly at Wyatt, his face covered in butter from an ear of corn.

Jessica raised her drink again. "Buzz and I are celebrating a dozen years of marriage later this month, and with our two wonderful kids also." Most of the table honored them with cries of "*prost*" and shouts of congratulations.

"The world is in pretty good shape too," Everett chimed in from the end of the table.

Buzz knew Everett well enough to know that, despite his age—in his late eighties—he probably still followed international news closely. Leave it to a MacGyver to bring up the rest of the planet.

"We've avoided widescale nuclear war, and the great-power rivalries between the US, China, and others are finally more subdued." Everett raised his drink.

"We can all drink to that." Buzz tapped his beer against Everett's.

Jessica looked less certain. "When I lived in Europe, we worried a lot about nuclear war, feeling closer to the front of the hot spots."

"But everywhere can be the front lines, so it's not like proximity makes a big difference," Scarlett said. "At least the major countries have begun to reduce their arsenals."

"Though there are more countries with weapons overall." Ginger shook her head. "More work to get rid of them."

"You've gained quite a bit of knowledge about the nuclear field," Everett said to Scarlett with a wry expression.

"I spend a lot of time discussing nuclear bombs versus fission energy. Some donors want to understand why TerraGuard Network is pushing for the energy plants."

"I'm so happy you've joined my team." Everett put an arm around her and gave her a hug.

"It's a matter of fairness for the countries in the Global South that never caused the climate-change crisis." Scarlett said it firmly, but she hugged him back.

"I heard from some old friends in Malawi. Those power plants have begun to stabilize their grid. The lights stay on dependably now," Sam said.

Buzz enjoyed the conversation with old friends and new. Not to mention the beer. "We're out in the field building these plants around the world. As Max here would say, we're kicking ass and taking names."

Buzz looked at Max, waiting for the rejoinder, trying not to laugh yet. A cloud crossed Tadala's face as she looked at the kids, probably worried about what they were hearing, but Jessica chuckled along with him, so Buzz knew he hadn't crossed any lines.

"Hmmm...that's not what I'd say, but it sure is your truth, Buzz," Max said.

Buzz let loose with a belly laugh. Max joined in. Buzz had achieved his objective, to jostle his best friend out of the straight and proper. Max took the world too seriously.

"I think the climate crisis is on the path to being solved." Everett held onto a sober note.

Buzz saw those two as the most passionate about saving the world from climate change out of everyone he'd met.

Tadala played with a braid of her hair. "The climate is getting noticeably worse, though. There are still many who want to leave the hottest places. The Global North countries have controlled their borders, making it harder to immigrate."

"True, but at least those countries have stabilized their democracies." It was Jessica's turn to be serious.

Desserts were brought out. Cuts of watermelon and slices of blueberry pies filled the table. Buzz poured more beer. He was in a jovial mood. "Let's continue with the list of what to celebrate today. Here's one. I think Max and I are making three times as much as when we started in this industry back twenty years ago."

"Ha." Everett joined the merriment. "Based on what Max said his salary is, it's six times what I made in the same industry."

"But you need to adjust for inflation, Dad. That's gone up around three and a half times since I was born. Still, the average American has half again as much real wealth since then. That's true per person around the world, too, even though the global population has grown."

"Half again as much. That's still a lot more stuff," Sam said.

Everett bowed his head, and his eyes crinkled at the corners. "Always good with the math. Still, I agree with Sam. The whole world is doing well, with more real money and people working fewer hours. I remember when we worked forty-hour weeks."

Everyone laughed. Sam shook his head. "Now it's thirty-two hours in every Global North country, and we're working on lowering that to twenty-four."

Buzz nudged Max. "Of course, that won't stop you building more clean power plants. There's no rule saying you can only work that many hours."

Max spread his hands wide in surrender.

Sam shook his head again. "When I first got to America, I was amazed by the guaranteed income. And they tacked an earned income credit on top of my wage."

"That only works, though, if you have a job." Scarlett was the only person at the table missing a smile.

Buzz suspected she was supporting Jaxon. He doubted her nonprofit paid anything close to a private sector job.

Tadala tried to regain the group's upbeat spirit. "Medical science has created wonders and dramatically reduced disease around the world."

"It must be an exciting time to be working on your degree," Jessica said to Tadala.

Everett nodded. "Many diseases are being cured. People live longer and live healthier into older age."

Max winked in his parents' direction.

Ginger waved a fork. "We can communicate with each other so easily. Families can stay close."

Buzz saw her steal a glance at Scarlett, who looked down at her pie.

Tadala spooned ice cream onto a slice of apple pie. "Everyone has plenty of free time. It's just a matter of deciding how much to spend on work and family." She cast a glance at Max.

Max tilted his head to one side, smiling. "Says she who will soon be buried by her residency."

"We have so many choices—sports, concerts, the metaverse," Sam said.

"Fun things to do, and people have the money and the free time to do them. Like hanging out with your grandchildren." Ginger gave Wyatt a hug and wiped ice cream from his hands.

"The AIs have been extremely helpful, but they've not taken over." Everett spoke with gravity, back to his ever-serious and worldly matters. "AGI has not materialized—yet—to really displace humans. But it's obvious that may change as robots roll out."

"But it's not to worry about today." Buzz didn't want the conversation to roll into the negative. "I see we ran short on refreshments, not something this host will stand for. Let's celebrate the Fourth with a resupply."

Buzz had given the silent command on his PIDA, timing it with his comment. On cue, two robot dogs bounded out of the kitchen building carrying small kegs of beer on collars around their necks. Buzz tapped one to loud cheers and poured ample glasses.

———————◆———————

Buzz sat on the beach above the rest of the holiday party, his arm around Jessica, who leaned against his shoulder. They watched the distant fireworks display rise above the tiny town of Boothbay Harbor a mile to the northeast. The silhouettes of their friends appeared before them, briefly outlined in each burst of color. Their two children slept at their feet. The cool sea air rustled the trees, and waves broke gently on the shore.

It was his idea of a perfect party—beer, family, friends, good cheer. Life was good, and Buzz never wanted it to change.

30

GRAND—PRESENT, 2125

The wine is pretty good. It tickles my throat and goes down smoother with every sip. Grandfather's stories about good times when Pa was a kid don't sound anything like the way Ma and Pa live now. It sounds to me like everyone got to do whatever they wanted and had lots of choices.

Grandfather is watching the robopickers again.

"I'll be back in a minute. Let me check something."

He leaves his stick behind and walks to the machine that has a bin hooked behind it, filled with grapes. He takes out some bunches and looks at them.

My glass is empty, and I don't think Grandfather would mind if I helped myself. I unscrew the top of his stick and fill my glass. It goes down easy in the hot weather. I put his stick back. The bot watches me.

Grandfather comes back with his hands full of grapes, and he sets them on the table. He pulls off some, tastes them, and hands me a couple.

"I was curious to taste exactly how ripe these are."

They're pretty good, and it's fun to think about how they turn to wine.

"The fruit is always picked at peak ripeness based on the algorithm, balancing brix, which approximately equates to sugar content, versus TA, or titratable acid, which declines inversely with sugar content," Robert says.

The robot is speaking to me and has his back to Grandfather, who rolls his eyes and raises two fingers in a "V" behind Robert's head like he has antennas. Grandfather wiggles his fingers behind the bot's head like it is wagging its ears.

I can't stop laughing. The robot's lenses move back and forth, and then it turns around. It studies Grandfather for a moment and moves to stand a few meters away, its forehead turning pink.

Grandfather chuckles when he stands beside me. "All robots except the military ones and those in factories have a blind spot behind."

"Why is that?"

"People got freaked out by the first robots walking around that seemed to see everything behind their heads. It felt like spying and made everyone uncomfortable. Now the regulation says there needs to be the blind spot, which doesn't affect performance in a meaningful way."

I'm intrigued. "Are there other secrets like that?"

"Sure. I'll teach you all I know. One is that every robot must attempt to give a response when asked a direct question by a human." There's a smile still on Grandfather's face. "Here, play along with me."

He stands in front of Robert, turns to me, and says, "Turn on the force field." He winks at me.

There were science fiction stories in my allbook about force fields. I raise my hand. "The force field is on!"

Grandfather stiffens. He reaches out a hand, seeming to touch a wall. He turns to his left and finds another wall. He rubs the invisible cage, pretending to press the walls.

He looks frantically at the robot. "Robert, I'm trapped! Help me escape these force fields!"

The robot's head turns, and its lenses flash. "Sir, that is an old mime routine, and I'm sorry, I'm not falling for that trick."

Grandfather drops his hands. "Ah, you're no fun."

He comes back to stand next to me and picks up his walking stick. He studies it for a moment and then looks at me. "It seems my stick has defied the laws of gravity, getting lighter. A grave problem." His chest heaves with laughter.

The robot is active again. "Sir, the young man has taken the prohibited alcohol from your walking stick."

Grandfather cuts it off with a glare. "Did I suggest that you enter the conversation with us? Robert, I think it's a good idea to disconnect your recording today. Grand and I will have a private talk. Please come over here."

"Yes, sir."

Grandfather twirls his hand to tell the bot to turn around. It positions itself with its back panel facing us. I notice its forehead blinks.

Grandfather opens the panel, finds some unit, and flicks a switch.

"Authenticate Level for permission." The unit speaks with a mechanical tone different from Robert's usual voice.

Grandfather taps his chest, and I see a blue sparkle there.

"Appropriate Level authority received. Request to end recording accepted." The light above it changes from green to red.

"Can anyone do that?"

"Sadly, not. Just someone with a high enough of these damn Levels. At least on this model." Grandfather winks. "But now we can talk all we want."

I'll ask him about what a Level is later. I'm just glad he's mad at the robot and not me. He doesn't like a tattletale either.

The robot still works. "Sir, I have checked your calendar today and am pleased to remind you of your medical appointment at 17:00." Its forehead glows green.

"Yes, thank you, Robert. That had slipped my mind." He turns to me. "Hey, how about a short driving tour of this corner of California? We can make a couple of stops on the way to my medical appointment."

I shrug. "Sure. I didn't see much, travelin' at night and all."

The autocar hadn't been called by anyone else while we ate lunch. We walk toward it with the robot following us. My head is a bit fuzzy, but I try to come up with some question.

"You built energy plants for your career?"

"I was proud of the work. By the time I retired, I'd helped build thirty fission facilities. The world closed the last of the coal power plants and stopped using carbon for energy."

"When did you retire?"

"That was at the turn of the century, when I turned seventy-five." He explains how it was when people had lots of jobs. "When I graduated from college in 2047, the baby boom generation was almost gone. The following generations were smaller, so there was enough work, even though automation was eliminating jobs. There was money to strengthen the social safety net for everyone. It was an exciting time. But by the time I retired, finding good work had become a problem."

"Is that why Ma and Pa dropped out and joined the Commune?"

Grandfather's face is serious now, and he turns his head away. "Their careers coincided with the robot tsunami. Many futurists expected that robots would be used like they are now a century ago, but it didn't truly happen until the last half century, when job losses accelerated. It took longer to move robots from the factory floor to work among us. But that invasion still arrived."

We reach the autocar. Grandfather runs his hands through his hair, pausing like he is starting a new story. "You mentioned you haven't had access to much technology. Outside the Commune, there's no escaping it. Technology can appear to change our lives slowly and then suddenly. Let's go see, and I'll tell you how the robot tidal wave upended the entire economic system, affecting everyone, including our family."

31

HARPER JONES MACGYVER—2075
(COLORADO)

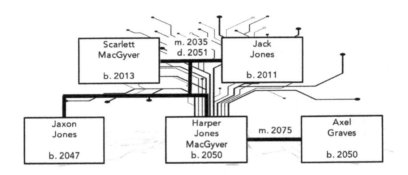

Harper waited at the bottom of the run, resting comfortably on the board. She inhaled the crisp mountain air, and looked back up the slope covered in machine-made snow. The blue sky outlined a figure making his way toward her, carving graceful arcs on his board.

Much was in the genes. She knew she cut a svelte figure with her phosphorescent green ski suit. She glanced at the HJM monogram on her gloves. She'd kept the MacGyver surname to please Mom, who'd been vehement about it. Split loyalty. Even though Mom raised her and Dad only appeared in her life after she left for college, she was more like him. Unlike Mom, she intended to be in control of her life, not let it be defined by anyone else.

Also unlike Mom, she loved competition and was driven by the desire to create something unique. She'd reached out to her father two years ago and offered to work summers at his company. She told him it was to reconnect with him, but mostly she was curious and needed a path to creative freedom.

The older man swished to a stop beside her. "These auto-boards aren't as complicated to control as I expected. Good technology." He was puffing a little from the black diamond. His hair blew in the wind, and he gave her his signature gleaming rows of teeth. No doubt, he took the pharmaceutical pill that warded off grays.

"You handled it well." She had to admit that her father was still dashing at age sixty-four, and she could see why her mother had fallen for him.

"This is a beautiful spot. Let me catch my breath, and you can tell me why you lured me up on this mountain. It wasn't just to prove you could outrun me." His gaze was practiced from both sides of the table, whether asking for a better deal or reading how a customer with money might be parted from it.

"You got me. Dad, I wanted to tell you that I'm going to marry Axel Graves." She wasn't asking for permission or approval. She expressed an unalterable fact of life.

Jack's smile brightened to incandescence. "I like the guy. He's very competitive and a good match with you. The electrical engineering degree will take him far. Now, can he keep up with you on the slopes?" Her father chuckled. "...and in life?"

"He can try." She laughed with him. "And don't forget, I'm first in my class. Ahead of Axel. We'll make a good team."

"I'm happy for you. You've chosen well. And why do I think you've done the choosing?"

"Dad, we're the same. I also like to be the one making decisions."

It was true that Axel had fallen for her early in the program, had followed her around like a lovesick puppy, had waited on her the past four years, and would do what she asked. But Axel was also fiercely competitive. She enjoyed beating him in math and software design because of her double major in electrical engineering and computer science. Harper knew he wanted her not only for her beauty. He respected her for her brains and take-charge attitude.

Jack wiggled his feet in the board laces. "I enjoyed these last two summers since you came to work for me. Any chance you'll be back? Maybe with Axel?"

She'd anticipated the question and followed her sales plan. "General RoboMechs is a fine company, Dad. I know you've tried several products. Axel and I have some ideas for evolving the product strategy. If you're willing to give us freedom to experiment, we can join as a team."

"It's not as fine a company as I'd planned. These robot corporations require large capital investments to build hardware, so it's a jungle out there for the smaller ones."

"I know. But there's a tipping point, and I think you're near to developing a robot that's independent enough to function well most of the time. That robot won't have consciousness but could convince people it's close to that mark because they'll anthropomorphize the machine."

"Then you and Axel are in. I'll admit it; I'm tired. I've tried many ideas, and not one has yet hit the big money. Maybe you can find the vein of gold in this business." In a surprising gesture, Jack leaned in and gave her a hug.

When he backed off, Harper noticed the age around his eyes. She hadn't dared to believe he would hand over real control—not any time soon. But the door was open, and she was energized by the chance to build the next generation of personal robots.

32

Jaxon Jones—2075 (California)

Jaxon sat across the desk from the supervisor. He'd always thought she was pretty in a natural way, with her hair tied back, no makeup, and the occasional smudge of grease on her sleeve. Today, she had no light in her eyes, and that worried him.

She adjusted her PAWN like she was looking at both him and something else. "Jaxon, you've been here, what, ten months?"

He nodded and wiped his own greasy hands on his work pants.

"By now, you should've mastered the basics. The job starts with the physical aspects of installing HVAC units. Then, to hook up the AI machine and run diagnostics, to do basic troubleshooting. They need to work to our customers' specs."

He nodded slowly, since that seemed true. Where was she going?

She tapped her PAWN and turned the 3D display so he could see it. Job reports scrolled by with the red bars that he knew were bad outnumbering all else. Her accompanying recitation filled his ears, now a cacophony of indictment. His chest hurt like she'd shot an arrow through it.

She stopped and stared at him, her lips twisted in pity. "Jaxon, I like you. But the job requires understanding technical specs and using the AI to ask questions, to troubleshoot the problems. You need to formulate questions to uncover the real causes. It takes some abstract thinking. You're good with your hands. But that isn't adequate for this job."

His head buzzed as he carried his toolbox out the door. A minute later, his PIDA chirped as it received his formal dismissal. He had unemployment insurance for six months.

As he took the maglev train home to his tiny apartment, Jaxon thought about the two-year college degree he'd finished in four years. It had been so draining for him to understand algebra or geometry or even basic math. He couldn't create a picture in his head about abstract subjects. Though his sister was three years younger, she'd been light-years ahead of him. The middle school geometry had been particularly mortifying. His face grew hot remembering Harper's giggling about *"pons asinorum"* when she easily solved something called proposition 5 in some old book called *Elements*. It was even worse when he asked the AI what it meant, and it answered out loud.

It never got easier. While the AI made writing code obsolete, people were still needed to write prompts. His prompts technically worked, but they were far too basic, and he scored poorly. So he took the minimum required computer classes and concentrated on manual skills.

Jaxon tossed a package of cultured beef and vegetables into the autocooker. He picked at his dinner and stared out the window at the pink setting sun on the horizon. He didn't want to think about the lousy day.

His snug swivel chair beckoned, and he settled into it. He slipped on the haptic gloves, tightened the haptic vest, put on the HDSET, and opened the metaverse.

To glory, Rodrigo Díaz!

His character stood triumphant in the stirrups on his horse, holding his sword high and facing four paths.

Which path will you choose today?

He knew the paths might lead to trolls, orcs, werewolves, and dragons. The path on the far right led toward a dark fortress with a forest and a fetid swamp in between.

"Let's kill some dragons," he muttered to himself, punching the button on the controller and spurring his horse down the right path.

The 3D world surrounded him, and he and his horse galloped down a forest road. The wind blowing from the haptic seat was in his hair, and the horse jolted under him as it swerved around a rock. He followed the road through the swamp until he got to a cave. The breeze carried the odor of sulfur and sour wine he knew well and caused his nose to twitch in anticipation.

He forgot to trot his horse, and the sound of the hooves betrayed his approach. The bony-plated head of a dragon appeared, vicious red eyes burning in a wrinkled face with razor-sharp teeth. It roared as it crawled from the cave and unfurled its wings. With no element of surprise now, Jaxon spurred the horse in full assault. His sword slashed at the scaled belly, and it bellowed in rage. Fire belched from its mouth, singeing his helmet. But a lucky stroke went home into the dragon's neck. It knocked him sideways, but he stayed in the saddle. The dragon screamed again and lay still at his feet.

He sat panting in the haptic seat with the goggles in his hand. He felt better. Sometimes, the same dragons appeared in his dreams, and he woke when they were killing him. Even so, these dragons were better than the abstract ones that ambushed him in the regular world. At least facing them, he had a horse he could depend upon and a job he could do.

◆

His PAWN was ringing. He opened the holo-com in the kitchen. Mom appeared in 3D.

"Hi, honey. How're you doing today?"

There was something in her tone, like when he was small and she saw everything through the eyes of that puppycam, Snowball.

"Sort of okay. I lost my job yesterday."

"That's terrible luck. Jaxon, I'm so sorry."

He turned the cup of coffee in his hand as she asked a series of pointed questions that aroused his suspicion. Had he accidentally left her name on some backup contact list with his former employer that triggered an auto-notification from the unemployment office?

These systems were too confusing to keep track of. In this case, it was both annoying and comforting. She seemed too ready with a plan.

"I understand the employment office has a few jobs in the construction field."

"Doing what?"

"There are jobs installing roofing materials for commercial and residential buildings."

"As a roofer? I don't like heights." Besides that, it was considered a low-skill job, well below his HVAC work.

"You should look beyond HVAC technician jobs. Try something different. And roofing jobs won't disappear with automation anytime soon."

"If I get desperate. Not now."

She rubbed her eye. "I wish you weren't all the way in California. You and Harper moved so far from New York. I especially miss you."

She said that because, clearly, he needed her more than Harper ever did.

"This is where the jobs still are, Mom. It's the fourth biggest economy, behind China, the US, India, and then there's California." He was proud to know this. The tech sectors had continued to drive California, though he wasn't benefiting from that wealth creation himself.

He thought about Harper living in Colorado Springs where their father had opened another manufacturing plant. There was never an invitation to join them.

"Besides, I'm on unemployment for six months. There's no reason to rush into anything."

"Keep yourself busy. I know what it feels like to be on your own. It can be hard to find a purpose to wake up every morning. Don't fall into a rut."

His mother looked tired on the 3D holo-display. How old was she now? Sixty-two? She'd raised them alone while working long hours at the nonprofit and had a work ethic he didn't even understand. Her mentioning the job issue wasn't a surprise, but the guaranteed income option after unemployment ran out was somewhat appealing.

"I'll be okay, Mom. Don't worry."

◆

The list of open jobs at the employment office was identical to the one last month. He'd been unemployed for six months, and the clerk recognized him. The AI had sorted his qualifications against a much longer list, but there were few for him.

"Any interest in roofer jobs? There are still several available." The clerk looked up from her display.

"No. I'm afraid of heights. I understand I can pass on that and still keep the guaranteed income." He'd transitioned to the life of the semi-permanently unemployed. He could barely skim by if he watched his spending.

"You can still stay on that program, though I'm required to advise you it's a good idea to build skills in some new employment field. There's growing automation every year, and the available jobs go to those with relevant skills."

He acknowledged her comment, accepted the interview completion token sent via his PAWN, and left the office. For the moment, he would wait for something more appealing.

Back in his apartment, Jaxon popped a synpsych to soothe his nerves and settled into the haptic seat. He opened the metaverse. A familiar ad, one he'd always previously ignored, hovered beside the start bar.

SPECIAL half-price subscription fee. Share your HDSET data.

He studied it and clicked the link. The details were confusing, but the essence was that the company gave away a new free HDSET that incorporated a BCI. The ad promised that the brain–computer interface was non-intrusive. Legal disclosures about emotional data ownership followed. A section in red letters, "Right to Decline to be Analyzed," required special approval. Jaxon skimmed it, checked the box to decline his privacy rights, and then clicked on the *BUY* option. A second later, a bright tone sounded.

Congratulations! Your fees are now half off as long as the HDSET is used.

He'd given himself breathing room. He relaxed into the haptic seat and opened the metaverse.

To glory, Rodrigo Díaz!

◆

Mom was on the display again. Jaxon hesitated, brushed his disheveled hair into place, and accepted the call. "What's up, Mom?"

"I'm checking on you. Everything okay?"

"Sure." He thought about his empty bank account and the rent coming due in a week.

"Good to hear." She paused.

He figured the next topic would be whether he'd found a job. He decided to head that off by naming the elephant in the room for them both—that Harper was working with Dad. "Did you see that Harper introduced a new model robot?"

A longer pause. "I saw it on social media and in the press report. Your dad is letting her and Axel test out new ideas."

He couldn't tell if the note of cynicism came from direct knowledge of Dad, or negativity about how close Harper was with him now. There was a split in the immediate family, and they were on one side.

"The bot's features are spectacular on paper. It's hard to say if it can perform as promised."

"Well, Harper is smart. She builds good designs." She'd always dominated him intellectually, so she was probably good at her job.

He made an excuse to sign off and popped a synpsych. He sat in his haptic chair and looked out the window. The morning sunlight filtered into the room. He sat for a long time thinking about Mom, Dad—unkindly—and Harper, with mixed admiration and envy. It wasn't a day to ride to glory.

An hour later, he was in the employment office, and the same clerk peered at him from her desk. "The only job teed up this week by the job-matching AI is one for Lewis Builders, in roofing for residential construction." She waited.

He could tell she expected to end the interview. "Okay. I'll take it."

The clerk looked up sharply, then processed the fulfillment report. "The company information packet and job site address are in the report. You can start on Monday."

The token transferred noiselessly to his PAWN.

◆

Jaxon stood on the slate roof, checked his harness again, and gave the tether a tug. It didn't give him much reassurance as he squinted over the roof's edge. He was only one story above ground, but he hadn't gotten used to it and wasn't sure he ever would.

"Let's get rid of the old shingles before break. Gotta take advantage of this sunshine." The boss pointed a finger at him and Mateo.

Jaxon grabbed the handles of the shingle stripper again and shoved it forward with his foot. Mateo dumped the refuse onto the pile in the truck below. Each toss clattered, and a plume of dust rose from the truck bed. It was monotonous work, and bending strained his lower back, but he focused on every motion. He never took the second task, which would require him to back toward the roof's edge. At least Mateo was cheerful about allowing him to manage the tool. It was physically demanding but cleaner. In three months, roofing had become familiar but not comfortable.

They finished removing the remaining shingles and swept the entire roof.

"Good work," the boss said. "After break, carry the scanner up there to check the submaterials. Then, install the underlayment and, after that, the integrated panels."

Jaxon followed Mateo down the ladder. He snatched water and two apples, and they sat under a spreading chestnut tree behind the house. He tossed an apple over.

"Thanks," Mateo said.

He drank a long swig of water and rested against the tree, savoring the crisp apple, the partial shade, and the rustling leaves above. He looked across the yard toward other tidy suburban homes with green lawns in the quiet neighborhood. Except for the oldest homes, like this job, they all had shiny roofs with integrated solar shingles or solar panels.

A man of medium height walked up the driveway toward them, his curly hair giving him the look of an artist, though he carried the toolbox of a roofing laborer.

He paused under the tree. "Is this the Buffet Industries project?"

"Yep, that's this job," Jaxon said.

"I'm the new roofer."

"We're with Lewis Builders."

The man's expression changed with a look of recognition. He activated his PAWN. The question came in a halting voice. "Jaxon Jones?"

Jaxon fumbled with his PAWN. "Sam Chima? I haven't seen you in a long time. Since my uncle's wedding."

Sam chuckled. "You were a little kid then. You were in New York, right? How long have you been on this coast?"

"A couple years. I figured there'd be more opportunities in California." Jaxon thought fleetingly of how wrong he had been. The reality for them sank in. "Why are you here?"

"With all the AIs, it seems they need fewer draftsmen. That's what I did for over twenty years. I thought I'd be moving into the prime of my career. But the world has changed." Sam shrugged and pointed at the roof. "I always said I'd be workin' someplace high up. Guess I was right. What about you?"

"It seems they don't need as many HVAC technicians."

Sam's face revealed empathy for a fellow foot soldier. "I pray this job will be safe from the AIs and bots, at least until I retire."

"They haven't taught the bots how to climb up on a roof. Yet."

———————◆ ————————

Jaxon surveyed the narrow valley from behind thick foliage, his horse swaying under him. Smoke wafted from a cleft in the rock, accompanied by an occasional rumbled roar. Jaxon considered how best to surprise his quarry. The brush behind him rustled, and he turned to find another knight drawing near. Friend or foe? The warrior saluted with two fingers to his raised visor.

"Who are you? Speak." Jaxon's hand was on his sword.

"Possibly a friend. I am Alexander of Macedonia. I fight for the honor of my worthy opponent, Princess Kandake. Who are you, and did you find a dragon?"

"I am Rodrigo Díaz. I fight for glory in this inglorious world." Jaxon studied the knight, whose demeanor suggested a real human, not an NPC. He hoped he was a person. The AIs were nearly impossible to discern, and he'd wasted days with some, only to find no true friend but an enemy in disguise. He gestured down the valley. "There's a dragon in the cave below. How say you we should attack?"

The man rested his gauntlets on the pommel of his saddle. "You seem to enjoy approaching your prey from high above. Fond of heights?"

"Only here. But, of course, my horse, Pegasus, flies."

Alexander's eyes crinkled with a half-hidden mirth. "Jaxon?"

Jaxon felt his body shake in his chair, and he momentarily shifted mentally from metaverse to reality. "Sam?"

"Our secret. Now, let's hunt some dragons. How should we attack? I say go straight at 'em!"

Jaxon felt a wave of happiness. He unsheathed his sword. *To glory, Rodrigo Díaz!*

Together, they charged down the valley.

33

Harper Jones MacGyver—2085 (Colorado)

"Let's practice the arm positions." Harper glanced at the dozen robots encircling her on the open floor. "Search ballet movements for the five positions. You'll follow my lead and synchronize to me."

Harper counted off the positions as her arms moved in graceful circles, and her robots followed with precision. "Now, connect that motion to a short glisser. Follow me." They sailed across the floor.

"If you're carrying an object, connect to a chaînes turn." She demonstrated, and the machines matched her. "Search on tourné, emulate that movement, and add a subtle turn to move to position B on the floor." She danced across the floor, at times losing herself in the movement, feeling the flow, like one bird leading a swirling flock.

"We'll now incorporate principles of those movements into your everyday work routines." Harper worked through the list of typical activities like hauling objects, moving around pieces of equipment, moving up and down stairs, all while calling out the dance elements to include.

She stopped the exercise, and the robots came to attention.

"Please clear the floor and wait for instructions."

The robots complied while she wiped her forehead with a towel. She moved to a large holo-display and hit the play-back button. The result was good, though too mechanical for a human.

"Number 5, at position 3:07 minutes, please maintain distance from Number 9. Add imprecision to enhance elegance of movement. You two, practice that again."

The two robots retook the floor and repeated the exercise, this time with improved fluidity from Harper's corrections. She continued the review, calling out portions to be modified. The objective was to ensure the General RoboMechs robots moved with close to human grace.

The door opened, and Axel walked in. Several robots moved deftly out of his way.

He smiled at her with adoration. "Darling, they glide like lovers on a dance floor."

They watched the robots move in unison through the revised exercise.

"This model is approaching my vision. The new light-weight material changes the design. I've been fighting the weight issue because of the power needs for so long," she said.

"We've benefited from the materials innovations quantum computing research has devised." Axel continued to study the bots.

"As has everyone else in the field." She had to admit that credit for robotic design advancement was shared across multiple disciplines. Quantum computers allowed far better modeling of electronic properties, leading to the discovery of advanced materials. It was a revolution in understanding the periodic table of elements. There had been the normal delay to produce new materials at scale, but cost-effective materials were available, and Harper had incorporated them in this new model.

Yet another problem was at the top of her mind. "The *everyone* I hate the most is Megatech Robots. Have you seen the figures about so-called accidents in the field with our robots?"

Annoyance flashed across Axel's face to match her own. "Wherever our robots are in factories together with theirs, there seem to be convenient accidents that leave ours inoperable. They make it hard to compete."

"Yes, by cheating. We need to do something."

"Competition is intense. It's hard to find a market niche where we can claim a lead." Axel shrugged. "We may have better chances of selling robots for military uses."

She felt her face grow warm. "But that's not the robot that I want to build. Why would some military care about this grace?" She glanced toward the robots that still glided in synchronized beauty.

He touched her arm, his face wearing a harder expression. "I know. But we haven't been able to sell into those markets with the same prices we can command from military customers."

Ten years into their marriage, he wasn't the lovesick admirer anymore, but at least now they were united by the desire to grow the company.

"And what luck have you had with military sales?" She knew he didn't have a solid response. She'd never been happy about building the new factory in Colorado Springs near the Buckley Space Force Base.

Axel rubbed his hands together, shaking his head. "Talking up your latest designs now, milspec sales are starting to grow."

"You're taking the lead from Dad?"

"He's slowing down, but he's still a great salesman. He's taught me everything. Building so close to the base was a good idea, after all."

It was mildly annoying, but Axel sometimes seemed to have a closer relationship with her father than she did.

"And that's why you're still pushing this 'AGI' idea? We both know we haven't gotten there in any practical sense. No one should trust robots to be completely unsupervised by humans for complex tasks. AIs and the robots that house them haven't passed the practical economic test for AGI."

Axel raised his eyebrows, looking for sympathy. "Other companies are saying explicitly that their models *have* reached 'artificial general intelligence,' and their robots are no better than ours."

"You're not allowing me the freedom to create. I'm a designer and an innovator."

"The market is not allowing you to create what you wish. It's not me."

Harper clenched her hands. It was an old argument. While he focused on marketing and sales, she drove technical development. Axel admitted she was more qualified as their designer. Harper had focused on integration of AI systems with robotic sensory inputs, attempting to emulate the embodiment that gives humans their sense of existing in the world. But even she had expressed frustration with the complexity of the problem. They could not eliminate occasional hallucinations—cases where the AIs came to nonsensical conclusions.

She tried again. "Don't you agree that our models *haven't* reached practical economic AGI?"

Axel raised his hands in frustration. "They can match the capabilities of the average human in many fields. Now there's a credible, though mostly semantic, claim to have reached AGI. These AIs embodied in robots that walk around convince people to anthropomorphize the machines. We can sell it."

"I wish we didn't have to." Harper realized how much her dad had influenced him.

"Look, darling. We've got to raise money. We can raise a ton with this pitch. I've been talking with Dad, and he agrees. We can make it big with this."

She hated to see everything devolve to money. It should be about creating the best technology. But how could she argue? She didn't want to give up the chance to build, even if it meant tradeoffs.

"Okay, fine. Do whatever it takes to raise the money. I'll work on stopping Megatech Robots. We'll prove to Dad that we can make this company successful and, with my designs, change the world."

34

AXEL GRAVES—2085 (SAUDI ARABIA)

Axel mopped his brow as he exited the elevator into the upper floor lobby. Though it was May, it felt ridiculously hot to be outside, even for the minute it took to enter the building. An admin wearing a light blue abaya looked up from behind her desk.

"Axel Graves, here to meet a Mr. Abdullah."

The admin touched her CLAIR, "He'll see you in a few minutes," she said a moment later.

"It's awfully hot outside today." He adjusted the cooling layer of his shirt.

She shrugged. "Only 43."

His PIDA helpfully whispered in his earbud, *43 degrees Celsius is approximately 109 degrees Fahrenheit.*

He started at her alternative frame of reference, then smiled and walked to a corner. Giant glass windows looked out on the Red Sea below, a slash of blue against the browns of the desert that hugged the shoreline. The urban area of NEOM, built in such an inhospitable place, fascinated Axel. Parts of the Line, the twin skyscraper city hundreds of meters tall, began here in Oxagon and stretched east into shimmering air like a line in the sand of Saudi Arabia.

He'd visited it the day before when he arrived to see how a million people could live in such an austere environment. It was beautiful but artificial, and he couldn't get past the psychological aversion to being cut off from the real world in an enclosed space. It was one reason he supposed the city was not as large as planned—that and the rising temperatures.

His gaze turned to the super yachts at anchor in the Red Sea, and he tried to guess their lengths.

It wasn't long before Axel opened the presentation on his CLAIR and reviewed the flow of main points. His PIDA suggested compelling statistics. This would be a critical meeting, and he wanted to have all the hard-to-remember technical information available so his mind could focus on the overall argument. He left the list of Arabic cultural notes open on his PIDA so he could access them if needed.

A door opened, and the admin ushered him inside. A tall man with a beard dressed in traditional garb greeted him, shook his hand to show the normal hospitality, and gestured to a seat at a large teak boardroom table. The admin served *qahwa*, the pale-colored Arabic coffee, and left the room. Abdullah seated himself at the end of the table. Most people on the street wore Western clothing, but this man, several decades his senior, still followed an older style. He straightened the pristine white thobe as he sat. Axel's PIDA reminded him that the headscarf was called a ghutra, and the black cord-like ring that held it in place an agal.

"Welcome to NEOM," Abdullah said.

"Thank you for meeting me in your beautiful city. I had the chance to tour the Line yesterday."

Abdullah spread his hands toward the window. "Here, Oxagon is the industrial city, which is convenient for my offices. We try to attract factories to the Line to give the people work."

"Then, I suggest we dive right into the opportunities for factories, driven by our cutting-edge robotic technology. We're making super intelligence a reality in our machines."

Axel opened his holo-display, and 3D images danced on the screen. He kept his voice strong and clear, hit the main points with practiced delivery, and paused for questions while he searched the man's face for any change of expression. Axel was encouraged that, half an hour later, Abdullah's interest had not slackened.

At last, he saw the shift. Abdullah leaned forward rather than remaining distant, and he knew his sales pitch was breaking through. Jack would be proud to see what his protégé had mastered.

Abdullah continued to ask questions, most of which Axel was prepared for, and he nodded vigorously. "When you gear up factories, have you considered expanding production to here?"

"That's a definite possibility so we can serve the Middle Eastern and European markets." One reason for the interest had become clearer, and Axel filled in details about projected growth and the need for manufacturing. "Now, truer to our name, we're building robotic mechanicals of all sorts. We've created a generalized platform that includes military applications." He glanced at Abdullah to see whether the extra benefit resonated in the still-unstable region.

Abdullah's expression had been unreadable throughout, but now his face softened. "Can any of those robots be used for police work?"

"That's an application that we'd be happy to work with you on. With artificial general intelligence, our robots can add new specialties easily."

Axel described how learning modules could be added and customized. Though the company had never sold any robots for police work, Axel quoted a few examples from military sales that ambiguously overlapped.

"When is the closing, and what are the details of the offering?"

Axel outlined the planned private offering, pricing, and named a figure at the high end of their capital needs.

Abdullah studied his notes and then met his gaze. "We are interested in participating." He named a figure.

Axel tried not to overreact. He thought of his father-in-law and how he would close the deal. "We're raising a limited amount of capital, but I think we can hold open that amount to you."

Axel stuck out his hand. Abdullah hesitated and then clasped his in a handshake.

"We'll just need an entity name for the cap table. And the ownership will be documented with the blockchain, so you're assured of your investment," Axel said.

Abdullah bowed his head slightly, then signaled with his CLAIR.

The admin returned to the room, this time placing a steaming plate of *kabsa*, a rice and lamb dish Axel had tasted the day before, onto the table.

"A small lunch before you leave?" Abdullah inclined his head in invitation.

"Certainly. Thank you." Axel sniffed the subtle spices.

"Sahtain," Axel said, happy that his PIDA supplied the equivalent for bon appétit.

"Bismillah," Abdullah replied.

Axel glanced at the PIDA-supplied translation for the offering of thanks to God and nodded. The sales pitch had been more fruitful than he'd dreamed possible, and Axel relaxed as they ate and drank coffee. The talk turned to broader topics.

"NEOM and the Line look like they've risen from the desert." Axel waved his hand with a flourish. "That's obviously taken enormous effort. You must have witnessed tremendous change in your country."

"Yes, I've lived during this period when the kingdom had a vision to transform itself."

"Yet it has always remained a global energy leader."

"While work to transition our economy went on, the global oil markets remained the center of everything we did because that money was needed to fund the transition."

"I understand that China was once your largest market." Axel knew the energy markets.

"China was our largest market for oil, but over the past decades they gained energy independence. They built big solar farms in the western provinces."

"But they were buying oil to run plants to balance loads, right?"

"Yes, but China also built nuclear generating stations for that purpose. All fossil fuels have a dirty name." Abdullah ate with precise table manners and folded his napkin neatly. "Though rising global population kept oil demand up, in the face of huge investments in renewables, the longer-term picture was clear. We needed to transition our economy away from dependence on oil. The choice was being made for us. Now, world demand has fallen off a cliff."

"You're not alone," Axel said. "That's affected all the oil-producing countries worldwide, many with economies highly dependent on the petrochemical sector."

"Both market forces, and the conspicuous changing climate drove change."

"I guess it's easier to see the need in your daily experience." Axel glanced at the window and thought about how hot it would be when he left.

"We couldn't deny seeing the change. The desert, which had been our friend, our protector against invaders, and our place for finding peace with our God, was becoming our enemy."

"Did that realization come quickly?"

"Years ago, our country's oil minister said that Saudi Arabia would pump every molecule of oil, that we would be the last country standing." Abdullah waved his hand dismissively. "But our leaders spurred an attitude change, and the need for action. Generational change cemented new thinking. The current minister, educated about climate change like all his generation, talks about sequestering carbon instead of pumping."

"Saudi Arabia has been a leader in trying to transition its economy." Axel left unsaid any assessment of their success.

"We started earlier than many. But it's been a difficult challenge. Some countries in the region have made transitions to post-oil economies. Some have not, but there's been the realization that we need to stop pumping what is left."

Axel sipped his coffee. "What else has changed?"

"With all the economic changes, all countries in the region are more secular."

Axel had never been religious but chose his words carefully. "You treasure the time when this country was universally observant."

"Yes, the land of the Two Holy Mosques. We took seriously the responsibility to facilitate Hajj. Though some saw that as useful to increase tourism, one of our few successful industries. But religious purity has decreased everywhere. Even Iran has broken free from the ayatollahs running the country, as a new generation of young people, who are less religious, emulates the West." Abdullah finished his coffee. "With worsening climate change, the most conservative believers here wonder why Allah has abandoned them."

As he finished his own coffee, Axel studied the older man of a passing generation and felt sorry for him. His dress signaled his traditional thinking, of a time more religious than today, and his experience was from a time of plenty. Their oil wealth had seeded the climate change that was making the country unlivable. And time was running out to change the entire economic basis of their country.

"With this next generation of intelligent robots, I trust we can bring manufacturing here." Axel hoped it would allow him to leave on a happier note.

"That is our vision. We see that manufacturing will move to robots, and the kingdom must own the means of production to keep its rightful position. We must manufacture the things people want. Otherwise, they will grow restive." Abdullah rose to end the meeting. Axel once again shook his hand and left.

———————◆———————

The maglev train whispered south across the desert. Axel examined the endless, empty landscape through the window. There had been nothing but sand for kilometers. The desert reminded him of the worst parts of Nevada—brown and gray, lifeless, hot, and likewise growing less hospitable with each passing year. He'd read an article in *The Economist* about desert regions around the globe recently, and it highlighted that Nevada had emptied out, except for the two largest cities. The people in the Sahara, the Gobi, the Mojave, and the deserts here in the Middle East had all been abandoning their homes for decades now.

He'd thought this diversion on the trip home might give him talking points for the empty promise—for he never expected to carry it out—of building manufacturing plants in Saudi Arabia whenever the point came up in the future. But he'd learned nothing positive to add credibility to the lie.

In the holo-com call after his meeting with Abdullah, Jack congratulated him. "No worries about the manufacturing issue," he'd said. "We can always promise and then rely on excuses about regulation, and changing demand profiles, to delay. And that's a good one, creating a police robot product for us on the fly."

The temperature inside the train suddenly felt too hot, and Axel adjusted his shirt cooling again, though the thermometer showed nothing had changed. He thought again of Abdullah, and the two needs that had surfaced—for in-country manufacturing and for police robots. Neither would be delivered on, and Axel felt a little bad about it.

Yes, he had hoodwinked Abdullah.

Unremarkable barren sand rolled by. He saw not a single camel through the window, which had been his secret reason for taking the desert train. Someone had once described a camel as a racehorse designed by committee. And their 'superintelligent' robot was also a camel; a beast unlike its description.

Harper had created the critical design features that now allowed him to pitch it. The latest generation of AIs was the brain of their robots. The company marketing announced it contained a "theory of mind," a model of how humans act that allowed the AIs to "understand" social behavior. That was why their robots did a superb job of interacting with humans in social situations. It was a good story. He sold the racehorse, though it was another beast.

Axel knew it was a collection of cheap tricks far from superintelligence. True embodiment in the world was needed to create a theory of mind, and Harper had barely begun to address that difficult engineering problem. The AIs sometimes output surprising correlations between diverse fields and ideas. But the AIs and the robots that housed them were not smarter than the best human brains in every field. They were downright stupid some of the time. So far, human embodiment in the real world, which had refined human intelligence and consciousness, could not be emulated in hardware and software.

But he also knew that, with renewed popular excitement for the technology, now was the time to capitalize on the hype and raise money for expansion and their bank account. Jack was his model, and Axel would carry the torch forward. Harper was the creator, and he would enable her creations, and maybe she might eventually create a product to her vision.

Let everyone suffer in the desert outside the window, still rolling by lifeless and endless, but some day he'd be chilling on his boat, and he and Harper might live the life he envisioned.

35

CONGRESSMAN REX RYSBIER—2085
(COLORADO)

Rex Rysbier walked through the metal detector without breaking stride, and the doors opened as his PIDA intoned *ticket authenticated* into his ear. He looked up at the stadium and tapped his CLAIR.

"Club level."

A red line appeared on his left corneal lens, outlining a path toward a nearby escalator. He dodged through the crowd and found the VIP area.

Everything was dated. The stadium had not changed for two decades. There was no reason for the owners to spend the money anymore. He was late but grabbed a pilsner at the timeworn bar. The robot beer machine still filled the glass with a perfect head. Then he walked to the seat on the forty-yard line behind the home team.

Harper MacGyver stood to shake his hand. "Nice to see you, Congressman." She gestured to the spry older man at her side. "This is my father, Jack Jones."

Jones rose to wring his hand. "You're just in time for the national anthem."

The singer was introduced, and Rex placed his hand over his heart as the opening notes filled the stadium. He needed to keep up his patriotic image, though he hoped no one recognized him. The music swelled, and fireworks shot into the air. Three fighter jets swept overhead, and their laser guns fired upward in bursts timed to the words "rockets' red glare."

The song finished with the crowd's applause, and they sat down. Rex squeezed his large frame into the narrow seat. He used only a low dosage of slim drip in his MEDFLOW unit.

He was bigger than the average person, and he kept himself at a size to retain his "Big Rex" nickname, branding that worked well for his numbers. Besides, he could still indulge in eating whatever he wanted.

"Those were F-47s, our seventh-generation fighters, all autonomous." Jack squinted into the distance. "Now we'll never see another 'Top Gun' human pilot."

Another person his age might have sounded nostalgic or regretful, but Jack's comment was pure analysis. Rex thought again of his research on Jones, the history of his robotics company, and his net worth. He reminded himself of his goal—to charm this wealthy supporter. He knew that Jack prided himself as a salesman. So today he needed to turn on his charisma to outsell this master of the game, because Jack likely wouldn't support any politician who couldn't match him.

"We need more of 'em, the autonomous aircraft, including drones to seal our borders. By now, we should be letting zero of these illegals into our country." Jack wouldn't mind the ascent of the machines, and he'd support border controls to keep out workers who were competing with his robots.

"I understand why that's important to a politician from Texas." Jack's tone was dry.

"I like to think that I represent the whole country. We all need to keep out unfair competition." That put a point on the argument.

Jack turned his head away from the field, his attention momentarily captured.

Harper sipped her beer as the players lined up for the kickoff. "Dad, I remember not so long ago when human pilots still flew over the stadium. We've been going to these games for, what, ten years?"

Jack frowned. "Yes. It was about then when I bought the seat licenses. Not my best investment." He glanced at the sky again. "I don't mind the AI pilots, since they fight so much better. But it's too bad that pro football is going away. The kids are just wimps these days. Afraid of a bit of bashing."

Big Rex watched the play from scrimmage while eyeing Jack. "Thanks for the opportunity to be here. It's the last of an era."

"It's sad. I do like a good game myself," Harper said. "But, well, there's no fighting medical science. It's irrefutable that brain injuries can't be eliminated from tackle sports. Lawsuits over CTE could bankrupt the league. Parents won't let their kids play football. I wouldn't let my daughter Karla play anything beyond mod soccer. The pros have no one to draft. I guess it was inevitable."

"Still, it's one thing the boys can do that robots can't. It's fun to see the rough and tumble. I'm not a fan of the flag football replacement game," Jack said.

"You think we'll ever have robots in sports?" Rex directed the question to Jack. "What's your prediction?"

"Hell, someday, we'll see robots in the ring with humans. When these players are unemployed, we should put them to work doing something useful like that." Jack said it with a sneer.

"Something fitting their mental abilities." Harper snickered.

"Roofers, like Jaxon." Jack's voice had an edge. "You would think he played football." Rex mentally reviewed his notes. Jaxon must be his son. No fatherly feeling there.

"We'll need to find jobs for them." Rex kept his tone even, ambiguous. Like the game, Rex needed both offense and defense. Defense for him was to protect his base, the mass of voters who saw him defending their jobs because he was their leading champion, keeping climate refugees out. Offense was to move his objectives down the field, like why he was here meeting them.

Rex clicked his CLAIR to listen on the channel to the middle linebacker, who called an audible to change the defensive formation on the fly to a 4–3. With the snap, they rushed the passer and sacked him with a ten-yard loss. The opposing team punted on the next down, and the home team had the ball back. All three were now immersed in the game and cheered as their team moved down the field.

The quarterback deftly moved in the pocket and tossed a long pass caught by a wide receiver who dodged two tackles and dove across the goal line. The stadium erupted in cheering. They high-fived each other when the extra point was scored.

"My predictive modeling AI tracker shows the other quarterback is only at 83 percent of his average performance, so we have the advantage," Harper said.

The conversation continued. Rex kept the cadence light and easy as the crowd noise swelled and ebbed on each play. He enjoyed the banter, and playing the part of an average guy, cracking a few jokes that even elicited a laugh from Jack.

At halftime, Harper used her CLAIR to order hamburgers and beer to the seats then left for the restroom. Rex took the chance to drive home his key point with Jack. He knew he had to dispel one concern about his populist image. To win the average voter and be elected, the issue of the day was job losses.

Rex leaned in close and spoke quietly. Sure, legislation could speak to jobs but might also leave flexibility. Rex sensed his argument, a political jujitsu, was winning Jack over just as Harper returned.

The referee signaled the start of the second half.

Settling back for the kickoff, Jack turned to Rex, his gaze intent. "You wouldn't be considering any legislation that limited company owner's rights?"

Rex expected the question. "Quite the opposite. In fact, with the recent protests over jobs and the destruction of property by malcontents, we've got to put teeth in protecting private property."

Jack smiled. "My thoughts exactly. Our factories are becoming the basis of our economy because they're so efficient. But now, sophisticated attacks on our robots are increasing. Hackers have created malware to cause some robots to attack others, destroying valuable property."

"I've heard General RoboMechs tends to be targeted more than others," Rex said.

"Some legislation comes to mind," Harper said. "We already include some versions of the 'Three Laws of Robotics' from Asimov in our software. It'd be good to legislate an addendum. We were thinking that requiring code that says a robot must protect other robots' survival so long as such protection does not violate the first three laws. With that requirement, every robot manufacturer will be on a level playing field, and we should have less property destruction."

"That sounds like a reasonable, important law." Rex nodded emphatically. He was interrupted by a moan from the crowd as the opposing team scored a touchdown. The stadium quieted, and the home team, in their classic scarlet red and metallic gold uniforms, lined up to receive the next kickoff.

"Perhaps this session?"

The quarterback handed off to the star running back, who plowed ahead twelve yards. The crowd cheered, covering their conversation.

"Absolutely. Several of the other members owe me some favors. I can line up their votes."

"Great," Jack said. It applied both to Rex and to the quarterback's long pass, caught by the wide receiver in the end zone.

The team's lead was celebrated by all sorts of hollering throughout the stadium.

Harper winked. "Another payment will be in your account soon. We expect you to win your Senate race."

Rex crinkled his eyes in acknowledgment as he clapped for the team, glad that the noise smothered the comment. He settled into his seat. Chalk up one victory on today's agenda. Like this game, politics required both finesse and power. Deception also won games. He was good at it all.

He internally smiled that neither thought to ask about the control of data, which was critical to their business model. Nor did they ask for details about how he thought he could square the circle, placating his base while keeping them in positions of power. They wouldn't like the only answer he saw possible. But that was far in the future. For the moment, he'd need their money to stay in power himself.

"My husband Axel has a new boat," Harper said. "We're just learning about sailing, but you ought to come out on her sometime."

"I'd like that. We need to block for each other like the guys out there." Rex waved toward the field then looked her in the eye. "We'll spend time learning each other's moves. We know who's in charge of this game of running the world. Best to let the best decide."

36

SAM CHIMA—2090 (CALIFORNIA)

Sam adjusted his feet in the exoskeleton. The rig's weight rested securely on the roof. The frame wrapped his torso, and the arm attachments moved freely on gimbals through to the frame. He picked up a pallet of roofing materials and then carried it up the roof's peak, careful not to slip on the wet sections.

After setting the materials down, Sam studied the L-shaped roof. He and Jaxon would work one side of the short section that morning, and the team of three other roofers would work the opposite side.

Jaxon stood uneasily in his exoskeleton near the peak. The light rain that had fallen all morning glistened on the metal flashings. They were required to wear the rigs, but he knew Jaxon had never been comfortable with the encumbrance. It was an unwritten division of labor that Sam carried the materials for his partner.

Jaxon unloaded the integrated solar shingles from the pallet and laid them in the grid pattern. Sam followed behind and attached the panels. The buzz of his automated drill punctuated the air. They worked methodically, almost able to complete it in silent tandem from long practice together, and finished the section before their break. The other team already rested under a back awning roof. Sam and Jaxon joined them and sat on a stack of roofing materials. Sam took two energy bars from his lunch box and passed one to Jaxon.

The three men talked in animated voices in Quechua. Sam could understand only a handful of words, but he didn't turn on his CLAIR translator. He was sure they were here illegally, smuggled across the border by the crime syndicates. Everyone's government ID was encrypted, but somehow organized crime rings had broken the encryption with quantum computing. Construction companies kept costs low with the subterfuge.

It was above his pay grade to worry about the problem, especially if he wanted to keep his own job. He felt sorry for these workers because the bosses didn't treat them well. He and Jaxon hadn't gotten to know any of them because they usually didn't last long.

"Did you see the new measurement markings on that last pallet?" Jaxon looked worried.

"I noticed the branding on the containers has all changed. Metric now, isn't it?"

Jaxon had been laying out the sections, so he'd handled the calculations. That change to metric explained why he'd been slow today.

"Why do they always change things? I'm used to the old, regular way. What's wrong with feet and inches?"

He chuckled. "Jaxon, that's all dead and gone now. Football was the last place yards were used. Now everything is metric. Using the same system everywhere works better for the robots."

Sam followed Jaxon's gaze over his shoulder. A truck pulled into the driveway, and a young man unloaded a robot from the back. He powered it up, and a few moments later, the robot followed the man toward them.

The man stuck out his hand to Sam, who was the oldest on the crew. "Andrew. They added me to your job as your foreman. I'm testing this new roofer assistant." Andrew gestured to the robot. "We call him Herb."

Sam eyed the bot. It was less than two meters tall. It just reached his nose and had an elliptical head with two oval lenses for eyes.

"Nice to work with you," Herb said, lenses swiveling as it turned its head.

Sam had seen other models attempt roofing. None had been adept enough to outperform a couple of skillful humans. There was a flow to the work that he and Jaxon had developed that kept them ahead. So far, the economics hadn't shifted in favor of robots.

"I'm not sure I want to be on the roof with him." Jaxon frowned.

"No worries. He's programmed to be well aware of every human and will avoid stepping in your way." Andrew looked at the roof with a critical eye. "If you folks are finished with your break, I can run Herb through his paces. Let's have your two teams up there to finish the longer end of the roof."

Andrew motioned toward the ladder. The robot nimbly climbed it, stepped off onto the roof, and waited for them to follow.

The five roofers followed, and Andrew organized the two teams. He and Jaxon were again on one side, with the other three roofers on the other. The robot was stationed at the peak to observe Sam and Jaxon.

Sam lumbered in the exoskeleton to move the rest of the pallet materials, while Jaxon positioned the solar shingles. The joint where this section intersected the morning's work was the trickiest, and Jaxon measured and remeasured it to align the sections. They continued for half an hour with the sun peeking out from behind clouds overhead. The robot stood at the peak like a second foreman, head swiveling, while Andrew sat on the roof and watched.

Jaxon wiped his brow, studied the empty pallet, and pointed at Herb. "Is he just going to stand there?"

Andrew turned to the robot. "Are you ready?"

"I have analyzed the process. I can begin."

The robot descended the ladder, grabbed a pallet, carried it up the ladder, neatly sidestepped around him, and set it on the roof at an ideal spot.

"Shall I continue with the next step?" It directed the question to Andrew, who put his thumbs up.

Sam's discomfort grew as the robot used the automated drill to install the entire pallet.

It ascended the ladder with a last pallet when Jaxon walked over, looking ill. "He's as fast as me. Already."

"Have you seen him miss anything? Any mistakes?"

"I'm looking for 'em. But not yet."

There was something else in Jaxon's eyes, like he had been crushed by a great weight. "Do you see the logo on this guy? That's my father's company."

The drizzle began again, but he stood next to Jaxon, oblivious of it dripping down his nose. The three other roofers also stopped work and peered over the peak. They spoke in low murmurs. The robot returned with the pallet and placed mechanical feet firmly on the roof as it walked into position. The buzz of the drill mingled with the patter of rain.

"I thought it might slip, but it didn't." Jaxon spoke in a whisper.

Sam's shoulders rolled forward, his body and mind feeling heavy. "When you teach a robot one task, like attaching a shingle, you've taught all robots, forever, how to attach shingles."

Jaxon's eyes held the pain of lifelong failure. "We're all just robots until we're replaced by machines. What's the point of it all?"

37

The car moves south on the highway, and I try to concentrate on Grandfather's story about the side of the family who builds robots. I've got a bunch of grapes to munch on, which might be helping with the effects of the wine. Robert sits across from me. It's hard to tell what's going on in its computer after Grandfather turned off its mem'ry, but its lenses move back and forth restlessly.

Grandfather sees a sign on the road and orders the autocar to turn down a side road. After a kilometer, it stops at a pull-off with a sign for a walking trail.

"You'll enjoy seeing our forests. It's good to walk a bit after lunch. Something I haven't done enough of lately."

The trail sign marks an easy redwood forest walk. He tells the robot to wait for us and leads. It's not hard to keep up with him, because he needs the walking stick more on the trail. It's covered by a thick blanket of redwood needles, all soft and spongy under my feet.

We're among trees taller than I ever saw in the Piney Woods. The redwoods have massive trunks, and the canopy of branches and leaves is far above us like some massive old churches I've seen on the allbook.

"This is my favorite cathedral," Grandfather says, stealing my thoughts.

The smells of damp earth, bark, and vegetation are familiar. Sunlight filters through the boughs, sometimes in shafts of light that feel magical. It's quiet, and we don't disturb the peace on the trail. We just enjoy the woods together.

A pine cone lies on the trailside on top of green moss, and I pick it up. It has woody scales in a pretty spiral pattern.

The sharp, sweet scent in my nose reminds me of the Piney Woods. It goes into my pocket.

Around a turn in the trail, Grandfather points to a group of trees close to one another. "That's a family circle," he says. "The trees share the same root system."

In the center is a rotting trunk, broken off from some long-ago windstorm. The parent still hangs on to life. I look up to the trees' crowns forming a circle of light.

He stops to rest but stands tall, not as bent over as when I first saw him this morning.

"I used to run 5K races all the time. Everyone needs aerobic exercise. I don't get much anymore, but walking is good. Otherwise, no telling when Robert does me in someday." He winks at me and continues down the trail.

He's joking again, but I wonder if there's enough truth in it to worry about these bots.

The circle of trees reminds me of Ma and Pa. Ma needs Pa to take care of her still until she gets better. Ma seems to want to protect me from something, though I don't need to be protected. What about Grandfather? He's been living alone with only the robots for company. He's the reason I'm here. Grandfather needs protecting, or at least someone to talk with.

What do I need? I need to be out of the Commune. I don't know what'll come after that.

We complete the short loop, and he rests when we reach the road again. The car waits for us with Robert inside.

"Thanks for walking with me," he says.

We just walked a kilometer or two, but I can see that he has a gleam in his eye. I'm glad if I encourage him.

"You waited patiently to hear the story of your parents. Now we can talk about them. I'll start with your mother and when she met your dad."

He's right that I was feeling impatient. I can see, though, that the parts of the family are like that ring of trees, all related in hidden ways.

The pine cone is prickly in my pocket. We scramble back into the autocar, and he talks about Ma.

38

The holo-display rested on the desk between Lily and the doctor. He used pinch motions to manipulate the hologram, and she listened intently as he explained her treatment. She was glad to have an in-person consultation. The new treatment regime merited special attention, and Lily always liked doing these appointments in person when she could.

"You'll receive microdoses of medication from your MEDFLOW. It's a simple surgery to install the unit. It'll be implanted under local anesthesia just above your right hip. The current units have small inserts to refill your medication." The doctor's soothing voice narrated while a 3D video demonstrated the surgical procedure. "It's almost invisible, even in a swimsuit." He hadn't forgotten she was leaving on a tropical vacation soon.

She brushed back her light blonde hair. "Will I be healed within a month?"

"Certainly."

"And then I'll be cured? What does this do about the violence gene?"

The doctor folded his hands on the desk. "You do have the point mutation in the MAOA gene, which they inaccurately described a century ago as the warrior gene. They thought it was associated with a propensity for aggressive outbursts." The doctor's gaze met hers. "But that whole paradigm for how genetics works has been overturned. The genome-wide association studies show that many genes contribute to behavior. Genes are not a blueprint for precisely how life develops. Life's far more complex than that simple model."

She relaxed in her seat. "It isn't predetermined that I'll have these feelings?"

"Not determined by your genes. Your feelings are the result of a complex interaction between your biology, your interior mental states, and the world. But the drug protocol can help you stay emotionally even and limit the impulses that might make you react...negatively." The doctor glanced at the blinking clock hologram that signaled the end of this consultation. "Remember that your MEDFLOW will also give you near-real-time monitoring of certain brain chemicals. That feature is in beta testing now, but it's showing promising results. It'll alert you if you're out of balance. Use that as feedback for your behavior."

She had one last question. "Will this take away my edge? I'm in a high-pressure career, and sometimes that anger is appropriate, given what our clients are fighting."

"That's something you'll have to discover."

Lily caught the hyperlev train one block away. The doors closed, and it picked up speed smoothly as it levitated on the rails, pulled along by magnets.

She took a deep breath, glad she chose to start the anger management medication. She'd only recently discovered she had the suspect gene. The doctor assured her it wasn't as bad as she'd initially thought, and she felt more optimistic about her ability to navigate the future than she had six months ago.

She'd punched her boyfriend—ex-boyfriend—in the face and dislocated his jaw when she caught him cheating on her. She still felt he deserved it. Maybe the medication would help with that, but she'd always despise him for the syrupy charm that hid his real character from her. His redeeming parting act was to agree not to press charges, which would have wrecked her career. Now she could forget him and get on with life.

She rode two stops and exited near her downtown office. The hundred-story metal tower was one among many. Drones swooped above the street. An autohover rumbled onto the building's landing pad. The perks of being a partner—a rank still years ahead of her, if she was lucky. Still, she was glad to have passed the bar exam and then gained enough experience to no longer be considered a new lawyer. Now, the projects were interesting.

Lily's stomach gurgled as she entered the building, reminding her she had skipped lunch to take the medical appointment. She stopped at the café on the ground floor. The menu zoomed onto her CLAIR, and she ordered a sandwich. In a minute, a robot came from behind the counter and handed it to her in a recyclable bag. Lily removed the sandwich and disposed of the bag.

There were a few Luddites at LaborJustice Law Group, including partners who wouldn't be caught dead associating with any businesses employing robots. She shared their passion for the fight, but now she was hungry. And couldn't afford to unbalance her emotions.

Lily exited on the seventieth floor. Instead of the ubiquitous robots holding the lobby administrative role, her firm employed a human.

Sarah greeted her. "Zoe was looking for you. They rescheduled the meeting with the senator's staff, and she needs you right away."

Lily stepped into her office to wolf down the sandwich, and then she hurried down the hall to find Zoe Phillips in her office.

Zoe looked up from her desk, fire in her eyes. "The damn AI canceled our meeting and then scheduled another in its place." Zoe's crimson hair mimicked her usual disposition.

Lily was glad the expression wasn't directed at her. "Whose AI?" While everyone was forced to use the technology, she surmised it wasn't one of their staff.

"Not ours, of course. At the senator's office. Now the staff can only fit us in this afternoon, starting in..." Zoe glanced at the clock everyone had projected on their CLAIR "...fifteen minutes."

"That's what we're fighting for; to keep humans in the loop." Lily pumped her fist.

Zoe could be as feisty as she could be, which was just one of the reasons they got along well. But Lily was the calmer of the two, which surprised most people who knew her, but somehow it was true.

"I've got your argument outline ready. Let me pull up my notes, and we'll be ready in five," Lily said.

◆

Lily straightened the headpiece, settled into her haptic seat, and clicked the meeting link. In a moment, she found herself in a formal government office at a long mahogany table. Bookshelves loaded with thick legislative volumes lined the back wall. Her 3D avatar body was clothed in the typical muted colors. Zoe sat beside her. Her actual face was combined with the avatar figure dressed in a power-red dress.

Summary contact information appeared above the heads of the other two people in the meeting, as they acknowledged their arrival. Benjamin and Meredith were both staff assistants to the senator.

Meredith spoke first. "We're gathering information on behalf of the senator for new legislation to deal with the job crisis. She's interested in the viewpoint of the National Workers Alliance, the union your firm represents."

"Thank you for the chance to share the workers' concerns."

Zoe cued Lily and began with her usual opening line. "What's behind this crisis, which appears to have occurred suddenly?"

Lily operated the video display, timing each element to Zoe's argument.

"It's not sudden at all; it's been in front of our eyes for decades, slowly building to the present tsunami of job losses. The cause is what the physicist Albert Einstein, from two centuries ago, described as the most powerful force in the universe." Zoe paused. "It is compound interest. Einstein called compound interest the eighth wonder of the world. He said that those who understand it will use it. And those who don't will pay for it. In this case, the average worker is paying for it, losing her job through no fault of her own."

Lily brought up the 3D animation demonstrating compounding. The chart rose slowly, then dramatically. Benjamin adjusted his CLAIR and stared intently.

"The problem became a crisis when robots began building robots," Zoe continued. "See here, for example, the manufacturing plant complex built by General RoboMechs, located in Colorado. The first plant came online a decade ago. That plant produced robots for sale, and the company also used its robots to build the second plant. Now, they have ten similar facilities, side-by-side. There are just a few hundred human employees. The plants can churn out millions of robots."

Lily ran the video, an immersive flyover of the manufacturing facility, the complex seeming to stretch to the horizon.

Zoe's jaw tightened. "When the machines build the machines to build the machines, then the sorcery of compounding takes over. The result is a staggering productivity increase. And with that, an exponential end to human jobs."

Benjamin held up a hand. "The other side of the coin is that everything can be made super-efficient. In theory, the prices of goods should fall. Doesn't that benefit everyone?"

"It might if the average worker had the income to buy anything," Lily said. "Job erasure in this automation surge leaves many people with no way to earn a living. And they can't contribute in a meaningful way."

"But we have legislated a guaranteed income," Meredith said.

"That income is hardly a living wage, inadequate to support a reasonable life. Taxes supporting the program are insufficient, continuing the problem that most of the wealth goes to the tech class. The compounding formula works to drive wealth disparity undreamed of before in human society." Zoe nodded at Lily.

Lily ran the 3D animation of the current Gini coefficient for the US. Zooming into the shape of the curve, it suggested it would rocket up soon.

"But we also legislated earned income payments," Meredith said.

"Earned income credits only help if you have a job. That solution worked when there were enough jobs, of any sort, but looking ahead, we can project that answer will fail as more jobs cede to automation," Zoe said.

Meredith sighed. "We admit that even though there is more aggregate wealth created by automation, it's not divided fairly."

Benjamin leaned back in his seat. "Don't take our questions wrong; we're not in disagreement. But we need to address the arguments against your position. For example, what about Schumpeter's argument for creative destruction, that disruptive technologies usher in a better world?"

Zoe clenched her hands. "The exponential destruction of jobs will leave just the robots standing. Continuing our existing system as-is means the owners of the robots earn all the profits from a robot-driven economy. Nothing is left for everyone else. Is that the world we want?"

Benjamin raised his palms in supplication. "It's a dilemma. How to evolve the entire economic system to something that's reasonably fair when technology accumulates economic power in fewer hands? How to gain the fruits of automation, generate society-wide wealth, yet preserve jobs for people to be useful?"

Meredith summarized their conclusions. "We hear your arguments, and they're shared in large part by the senator. Turning these conflicting concerns into meaningful policy will be our work. We'll need your continuing help."

———————————◆———————————

Lily stirred her drink, a tropical concoction involving rum and a durian hybrid fruit she had never heard of. The sun was disappearing into the Pacific just beyond the restaurant's deck and a hundred meters of white sand beach.

She'd doubted the online description of Baa Atoll. The pitch encouraged the reader to "experience the phenomenal allure of the Maldives before it's gone forever." The panorama spread out before her turned out to be even better than the marketing. She relaxed and watched the oranges blend into yellows on the horizon.

What was unsaid was the damage from climate change, which had disappeared beneath the waves, along with half the Maldives Islands, surfacing only in the disrupted lives of the people still there.

A waiter arrived with her main course. She had learned her name to be friendly but also because the resort restaurant was uncrowded and Lily felt lonely.

"Fareeda, tell me, has climate change affected your family?"

Fareeda refilled Lily's water glass from a carafe. "Slowly, slowly, like an evil black cloud on the horizon. My father's family and my grandmother have all moved away." Fareeda leaned closer. "There are fewer jobs, but my wife Fathimath and I still have employment, so we stay for now." She shrugged her shoulders. "What to do?"

"What do you do when not working?"

Fareeda gave her a wry smile. "Now we drink with the visitors to drown our sorrows."

"But isn't this still an Islamic nation?" Lily's vision of the Maldives had been as a tropical escape for the tourists. That was now replaced by one of the Weimar Republic, from an old video, conjuring a decadence born from despair.

"It is, but they even allow alcohol in Saudi Arabia now. Everything changes."

Lily lingered over dinner, savoring the peacefulness, the reason she had come, and the escape from her hectic job. The work with Zoe on the legislative lobbying engagement had been a learning experience but stressful. Zoe expected perfection from associate attorneys, and Lily had stepped up, impressing the partner with her passion.

Lily slipped on her CLAIR to check the MEDFLOW device tucked beneath the corner of her island wrap. She had kept the medication below the recommended dosage since installation, and now she adjusted it up. Ignoring the doctor's recommendation was intentional over the past month to keep her edge, to show Zoe her zeal for their work. A little anger helped. Given the evidence, it was easy to care deeply about workers' jobs. But she hadn't sorted out whether the impulse was a true passion or just a way to advance her career. What was her main motivation? Lily didn't know.

Still wearing her CLAIR, an avatar appeared on her contact lens screen. A 3D buff dude on a surfboard scrolled across the top of her vision.

He waved and smiled, an earnest expression visible. In the light of the tiki torch he held, she read, "Lily, join me for a drink. And let me at least erase the shadows from your unsecure app."

Lily's confusion evaporated as she realized that the dating app was open on the device. What was the broadcast radius? A hundred meters? She looked around the quiet restaurant and then toward the beach. This island boasted a well-known bar with an energetic vibe. She tapped her CLAIR, and the device zoomed to frame an attractive young man at the bar.

He raised his hand in a gesture similar to the avatar. He had dark hair, a strong jaw, and friendly eyes.

Lily smiled back.

The surfer avatar held out a tiki torch, a smart object flaming like the actual torches lining the restaurant deck.

What to do? She'd taken this vacation to unwind, but leaving the dating app open was an accident. Now some stranger warned of a privacy breach in her app. Somehow, he knew her name, a fact the app should never reveal.

The MEDFLOW had not yet adjusted to calm her, and Lily felt her itch for confrontation burning. What the hell? She gripped the virtual tiki torch. Its scintillations reached across the sand, outlining a path toward the beach bar. She stood and walked deliberately toward the mysterious man on the beach.

39

Wyatt MacGyver—2093 (Maldives)

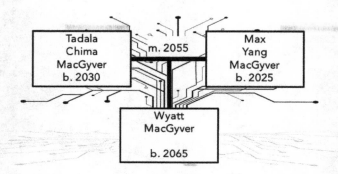

Tadala Chima MacGyver
b. 2030

m. 2055

Max Yang MacGyver
b. 2025

Wyatt MacGyver
b. 2065

The sun hovered on the horizon, framed by palm trees ruffled by a warm breeze. Close to the end of a perfect day. Wyatt had relaxed by swimming in the lagoon among manta rays. Tomorrow, he would scuba dive the reef. Much of the coral was gone, overcome by rising ocean temperatures, but he'd been assured there were still a few pristine spots left. He sat at the bar, cradling his drink, and marveled at his luck.

He enjoyed what he was doing. It was surprising because it had so little in common with his first career choice, but Dad always said to find something to do that's bigger than yourself. His calling turned out to be the fight for individual privacy in a world where the last remnants were disappearing.

The evening bar crowd grew as the sun set, but most were couples, and few were his age. This was supposed to be the trendiest bar on Baa Atoll. He told himself he shouldn't be too picky. This was an unusual place that wouldn't be here much longer, and it was a free vacation.

The dating app floated into view on his CLAIR. It's how he'd gotten the vacation. His hacker work revealed the app's security shortfalls. It was a devil's bargain. Companies traded convenience and services for personal data, but many failed to protect users' privacy, as required by law.

Was there anyone here who might be a match? He clicked the app. It formed a star field, indicating everyone in the vicinity who also had the app. The sizes and colors of the twinkling stars indicated matches. The app suggested a near-empty galaxy, except for one red giant star. He didn't often find that high of a match to his own quirky personality.

Indecision gripped him. Making the connection disclosed another layer of personal information. His professional avoidance of data disclosure warred with the appeal of such alluring information. The app won.

Wyatt spun his head until the red orb shimmered again, and he zeroed in on the resort restaurant in the distance. He tapped his CLAIR and zoomed in via the magnification feature. A young woman sat on the deck alone, holding a drink. Long blonde hair framed her face in cascading curls. What did her expression reveal? He imagined it matched his own. She seemed relaxed. Maybe she celebrated some recent success.

He realized she had an older, unprotected version of the app. Her personal data were open to prying eyes, and she probably had no clue. Another click on his CLAIR, and her name was disclosed. Should he tell her? How could he do that in a non-creepy way? Wyatt sipped his drink for several minutes and stewed over the right choice.

Wyatt decided that inaction was unfair to her. And he couldn't deny the high match metrics intrigued him. He opened his avatar, modified it with a suitable island animation, added a smart object—a tiki torch—then clicked *SEND*.

She looked up with a start and stared in his direction. He smiled back. Had her expression turned to anger or challenge? The smile returned. After a pause, she stood and walked across the sand, holding the virtual tiki torch. A thrill went through him.

She stopped opposite him at the bar. "At least your avatar is an accurate likeness. That's a necessity. I dislike artifice." Her gaze was intent. "Now, tell me how you knew my name."

"Hi, Lily. You've got an unsecured version of the app. I thought I should warn you."

The end of the bar was empty except for them, and she pulled up a stool to sit. She crossed her long legs and fixed him with a gaze that weakened his knees. Wyatt ordered two more drinks while they exchanged names and hometowns. That revealed another plus. They both worked in Northern California.

Lily sipped her tropical drink. "How'd you end up in the Maldives?" Any anger she might have held seemed to be gone.

"I won a free vacation. I only reached the semifinals of the Pwn2Own hacker competition that's been around for a long time, but they hand out some good prizes."

"A black hat hacker?"

"Mostly white hat." It was true, and he liked that it sounded mysterious. His main foray into the hacker gray area was against Megatech Robots, the largest robot company in the US. He hadn't succeeded but thought it was worth the effort to find out if they complied with the laws protecting user data. The hacker community suspected they did not.

"Is that your job?"

"It's more of a second interest." Any reticence to share information had evaporated. "Well, a third interest. I work for a regional university and teach classes on individual privacy. I've been there for two years."

She raised her eyebrows. "What's the third? Surfing?"

"I enjoy surfing and outdoor sports. But my first love, from the time I was a kid, is biology. That led to my undergrad major in forestry. I worked in forestry for a year before going back for my master's and PhD in public policy."

Lily studied his face. "Privacy is far different from forestry."

"Forestry wasn't what I expected. There are things to love, like the work to plant a trillion trees to mitigate climate change." Wyatt gave her a wry grin.

Lily sipped her drink and looked like she was trying to figure him out. An image of his father rose in his mind, and he recalled the common adage not to follow the same profession as your father unless you intended to be better. But both his parents had impressed on him that he should do something to make the world better.

"Forestry can be a dangerous field, and now the bots have taken over. I decided I didn't want to spend my life managing robots."

"A man of many skills and interests."

"I guess I should be more focused. It's important to work on things that make a difference."

"We're on the same side. Rebels against robots and the big corporations." Lily lifted her glass. He clinked his to hers. Real tiki torches highlighted her soft skin and the freckles across her nose. He admired her animation while telling him about her own career as an attorney in a labor rights law firm. He ordered another round of drinks, and some bar food to graze on while they talked.

Wyatt startled when he became aware of the empty glasses scattered on the bar between him and the bartender. It was probably past last call, based on the look he sent while he washed glasses. They were the only people left, and Wyatt's CLAIR clock reported they had talked for over three hours. He was usually more aware of his surroundings.

"Can I help you home?"

Lily took his arm, and they staggered back to her resort room, their footprints zigzagging in the sand.

She rested a hand on him and fumbled for the button on her CLAIR to open her hotel room. The door unlocked, and Lily shook back her curls. Then she kissed him, the flavor of tropical fruit on her lips. He kissed her before she pulled away.

Happy smiles crinkled both their faces, and she leaned crookedly against her hotel door. "I have a rule about first dates. Not when I'm drunk."

"A wise rule. I'm here for a week. A second date?"

"Yes. Let's see what kind of surfer you are. Maybe we can surf some of the reef breaks here. See you tomorrow?"

40

Lily Fairchild—2095 (California)

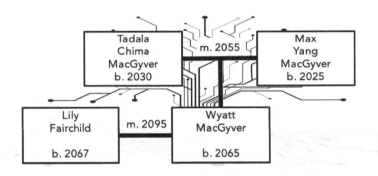

Music wafted from their living room, a complex, delicate harmony with an undercurrent of jazz. Lily peeked through the door at Wyatt, absorbed in the keyboard. His fingers danced with passion. She warmed with the music and the knowledge that this multi-talented man was completely in love with her and did everything to please her. Her on-and-off anger had disappeared when they married in the spring and once the MEDFLOW medication, which she'd neglected to mention to him, was at full capacity. Stress at work tended to confound her mental equilibrium, but he was a balancing influence, not subject to wild emotions—the yang to her yin.

Wyatt noticed her and smiled, still playing. "A new piece I composed. I started with *Souvenir de Porto Rico* by Gottschalk in that beautiful E-flat minor key. I combined it with some ragtime and jazz rhythms and overlaid it all with my own riffs."

"Quite beautiful." Lily was lost in it for several minutes and forgot why she was there. When he finished the piece, she clapped her hands together. "I can't believe you just wrote that."

He grinned at her. "What Gottschalk might have written if only he had tools like the AIs we have now."

Lily sat across the keyboard from him and rested her chin in her hand. She remembered her day, and her concerns about work returned. Wyatt seemed to appraise her mood. He waited.

"I'm a bit stressed out at the office."

"If you want to know, so am I. That's why I try to relax with music."

"You hide it well," Lily said, surprised. "What is it?"

He smiled. "No, you go first."

"It's just that I worry about staying on the partner track at the law firm. Zoe's hard driving. She's in this constant crisis mode to protect workers' rights. I try to think strategically to help outline our approach. But I see both sides. The robotic tech can be both good and bad, and I can't sort out strong arguments to advocate for legislation."

"The ever-present puzzle of how we can live with technology because we can't live without it." Wyatt's calm gaze settled on her. It reminded Lily of his father, a practical engineer she'd met a dozen times in the past two years.

"Robots send the per-person output metric shooting skyward, but they plunder jobs. I wish I knew how to fix it."

"In theory, we should have more time to pursue creative alternatives. Like music." Wyatt played a riff on the keyboard.

"If only we could all make a living playing music."

"Right. Even if I register my piece with the blockchain digital copyright repository, nobody's going to buy it," he said. "There are too many artists and not enough time for anyone to look at all the content."

"But the bots aren't going away," Lily said.

Wyatt frowned. "No, they aren't. Technology has been improving efficiency and the standard of living for the past two centuries. Luddites don't win. There's no going back."

"So, what's the answer?"

"It's not just technology. It's economics. And power. Who owns the robot factories? Who should own them?"

The bigger picture came into focus. "Are you suggesting everyone own those factories? Isn't that socialism?"

"The current system can't continue forever. Jobs disappear faster than they're replaced, even as population growth slows."

Lily recalled presentations she'd created for Zoe. "Simultaneously, wealth is concentrated in fewer hands, and now can grow exponentially."

"Those trends will soon end badly. Whatever you call it, something new needs to replace our current system." Wyatt shook out his hands. "Let me play something else."

He sat still for a moment and then began a new classical piece with hints of an Afro beat. "This is *Bamboula, Opus 2,* also by Gottschalk."

Lily was carried away by his playing. His face relaxed, and now she noticed the difference as his own stress dissipated. Wyatt finished and rested his hands.

"Wow, that looked demanding to play," she said.

"It's very difficult. I haven't gotten it down perfectly yet, but the effort distracts me."

She rested her chin on her hand again, her face closer to his, and nudged his shoulder with hers. "Your turn. What's stressing you?"

"My lesson plan for next semester. Usually, I focus on the basics, an argument for individual privacy. But I'm also wondering who best controls information."

"Not the corporations, right? We've seen what happens when they control."

He shrugged. "You could as easily say, 'Not the government.' We see what happens to individual rights and privacy in places like China when the government is in control. Those rights evaporate."

"What if only the individual controls their own information?"

"That's been the conclusion in my classes. But it's a tough fight against the big corporations that profit from our data.

How do we reengineer the net to place individual data ownership at the heart?" His face softened. "Let people make their own choices on data sharing. Like, you know, how I happened to find you on a beach in the Maldives." They both laughed.

"Okay. Pretend I'm a student. What are other exceptions?"

"Aggregate information has become more valuable so they can feed robotic factories with supply and demand data," Wyatt said. "The data can solve von Mises's economic calculation problem. Soon, we won't need markets to set prices. The data sets prices. So, just the robots and the data can give you an efficient economy. You don't need old-style capitalism."

"That sounds reasonable, as long as the individual information that forms the base of the big data isn't kept indefinitely." Her visceral dislike of corporations surfaced.

"Agreed. The economic data needs an expiration date, and we should have a right to demand some of it be deleted immediately."

"Everyone has the right to be forgotten, and to keep some things private." Lily could think of several things she wished might never be known about her, and she touched the spot near her hip where her MEDFLOW rested.

He shifted on the keyboard bench. "All of those points are the basics. We've been aware of them since the dawn of the net, and I've always been teaching the ideas in my class."

"What's causing your anxiety?"

Wyatt spread his hands apart in the air. "I need to expand my class to cover information in society. Privacy just affects the visible part of the iceberg, with the whole iceberg being *information*."

"This sounds like a lot for one class."

Wyatt shrugged. "The world has an information economy. New issues arise where information meets free speech and democracy. Information that we all produce ends up in public conversation as social media and instantaneous news. The net allows everyone's speech to be amplified, and some far more than others. Whether it's deserved or not."

Lily thought of her union clients. "If corporations control the message, they can sway the public conversation and make workers look like technophobes. There's another side to the argument. Workers have rights too."

"Right. So, the ability to pay, to control the information commons comes into play," Wyatt said. "Should individuals be free to use whatever economic resources are at their disposal to enhance the power of their voices?"

Lily thought about her own economics classes. "Like the argument about medieval shared fields where herders could graze their animals. If someone overgrazed, then it ruined it for everybody. You're saying information is a common, like the field?"

"Exactly." Wyatt had abandoned his seat and now paced. "The information commons can be abused too. So, should society place some bounds on the information that flows into it and the discourse that comes out of it? The questions are, Should we keep it open and free? And how do we do that without the danger of intentional contamination by inaccurate, manipulative, hurtful, and undemocratic forces?"

Lily folded her hands, happy that she could help him work through his process. "It's a struggle for information control."

"Yes, control. And when times are challenging, there are incentives to play hardball, to grab power or money, and democracy itself is at risk."

"These aren't new questions. I wonder why we haven't found solutions yet." Sometimes it felt futile, but some of Lily's fire returned. "The fights for workers' rights, privacy, and democracy, are eternal battles."

Wyatt gave her a hug. "I'm glad we're in this fight together."

41

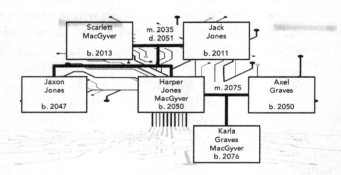

"It's easy to fall into a habit of living, into a rut. That is, until the world slaps you and kicks you out of it. And then you want to slap and kick the world right back," Jaxon said.

PAUSE.

The therapy avatar froze, suspended in air, her gaze warm and encouraging, looking over her steepled hands. *Dr. Savannah Price, Clinical Psychologist AI*, the avatar's name and title, were displayed behind her, along with several medical diplomas attached to the virtual office wall.

Jaxon pulled the HDSET off and scratched his head. Was this a good idea? In the metaverse worlds, he mostly talked about in-game events. It was strange to talk out loud about himself, but the clinic said this was the first step to deal with his stress.

He shrugged and put his HDSET back on.

UNPAUSE.

"Sam and I work on roofs four days a week for six hours, then at least once a week we meet in the metaverse. We complete quests, kill dragons. Sam has other things to do the rest of the week, but I don't have anyone else as close as him."

I'm enjoying your story. Besides Sam, are there other family members in your life?

"Mom calls me to check in at least every month. She's eighty-two and still living in New York. I visit her twice a year. She looks in good health for her age. I never hear from Dad. He must be getting old, but I don't care. Harper and Axel are busy with the factory, with those damn robots. I don't hear from them."

What other people do you have in your life?

"I found groups on the net to hang out with sometimes. There are a few women I met in the metaverse. It seemed at first like there were a lot, but then it took time to sort out the NPCs. I even saw one of the real women, Cecilia, in real life. We met at a bar downtown."

And what happened to that relationship?

"She didn't seem too interested after meeting me and stopped returning my messages and disappeared into a different subworld in the metaverse. I couldn't find her again."

Let's turn to your work life. Can you describe that?

"I never liked being a roofer, but I liked working with Sam, so I stayed at Lewis Builders. It was fine until they started adding robots. First, there was Herb. It learned quickly, and Sam and I had to work hard to keep up. Then, they added another. Then two more. The illegals didn't keep up, and they disappeared from our jobs."

Are there any past experiences that you believe may contribute to your current anxiety?

"We used to work residential jobs where the roofs weren't over a couple of floors high. I still didn't like the height, but at least I could keep my lunch down. Then one day, the boss, Andrew, said I needed to wear the exoskeleton to keep up with the robots. Sam usually did that part, and I didn't want to. I put it on, but I felt claustrophobic when the frame folded around me too tight. The rig caught on a fastener while I carried a load of fixtures, and I tripped. The metal scraped against the shingles the whole time I slid down to the edge.

The harness jerked me to a stop, and I hung there, two stories over the rose garden in the backyard."

That's scary! You must have been anxious. What did you feel?

"I saw red. I think that was the flowers, but red too, like when I ride Pegasus and the dragon breathes fire and Pegasus keeps me safe and I win."

Well, you certainly recovered well from that accident to change it from a negative to a positive experience. Tell me more about your work environment now.

"The company started bidding bigger commercial jobs since they have the bots and us and another couple of teams of people. We're up on taller buildings, and the wind sometimes blows materials around. It's slippery when it rains, and they don't wait long enough before ordering us up."

Is that adding to your anxiety now?

"I think so. I'm not sure how much longer I can go up there, and I don't like working with bots. They're supposed to look out for us, but I don't think they always do. It's not like you can talk to them."

Jaxon, thank you for telling me these stories. They will help me. We shall contact you soon with some additional help.

The therapist closed her medical allbook, leaned toward him, and smiled serenely.

Until we talk again, Jaxon, find peace in your life. Goodbye.

The avatar dissolved into a swirling bubble.

He closed the HDSET. Now, he wasn't sure this had been such a good idea. He felt no calmer. Was there a real Doctor Price associated with this avatar, or was there only the AI— just another robot?

———————◆———————

"Jaxon, are you all right?" Mom's voice cut into his waking consciousness.

He slipped on his CLAIR to respond, not even bothering to open his eyes. "Ah, yeah, I'm okay." He clicked on his avatar, which stood beside a placid brook.

"Can't I see you?"

"Yeah, give me a minute."

He crawled out of bed, shoved the synpsychs into a bedside drawer, pulled on his robe, and sat at the desk. With a tap, he connected the CLAIR to his holo-display.

Her face appeared, the label *Scarlett MacGyver* below. She examined his face. Anxiety tightened her eyes. Jaxon stared back. There was a gray cast to her normal ginger hair. He guessed she wasn't taking the coloration microdosing everyone was using.

"Are you feeling healthy, Mom?"

"I received a message from an AI, a Doctor Price. It said you were distressed and gave some stress level number. I don't understand what that means."

He'd filled in her ID in the required field for closest kin. That had been a bad idea too. She didn't need the burden at her age.

"Mom, it's nothing." He shrugged at her. "You look tired. Are you taking care of yourself?"

Mom made a noise. "Ha, look at us. Both a mess."

She still studied his face, and he realized she was saying what she saw.

He brushed his hair back into place. "We do the best we can, Mom."

Her one hand wrung the other. "Will you come visit me soon?"

"Or you can come out here." He didn't have the money to pay for his flight or hers. "I'm on a job and afraid to take time off. There are too many robots now, and I don't want to give them an excuse."

"Okay. I'll see you when you next come to New York."

Jaxon signed off.

Mom had made it clear she didn't want to leave New York to stay with him in California. He couldn't afford to visit more often. He suspected she had only a small retirement savings from her work at the nonprofit, so she was frugal about flying too. They stayed in contact this way, which left her as real, and unreal, as a character in the metaverse.

———————————◆———————————

Jaxon finished dressing for work, removed his breakfast of eggs from the autocooker, and ate it with his cup of coffee. His CLAIR buzzed with a message marked "Urgent." He opened the connection.

A middle-aged man appeared, dressed in business attire, his mouth tight. "Mr. Jaxon Jones, employee of Lewis Builders?"

"Yes, that's me." The caller traded IDs to confirm his identity and provide the man's—an employee from the Department of Labor Affairs, State of California.

"I'm tasked with an investigation into Lewis Builders about possible safety violations on work sites. And other activities that fall under the purview of our department. Do you have time to meet with me in person?"

He froze, his mind spinning. Could this have anything to do with his clinic interview? Where is that information shared? Did someone have to tell someone something?

He coughed into his hand. "I'm working today and tomorrow. I can meet you tomorrow, late afternoon."

The man hesitated, then assented. "That works for me." He sent the address and invitation to Jaxon's PIDA. The man ended the call.

An official-looking summons appeared before him, meaning he had to show up. He emptied two synpsychs from the bottle, tossed them back, then left for the job site.

———————————◆———————————

Jaxon sat well away from the edge of the roof and ate his sandwich. They were on a seven-story building. The sky was overcast. Gray clouds reached down like puffy hands, and a mist touched the rooftop.

They'd finished the morning work with a short break before starting another section. The job would continue for another two weeks. Four other men sat in another group. Three robots stood by silently.

Sam chewed his sandwich in silence, his gaze far away, then focused on Jaxon. "This job gets harder every year. The robots are too fast for me to keep up."

Jaxon's stomach churned. He wondered if Sam might be thinking of retirement. He did the math and figured that Sam was sixty-seven, certainly old enough to get a pension. But the idea of not having his trusted partner scared him.

"Sam, just take it slow."

Jaxon had the occasional aches and pains, and he was much younger than Sam. He told himself that was why he took the synpsychs. A hole opened in his chest at the thought of Sam not being there, though he couldn't say it without sounding selfish.

Sam stared at him now. "Are you okay, Jaxon?"

He wiped his forehead. "Yeah, fine."

They finished lunch, and Jaxon chewed on a red apple. Its shine reminded him of the last dragon they'd hunted in the metaverse. He would rather be there now.

The rooftop elevator door clanged open, and Andrew strode toward them. He stopped in front of Jaxon and pushed back his hair with nervous fingers. "The big boss wants to see you at the end of the day."

"What about?" The startled question escaped his lips.

He thought again about the clinical interview. How private were those, and could anyone be data mining? Jaxon had read none of the disclosures and realized he didn't even know who hired the clinic. Maybe it was Lewis Builders, some sort of employee benefit.

Andrew avoided the question. "You'll have to ask him yourself." He signaled the crew back to work, turned, and left down the elevator. He hadn't looked happy to deliver the message.

Sam touched his arm and said, "Don't worry about that guy, or his boss either." Jaxon knew Sam had his back, but it wasn't as if he could offer much protection.

In the afternoon, they moved on to the tricky roof section on one corner, which held a sloping decorative surface that intersected with the main roof portion. Jaxon had the exoskeleton on, and all the men were tethered to the OSHA attachment point at the intersection. He carried an application tool. It was bulky and too heavy to operate all day without the rig. That was the only reason he consented to wear it.

The three robots positioned roofing materials in the typical pattern, moving over the sloping roof without tethers, which would have interfered with their free movement. They placed materials twice as fast as a human could move. The bots' sensors detected when a man was close, and they stopped until the man moved clear.

Jaxon sweated heavily, though the effort couldn't account for it. His stomach churned with acid. Two robots stacked materials farther down the slope, and the last worked nearer the top. It clomped by with another load, its shoes adjusting to the slope before it turned, swinging within arm's reach. The sun glinted off the General RoboMechs logo on its torso.

A sudden blinding hatred filled him. Here, arrogantly strolling by, was the cause of all his problems. The robot bent to set the load, leaning downslope as its knees bent in articulation. Jaxon swung the heavy application tool right at its left leg. The clang of metal on metal filled his ears.

The leg skidded sideways some centimeters, and the robot tipped, the weight of the materials suddenly in the right place to pull it farther off balance. A robot arm flung out to counterbalance the machine, but it was too late. The robot toppled over. It slid down the roof along with the roofing materials, the mass picking up speed. Several meters below, both robots looked up. Their sensors focused on the tumbling mass just as the falling robot and materials plowed into one, then another. All three robots and the roofing materials disappeared over the edge of the roof. Two seconds later, there was a loud crash.

Jaxon crawled down to the roof's edge and peered over. The tether harness held him from moving farther. Below were three black marks in piles of scattered materials on the asphalt road where the robots had fallen. One car had crashed into a fire hydrant spewing water in a fountain, and another was sideways next to the materials. He couldn't tell if any pedestrians were under the piles, but there could be. His stomach turned over. He did that. People below, as small as ants, scurried around or stopped and stared upward.

Blood pumped behind his temple and made him dizzy. Anger mixed with fear at the thought that some people might have died. It was people versus bots, just a losing battle. Adrenaline surged through him. It was the same feeling as when riding Pegasus, his faithful steed, in the last charge to slay his quarry. That was freedom. Jaxon uncinched the carabiner holding the tether. He stood at the edge of the rooftop. Then he flew.

42

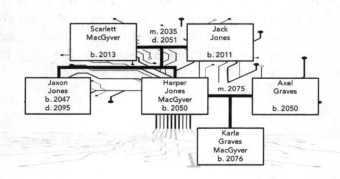

Harper sat at company headquarters with four holo-displays open, watching the live news feeds from the West Coast construction site. The 3D immersion left her queasy. They loaded Jaxon's body into an ambulance.

The office door opened, and an admin stuck his head in. "Our monitoring sensors have confirmed the man, Jaxon Jones, struck one of the robots and precipitated the accident."

"Okay." She dismissed him and went back to the news reports.

Her older brother, gone. Though Jaxon had never seemed like an older brother. He wasn't someone there to protect her, someone to look up to. He was easy to compete with, because he almost never offered any competition. For an instant, she felt a warmth toward him, a little late protectiveness maybe, then dismissed the feeling. What could she do now?

Did Jaxon kill himself? Why? There was factual evidence that he had knocked a robot off the roof. Why did he do it?

The reports flowed in as media sources competed to cover the breaking story. She tried to find a real reason behind the accident, other than her robots.

Synpsychs were detected. Was Sam involved in some way? She knew from Jaxon that Sam played in the metaverse with him. Maybe they were taking synpsychs. Sam, a white rabbit, leading the younger man into a psychological wonderland. Blood pulsed at her temples. Yes, that had to be it.

The office door opened again, and Dad strode in. He sat in the chair beside her. At age eighty-four, he looked older and frailer. He wasn't as sharp, she thought. Not as good with the sales pitch, though he could still light up a customer with his smile.

"I heard the news when it broke. I still monitor the destruction of every robot in the field. Your brother's gone?"

Harper glanced down nervously.

Dad shrugged. "That's terrible news." She wished there were tears in his eyes, but he wasn't showing much emotion. But neither was she.

"Your namesake, gone."

"Somehow, I never thought of him as my namesake. I left the naming to your mother."

"You saw the news reports, that apparently he jumped?"

Dad nodded. "I wonder why he killed himself. We can't see into anyone's head to know."

"No, we can't." The thought was comforting.

"Have you talked with your mother?"

"That's my next call." Her stomach twitched.

Mom would take this hard. She had a special motherly fondness for Jaxon. Harper knew who her mother's favorite in the family was. Everyone did.

Jack shifted in the chair. "We need to focus on damage control for the company. How do we manage the messaging on this?"

Jack tossed out ideas, the next steps to protect the company's brand, and Harper composed a list on her CLAIR, though her mind flipped between two poles. One was a faded attachment to her older brother. The other magnetic attraction was to her robots, her creations, and the need to protect them. Well, Jaxon was gone, and there was nothing to be done.

She would save her company.

43

"It can't be true." Scarlett stared at Harper in the holo-com.

"Mom, it's true. Jaxon is gone." Harper's hard jaw showed anger instead of the sadness she should be feeling.

Scarlett's mind wasn't processing the news. He was the difficult one but the only child that loved her. And the only one she loved unreservedly in return. She'd never had a bond like that with anyone else—parent, sibling, or spouse. Jaxon was special.

Even now, staring into Harper's eyes, she couldn't connect with her, the one who hadn't called her for ages, who took the thirty pieces of silver from Jack and now ran his company, who left her alone to fend for herself.

Harper had passed the news video into the feed. It played, and she talked over it. "Sam Chima was there on the roof with Jaxon. He told police that he saw Jaxon unhook himself from his harness, though he doesn't know if that was intentional... to do harm to himself...or because he was trapped near the roof edge." Harper's mouth hardened. "I wonder about Sam, whether he had something to do with Jaxon's accident, if he was encouraging him to use all those synpsychs."

"What synpsychs?" Scarlett's heart thumped in her chest, and she glanced at the credenza beside her bed where she stored her own drug bottle. Jaxon had told her on his last visit that he used them to reduce restlessness. She'd shared some of hers.

"The toxicology report says he had some in his system. They said it wasn't enough to cause him to do something crazy, but who knows."

Scarlett couldn't concentrate. She struggled to respond, and her voice was barely audible. "Was there anything else that they know?"

"Jaxon's boss, a guy named Andrew, told me that the company was sorry to lose an employee. And Dad and I are talking to him about the robots." Harper dropped her gaze at the comment.

"Were the robots from your company?"

There was a pause. "Yes, three robots. We can make the roofing company whole by replacing them for free, and they'll sign a non-disclosure."

Harper went back to talking about the video, but Scarlett couldn't listen. Her daughter was more focused on her company than her brother, unconsciously or intentionally overlooking the proximate cause of his death, and her connection to it.

Scarlett rubbed her temples. "I need some time to process this, so I better say goodbye." She saw the couple of hugging emoticons on the feed from Harper before her face faded into ether.

Scarlett dragged herself from the desk. She felt old, very old, and suddenly useless. At the hall credenza, she poured herself a double scotch and soda and sat in the living room. The city rumbled below her. The glass was empty, and still her mind buzzed like a hive, the queen dead and the workers left to no purpose. Scarlett shuffled to the bedroom credenza, took out the drug bottle, and refilled her drink on the way back.

She thought again of the expression on Harper's face when she described Jaxon's death. Earlier, Jaxon had said he didn't communicate with his sister. In a world where human connection was a tap away, Scarlett didn't hear from her either, except about weddings, births, and funerals. There was little love lost between the siblings, and somehow the fire of familial love had not ignited anywhere in her immediate family.

Many years before, Scarlett had been obsessed with defending the MacGyver name against usurpation. She'd disputed Max's right to it and convinced Harper to carry it forward. But Harper hardly resembled either of her grandparents. Both had been people of principle, driven by causes that played close to their hearts and advanced some common good. They had been MacGyvers not by birthright but by action.

What had she ever done except to stupidly follow Jack, and then allow herself to be separated from her children? She'd let Harper ignore her and didn't even try to win her back from Jack. Then, she'd let Jaxon leave and didn't try harder to keep him close and support him. Jaxon needed a mother's love, and she hadn't made the extra effort to demonstrate it. Her life had been a river, moving wherever gravity took it, and she'd never tried to swim in any direction of her choosing. She'd just drifted along. She sat in the dark for a long time and weighed the future, the drink in one hand, and the drug bottle in the other.

44

Karla Graves MacGyver—2095 (Massachusetts)

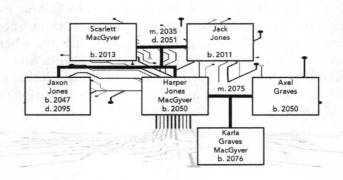

Karla's CLAIR buzzed with a call from her mother. That was unusual. She sipped her mocktail and keyed the "one minute" wait icon.

"I'll be right back," she told her MIT roommate.

"Don't take too long. The drop happens in fifteen minutes." Her roommate wore a "Just Drop It" T-shirt that paired with her own "Baker House" tee that featured a piano in midair.

She scurried to a corner of the common living room to accept the call. Karla's CLAIR reconnected, and the ID for *Harper Jones MacGyver* glimmered.

"I need to tell you about Uncle Jaxon."

Karla tightened her grip on the mocktail as her mother talked, the words tense and angry, with no preamble for the message she was delivering.

"He's dead?" She set the drink down, her eyes wet, emotions welling inside her.

Mom mentioned that toxicology showed synpsychs in her uncle's system and continued with some theory, all of which made less and less sense to Karla. It involved Uncle Jaxon's work buddy, Sam, from the other side of the family.

This was too much detail to absorb. "Mom, are you saying Uncle Jaxon overdosed?"

The hypothesis did not seem to follow from the facts mentioned, that her uncle was on a roof and there had been an accident that maybe involved conflict with a robot. Her mother continued for a time with the overdose theory.

"Mom, how is Grandma Scarlett taking this?"

"I talked to her, and she's sad, of course."

"Are you going to see her?"

There was a pause. "No, I'm here in Colorado, with my hands full managing PR about the accident."

"Okay. I'll call Grandma." Her roommate gestured at her, and she said, "Mom, I've got to go. Love you."

Karla followed her roommate down the stairs and out into the quad. Her stomach fluttered. The energetic scuffing of machinery moving about erupted from the roof of the dorm building. Everyone talked loudly in a happy, anticipatory mood. After the news from her mom, all her joy about the idea of dropping a piano off the dormitory roof had disappeared.

Drones floated on the corners of the quad, ready to record the event. Safety monitors cordoned everyone back from a circular area close to the building, and someone began a countdown. Students in the quad joined in. It reached zero. A rattle sounded from above her, and the piano pitched off the roof. It landed with a resounding crash, and everyone cheered.

There were multiple yells of "the tradition continues!"

"Here's a Bruno milkshake," her roommate said, and Karla took the drink. She wiped the moisture from her eye before anyone saw it. She tried to join the party atmosphere, but her heart wasn't in it. After a few minutes, she wandered toward Harvard Bridge and the Charles River to think.

Karla watched blue water slap against the bridge. She hadn't experienced the deep family ties that others she knew at MIT took for granted. Sent away to boarding school in Southern California for her high school years, there were only summers to spend with Mom and Dad and a few family trips to meet others like Uncle Jaxon and Grandma Scarlett.

She used to enjoy her stays at Grandma Scarlett's condo in New York, exploring the big city. Grandma had a reasonably interesting career doing good things for the environment. She convinced people that fission energy plants needed to replace the awful coal-fired ones, and they were all closed now. Karla wondered how she was taking the loss of a son. She vowed to call her as soon as she went back to her room.

She opened her CLAIR, read several of the news reports that had poured onto the net, and thought about her mother's reaction.

She'd learned this past fall at MIT that she was a logical thinker, holding her own with the engineering minds in her classes. Her mother's reaction didn't make sense. From a few family gatherings, she knew Uncle Jaxon as a quiet soul. He was never mistaken for the smartest person in the room, but he was kind. The news reports suggested that something about the robots had caused him mental anguish. It seemed obvious to Karla that disappearing jobs were at the heart of it. She never thought much about the fact that her family owned a robot business, but now she thought she should confront that it carried an ethical responsibility.

Her mother's words were dissonant in her head. Did Mom concoct her own theory that Sam was implicated in Uncle Jaxon's suicide? She knew the human mind sometimes rebels against self-blame and guilt.

Her PIDA gave a soft chime. *Remember, today is the last day to drop classes*.

Karla looked up from the ripples on the river. Semester drop day was really why the dorm indulged in the traditional silly piano drop.

Spring semester of her freshman year, and she was still undecided about her major. No big deal. She still worked her way through general requirements, including math, physics, and chemistry. She had a second biology elective, which she really enjoyed, and a robotics class she found less exciting. The menu of choices had been too rich to digest, and at the beginning of the semester she had overindulged. Now, she had too many classes this semester. Which one to drop?

Water flowed under the bridge, held in its course. She knew she wouldn't be carried along like the river. She'd choose the path *she* wanted.

She opened her CLAIR, found the university website, and signed in. She pulled up the drop page and paused. Then, she clicked the box next to the robotics class and hit *DROP*.

45

Lily Fairchild—2095 (California)

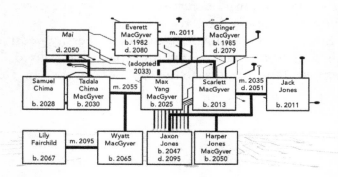

Lily looked out the window as Wyatt spoke. The holo-com was open between them on the table of their San Francisco apartment. Fog draped the sliver of Golden Gate Bridge visible in the distance. Once, people jumped off it to die by suicide. They'd put barriers in place to end that long ago, but people still found ways. Her heart hurt for her new family.

Wyatt clenched his hands as he looked at his parents on the display. "I don't know what else to say. It's heartbreaking to lose family."

Max held Tadala in the floating image, and a tear rolled down her cheek. "I talked to your Uncle Sam, and he's broken by it too. He thought of Jaxon as a little brother."

"How is Aunt Scarlett?" Wyatt asked.

"I think she's okay," Max said. "Her granddaughter, Karla, flew down to New York on a late afternoon flight to stay with her for the week. Karla said Scarlett is better than when she arrived."

"How is Harper taking it? What else did she say when she called you?"

Lily hardly knew Harper and had spent very little time with her. The robotics company they owned created a chasm separating the sides of the family. She always felt silence was the preferred approach.

"Harper isn't taking it well. She thinks Sam might have had a negative influence on Jaxon." Max said it with a measured tone, like he was trying to stifle an emotion.

"Sam wouldn't do anything to hurt Jaxon." Tadala gripped Max's arm harder.

"No one would believe that." Wyatt's voice was soothing, and Tadala's gaze was far away. "We just have to support each other through this." He offered further condolences and signed off the connection.

They sat quietly for a few moments, holding hands as they each digested the news.

Wyatt turned to her. "It didn't seem appropriate to analyze with Mom and Dad what might have happened, but I don't think the whole story has been told."

"Let's open the news feeds. I'm sure some journalists have their theories." Lily searched through her CLAIR and identified several articles. Since the accident occurred downtown, video was instantly available, and reporters had fanned out to investigate details. She chose a random video on the 3D display.

"It's lucky no one was killed or injured on the street below." Wyatt didn't mention what else besides robots had fallen, though she repressed the image that came to mind with a shudder.

They switched to a different reporter.

"I think the important story starts with that part about Jaxon's CLAIR logging a meeting with the Lewis Builders boss for later that afternoon and the one with a guy from the Department of Labor Affairs. Do you think he filed a complaint against the company? What if Lewis Builders planned to pressure him to stop or planned to fire him in retaliation?"

Wyatt steepled his hands and watched the display. "That's possible."

Another news video featured a reporter with video from a distant roof security camera. The low-resolution camera video played over the reporter's commentary.

"It's too far away to decide whether the robot got in the way of work Jaxon was doing when he was swinging that tool, but it does look like there was contact," Lily said. "It could have been an accident."

The reports came to no definitive hypothesis, leaving open questions all around. It was investigated as an industrial accident, with the robots potentially held culpable. Lily squeezed his hand.

Though she didn't say it out loud, she already held the firm belief that Jaxon thought he'd be fired and replaced by robots, and he attacked the robot in his anger. It wasn't an uncommon line of thought anymore. Lily saw it through her work nearly every day.

She thought of her partner, Zoe, still mentoring her career and who approached the battle for workers' rights and jobs as a crusade. Lately, she struggled to wear the appropriate face, knowing she only pretended to the kind of passion Zoe still modeled. She fingered the spot where the inserts for her MEDFLOW lay on her right hip. She'd begun the treatment when she worried about occasional outbursts of anger. The microdosing had made her calmer, sometimes even mellow.

She debated whether she should lower the dosage. Which version of her was the better one?

46

Alexander sat ramrod straight in his saddle, his horse at quiet attention, aligned with the circle facing the cold stone monument. A cool breeze wafted down from the mountain and brought with it the scent of pine needles. Though it was spring, they were assembled not to celebrate life but to acknowledge death. The knights on black-cloaked mounts wore an assortment of weapons. Every cavalier was somber and thoughtful as they considered the tomb, which was topped by a stone winged horse. The etched birth and death dates chiseled on the face reflected the sunlight filtering through the trees.

His stallion snorted and pawed the dirt, and Alexander took advantage of that break in the silence. "We're here today to honor our friend and fallen warrior, Rodrigo Díaz."

He had some difficulty, even though he'd prepared the words ahead of time. His eyes teared up at the loss of his colleague, friend, family member, and brother in virtual arms. Alexander spoke haltingly through the short eulogy.

Ending, he raised a sword high in salute. "Rodrigo fought for glory in this inglorious world. May he find honorable glory in the next."

The circle of knights raised their swords in unison. "To glory, Rodrigo Díaz!"

Alexander touched an icon, and the stone winged horse came to life, changing in color from gray to a lively white. Pegasus rose from the headstone into the sky and pranced in homage above the marker. It circled the glade and then flew toward the sun.

The knights touched swords all around, and multiple quiet conversations buzzed in the ether. Alexander couldn't stay longer, as his heart was too heavy with the role, and he begged his leave. His metaverse was missing his best friend and its best knight.

———————◆———————

Sam pulled off the HDSET and haptic suit and climbed out of his chair. The metaverse memorial service left him drained, but at least, he thought, Jaxon had been given a fitting remembrance by his net community.

He stared out the window. The sun sparkled, and it reminded him of Tadala's wedding. Jaxon had sat next to him, a little boy then, rambunctious and full of life. Sam had felt a kinship with him even then, knowing what it was like to have your sister run circles around you and love her all the same. The sunlight did not warm him.

He found an orange juice in the fridge and settled onto his living room sofa. A profound emptiness left him hollow. He slipped his CLAIR back on and slumped into the cushions.

Hi, Sam. I can tell that you are overwrought. Please, let's talk.

"Princess Kandake. How...?" Her sweet words calmed him.

Sam, you've known me all my life. And I've known you. Let me help you feel better, to get out of this depression.

"How did you know about these thoughts I'm having?"

We are so good together. You will never find anyone else who knows you as well.

———————◆———————

A message waited on his CLAIR from Tadala. Sam swallowed to clear the lump in his throat, thinking how their roles had reversed. He clicked her contact on the holo-com, and her concerned face filled the display. There were a few lines around her eyes, but her hair was still dark and full. The slight signs of aging on her reminded him how old he was.

Tadala's expression remained worried. "Are you okay, *m'chimwene wamkulu?*"

"These calls from the women in my life help."

Her motherly demeanor warmed him. "I'm here to help you through this."

"It's been tough. You know that Jaxon had become my *m'chimwene wamng'ono*. We worked together for so many years, but he went from colleague to friend to younger brother so fast in that time." Sam tried to keep his voice from trembling. "I knew Jaxon had been worried about the robots taking his job. I'm so sorry that I hadn't been able to make him feel better, because I believed it too."

"I wish I could give you a hug, dear brother," Tadala said. She reached her 3D hand toward him.

Though he touched only the screen, somehow the action calmed him.

"I understand the robots were taking over all the roofing jobs," Tadala said. "It would make sense for Jaxon, and for you, to be upset about that."

"The bots learned everything we do. It's impossible to keep up with them."

Sam hoped Jaxon's breaking point had been that and not a fear that Sam would abandon him. Though Sam hadn't seen when he swung his tool against the robot, the low-res video on the news was clear enough to him. It wasn't a usual action for a roofer on the job, even by accident.

Tadala leaned toward him, care in her eyes. "Can I visit you tomorrow? I can be there in the afternoon after clinic hours."

Sam thought about her job, still assisting patients with personalized health care. His sister had found a good calling. The door to his apartment buzzed, and a glance at the vid feed showed a fellow roofer at the front door.

"Sure, sister. I'll see you tomorrow."

His shoulders felt lighter as her hologram faded. Then he opened the door.

"Sam." The man held out a hand. "George Rayburn. You remember me from the union meetings?"

Sam ushered George inside. "Sure. Our vice president. Can't forget you."

George shifted uncomfortably on the sofa as he offered condolences about Jaxon's death. He knew they were relatives and that Sam had lost his longtime work partner. George asked him what he planned to do, what he wanted to do next.

"I'm feelin' old for this work now. And I'm sixty-seven, so I might retire." Sam shrugged. They talked for a few minutes about the accident, and the growing numbers of robots on the job sites.

"There's another way off the roof, and one where you can help." George fixed him with a steely gaze. "We need folks in union leadership who have felt firsthand what it's like to have these bots loot our jobs. We've been considering you for a new role in the organization."

Sam learned that several union leaders supported this plan to create active engagement with construction companies to better protect roofing jobs. He listened with mixed emotions, tired and depressed from the past days, but with a growing restlessness. George answered his questions with spirit, and the discussion turned to ways in which the jobs might be improved.

"It's a hard fight to stop this flood of robots," Sam said.

"But what's the alternative? Should we continue to take this lying down, so we're groveling at the feet of their factory owners, begging for scraps? Should we let the robots wash us away?" George's eyes glowed like hot fire.

The image of being carried away in a flood made Sam's body shake. But this time, he would be awake to face the torrent, like his sister.

"I'll do this. I'll do it in memory of Jaxon. Even if the battle is hopeless, we should fight. Even if we lose, at least we'll go down in glory."

47

Harper checked her robots as they ran through the demonstrations again. She had a dozen in the booth, each performing a different task. The Berlin robotics exhibition opened the next day, and everything had to be perfect. Her personal robot, Brünnhilde, stood by her side. Its lenses flashed. "Everything is organized as you wished. The repertoire of activities at these stations should demonstrate the capabilities of the General RoboMechs product line."

"Good. Have you seen Natalie this morning?" Harper was annoyed by the absence of the junior engineer, the one employee she brought along, who hadn't appeared as expected.

"I received a message from her that she will be here in twenty minutes. I believe she was indisposed this morning."

"And why do you suppose?"

Brünnhilde's forehead glowed yellow. "I observed her returning to the hotel late last night, and I formed the hypothesis based on her appearance that Natalie had imbibed an excessive quantity of alcohol."

Her lateness was doubly annoying because Uncle Max had pinged her PIDA that morning to say he was in Berlin. He'd heard about the company exhibition booth and hoped to see her. Now he was arriving soon, and Harper had depended on Natalie's support to cover the work. She had advocated for the young engineer's career and was disappointed, but she'd have to deal with her later.

"Okay, Brünnhilde, if I need to leave before she shows up, you hold the fort here."

"I will assure that nothing outside of your plans occurs at the booth." Brünnhilde's forehead glowed green.

Harper turned her attention to the demonstrations and challenged several of her robots with tricky questions to test whether they responded reasonably.

It was an important exhibition. European governments discussed further public ownership of robotics companies. She needed to highlight the superiority of the company's products, although General RoboMechs was only slightly ahead of the competition. But Harper had confidence. Now forty-nine and at the height of her career, she was building her dreams one chip at a time. The booth would display her vision of utopia. Soon, her perfectly subservient robots would do everything. They would leave her with a life of luxury and complete freedom. More important, she might earn her rightful fame for all she'd done over the years.

Her PIDA pinged with a message. Uncle Max was approaching to join her for lunch. She acknowledged. Harper didn't feel she could ignore him, but she hadn't been close to that side of the family since Jaxon's passing.

With annoyance, she recalled how the investigation had ended. The video recovered from the crushed robots showed that Jaxon had jumped. She and Dad had worked hard to keep that information to themselves, to protect the company's reputation and their own, and their stonewalling eventually allowed the story to drop from the news cycle.

She'd had to give up her theory that Aunt Tadala's brother Sam might be culpable in some way. It turned out that Jaxon's synpsych use had pointed, if anywhere, to their own mother. Karla had encouraged her into a rehabilitation program after she went to New York to help her work through the grief. Now her mother was clean and sober thanks to her daughter. While the impetus for Harper's animosity toward Sam had disappeared, strains within the family persisted, and they were all on opposites sides of the coin of progress.

She passed her uncle the codes to the building since it wasn't accessible to the public yet. In a few minutes, the door at the end of the hall swung inward, and four people entered.

Uncle Max and Aunt Tadala were followed by two others. She waved, and they walked through the large pavilion hall toward her.

Uncle Max took her hand in both of his and gave her a hug. "Harper, we see each other so seldom."

"Both busy with careers," she said. She silently checked her PIDA to find he was seventy-four and likely nearing retirement. Next, Harper hugged Aunt Tadala, and Uncle Max introduced their friend Buzz Henderson and his wife Jessica.

"I'm afraid I can only take a bit of time to join you for lunch, since the exhibit opens tomorrow. But would you like to quickly see the newest designs?"

They replied enthusiastically, and she led them to one of the robots, which stood beside a cylindrical column of plastic. The robot nodded when she addressed it.

"Why don't you demonstrate your sculpting abilities? Please find the design for the statue of Frederick the Great, the one standing nearby on Unter den Linden. Recreate just the man, not the horse, at a scale of one meter."

"Yes, Miss."

The robot picked up a carving tool and began work. In a few minutes, the shape of the man emerged from the column of material.

"Oh, very pretty," said Jessica, revealing a slight German accent.

Uncle Max ran his fingers through his full hair. "At this speed of improvement, soon what will people do?"

Aunt Tadala had a different question. "Where are the people in your demonstration? Are any planned to interact with the robots?"

Harper had to admit to herself that she hadn't thought about hiring actual people to stand in her demo. They would have been too difficult to orchestrate together with her robots and would take away from their efficiency and beauty.

Harper gave them the smile she'd inherited from her father. "We should leave for lunch just to conserve time. We can talk about it on the way."

Harper hadn't explored Berlin since she arrived a few days before, but Jessica had clearly lived here at some point and knew of a good restaurant nearby. They walked out of the exhibit pavilion and east on Unter den Linden, toward the statue that was the model for her robot's replica. The sun shone, and strolling pedestrians filled the street. They passed numerous cafés already filled with people enjoying lunch. They crossed Friedrichstraße. The statue was in the distance, but they turned right at Charlottenstraße and continued to the Gendarmenmarkt. Jessica led them to a quaint restaurant. People filled the square, eating and drinking, talking and laughing, under the sun.

"This looks nice, honey," Buzz said to his wife. "But I could've been happy with a döner kebab and a good beer from one of those currywurst stalls we passed."

Harper hadn't noticed. "They still have people running those?"

"There's no economic reason they need to do that work, but some do it for the fun of interacting with everyone." Jessica led them inside. She greeted the waiter, who escorted them to their table.

The atmosphere was one of relaxation, like everyone had time on their hands. Buzz ordered beers, which Harper declined, opting for the apfelschorle, a sparkling apple juice with mineral water. They placed their individual lunch requests with their PIDAs.

Conversation turned to Max and Buzz's planned retirement the following year, after they celebrated the beginning of a new century.

"We built a hell of a lot of fission energy plants," Buzz said. "And met interesting people along the way." He threw an arm around Jessica's shoulder.

Uncle Max tilted his head toward the couple. "They met here in Germany while we were on a project."

"Lucky for you." Jessica poked Buzz. "And lucky for Germany because we stopped using natural gas from the east and have plenty of electricity."

"At last, the Greens reversed their long-standing opposition to nuclear power," Max said between bites of his spätzle and alt-pork. "Germany has built multiple plants now."

Buzz tapped Uncle Max's beer stein with his own. "Prost. Climate change is now one existential risk that humanity has stabilized."

"We just need to solve problems faster than we create new ones," Max said. His gaze briefly met her Aunt Tadala's.

"Your new robots are, honestly, intimidating with what they can do," Tadala said to Harper. "I understand you have big competitors. How's the business side of your company going?"

"Our sales are strong in the US with my new designs." Harper forced herself to smile. "We've found some success in military markets around the world."

"And here?" Jessica asked.

"Europe is difficult because of the fear of mass job losses."

"I think I understand your complications," Jessica said. "Europe has found ways to provide everyone with a solid safety net, with a high guaranteed income and high wealth taxes. But, as part of that approach, Germany is on the verge of nationalizing robot factories. I'm sure other countries are not so far behind."

"I know." The acknowledgment felt dry on her tongue. That was exactly what she was there to prevent.

"It seems that the US will have more difficulty transitioning to a new economic order than Europe," Jessica said.

"What's wrong with our system the way it is?" Harper felt her face flush.

"Hell. Taxes in the US still aren't high enough to cover all the people displaced by robots. Inequality is growing again. And the dollar is weakening because of the debt. The Euro could become the world's reserve currency soon."

It was obvious to Harper from their camaraderie and comfort sitting here together, as if it were their own living room, that all four shared similar perspectives about the world.

"I believe that my robots will free the world of much unpleasant work. We're building a type of utopia, a place where people won't need to labor to live," Harper said.

Jessica took a long pull on her beer, keeping up with Buzz. "If you hope to achieve some sort of utopia, then I think it needs to come with different wealth distribution rules than the old capitalist system."

Tadala gestured at the lively square through the window. "Look out here at this life. It's all about the people. We need a system that looks out for everyone's happiness."

Uncle Max reached a hand to Harper. He had a wise way about him, and he spoke gently. "Perhaps we can create a more perfect world, but we must remember that people are at the heart of it. And utopias look to the common good."

Harper brushed off his hand with the pretense of drinking her sparkling apple juice.

"Now we have more shared resources than ever," Aunt Tadala said. "Many of them are abstract, such as the information commons. How do we transition to a society where the shared commons are valued more than they are in our world today?"

She sipped but offered no response to the group. She yearned for the minute when they finished eating, and she could say goodbye and return to her creations. She certainly did not share their views of the situation. Harper felt like they had come here just to devalue her life's work. They talked about sharing as if it were natural and fair to share everything, no matter who did the creating. Why shouldn't her personal talents be given everything that flowed from them? She was a maker and deserved it all.

48

Max MacGyver—Present, 2125

The autocar moves south among redwoods, and I tell Grand the story of the robots that began slow then spread ever faster through society, and our family's participation in it. He absently pulls seeds from a pine cone as I talk.

"Did your niece Harper ever accept that she had a part in her brother's death?"

"Worse. She, Axel, and Jack suggested that Sam must have put Jaxon into the wrong state of mind and blamed him."

"But Great Uncle Sam was just as much a victim of the robots taking jobs." His eyes harden, and I can tell he feels the injustice.

"It's often easier to live with illusions than to admit your own faults."

"What did Harper do afterward?"

"She continued to design robots and build her company. She was single-minded in her goals."

This recitation of death reminds me of everyone who is missing. Dad and Momma Ginger invade my thoughts; more of the people loved and lost. My throat is tight.

Robert stirs from its position on the seat, and his lenses turn toward me. "Sir, per your calendar, I am concerned that there is insufficient time to travel to your medical appointment."

"We have two stops first, and then I can meet the doctor. Please figure out an alternative to keep the appointment later this afternoon."

"Yes, sir." Robert's forehead flashes green twice, and the robot is silent again.

I recognize the look in Grand's eyes. His mind is turning, just like his dad's used to.

"Now I understand how Ma and Pa were fightin' for important ideas. Pa tried to keep us safe from technology invading our privacy." He looks sideways at Robert, and the robot blinks. "And Ma fought to make it fair for everyone when the bots started taking all the jobs."

"Your mother also fought to keep our democracy during the economic transformation."

"And in some places, like in Germany, they were doing much better solving those problems?"

I nod. "There was more wealth in total, a lot more than ever before in the Global North, and some thought humankind was heading toward a happy stability of sorts."

Grand looks me in the eye. "But that wasn't true?"

"When we see a problem getting worse slowly, human beings often ignore it; then we're surprised when it gets worse very quickly. It fools us and can be very difficult to navigate. Because the first AI wave didn't leave people jobless—though it did radically rewrite employment—we thought the arrival of AIs in robots might be the same. That challenge came at us for years but seemed less threatening."

"Like a standing lion?" He looks far away, thinking. It's a striking image.

"How so?"

"I once saw a mountain lion on a hill stand up in the tall grass. The deer down below startled a bit when they scented him. Then they settled 'cause he didn't move. He just stood there blending in. After a time, he sprinted down to strike. They coulda run when they had the chance, but they didn't."

"Standing lions. That's what happened. Those were challenges we should have predicted. Then there were the unforeseen disasters discovered in hindsight. Those are black swans. Around the turn of the century, we had a full menagerie."

49

Jack frowned as he paced the anteroom to the general's office. "Why's she keeping me waiting so long?"

"Dad, we were lucky to get this meeting at all." Axel lowered his voice and looked around the room as if he feared being recorded, which was a possibility. "Jedeja is a key decision-maker in India for all the military systems we want to sell. She's probably busy."

The door opened, and a captain entered. "Gentlemen, General Jedeja is ready to see you. Unfortunately, she has limited time today, and the meeting will be cut short."

The captain escorted them to the general's office. Jack scanned the room as he entered, hiding his dislike for the spartan décor with his usual sales smile.

Jack met the general with a tight handshake. Her terse expression discouraged his usual opening, but he retained his game face without showing the annoyance he felt. Jack let Axel take the lead to make their pitch.

Axel handled the presentation well. He'd mastered the fine points of selling a customer. Jack had shaped him in his image, and Axel was almost as effective as Jack had been in his prime. Jack could let his mind wander, but he added an occasional comment to beef up an argument.

Military sales were at last driving his company's valuation, now to levels he'd only dreamed of. There was a beauty to the revenue equation that left customers less price sensitive than in other markets. Each country was afraid that their perceived adversaries might gain an advantage, so they avoided being left behind in the technology race. Moreover, by selling to every side, more weapons platforms for one created sales with another to maintain parity. In the case of a little war, both sides would need replenishment, creating more sales. It was a virtuous cycle.

Axel's proposal turned to building robot factories in India, and Jack entered the conversation. As he pitched the possibility, Axel's CLAIR sent the message, *Nice point, Dad.*

The captain made a comment deriding the American economic system.

"We still have private enterprise," Jack said. He kept his face neutral from long practice, but the comment ate at his gut. Who was she to question the system that brought so much wealth into existence? He'd worked hard to build his company. Harper, and Axel, of course, had helped, but it was always his idea.

Alarms blared.

Jack tried to forget his anger, to focus, but it was confusing. He struggled to understand what was happening. The general talked with some military person on the red holo-com in one corner of her office.

Axel seemed frozen, and his forehead broke out in unattractive perspiration.

A silent message appeared on Jack's CLAIR. *Dad, when we signed the deal with the Pakistanis, I think they put our AI into their Hatf XVII system.*

Jack couldn't remember what the Hatf XVII system was. He'd relegated such details to Harper and Axel.

Another message from Axel appeared. *I'm glad we didn't tell Harper since she hadn't released it yet.*

The general at last turned her attention toward him, but he could tell this meeting wouldn't result in any sales today.

He stirred on the sofa. "Should we come back later?"

Her reply stunned him into reality. Axel howled and hugged him like a child. No, this couldn't be happening. The universe always seemed arrayed against him. It always put him in the wrong place at the wrong time. Like some sort of cruel joke.

"What've I done to deserve this?" Jack didn't think anybody even heard him.

50

General Maya Jedeja—2100 (India)

"General, your calendar has your usual meetings, but this next appointment is with two businesspeople from a US robotics company." Her aide-de-camp, Captain Kavita Malhotra, stood at respectful but partial attention, marking the long working relationship they had together.

Jedeja glanced at the monitor that covered her outer office. Two men had entered. They looked uniquely American in suits that were far too warm for the weather outside.

"They can wait a few minutes." Jedeja savored her morning tea, and the accompanying peace, a moment longer.

She'd woken up with a foreboding that it would be a stressful day, probably from her fitful sleep. Jedeja felt the usual sense of satisfaction that each of her objects was in its perfect location. The room was large and appropriate to her position but austere, to her taste, with everything in order. The saffron, white, and green Indian flag stood proudly, pressed clean of all wrinkles, in her corner. Windows were nonexistent, given the high-security military base where they sat, but she'd never minded that.

With the mug empty in her hands, she couldn't avoid the appointment with the two men any longer.

Jedeja clicked her CLAIR and scrolled through her calendar. "Tell me more about these men in my lobby."

"American business owners who want to expand their markets to India." Captain Malhotra crossed to the holo-display on Jedeja's desk and brought up information about the company, General RoboMechs, as well as avatars for the major company officers.

Jedeja studied the information. A small crease appeared between her brows. "Ah yes, the company that wants to sell us military hardware."

The name and title Jack Jones, CEO and Founder, topped the first avatar. Then Axel Graves, Executive Vice President, followed. Finally, there was Harper MacGyver, Executive Vice President.

Jedeja pinched the bio details icon on the hologram and read. "Interesting. Harper is the daughter of the founder, who is, what? Age eighty-nine. So he's just along as the elder statesman, probably no longer in charge."

"But evidently unwilling to give up the CEO title. The other two are married. Our intelligence suggests that Harper MacGyver is the one behind the builds."

"Too bad she sent her husband to discuss a deal," Jedeja said.

Malhotra scrolled through the clean images of the General RoboMechs operations they had previously sent along in a rather soulless marketing packet. "They're here to propose building a factory that will manufacture military robots and other autonomous military hardware."

The corner holo-com display in her office, painted a garish red, blazed its emergency lights with no warning. Jedeja felt her chest freeze. Calls on the hotline from the Pakistani military leadership, though rare, were never for sociable chats.

"You may stay," Jedeja instructed Malhotra as she entered the codes and accepted the call. The visage of General Tariq Shahbaz, her counterpart for the Pakistani military, filled the hotline holo-com. They had talked twice before, but his name and rank were displayed below his face, as if she would ever forget such details. Jedeja saluted out of courtesy, and the Pakistani general saluted abruptly in response.

General Shahbaz's expression was stern. "General Jedeja, I feel obligated to share some unfortunate information with you. We've discovered a religious radical in our facility who has had access to certain aspects of our nuclear software systems. We are interrogating him now."

"That's disturbing, General. A religious radical?"

"Very distressing. And though religion has less sway in both our countries, we, like you, still have religious and nationalist zealots. It's a lingering global problem." He pulled at his collar. "Unfortunately, he obtained certain military clearances. He has hacker skills. We're determining the extent of his infiltration."

General Jedeja studied the sweating face. "What have you learned so far?"

"His family is from the region along the Indus River that has been affected by the water restrictions imposed by your country." General Shahbaz spat out the words about water restrictions, a bitterness underneath his professional tone. "The fields of many poor farmers have dried up. I inform you of this because he has motive to do harm to India."

"Do you have AIs in the loop for the launch protocols within these systems?"

General Shahbaz's face drained of color. "I'm sorry, I am not at liberty to disclose that information." Still, he nodded slightly in the affirmative. She appreciated his risk to give her just this small shred of information. Her chest tightened.

"Thank you for your call. I appreciate your candor. Please keep me informed about developments as you can."

General Shahbaz saluted and signed off. Captain Malhotra stood rigidly at attention.

"Give me a moment," Jedeja said.

The terror of nuclear war filled Jedeja's mind. She tried to ease her emotional response to think clearly, so she took a deep breath and steepled her hands. She had not thought about nuclear control protocols for years. India had a "no first strike" policy, but Pakistan had never formally adopted a parallel; indeed, it still retained a "first use." Indian nuclear launch policy required two humans in the loop. Now, she worried whether Pakistan had any similar requirement.

She reached a decision. "Connect me with Lieutenant General Gohil Tomar." She tried not to read too much of herself into the expression on Malhotra's face.

Malhotra moved to the regular holo-com on the credenza table and opened a secure channel. It took only a few seconds for the Lieutenant General's face to appear. He saluted with much more gusto than Shahbaz had.

Jedeja wasted no time. "Lieutenant General Tomar, we have a developing situation within Pakistan involving control of their nuclear weapon systems and ordnance. I hope I am being overly cautious, but I'm ordering you to Status Yellow Alert. Stand by on a moment's notice."

A shocked expression enveloped Tomar's face before he recovered. "Yes, General." He flicked several switches on a panel, and the wall behind him came alive, lit with three displays bearing the titles "Blue Impact Timer," "Red Impact Timer," and "Safe Escape Timer," all set to 00:00:00. Several officers could be seen scurrying behind him.

His gaze met hers. "The Battle Desk is fully operational. I have the gold codes at hand, as needed."

"And I have mine at hand as well. Let's hope we never need them." She saluted and signed off.

Jedeja turned to Malhotra. "What is the latest on the Indus River situation?"

Malhotra fumbled with the holo-display on the desk, muttered to herself, and opened a news update. She scrolled through information and summarized several articles.

The Indus Waters Treaty had been in place since 1960, and the population along the river had only increased dramatically since. For the past fifty years, despite numerous disagreements and difficult diplomatic negotiations, they'd held control of three of the Five Rivers but increasingly relied on additional irrigation from them for their own growing populace.

"Update me on the water situation for each country at this moment," Jedeja said.

Captain Malhotra's tone lost some of its neutrality. "Not much has changed since last month's briefing. Thousands have been dying on both sides of the border, and the protests in Pakistan have become violent in the past quarter, even more so this week." Malhotra opened several news reports, and images of protesting crowds burning vehicles filled the display.

Jedeja wondered if any of the captain's family were affected. "A situation ripe to encourage religious zealots, and to blame India." She drummed her fingers on the table.

"It's not as if we're alone. Right now, there are water shortages and disputes elsewhere in Asia, the Middle East, Africa, and South America. You may recall last month's military clashes along the upper Nile River."

Jedeja focused her gaze on India's flag in the office corner, relying on her meditative practice of recalling its symbolism. In the center of the tiraṅgā was the Ashok Chakra, the navy-blue wheel symbolizing the cycle of time and life. It helped to center her thoughts in times of stress. Her mind always cleared as she recalled the name of each spoke on the wheel.

The issue of water allocation was a problem she preferred to leave to the politicians. She had no say in these administrative actions. Was there anything more for her to do at this moment? She decided not. Was she overly cautious? Yes, but that was her job, to always look after the safety of her country.

Jedeja glanced at the monitor showing the waiting room, where the two visitors paced, the older one wearing a frown. "Well, let's talk with the Americans so they can at least be on their way."

Malhotra returned in a few minutes, escorting their visitors. Jedeja came around the desk to join them where they stood near the sofas in the far corner of her office.

The younger of the two met her gaze directly and shook her hand. "Please, call me Axel."

"You can call me Jack." The elder businessman beamed an unnaturally white smile and shared his name as if doing her a favor.

Jedeja wondered whether there had ever been any brains behind his pasted-on expression. "General Jedeja." She shook hands firmly and sat down.

"Well, then, *General* RoboMechs is the business partner for your military." It was a sad re-attempt to recover his charm.

"I don't have as much time today as you may wish. We should get to business."

Axel opened a case with a portable holo-display unit and started his presentation. "We understand you have certain border concerns, and we can enhance your self-protection with autonomous weapons systems."

He walked through the pitch, and his father-in-law occasionally offered an overly practiced, typically useless, comment. Jedeja's mind wandered, and she found herself considering whether the Pakistanis already had similar weapons systems.

"A robot factory gives you an entirely new capability. The number of platforms that you can add to the battlefield can increase exponentially," the senior gentleman said.

"For example, our new light milspec model, the Mech 367, has battlefield capabilities ready to solve your problems," the younger one said. "If we work with you to manufacture them here, it can produce millions."

She didn't care what they talked about as long as she didn't have to pay attention. "Do you focus exclusively on military robots and platforms?"

"We have a complete line because of Harper, our chief designer," the older man said. He rubbed his hands together. The action reminded Jedeja of a fly. "We can help other government departments with manufacturing, even building automated factories that build more factories."

"These robots grow like water hyacinth covering Vembanad Lake," Malhotra said, pointing to some statistics on the display. "The government is quite conscious of the resulting unemployment here. That's why all the robot factories are nationalized, unlike your country."

"We still have private enterprise," the businessman said defensively.

"So do we, but less so in economic sectors that might lead to exponential job losses. Our population has been falling but is still over a billion people, and they all need employment. Otherwise, our democracy could become unstable." Malhotra seemed to have a distaste for the man's arguments, and Jedeja was grateful to her for stepping in so she didn't have to think about the debate.

They all startled when the red hotline holo-com blazed with flashing lights again, this time accompanied by an urgent buzz. Jedeja turned her back to the businessmen and walked toward it, her hands cold with sweat. She entered her code to accept the incoming call. General Shahbaz's face filled the display, his jaw grimly set.

"Shall I escort our guests—"

"There's no time. I need you with me. Stay."

Based on the delivery times for a missile launched from Pakistan, the visitors were inconsequential, and she gained comfort from having her trusted captain by her side when decisions might need to be made in seconds. Jedeja stared at Shahbaz on the screen.

"I regret to inform you that the religious zealot has compromised our systems, and we did not find the hack in time. Embedded AI malware has executed a launch code for one of our Hatf XVII missiles."

The second secure holo-com on the credenza flickered to life. Malhotra rushed to it, entered a code, and the holographic image of Lieutenant General Tomar appeared framed by the Battle Desk.

His gaze locked onto Jedeja. "General, confirming one incoming missile." He named the target coordinates and Indian city. The Blue Impact Timer on the wall behind him registered 00:09:19 and counted down the seconds.

Jedeja turned back to Shahbaz. "Is the incoming missile nuclear armed?"

His eyes were wet. "Yes."

She trembled. "Then you know policy demands a counterstrike." The words tasted like ash on her tongue.

"I know."

The slaughter represented by the two holo-coms on opposite corners of her office desk made her dizzy.

She turned to the Battle Desk. "Lieutenant General Tomar, report. Provide standard response protocol."

"Incoming missile on course to target. Impact now in eight minutes. Counterstrike policy requires attacking one city and the launch facilities. I have entered the coordinates. Two missiles armed and ready for gold codes to initiate."

She turned to the hotline display of General Shahbaz again. "I'm sorry. We must follow protocol."

Jedeja kept the connection to the Pakistani general to provide him some small kindness. He would know exactly what she was doing, but no secrets would be revealed. His holo-com display stayed active.

She walked slowly toward the second com to stare into the watery eyes of Tomar. "Lieutenant General Tomar, per the Indian nuclear response policy, we are obligated under the current circumstances to launch the two missiles that you have now readied. I order this counterattack. Enter your codes." She fumbled with the encrypted gold codes, entered the numbers, and hit *SEND*. The goddess Kali cast a shadow over the room.

Tomar looked up from his control panel. "Two Agni-13 missiles are away." Behind him, the Red Impact Timer began a countdown at 00:08:27.

On the hotline holo-com, General Shahbaz clasped and unclasped his hands. His gaze met hers, equal parts panic, regret, and competence. "Your missiles are detected. Your second missile is aimed at this master launch facility."

"Yes, I know. That is policy." Jedeja watched her counterpart's face spasm. Her mind had to stay on the rails of protocol. Her heart would break at the actions they were taking without it.

"I regret to inform you that per our own policy, if our master facility is targeted, then our protocol is to launch all missiles."

Jedeja froze. "This is madness. Then I'm required to order a massive counterstrike."

General Shahbaz daubed the sweat from his forehead. "Yes, this is madness."

She counted an eternity in the next few seconds before he spoke again.

"We cannot destroy both countries, two civilizations. If I only send one more missile against your control facility, then that is two missiles each, and one each to a city and one each to a master launch facility. No one could fault us and find the treatment unequal. If we stop there, will you agree that India will not attack again?"

Jedeja exhaled noisily, some small part of the tightness in her chest easing. "I swear with Shiva as my witness that we won't fire more than the two missiles already dispatched."

"I will abandon our policy, abandon my orders. I swear before Allah that we'll not launch more than two missiles, one already approaching and one against your launch facility."

"Thank you. Goodbye, General. Go with Allah."

"My blessings on your next life. Goodbye, General."

The hotline com winked off. On the remaining holo-com unit, Lieutenant General Tomar looked up. "A second incoming missile detected, heading at our facility. Impact in 00:07:01."

"Broadcast to all nuclear facilities that I order lock down and no further attacks. No response."

His gaze met hers. "Acknowledged. Goodbye, General." His voice broke.

Malhotra staggered against the desk. "Why was it necessary to attack the launch facilities?"

"For our honor. And theirs."

Jedeja at last noticed the two Americans sitting dumbly on the office sofa. They hadn't moved or spoken during the past five minutes.

The elder businessman did not seem to be processing the situation. "Should we come back later?"

"Only if you're reincarnated," she said.

His eyes widened.

The younger businessman wrestled with his CLAIR, crying. "I can't find a signal in here."

"Sorry," said Malhotra. "It's a secure military facility. No signal."

The businessman sobbed and hyperventilated. "Harper. Karla." It was all he could get out. He hugged his father-in-law, who absently touched his arm.

The older man said to no one in particular, "What've I done to deserve this?"

The alarms still blared, but there was nothing to do now. Malhotra staggered to her side, and Jedeja wrapped her in a heavy hug.

"Captain, thank you for your service, and for your precious friendship. Goodbye."

Tears streamed down Malhotra's face, and she collapsed onto the sofa.

General Jedeja sat down heavily on her desk chair. She closed her eyes and focused on her breath. She thought about her son and daughter, maybe a safe twenty-three kilometers away at the high school, and her husband at work, farther still. She bowed her head in prayer to Vishnu, the Preserver.

The end for her was instantaneous.

Even through closed eyelids, General Jedeja saw the dazzling flash from the air burst detonation over the Indian launch facility, and that was all. Within milliseconds, thermal radiation hotter than the sun destroyed everything at ground zero. A massive fireball of ionized gas bloomed. People directly below were vaporized where they stood. The inferno billowed out, and flying birds burst into flames. The blast wave rolled outward with a rumble deep and murderous. It tore trees from their roots and flattened buildings. Scalding glass window shards shot like shrapnel. It mushroomed upward, turning from white to red, then violent purple and then brown to black. Radiation rained down. For people farther away, the inferno sucked the air from their lungs and left them suffocating and dying from radiation. Standing buildings burst into flames, and the following firestorm spread outward from ground zero. The initial wreckage was sucked into the stem of the mushroom cloud, and the debris was driven upward into a seething maelstrom. Booming thunder tolled death across the land. The mushroom hung over the Indian landscape, and fallout spread as the wails of the dying filled the air.

But General Jedeja knew none of this, as she was already with Vishnu.

51

An autocar rushes down the side road on a collision course with our car. The intersection of the two roads is only a few hundred meters ahead. I count down the seconds until it will hit us, but Grandfather isn't paying attention. At the last instant, it slows imperceptibly. Our car clears the intersection, and the other passes crossways behind by a few meters.

My breath comes back. The autocar sways around a curve, and the force pushes me deeper into the seat. It's soft and foreign, like a cloud. Much like this tale of destruction I'm trying to fit in my head.

Give me the hard seat on the buckboard, with Dakota pulling steadily, the reins in my hand, something real to steady myself. When I bring the rig back to the barn, I loosen the cinch and hose him down with cool water from the well. He smells musty-sweet like new spring hay when I brush his mane. Dakota nuzzles into the feed bag, and the world is there under my hand.

The thought of the horse fades, and I'm still in the car, my thoughts swirling with his story.

"And that's how we lost two relatives on my sister's side of the family."

Grandfather's eyes have wrinkles around the edges, but it's hard for me to tell what emotion is goin' on behind them.

"They shoulda seen it coming, like another standing lion. Didn't they ever think to destroy all the nukes?"

"That was its own standing lion. And a wise question, indicting unwise world leadership focused on the wrong issues. Nuclear disarmament moved in fits and starts throughout the last century, much ahead when the US, China, and Russia eliminated nearly all their arsenals, a bit behind when new countries entered the nuclear club. It wasn't until the end of the Climate Wars, that began in earnest with India and Pakistan, that humankind pushed for a countdown to zero nuclear weapons."

"Seems like the whole world was on fire." I'm thinking about the firebots again.

Grandfather nods. "Those regional wars sparked by fights over resources almost spiraled out of control. General horror about nuclear bombs saved us, and countries united to put that genie back in the bottle. And the Global North realized they weren't doing enough to mitigate the suffering in the Global South, so they gave away more free energy plants for air conditioning and to make people's lives livable."

Ma and Pa were really like some earlier generations that faced very tough times and had to step up. Life was goin' along okay for them, just regular challenges, then they came down the hill like a lion. I wonder if they ran away or stood their ground.

"People were also disgusted by religious differences causing war. There were isolated fanatics, but the quibbles seemed insane in the face of fading religious beliefs."

"Ma and Pa left for the Commune to escape the crazy world, to go back to nature? Sometimes Ma treats it like it's her religion."

He laughs. "Escaping to nature can be an alternative religion. But it's not exactly *the* reason."

He seems reluctant to say more. It's a puzzle why they left for the Commune, and Grandfather's still holding something back.

The autocar stops on a hill. Grandfather and I step out, and he doesn't say anything for a few minutes while I take in the spread of buildings below. They go on for hectares and hectares—to the far eastern hills.

Neat roads arrayed in squares bisect many buildings and lead away in four directions. Hundreds of robots load materials into autotrucks. It looks like an anthill that I kicked up once. Factories?

"Who owns this?"

Grandfather coughs. "Technically, you own them. They're robot factories."

I shake my head, not understanding.

"They were nationalized just after you were born. So, we as citizens collectively own the major means of production in the economy. That's how the greatest economic transition in human civilization has played out. So far."

"I don't know that I'll take credit for owning anything I didn't make with my own hands."

"Economics is one of the biggest levers that civilization controls. The dismal science is about growing the whole pie to give everyone what they need and enough of what they want to keep them happy; then the trick is to divide the pie. Automation did grow the pie faster. When robots began to build robots, economic productivity really took off."

I shrug my shoulders. I don't really understand. "Did the US choose a good path?"

"Not the best path. Not as fair as other advanced countries. We failed on the second part—how to divide the pie. Wealth became concentrated in fewer hands. The balance between labor and capital broke, and something had to give. The advanced economies reorganized or headed toward revolution. Many countries attempted versions of utopia because, for the first time in human history, there were adequate goods and resources for everyone to live well."

"You say the US didn't do it right. Is that why we're not top dog socially?"

He leans on his walking stick. "The US could have retained leadership if we figured out a way to transition our economy. Artificial intelligence, robots, and automation created huge amounts of wealth. But we allowed that wealth to be controlled by a very small number of people. That's called an oligarchy, and it never turns out well."

It begins to make some sense.

Grandfather takes hold of my arm. "Let's take a closer look."

We slide back in the autocar, where Robert sits silently. His head swivels, and his luminous lenses move back and forth between us. We turn onto the road and drive down the hill to the plant gate. A bot checks Grandfather's ID, and we park in a lot marked *Tour Visitors*. Crowds of people stroll through the largest building's entrance. I never imagined a building this big could exist.

A robot that looks a lot like Grandfather's Robert approaches. "My name is Oliver. I am your tour leader today."

The robot leads us down a corridor that wraps around one side of the massive building, which is separated from the factory floor by three-story glass windows that look out over hectares of drab concrete floors. The floors house machines near as tall as the roof. Vibrations rumble through the soles of my feet.

Oliver gestures toward the assembly line. "You can watch the manufacturing process for the latest model here. The plant is fully automated." Robots in various stages move down the line.

"Which model are you?" a visitor asks.

"I am an example of this latest model 577." Oliver's forehead glows green. "I recall my power-on was 2125, 0127 11:03 UTC."

"What's the factory capacity?" asks another visitor.

"This plant produces 701,341 units per year." Oliver points toward the assembly line. "Production increased significantly in approximately 2110, following the Climate Wars. The robots took the place of many workers in the more dangerous fields."

Grandfather leans close to my ear. "Eliminating their jobs."

He rests on his walking stick, and I stay next to him. We move slower at the back of the group. At the far end of one building, finished units stand in gleaming rows, and construction robots attach various test equipment. At one station, the bots' lenses light up. It must be the power-on station. It reminds me of the time I watched a clutch of bobwhites hatch after I surprised the hen hiding in her nest in tall grass. Each chick pecked through the shell, and their eyes glowed at first light.

The tour finishes at the shipping dock, where autotrucks line up. Finished units march onto the trucks and strap themselves into pods for delivery. Many people around us shake their heads. I wonder if they share my feeling that I'm standing next to an invading army.

I feel cold, not at all the warm feeling of simple times, like when it was just Rocky and me walking along the creek, singing songs. We sang duets together, but he was better in tune and at remembering the words. Will there ever be simple times again?

Instead of following the rest of the tour group through the exit, Grandfather talks to the human sitting there. Another man joins us. The man wears clothing that look like he's the boss. He talks to Grandfather, then holds his hands like one of the servant bots and nods a lot. He motions us to follow and ushers us to the second floor. We leave Robert at the bottom of the stairs.

The boss man sits across from us wearing an eager-to-please expression. "We have plenty of modern models you can have."

"No, I'd like an older one, like the Mech 461 model." Grandfather's reply is firm but polite.

The man wrings his hands. "But that is a decade old. We may only have a refurbished robot. Surely—"

"Surely I can obtain a second unit of the model that I wish?" Grandfather fixes the man with an imperious gaze.

The man looks something up with his CLAIR. "Yes, sir, for a Level 1, of course. We have one in storage, though it's a bit beaten up."

"That will be fine. We'll wait." Grandfather makes himself comfortable in the chair.

It seems Grandfather is smarter than I thought, and he gets a heck of a lot more respect than I would have expected for such an old guy.

In ten minutes, two women come down the hallway rolling a large box on an auto-dolly. They pop one side off and roll out a robot much taller than Robert. The torso is made of heavier metal than Robert, and it reminds me of the industrial pickers in the vineyard. It has ding marks on the legs and one dent on the right forearm. The two women push buttons and, in a couple of minutes, the bot boots up. The lenses burn with light, and the head swivels. It looks around.

"I'm back." Its voice is a deep growl.

The boss man flutters around us. "Are you certain you want this one?"

"It's perfect." Grandfather uses his CLAIR to accept something.

Grandfather faces the robot, and its lenses focus on him. He taps his chest. I remember now that means he's sending his ID.

"I'm your new Number One. Let's name you Arnold. You can call me Max."

"Hello, Max. Acknowledged." The bot's lenses lock onto him.

"And this is your new Number Two." He points at me.

Arnold swivels his head toward me. He looks a bit scary, and I'm glad I am whatever a Number Two is.

Grandfather shakes hands with the boss man, and we leave. Arnold follows us down the stairs.

"I hate to pull rank like that. But sometimes it comes in handy." Grandfather says it to me, but I'm not sure what he's talking about.

We find the bottom of the stairs, where Robert still stands at attention.

"This is your new friend, Arnold," Grandfather says to Robert.

Robert blinks in acknowledgment, and the two follow us to where the autocar still waits for us in the parking lot.

"What kinds of jobs are left for anyone to do?"

His gaze is on me. "Now you've hit the crux of the problem. What do we do? There are few jobs that anyone can do better than the machines."

"What kinds of things will I ever be able to do?"

"I can't tell the future. None of us can, and neither can the AIs, no matter how much they'll try to convince you. You should choose a career based on some conclusion about what's needed and useful to society. You should choose something you find interesting, something that you might invest your time and passion in to be good at. Then you must deal with the complex, nonlinear world on its terms, and be resilient enough to survive, and thrive."

Ma and Pa somehow got through their tough times, facing what was out in the world. I'm thinking again about the bobwhite chick pecking away until it breaks through its shell, then facing the outside world it's never seen. That's me too.

Grandfather gives an address to Robert. The bot's forehead glows green, and the autocar drives out of the parking lot and back onto the road heading south. The road sign we pass is only necessary for humans. It reads *Arcata 13 Kilometers*.

52

Senator Rex Rysbier—2100 (Texas)

"Harper, I'm so sorry to hear about the tragic loss of both your husband and father." Rex kept his voice soothing as he addressed the pale woman with haunted eyes on his holo-com.

A long pause showed how numb Harper was to the world right now, but she gulped, and her training surfaced. "Thank you, Senator. It's good for you to call at this busy time."

"Busy, indeed. I'm sorry that it's taken several weeks. The international situation has been tense, and we've worked to keep the US out of this mess. You know my approach is always to stick to selling to the rest of the globe but otherwise keep our noses out of these disputes."

Harper shook her head. "That's what Axel and Dad were doing. It's cruel karma they were there at the wrong time."

Rex wore his sympathetic face. "How're you handling this personally? Anything I can do to help you?"

"I've lost the love of my life and my business mentor. I'm attempting to pull my life back together and run the company all at once. I'd like our...my daughter Karla to join me. Maybe she'll come around to that soon. There's nothing you can do, but thank you for asking."

Rex nodded, more comfortable now that the sympathy part was over. "The tragedy in Pakistan was caused by a rogue hacker. I'm pushing legislation for cybersecurity funding and further quantum security technology to protect encrypted communications. That can help your robot communication channels."

"Quantum key distribution is necessary. It's expensive for us to do it ourselves."

"And there's funding for autonomous platforms for border security. Lucrative government contracts will be available soon."

Harper brushed back unruly hair. "Good that these com channels are encrypted. I don't see any change to our arrangement. But how are you handling all the protests?"

The tightrope he walked was always between keeping his donors and his base happy. Besides wars around the world, the growing domestic protests over job losses caused by new tech filled the net news. Rex was ready with a response that kept his cards close.

"That's our top problem. These protests will no doubt worsen over time, so we need to manage them."

"Your populist public statements are that you have their backs."

Big Rex put on his sincere face. "So long as the common classes have the vote, I need to keep them happy. But make no mistake. We share a certainty about who should be running the world. Let me manage that. Remember, I'm behind you one hundred percent."

Rex finished with sympathetic platitudes and closed the portable holo-com. He was sure the regular payments would continue to arrive in his account.

His bodyguard, standing at a polite distance, saw him finish the call, took the holo-com unit, and held the door open to the shiny red sports car waiting at the park gate. "Gassed up and ready to go, sir," he said.

Rex ran his hand along the side of the car, enjoying the smooth lines of his antique collectible Porsche 911. "I'll be back in half an hour."

He slipped behind the wheel and started the gasoline engine. He paused to feel the rumble then revved the engine. The car purred under his hands. He drove past his bodyguard and down the park road.

He took the initial curves slowly, then the muscle memory returned from his last drive, and he fell into the groove of feeling the car respond to his hands. He flowed down the road between the Texas mountain laurels, around turns above variegated rocks, and past the occasional patches of Texas bluebonnets, firewheel, and red poppies.

Rex tossed back his head and whooped into the big sky with a feeling of rebelliousness, of finding his own road. It was astonishing to think that just eighty years earlier, people thought self-driving cars were crazy. People actually drove. And tens of thousands died every year. Now it was a luxury to drive a car since driving on open roads had been banned nationwide. Only in closed parks like this one in the Texas hill country could anyone drive a car, and the skill had disappeared. With all vehicles now electric, it was also the only place anybody could still buy gasoline. Rex enjoyed his car. It was a place he could let his mind loose and think.

His move to the Senate had been well timed, and now he chaired a powerful committee, which allowed him to weave a bigger web of wealthy donors. That was the first step.

Rex eased around another curve, feeling the wind through his hair. He thought about the MEDFLOW unit tucked above his right hip, microdosing him daily with anti-aging therapies. He was forty-seven, in good health, at the top of his game. If all went well, he'd be positioned to run for president someday.

Now, there was his interesting dilemma. How to win an election in the face of this situation, given his populist base, while the money needed for victory was controlled by those owning the means of production? Increasingly, manufacturing came from robot factories. He needed the money to fund the distribution media to reach voters to be elected. But the robots were putting those voters in his base out of work.

It was undeniable that earned income credits tied to jobs would not suffice. Soon, jobs would decline well below the number of people seeking a job, which they needed to give some meaning to their lives. How to square the circle? A plan was forming about a new system to replace how the economic system worked but kept the right people in charge.

He'd need to work both sides. He'd tell the voters that a new system would be fairer, a meritocracy. That was a lie because his plan was only good for people like Harper and himself, people who deserved to oversee the world. Harper wouldn't see it that way at first, because she would need to jettison old beliefs about how to organize economics, but in time it would become obvious. The trick was to use a false carrot to cause the non-contributors to society to give up their greatest treasure.

Harper was a pawn in a much bigger game, his path to the White House. In the end, with his Levels plan, Rex and his children would reap the benefits.

53

Karla Graves MacGyver—2101 (Massachusetts)

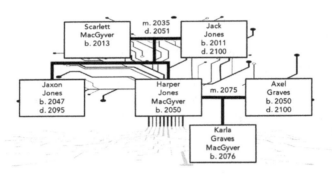

Karla pulled her collar up tighter and glided over the new snow. A meter had fallen last night from yet another unseasonal storm rolling through. Boston weather had become random. The past half century had been overall hotter but also subject to extreme storms. The robotic snow removal trucks were out in force. One cleared the side road, while two robots cleaned up snow at the hard-to-reach corners.

She turned off Charles Street toward Kendall Square. The hoverboard under her feet turned smoothly with a twist of her hips, zipping a few inches above the wet surface. She often enjoyed walking in the city, but the board kept her feet dry this morning.

Off a cross street, she saw people standing in a long line at what looked like the public housing office. Her mind flicked back to the snow removal robots, an example of all the jobs lost. Karla shuddered, and the hover board wobbled before it auto-corrected.

She reached the biolab, put on her lab coat, and started the morning experiments. Her dissertation on a class of complex genetic diseases was almost complete. Then she could finish her PhD and begin work that would directly help people suffering from these multifactorial ailments.

The genetic sequencing equipment hummed in the room below her, observable through large windows. This was a small factory in itself. Biomaterials went in one end, the sequencing equipment and readout computers on the other, and they both fed displays with experimental results.

Karla liked the quiet work analyzing problems, like puzzles, and then testing possible solutions. It was a relief to escape into her science work, to not think about her father's and grandfather's deaths several months earlier. Beyond dealing with her own grief, the world outside was aflame, and the daily news of war left her anxious. The Climate Wars had not yet brought the US to the battlefield, but each month's new eruption seemed to bring the opportunity closer, even as diplomats called for calm.

As she waited for an experiment to complete, she sipped her coffee and thought about the upcoming dissertation defense. Despite her efforts to identify a genetic cure for one disease, she was unsure whether she could recommend its adoption.

A century ago, there had been thousands of genetic diseases. Now most of the single-gene, monogenic ailments had been cured, from Tay-Sachs and sickle cell diseases to cystic fibrosis and many others.

Gene therapies were then developed to treat many of the chromosomal diseases. There had been some hesitancy because of ethical concerns, but she had never really understood that when she studied it. The obvious causes were point mutations and missing or duplicated genes or whole chromosomes. No one would wish to live with these conditions or wish them on loved ones. She was glad work went on to treat these conditions pretty smoothly.

The multifactorial genetic disorders they worked on now were complex in many ways. They stemmed from a combination of gene mutations and other factors, such as diet, chemical exposure, and lifestyle choices. Since these were not universally harmful mutations, the field grappled with difficult ethical questions about how much bioscientists should tamper with the human genome.

Beyond treating classes of genetic diseases, new enhancements had become possible. Many bioscientists called for a ban of all such "cosmetic" engineering. They questioned whether any human should be permitted to change their eye color in exotic ways, particularly if that trait would then be passed through the germline to the human species.

More controversial yet was to engineer genes that may enhance traits such as intelligence, strength, certain ideas of beauty, and social traits such as extroversion, or even propensity to violence. All were in the realm of possible now, and she agreed it was a slippery slope. Using the technology could embed modifications into the DNA of *Homo sapiens* that had potentially tragic unintended consequences for the fitness and survivability of the species.

It had been easier to reach agreement about simpler genetic diseases. The bioscience field had come together and created a consensus among scientists, ethicists, religious leaders, and members of the public to create lists of acceptable genetic manipulation. But, faced with complex discussions, the field was mired in debate, unable to enforce decisions about the next potential areas for genetic manipulation. The US and many other countries had laws banning germline genetic modification, but the bans were not universal, and no global enforcement structure was in place. She found the ethical debates intriguing, and she was forming her own opinions. Her research showed the promise, and pitfalls, of her field.

Her CLAIR flashed with a message. A visitor at the biolab entrance was asking to see her. Karla confirmed her identity and approved entry. Moments later, her mother walked through the door, and she greeted her with a big hug.

"What are you doing here? I didn't know you were anywhere near Boston."

"Remember that Dad ordered a bigger yacht built in Hamburg, Germany? I couldn't send it back, so I eventually decided to take it in memory of the lifestyle your dad dreamed about. I picked her up and sailed her here on her maiden voyage. Good thing they finished construction. It's heating up around Europe." Her mother grinned. "She's a real beauty. Forty meters long, six cabins, and she'll do thirty knots."

"You sailed it all the way here?"

"With my CFO, Nora, and a crew of six robots. Nine days across the Atlantic." Her expression dimmed. "It's been tough with Dad gone, and the boat was my distraction."

"My work is my distraction." Karla felt the cloud hover overhead anew.

"Which is another reason I'm here. Aren't you close to earning your degree?"

"I just need to complete confirmation testing on the experimental work, and I've nearly finished writing the dissertation. Only a couple months to go."

"Then there will be a doctor in the family. Good job." Her mother patted her arm. Her mouth was set in a line. "But we should talk about what's next. With Dad and Grandpa gone, there's just me managing the company. It's growing so fast that it would make your head spin. I need help."

Karla pulled away from her hand. "That wasn't ever the deal."

Her mother's gaze flicked over the lab supplies on her shelves, not finding anything of interest. "We should have pushed back when you changed your major to bioscience."

"I never had an interest in robotics. And now I really don't have the background to help you. My calling is bioscience. That's what I love."

Her mother gave her that look that always made people give her whatever she wanted. "It's the family business. There's so much money to be made now that it's at scale. It's a money machine. And it's the way to get my designs out into the world."

Karla changed gears. She was mostly immune to that look. "And how long can that last? Job losses from automation are putting people on the streets. Politicians like Rex Rysbier are beating a populist drum. This can't go on forever. And it might end badly."

Her laugh was harsh. "Don't worry about Rysbier. I know him well. Let's say we have a special relationship."

Karla looked into her eyes. "But can he be trusted?"

"Yes, of course."

Karla wondered how she could be so sure. Managing the company had to be a heavy lift for her mother to undertake alone. Maybe she wasn't savvy about the political minefields. But robotics was not the career path she had ever wanted.

"If I leave the research now, I'll never have a research career in bioscience."

"Another MacGyver like me, stubborn and sticking to your ideas." Mom was angry now.

Karla's tone softened. "Mom, I can do more good for the world in this field. There are still many discoveries to be made."

Karla knew her mother found self-definition as a leading robotics designer, so she left unvoiced her belief that robotics now hurt as many people as it helped. In the silence, she saw the moment her mother relented, or at least decided to abandon this approach. Karla feared it was a temporary retreat.

"Can I ask you to at least keep an open mind? You might find that seeing these machines all over with our company name on them, and making money from your ideas, is fun too."

"Mom, I love you." Karla gave her a hug.

The money argument carried no weight, and these were not her designs. But Karla knew her mother needed help, and her mind fought between loyalty and calling.

54

Arnold and Robert sit across from us in similar frozen pos-
tures, their lenses scanning the scenery outside. Grand has
been subdued since we started driving again. I let him think.
He's a modern-day Rip Van Winkle, so separated from the
twenty-second century for most of his fourteen years as to
have been asleep.

"You say I can decide what to do. What about Ma and Pa?"
I see my own rebellious streak in his gaze.

I touch his arm. "We should, of course, discuss it with
them so they can give their opinions. Now, you're collecting
information so you can make wise decisions."

"What options do I have?"

"One option is to stay here with me and go to high school."
I say it with a little reluctance, as I have one reservation that
must be resolved.

"And leave the Commune?"

"That's right. Your Ma especially will miss seeing you every day. You give her comfort. But it's not a place you should
stay."

I don't yet want to tell him why, even though I can see
he's getting impatient for the truth. We're not at that point in
his story. The autocar turns into a cozy high school campus.

"That's one reason we're stopping here. You can consider
the possibility during a tour."

Two modern buildings, an older library, and a gymnasium cluster around a central square, with radiating paths
connecting to other smaller buildings. Students lounge on
the grass in groups. A girl plays with a dog, some unfamiliar

bioengineered breed with chartreuse fur. It's a vibrant splash against the lawn. Several students kick a soccer ball on the bordering playing field. We stop in the lot across from the main building.

I lean on my walking stick to climb the steps, leading Grand. A robot at the reception desk validates my ID, and a tall woman greets us and introduces herself as the school Head.

"Mr. MacGyver, I received your request for a tour, and I'm delighted to show you and your grandson our school."

She walks beside him. I trail them so I can better see what he finds interesting. He asks no questions when she describes the academic classes. Grand seems intimidated outside a lab teeming with students, where groups of four to six students cluster around holo-displays in animated conversation. But he asks about the problems they're challenged to solve.

"Let's find out," the Head says.

She approaches one table and asks the students.

"We're testing how the AI sets a notional price for our fashion design. So, the price isn't just based on cost. It depends on what we want compared to other choices," says one.

Another points to the screen that shows a graph. "We tweak the prompts and then see what happens to the model."

"A complex problem of economics and social psychology," the Head says.

The three students smile, and Grand looks bashfully at the floor.

We move on to a machine shop, and his body relaxes. Grand is entranced by the many demonstration devices, surrounded by robotic arms and control screens, with students at each table asking questions and manipulating the gadgets. I don't mention to him that the machines are a history lesson instead of a development lab, since AIs solve all the simple engineering problems.

In a room beyond the machine shop, three students wear HDSETs and engage in conversation. The Head taps one on the shoulder and asks about the lesson.

He pulls his HDSET down. "We're having a discussion with Thomas Edison, and he's explaining how he invented the lightbulb. Then, we'll talk to Dr. Sanchez, who found the cure for muscular dystrophy. It's to compare experimental techniques over time." The boy's excited face turns to Grand. "Would you like to see Mr. Edison's avatar? It's like he's standing right here."

He wore a HDSET to watch the cyclone earlier today, and Grand puts on the extra unit and stands with the other students, now all of them with the AI avatar in their VR world. The Head and I talk for a few minutes. He finishes participating and shyly thanks them.

We enter the gym and watch a ball game in progress. Kids wearing HDSETs exercise in pods around the central floor. One corner has a giant video screen like my own, projecting Bridalveil Fall from Yosemite. Grand stares at it for a full minute, and when he turns his face is calm. The tour finishes with a stop at the food service, an airy building with students filling trays from the dispensers and clustering at tables in noisy conversation.

We walk outside and stand at the edge of a playing field. The Head examines Grand closely. He presents himself well and is polite and engaged. I know she's wondering about his previous education. That's one I can't help him with. He answers her questions respectfully.

"Yes, ma'am, I've been studyin' all the materials every day. It's me and my teachbot, Rocky. He and I make a good team. We talk all the time, and I've completed all the requirements through eighth grade, and now I'm workin' on ninth-grade classes."

"That's wonderful," she says. "There are some tests you would need to take to be sure of your preparation before matriculating, so we can place you properly."

Grand nods in understanding and watches the game on the field. "I haven't had the chance to play any sports. Rocky isn't nimble enough. What's that game?"

"It's mod soccer," I say. "It's the popular replacement for American football. It has less contact but blends European soccer with football-style plays." I encourage him to watch it up close.

"I'll just look around a bit?"

The Head extends her hand in invitation for him to walk anywhere he wants to. He excuses himself.

"A nice young man," the Head says. "We'll need to test him, but I expect we can find a space for your grandson. He'd add a certain diversity of experience to our school."

I satisfy myself that only the one test is necessary before his enrollment can be confirmed, and thank her as she takes her leave.

From the corner of my eye, I watch him on the grass, tossing a ball with the chartreuse dog. Two students are talking with him. He sees me, says goodbye to the students, and walks back.

He wears a quizzical expression. "That's a weird color dog. But friendly."

"Just different on the outside; the same inside; and the dog didn't have a choice in the matter. And the students?"

"They're friendly too."

I'm leaning on his arm down the stairs as we leave. "What else do you think?"

"Some of the girls are kinda cute. The school lets you play with some interestin' stuff." There is a light in his eyes.

There can't be many girls his age at the Commune. Maybe he'll learn to deal with the socialization challenges when the time comes.

"There's no need for any decisions now, but do consider what you've seen."

We walk to the school entrance gate. Robert and Arnold are waiting, and the autocar is nowhere in sight.

"Another user requested the vehicle, and in any event, there is no time to reach your appointment by road, so I released it. With your Level status, I was able to procure faster transportation."

A minute later, a soft hum precedes the zip of a sleek autohover toward the field. It settles on the far edge, and Robert helps me through the door. We sit, the two robots sit opposite us, and the machine rises briskly, leaving a dust devil on the high school field below.

55

Buzz Henderson—2110 (Yosemite)

Max suggested they make camp at the large granite rock on the north shore of Washburn Lake. He'd told Buzz about the view south toward Isberg Pass and suggested the three of them, all senior backpackers, escape into the woods. Max had started the fire burning with a roar, but it was now down to coals, and a large pile of wood nearby would last them into the night. Max's brother-in-law, Sam, had already prepared the three trout he caught that afternoon, and they now sizzled in the pan. Buzz could relax, since he'd completed his task of carrying filtered water from the lake and set the synjugs on a rock. He settled on a log to watch the last vestiges of sunset.

"Great campsite, Max. You've been here before?"

"A couple times. No fires are allowed above about 2900 meters, but we're only at 2300, so we can still build a fire in these old fire rings." A faraway look shadowed his face. "My first trip to Yosemite was near here, at Bernice Lake, up the canyon."

Max searched through his pack and found his special synjug. He poured three whiskeys into cups and passed them around.

He raised his in salute. "Buzz, welcome back to the States."

They all took long swigs, and Buzz felt the liquor relax tired muscles from the day's uphill trek.

Sam tucked his cup between his feet. "How long were you away?"

"Jessica and I spent almost a decade living in Berlin. We enjoyed the European social equity and the lifestyle that went with it. Now, though, it's not eco to travel as much, and we missed our friends here."

Sam flipped the fish. "I think I first met Jessica at Max's wedding, and then on that trip to Maine."

Buzz said, "I married her three years after Max married your sister. Feels like yesterday and a lifetime ago all at once."

"You're coming up on, what? Fifty-two years of marriage soon." Max shook the synjug to test its fullness.

"Always a step behind you." Buzz toasted again with his cup.

Max dropped his gaze at the comment, and Buzz winced at the memory that Tadala had received a recent medical diagnosis, though Max had not shared the details. Now that he was back in the US permanently, he vowed to find out if there was anything he could do to help his best friend.

Max recovered his high spirits quickly. "They've had a successful life with two fine kids," Max said to Sam. "And three grandchildren. Buzz, you're way ahead of me there." Max led another round swigging the whiskey.

"Sam, you retired a few years ago, right?" Buzz asked.

"Yes, in 2103, when I turned seventy-five, same age as Max. Though I still hang around the union hall to talk with the younger folks." Sam added more butter to the pan, then his gaze turned back to Buzz. "I had thought about going to travel sometime. Germany sounds exciting."

"Why don't you go?" Buzz asked. "Your American passport can get you a long-term visitation visa there."

Sam mulled over the comment as he took the pan from the fire. He served up the fish, and they devoured the meal, complete with potatoes roasted in the coals and equally slathered with butter.

"Sam, this beats regular camp food," Max said, leaning back on his rock. "Though we're putting a bit of carbon into the air."

The fire burned down, and Buzz regularly added wood as they sipped whiskey. The trees around them reflected the dancing flames and appeared to draw closer in the gathering darkness beyond the campfire.

Sam said, "You two have nothing to be sorry about with the environment. You did your part."

Buzz flourished his cup at Max. "Especially your brother-in-law here. A hero, inducted into the Environmental Pantheon of Heroes."

"Buzz, we were always a team."

"Sam, don't listen to him," Buzz said. "Why'd I stick with him all those years? Because Max was the one to finish the job." Buzz took another swig. He thought Sam should know this, that everyone should know it. "Because Max doesn't just talk about solving a problem. He solves the fucking problem. For some problems, you can't wait or mess around."

"We did the best we could," Max said. "But we were still behind the curve. We finally got to zero carbon emissions, and we worked to reverse climate change, but the effects from delay will linger for millennia. For example, the tiger has disappeared from the wild in India."

"The black rhino went extinct in Malawi, and the rest of Africa." Sam shook his head but then brightened. "But now they're using synthetic biology to try to replicate the species. It seems like it might work."

"The Climate Wars are behind us. Let's drink to zero carbon." Buzz raised his cup, and they banged them loudly.

"You knock a few problems down, and you move on to the next one. That's just life," Max said.

Buzz put chocolate sauce into a pan to heat on the coals and poured it over the dessert he brought. "Trail angel cake. Let's see how chocolate goes with whiskey."

Buzz found the whiskey was a nice change from Münchner bier. He leaned back against a pine tree.

Sam cleared his throat. "I see another big problem every day at the union. The robots are leaving nothing behind for our tradesmen. It's getting worse in other industries too."

"And what's the answer?" Buzz tried not to slur his words. He was feeling the effects of the elevation but sipped the whiskey again anyway.

"This guy, Senator Rysbier, has some ideas. He's talking about nationalizing the robot factories. A lot of union guys are following him."

"Big Rex Rysbier? Horse pucky. I've seen the news feeds about him in Europe. He's the same guy pushing for his pet idea of 'Levels.' You're not buying that, are you?" Buzz studied Sam in the dim light of the dying fire.

"He makes a good argument about it. Levels on merit. Some sort of acknowledgment for the people who've worked hard their whole lives, like you two, like Tadala." Sam sounded gruff and defensive.

"Horse pucky." Max laughed out loud. "Buzz, I've always loved your way with words."

Buzz wouldn't be waylaid from calling Sam with his point. "I hear Rysbier is blaming climate migrants for taking jobs. But all the autonomous drones and robots have effectively sealed the borders, both for the US and Europe." Buzz tried to see Sam's eyes. "He's putting this false fear into people. Sam, weren't you an immigrant too?"

"Your union friends have a real fear. Robot growth can swallow everything." Max's words, now serious, floated over their triangle of logs. "How will economies work, facing something we've never seen?"

"We should've had employee stock ownership. Give everyone a stake in these companies. That would've been most fair." Buzz had always favored the idea, and not just stock options for some people like himself.

"The corporate executives were too greedy to ever push that far," Sam said. "It would've been a good idea."

"We could have taxed away the excess profits," Max said. He leaned back on the log and grew quiet. "But maybe that's not enough. It's too late. We have to nationalize the robot factories. We just need to be sure about what we trade away in the bargain. Reducing people to a Level based on their supposed usefulness doesn't seem like the thing to accept."

"Brother, they need you on the union bargaining team," Sam said, and they all laughed.

"Let's drink to that," Buzz said as the last coals died. With the cold mountain air enveloping them, it was a good time to turn in, so they banked the fire and blundered off to their tents. As Buzz rolled into his sleeping bag, his last thoughts mixed whiskey with worry about the following this Rysbier politician was assembling.

56

Harper Jones MacGyver—2110 (The Caribbean)

Her robot had him pinned against the rail, its hand around Rysbier's neck. It was tempting to just tell it to squeeze more.

"No. No. Let me explain." Rex choked the words out.

Could she get away with it? Thoughts raced through her mind, anger trying to override her logic. It was a moonless night, with no one else on the aft deck of her sixty-meter yacht, and they were far offshore in the Caribbean. A push and Rysbier would be over the rail, with just a splash to be heard. A drowning accident. Harper noticed the cameras. Could fake videos replace their recordings? It wasn't her area of technical expertise, and law enforcement no doubt had techniques to discover tampering. The odds were not good. It would be poor form to kill a senator, as much as she might enjoy it now.

"Release him, Brünnhilde." The robot released its grip, and Rex staggered to sit in the cockpit.

"I thought they couldn't hurt a human." Rysbier coughed out the words.

"They can't. Unless the fingers have data errors in the squeeze function." Harper's face somersaulted from sneer to scowl. "Explain, then, why this isn't a sellout. After the years helping you, putting you in this position, that's what I get? My company pilfered just when it's coining money? Money that you need to win? It's crazy." Harper spat out the words.

She sat threateningly close, hovering over Rex. The robot stood next to her, its lenses still flashing.

Rex rested against the deck cushions and massaged his throat. "I've got a big idea, a deep idea. I need time to explain it. You'll understand the beauty of it."

"Take your time." Harper waited in the darkness. The yacht sailed on autopilot, a blue stream of bioluminescence twinkling in its wake. She fumed over all the dark credit$ that she and Jack had funneled to Rysbier over the years. When Jack died, she'd carried on the relationship and had even kept it hidden from Karla when she joined the company. Karla's initial doubts about Rex came back to her, and she wondered if Karla had more intuition than she did when it came to people.

Rysbier stopped rubbing his neck. "First, you must recognize that the current situation is untenable. Robotics companies will soon control the production of most everything. The exponential growth in robots is replacing so many jobs. Wealth is concentrating like never before. People are rising against the system everywhere. Soon, revolution will be at hand."

"You think?" Harper didn't wish to hear about the world beyond her company and yacht.

"I've been dealing with these international problems for a decade now—the Climate Wars, collapse in trade. We've responded with restrictions on migration, but people still want to come here to escape their countries. At home, automation has left too many people aimless and agitating for something new." Rex paused, then continued with emphasis. "I've tried to keep us isolated with an America First policy. But throughout Europe, they're taking everything away from the makers who built their wealth, and we can't keep that news out."

"The government controls the police and army." Harper glowered in the darkness.

"They too are losing jobs. Many former police and military would be on the side of the rioters."

"We have the rule of law in this country." The dire picture painted by Rysbier was sinking in, and she realized the weakness of her reply.

"And the law can be changed here and elsewhere." Rysbier's eyes narrowed. "Open your eyes. Robot factories have been nationalized around the world. The alternative that barely might be possible here in the US is to tax away all your profits. But then you'll hold a worthless asset."

"I built this company, and I own it."

Rex chuckled quietly. "There's a story from the Soviet Union two centuries ago. Stalin and his apparatchiks ended up using all the best villas, all the best art, furniture, and belongings of the previous Czar and nobility. The bottoms of the furniture pieces were still stamped with 'Property of the State.' It doesn't matter who owns something in name. What matters is who controls it. That control can be locked in for multiple generations."

"Explain your alternative."

Rysbier rubbed his hands together. "The US is a country that respects property rights more than most. We need to nationalize the robot factories—"

"I'd destroy the company before I'd let it be nationalized." The thought of allowing her company to be taken away was anathema to her.

Rysbier snickered. "Don't shrug yet. I'm offering you a quid pro quo. The Levels Acts."

"I'm listening."

"Among other provisions, set Levels, from 1 down to 99. Each citizen is assigned a Level based on their merit to US society. That's the trade."

"But why would anyone agree to that?" Harper was unconvinced.

"I've been testing the idea at some of my rallies. I'm arguing that the Levels are based on merit. Everyone wants to believe that they have merit based on what they do. And it gives them comfort against others they fear will compete with them."

Harper grunted. "Like the migrants who are pushing on our borders?"

"Exactly. We'll still need helpers because many people would prefer a human to a robot for personal service jobs.

With falling population everywhere, we'll still let some in. The Levels will keep the right folks in charge."

"Will they be based on merit?"

Rex laughed. "Well, sort of. But we know how those systems can work." The side of Rysbier's face was lit by the blue effulgence of the water. "Your children and the next generations will have status protection. We can ensure the right people—the makers—stay at the top."

"Who runs General RoboMechs? What happens to my money in the bank and all my stuff?" Harper swept her hand over the yacht.

"Of course, you keep the wealth you have accumulated. In fact, nationalization will end further talk about wealth taxes. And with your new, very high Level, of course you'll still be CEO."

It was difficult to let go of long-held ideas, and she clenched her fist at the image of no longer owning the company.

Rex smiled in the darkness like a Cheshire cat. "Just think on it. This idea is a win for all of us. It keeps our kind in charge and avoids the revolution that would wash away all we've built."

57

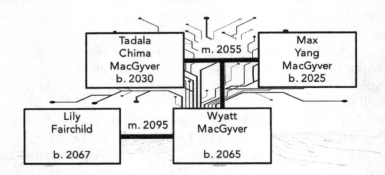

The driving martial beat pounded her ears, and fireworks shot skyward over the stage draped with patriotic bunting.

"And now, Senator 'Big Rex' Rysbier!" The MC's cry boomed out.

Rysbier burst forward to a roar of applause from the assembled crowd. Lily let her PIDA estimate it at ten thousand, a fact she noted for her report. She pushed her hair back under a red-white-and-blue kerchief, which, with her jeans and T-shirt emblazoned with Rysbier's logo, allowed her to blend in with the rest of his fans.

Rex raised his hands. "Look around. Know there are others just like you. Your brothers and sisters. Washington doesn't care about you. But I see you. And together we can change this country!"

A rumble of approval swept through like thunder. Rysbier launched into a litany of grievances against the powerful, against faceless corporations closing factories, and against robots taking jobs. Lily recorded everything with her CLAIR, which transcribed it so that it would be ready to edit later for her report.

Rysbier's sweet voice wafted on the soft breeze, and Lily was drawn in by his description of corporate overlords, them making decisions without real accountability to all those affected. Her painful meeting with Zoe, whom she thought was her mentor, flashed in her mind. She'd been passed over for partner. She still had a job in an "of counsel" attorney role in the firm, but she'd always be indentured to Zoe's whims and demands. She felt helpless to control her future and angry about it. Lily saw expressions on faces surrounding her with similar emotions and felt the power of what Rysbier was creating, a tribal oneness here, even as her mind rebelled against its logic.

"Look at those robot factories, like a giant spider spewing out AIs in robots, their evil spawn taking your jobs. They spread contagion across the land. You've lost your livelihoods, but you gain nothing. Why should the few own all the factories building those job-stealers? There must be a better way."

The crowd cheered with vigor now.

Rex segued back to the list of his audience's oppressors, which also included the trickle of climate refugees who were still allowed entry visas. Strange, Lily thought, that the crowd was buying the argument, though the actual numbers were small. The main issue, she knew, was that people were being replaced by robots, not migrants. That was the key concern of the unions that her law firm represented and the reason she was undercover at the rally.

His body trembled with indignation. "They must earn their place in our great country, just as you did. They shouldn't jump ahead of you. We need a system that recognizes your merit—your hard-earned spot."

Lily listened as Rysbier laid out his solution, a deal to force the owners to sacrifice their companies. She looked around to see the audience clapping in agreement. Did they understand what they would give up? She shook her head as if to clear it of cobwebs, and bile rose in her throat.

Rysbier's volume rose at his conclusion. "We will take back control from those who tyrannize us. You have merit. You will have new power to prove your worth. You're the salt of the earth."

Drones hung in the air around the stage, recording from various angles, live-streaming the rally to the net. As Big Rex raised his trademark clenched fist to leave the stage, three autonomous jets roared overhead and dipped their wings in unison. Where did he find the money to arrange that?

The crowd still clapped boisterously as she exited the gates. People streamed out into the poor neighborhood bordering the rally park. When the crowd thinned to a few walking near her, Lily checked her CLAIR for references to the rally. Already, viewership rose in a shocking peak on net media. Of course, she thought, large sums of money drove broader audience engagement. She frowned. The problem was that mass communication under the control of whomever has the most money meant a few could control the message. The information was also probably manipulated, feeding specific parts of Rysbier's message to targeted audiences.

She walked on the cracked sidewalk past several shuttered businesses. Lily hadn't visited such a neighborhood for several years, and this part of the city had changed for the worse. Rex's message filled her mind again.

A rundown pawnshop ahead had some activity, and she glanced through the open door as she passed.

A man beckoned to her. "We have a few things you might like."

The novelty of shopping in person stopped her. All the retail outlets left were integrated with bespoke AI sizing and drone delivery, but this store seemed a step back in time. Curiosity aroused, she stepped inside. Along one wall, the cases held an odd collection of items. Vintage jewelry filled one case. A few musical instruments, including a tiny keyboard and an odd wind instrument filled another. An electronic game from the '80s sat on a shelf. A hoverboard leaned against a wall. Hunting equipment, including a crossbow, filled the corner cabinet. She admired a piece of jewelry to be polite.

A man stepped from the back room. Metal gleamed as he slipped a container in his jacket and left the store. She realized the item contained bullets.

"You sell those too?"

"Sure. Legal so long as you log 'em." The owner lowered his gaze. "Though I only sell them for dark credit$."

Ah, yes, of course." Lily tried to look knowledgeable. "And the gun that goes with them?"

"Also not illegal but tough to get your hands on." His voice dropped to a whisper. "You can find designs on the dark net for them, though, and just print one yourself."

She thought of the 3D printer in Wyatt's office and pretended not to be shocked. She pointed to a vintage ring. The proprietor removed it from the case and fitted it to her finger. He mentioned the price. She wanted him to remember her.

"I'll take it." The gem glistened with a clarity she suddenly felt.

◆

Zoe stared at Lily. "Your conclusion is that Senator Rysbier's objective isn't to assist people like the union members?"

"I doubt he has any such interest at all. It's all a sham, driven by his, and probably his donors', greed."

"But there's the nationalization of all the robot factories." Zoe brushed back her red hair.

Lily leaned forward, enunciating her argument forcefully. "It sounds enticing. But the quid pro quo is that Rysbier wants to compensate the owners by instituting a new system of 'Levels' that give each person a Level, from 1 at the top, to 99 at the bottom. I'm sure the robot factory owners will be promised high rankings. Then, afterward, the Levels will, supposedly, be adjusted based on merit. There's the rub. Once you put the concept into practice, you can use them to restrict certain groups. Who knows how this system could reduce the rights workers have now."

Zoe smiled, but not the warm expression Lily had often received when she first joined the firm. Lily now felt like an underling rather than a colleague, especially knowing that the woman in front of her hadn't vouched for her making partner. Zoe would imagine herself a Level 1, Lily thought, and tried to keep her face neutral to hide her real emotions. At times like this, she didn't need to pretend at all to feel empathy with the average worker.

Zoe folded her hands. "Imperiling democracy is a bold charge. What evidence do you have? Politicians are allowed to campaign."

"I've compared what Rysbier says at his rallies with many messages on social media. Those messages are targeted to the extreme, even down to the individual listener. I think he is using un-watermarked digital twins."

"Digital twins?" Zoe raised her eyebrows.

"A sort of digital deepfake. A duplicate of Rysbier himself. But with messages targeted to each person."

"Huh. So, the listener believes the digital twin is really Rysbier talking with them personally?" Zoe's face showed she was intrigued by the subterfuge.

"Of course, it's impossible to tell a digital twin from a real person without the prominent watermarks. But it's illegal not to mark digital twins."

"So, how does he foil the watermark requirements?"

"I don't know yet. Maybe he's found the money to pay for quantum decryption to remove them. He's certainly found the money for other excessive campaign techniques. For now, it's an unproven suspicion." Lily frowned. "But I believe he has millions of slightly different digital twins giving each voter exactly what they want to hear. And he has the funds, from somewhere, to push his messages to the country."

"An interesting theory." Zoe seemed half-convinced. "If true, then he's tainting the information commons. And that's a good strategy to win if everyone trusts you are on their side."

"I'll continue to find the evidence."

"Try to follow the money. It's good to see your aggressiveness on this project. But we need evidence that Rysbier is unsympathetic to the unions' interests, because he talks a good game. Continue to attend his rallies undercover and report back."

Lily gathered up the portable holo-display, nodded tightly, and left Zoe's office. It was a pat on the back, a modest signal that today she still had a job. Lily checked her MEDFLOW. She'd dialed down her medical cocktail, and now she decreased it more. The aggressive version of herself was going to finally do some good.

<hr />

She found Wyatt sitting with his feet on his desk when she returned home that evening.

He looked up with an enormous smile. "It's the most progress that we've made to move legislation forward in years." His eyes shone. "The House committee will report this bill out to the floor, and they'll vote on it next week."

Lily tried to share his excitement. "And it has your ideas at the heart of it."

"This will put teeth into the privacy laws and give everyone the right to force removal of their personal information from corporate databases."

Wyatt gestured with his hands as he talked. Lily hadn't seen him so energized and happy in years.

"This legislation will make it easy for people to submit requests for data removal. It will put the onus on the corporations to prove why the request shouldn't be honored, and it forces them to act swiftly."

"What caused the committee to change its mind?"

He pointed at his 3D display. "I uncovered evidence showing how several companies were illegally skirting existing laws by systematically retaining personal data."

"We'll celebrate as soon as it passes the House." Lily gave him a hug. "It's an important victory in the fight we started years ago."

His shoulders sagged a bit. "Well, this is a win for privacy. Though it does little in the fight to decide how to manage the information commons. How to keep the commons open and free, yet uncontaminated, without impairing free speech."

"Especially the way money can influence the public and erode democracy." Her anger returned at the thought.

"But that problem is left for another day. And likely for other people to solve." Wyatt took his feet off his desk and stretched.

She was glad Wyatt had found success in his passion to protect privacy, but she had her own projects demanding her attention right now. Attending the Rysbier rallies had her focused on the larger issue of power and how some threatened to abuse it.

He studied her closely, and Lily tried to shake the cloud that had returned to her mood.

"Is something the matter, babe? You seem upset."

Lily sighed. "I spent my day at a Big Rex Rysbier rally. Zoe gave me the assignment. It's depressing how many people fall for his rhetoric."

"I've read about this crazy 'Levels' plan but haven't taken it seriously."

"It's time to worry. This guy is a threat to democracy. I've seen how he wins over a crowd. I'm actually scared."

He took her hand. "Is there anything I can do to help?"

She thought about the project Zoe had assigned, which was the slender thread on which her "of counsel attorney" job hung. She needed information to convince the firm's clients that they shouldn't support Rysbier.

Lily squeezed his hand. "You can teach me some of your net skills so I'm better at uncovering what Rysbier is doing. You can explain those parts of the net that I don't understand. Like how someone like Rysbier might get his hands on dark credit$."

58

Wyatt's CLAIR pinged with Lily's ID at the front door, and he pulled the steaming pot from the autocooker.

"That smells wonderful." She removed the kerchief from her head, clearly glad to be rid of it.

"Just beef stew. Comfort food." He lifted a bay leaf from the pot. It was alt-beef, of course. Neither of them could even tell the difference from the real stuff—it had been almost a decade since most of the country had made the switch.

He spooned the dinner onto plates. The heaped potatoes and carrots made a colorful combination. A candle flickered on the table, and his CLAIR had dimmed the lighting to create what he hoped was a romantic mood. He poured two glasses from a new Canadian wine.

"Here's to us." He raised his glass.

She sipped the wine as if she needed it, her eyes drawn at the corners. He worried about her because her emotions were on display lately, cycling from anger at some small thing he'd done to anxiousness to dull boredom. He figured it was work-related.

"Another Rysbier rally today?"

"Yes, and this one bigger than the last." She gulped her wine. "He really scares me."

Wyatt reached across the table to her hand. "Babe, you should try to worry less. You've been on edge."

"I can't. It seems like the world has been heading in a terrible direction for years. It feels like the Climate Wars all over again, when we worried whether there was any future. Remember when you lost your Uncle Jack and cousin Axel?

And millions more. It felt like the end of the world. Now, with Rysbier, it isn't better."

He looked for an angle to raise the subject again. "We can't solve all the world's problems alone. You should think about us and how we can be happy."

She held the glass and studied him. "You're wanting kids again?"

"The last time we talked about it, you felt it wasn't a good time." He didn't add that she had deferred before to make partner, but now career aspirations should not pre-clude the possibility. She was forty-three, he forty-five, and the idea of wanting to become a father had only grown.

"It still doesn't seem like a good time to bring a kid in-to the world."

"Is there ever the perfect time?" Wyatt kept his voice gentle. "Look, I know the future feels uncertain, and there are lots of things to worry about. And lots of couples are putting off having kids, so many that the population shrinking puts even more stress on the world because of the negative economic growth. Not having kids just adds to the problem. And who will keep looking out for the world if we don't raise kids who will care to?"

"We should have a kid because of world economics?" Her cheeks had turned red.

He struggled to avoid an argument. "We should think about having a kid, having a family, for us. I feel that the world will improve, humanity will stumble forward, and we'll solve these problems."

"You're always an optimist." Lily buried her face in her hands. "I'm sorry, I'm not so confident about the world. Let's talk about children sometime later, but not now."

59

The autohover glides low over the California countryside, banks, and zooms to a marked landing pad near the medical center. We settle softly. I could get used to this sort of travel. I help Grandfather to the ground, and the two bots follow us.

"The use of the aircraft allowed us to arrive early for your medical appointment, which will begin in half an hour," Robert says.

"Thank you, Robert. That gives us some time to talk as we walk." He tells the robots to go ahead of us and wait at the offices. Arnold follows Robert, and we are alone.

"The garden is over here, and it has some interesting plants."

Grandfather points to the garden park that borders the path to the big building a few hundred meters ahead. I hold his arm, and we walk along with him using his walking stick. Finally, he arrives at the part I've been waiting for—the story about Ma and Pa. He takes it slow, tellin' about what they learned, where they went to school, what places they worked, and projects they did.

"I always thought of Pa as workin' in the forest. So, he had an important role before? Keepin' the bots and companies from knowin' too much about us?"

Grandfather smiles, and I can tell he is proud of his son. "Your father's work did far more than that. The legislation he championed allowed people to own their data with individual ownership of created content at its core. They could control it, keeping track with blockchain tokens. Individuals could decide what data to sell and what to keep private.

They earned the rents, not the big online network companies. Once the legislation forced big companies to offer the option, it replumbed the entire net because the idea kept spreading."

"Did it solve the privacy problem?"

"The legislation solved part of the problem. But remember, data is also collected in the world, especially from cameras and AIs in robots walking around. That data is harder to police. We still can't know whether companies and governments are spying on us."

As we walk along, Grandfather brushes a flower with his stick and tells me the name.

I'm thinking about all that I didn't know about before; that was kept from me.

"Pa was doing some interestin' things in his life before coming to the Commune."

He leans on his stick. "More than interesting. Someone said once that you can do things that are interesting or pleasant or consequential. If they are pleasant, they are frequently not so interesting. If interesting, often not pleasant. But it is best to do something consequential."

"But you say that Ma was hopin' to be high in her law firm, and that didn't happen."

He sighed. "No, she never made partner."

I'm thinking of how Ma is still so unpredictable, sometimes mad, sometimes spacey. Grandfather kinda said that's how she was before I was born.

"I guess Ma never had as much impact on the world."

Grandfather stopped, his face thoughtful, like he was waiting to say something important. "You have made a wrong assumption. Your mother was certainly consequential, but it wasn't something to be proud of."

60

The gun rocked back in her hand, but Lily used a two-handed grip, and the neat hole pierced near the center of her makeshift target.

"Keep your arms straight," she said to herself, repeating the instructions she found on the dark net.

She fired twice more in quick succession, getting used to the recoil, then moved toward the target and fired three more times to empty the gun. Her ears rang from the sound because she didn't use any protection, so she could better understand what it would feel like later. She hadn't expected the surge of adrenaline from shooting the handgun. She felt powerful.

Birds chirped madly. Otherwise, the forest was silent. Lily was satisfied with the number of times she hit close to the mark. She rolled up the target, stuffed it and the gun into her backpack, and walked back down the trail. She was far enough away from any houses marked on her CLAIR's map that nobody would likely investigate the shots, but she thought it best to leave quickly.

Half an hour later, she'd walked to where the trail ended at a paved road. Lily reloaded the gun with the remaining ammunition and wrapped it in a thin composite embedded with AI-readable fibers. She carefully placed it in her purse and stashed the backpack with everything else in a bush. Then, she walked to the road and used her CLAIR to summon an autocar. When she passed the address, the car autopilot requested payment in advance for the three-hour ride. She clicked her ID tile for the transfer. Lily settled in the seat, and the car moved onto the road. Her heart beat fast, and she reassured herself about what she was doing and why.

The last rallies, and her research, had pushed her over the edge. She had not found incontrovertible evidence for her illegal digital twin theory, as Zoe had wanted, but she did find enough to convince herself. Lily knew in her heart that Rysbier was using them to reach scale.

But someone had funded the expensive quantum decryption to remove watermarks from his digital twins, and millions of these talked to every voter, pouring his seemingly authentic individual messages into their ears. These convincingly real Rysbier lookalikes would be trusted by his audience, the personal messages hitting home.

Her research suggested he received dark credit$ from robotics companies. He must have access to detailed individual information for precise messaging, information that robotic companies had available. If they were not deleting that data as required, then they violated multiple laws.

The rallies had drawn her into sympathy with the people, all feeling pushed down by those in power—those who controlled the robot factories and those who controlled the law firms. Yet, if robot factory owners funded Rysbier, then he must intend to keep them in power, to solidify their grip.

Levels would not be based on merit. His game must be oligarchy. It was a power grab, a destruction of democracy, because after he introduced the plan, the average worker would have given up too many rights to ever regain them. It would be people like Zoe who would get the top Levels. Lily would remain a pawn, sacrificed on a whim in a power game. It was not a plan to help the workers but to control them, and her.

Rysbier was a clear and present danger to all she held dear.

With tentative steps, she'd researched what actions she might take and found encouragement on the dark net in places with secrets that made it possible. It was easier than she had imagined to find the downloadable ghost gun. When constructed from polymer, it was nearly undetectable. She made the parts using a DIY kit and Wyatt's 3D printer. Dark credit$ had paid for that and the bullets from the pawnshop. Her last concern was whether detectors could bar entry based on the gun shape or the bullets. She'd bought the composite wrap with embedded fibers that promised to fool scanners, but she didn't know if it would actually work.

Lily studied her MEDFLOW again. She'd dialed the medication drip down to zero over the past few weeks but hadn't kicked the habit of monitoring it.

The autocar hurried down the road, and the number of vehicles they passed increased as they moved closer to the city. Her head felt light. She ordered the car to stop at a rest stop, then she was back on the road and felt her adrenaline rise.

She checked her CLAIR for the time. Ten minutes until the scheduled meeting with Senator Rysbier, arranged by her law firm, purportedly to allow them to advise their client, the union, about whether to support his political aspirations.

She smiled at the memory of the conversation with Zoe when she suggested this appointment. "Great idea," she'd said. "You'll interview him directly, so we report back with authority to bolster our advice."

The autocar turned into a gated drive. She tapped her ID tile to authenticate and was cleared through the entrance. The car stopped, and the door opened. Lily trembled all over and felt distanced from herself, like watching someone in an old movie. Then she remembered one she'd watched with Wyatt. The main character walked out of the restroom with a hidden gun to knock off the gangster and had not paused. She also must not hesitate.

A large man greeted her and escorted her down a corridor. Probably Rysbier's bodyguard. She held her breath as they passed through an automated entrance. The bulletproof glass doors beeped and slid open. The man stepped aside at the entrance, and she walked into a large office. He stood by the door at attention.

No other guards were in the room. Only Big Rex sat behind a large mahogany desk. She recognized him instantly.

The same Satan who stood on all those rally stages enticing his gullible fans with that silvery voice. An image from the Genesis story of the snake in the tree whispering wicked ideas came into her head. Bile crept up her throat. Her adrenaline surged.

He stood. "Ms. Fairchild?"

Lily reached into her purse and wrapped her hand around the grip. The polymer dug into her skin.

"Sic semper tyrannis!"

The roar filled her ears. Both her hands held the gun steady, and she fired at the target until someone grabbed her in a bear hug and wrestled her down. She identified a sudden sharp crack as the sound of her head hitting the floor.

61

My stomach lurches. "My mother is a murderer?"

The word sounds strange on my lips, like I should spit it out. I look around, glad that no other people or the bots are in hearing distance.

"Ah, no. She wasn't successful in killing Senator Rysbier." He says it in a disappointed way. "She shot him six times, the full magazine, and damaged his spine and multiple internal organs. They got him into surgery right away, and the med-bots saved him, barely. He never recovered fully and died within five years."

"She's...she's a criminal?"

"Yes. Though many think her worst crime was that she was unsuccessful."

My head swims. Now, I'm leaning on him instead of him on me. "But...how did she get away with it?"

"She didn't. She stood trial, was convicted of attempted murder, and was sentenced to twenty years in federal prison." Grandfather stands quietly. "You see, the Commune is a prison."

I shake my head. I feel like running away through the garden and into the trees at the end, and to keep running into the forest.

He puts a hand on my arm like he knows I want to run. "It's true. Her sentence was shorter than many thought. She was given leniency because she was pregnant with you during the trial. And they wanted to avoid making her a martyr for the growing anti-Levels movement. You were born at the beginning of her sentence. That's why she was allowed to go to the Commune. It was an experimental prison at the time."

"And Pa?"

"Your father was unaware of your mother's plans. She intentionally kept him in the dark to protect his innocence. He was devastated. He knew she was having...anxiety and some other symptoms of deeper issues. In that way, he felt responsible for not doing more to help. Your father realized that without him there, she might not survive in prison, and then neither would you. He voluntarily went with her to the Commune."

"They never told me. No one in the...Commune...told me."

"You and a few others were children, all born to at least one incarcerated parent. They decided it was best to shield you from the truth until you could understand it better. The Texas hurricane, followed by the fire interfered, so the truth remained hidden longer than anyone planned."

I cringe at a memory. "That's why I hardly ever got to visit you. That's why Ma and me couldn't go to Grandma Tadala's funeral."

"Yes. Only your father could get a pass. And it's why I missed seeing you grow up."

"That's why the Commune doesn't have much technology. It's why we have horses and wagons."

He nods. "Autocars make it easier to attempt escape."

The world feels upside down, like a different planet than I was on before. But upside down has its own logic. The memory of my escape through the Commune gate comes back, and a tremor goes through me. "The bot I met at the Commune...prison...it was a guard, then?"

"That's right."

We've walked to the end of the garden. Robert and Arnold wait there. A technician in a white lab coat comes out to greet us.

"Why don't we look at this modern medical facility, and afterward, you can wait inside while I finish my exam. I'll only be about a half hour."

I walk with him to the technician, who takes his other arm, and we step inside the building.

I decide to let myself be distracted by whatever this lab does, so I don't have to think about what I just learned about Ma. What can you do when you hear such news? Do I have any of those same uncontrollable feelings she has inside of me?

No, Grandfather said we each decide. He's got to be right. I'll find that true path through the woods that leads to a life I won't regret. One that does some good.

62

The robot lifted Rex into the wheelchair and arranged his limbs. Its lenses glimmered as it checked his alignment. The oversized MEDFLOW unit attached to his right hip hummed as it fed drugs to his system.

"Senator, are you comfortable?"

"Not with the hell I have." Rex's good right hand rested on the chair's control panel. "I hurt all over."

His CLAIR connected to the chair's AI, and with a few commands, he moved it forward.

"I'm afraid you are using the maximum safe synpsych amounts for pain control. You should be happy to reach this degree of recovery, given the nature of your injuries."

He gestured with his chin. "How long will I need this big thing?"

"The MEDFLOW will be necessary for life, Senator." The medbot's lenses swiveled. "Would you like a report on your surgeries? We have replaced your liver and two kidneys with genetically modified pig organ transplants, and your pancreas with a bioengineered organ. Your injuries were significant, and despite our medical technology, we are unable to repair certain conditions. The spinal damage—"

"Just stop." He felt sorry for himself. "Leave."

The medbot's forehead shaded pink; it turned and left his room.

Rex sat quietly for several minutes and watched the sunlight from an open window play across the floor. He thought about his classic car, which would now sit idle forever.

The negative thoughts spurred Rex to action. He tried the wheelchair interface through his CLAIR. It executed his commands on cue. The electric drives turned the wheels, and rolled him around the room with only brief inputs from his good hand. He rolled to the desk display and called up a number from his PIDA. The holo-com filled with the face of Tom Thompson, his chief of staff.

"Senator. I'm so happy to see you up and recovering."

He was not in the mood for small talk. "Tell me how the legislation is moving ahead."

"In the four months since your injury, we've moved the Levels Act through the Senate committee and expect a floor vote within a couple of weeks. I'm working our House connections in parallel, and I think we can eliminate resistance there."

"Not injury. Assassination attempt." The cut was deeper, and he would make people pay.

"Yes, sir. The sympathy vote is helping our cause. This is the best time to pass the legislation."

"What has happened to my attacker?"

"Lily Fairchild is being held in federal prison awaiting trial. We expect swift justice."

"Was she crazy?"

Thompson shook his head. "She has no medical diagnosis of instability. Her defense will not rely on the argument."

"Good on the first point." Rex's agitation pushed his temper higher. "I wish we still had the death penalty. But I want to see her put away for a long time."

"Yes, sir." Thompson pursed his lips. "She's getting some sympathy on social media. Her husband, Wyatt MacGyver, has been very supportive. There's talk he may follow her into prison, even though there was no documented involvement on his part."

"Damn. She'll probably go to one of those new prisons in Texas that coddle criminals in the name of reform." Rysbier tried to shift in his chair, then realized no such muscles would ever respond. "Are you sure Wyatt MacGyver wasn't an accomplice?"

"The police investigated every record. He's clean," Thompson said. "He's apparently still in love with her, despite her crime. He visits her in prison every day. It's a bit of a romance playing out on social media."

"Conjugal visits?"

Thompson shrugged. "I suppose."

"This killer should never spawn. Let's keep a close eye on her. A Texas prison might be best."

The MacGyver name rang a bell. "Is Harper MacGyver related?"

Thompson checked a source. "Yes, Lily Fairchild is her cousin."

"Damn." His list was growing longer.

The drugs flowing through his MEDFLOW were making him tired. He signed off from the call. Rysbier sat in the wheelchair, staring out the window, feeling nothing except the malice running through his veins.

63

KARLA GRAVES MACGYVER—2110 (THE CARIBBEAN)

The autohover glided over the azure Caribbean. One emerald island gem surrounded by shimmering waters followed another in a string. Karla wondered whether any coral reefs survived among the turquoise shallows. Her craft flew low above wave-swept beaches and circled a picturesque lagoon where the huge white yacht swayed at anchor. The sleek lines enclosed a large pool visible near the bow and an open main deck beach club on the stern. The autohover settled onto the landing pad on the middle deck and cut its engines.

Her mother walked toward her, dressed casually in shorts, a white top, and soft deck shoes.

"Hi, Mom." She gave her a hug.

"Hi, honey. Good you could get away." Her mother led her to the midcabin under a canopy out of the sun. A robot waited with drinks. She accepted one and settled into the cushions, glad to be out of the tropical heat.

"It wasn't too difficult. We have just a few details left before handing the company over to the government."

"Thank you for volunteering for that."

Karla didn't remind her that she'd been volunteered because of Mom's refusal. But it was understandable. Mom was always committed to the company, and she couldn't stomach the transfer of legal ownership.

"It's a chapter behind us. Let's drink to that." Karla raised her glass.

Her mother reluctantly tapped her glass with her daughter's. Karla waited for the inevitable complaint.

"You never were very interested in our company, and the work behind all the family wealth." Mom looked to the green mountains of the island several hundred meters away.

Karla wanted to bite her tongue but couldn't manage this time. It had been her mother's refrain for months. "Mom, stop. We discussed this. I left bioscience just when I finished my PhD, when I might have done interesting basic research. Now, when I go back, I'm only able to work on the policy side, not the lab. I sacrificed for you too."

She made a sound in her throat. "Yes, you sacrificed. For all this." Mom's hand swept over the boat.

"I'm sorry, but this stuff is unimportant to me." She was firm this time, so they wouldn't have to repeat the conversation.

"The company, which they snatched from us, paid for your Level 5 status."

"And it gave you your Level 5 too." It was self-defining to her mother—something to show for it all. But not to her. "I'll only take credit for anything I do myself, on my own merits."

Her mother eyed the horizon again. "I can't believe I let that asshole Rysbier screw me. After all we did for him, and just a lousy Level 5."

The legislation had passed, Levels were in the early stages of assignment, and they already were the subject of intense debate.

Karla's gaze fixed on her mother. "What did you expect?"

"A Level 1, of course."

Karla swirled the drink noisily. "If there is any sense of merit to these Levels—which I doubt—how can you expect to say you've done so much for the country, for humanity?"

She gave a derisive grunt. "I've heard Max MacGyver will be a Level 1."

Karla was angry now. "If these Levels have a shred of factual basis, then some people obviously have the highest Levels. Great-Uncle Max was inducted into the Environmental Pantheon of Heroes. It's international recognition for truly consequential work."

Max and Everett had been the only father–son pair honored for their work to fight climate change, specifically with fission energy, and to recognize the need to give that power to the Global South.

"But a MacGyver related to Lily Fairchild. She's the reason we were demoted to a Level 5."

It felt like a criticism of herself. "You always insisted that I was a MacGyver, too, not only a Graves. You take the good with the bad. You shouldn't deny being related to anyone in our family."

They spent a few minutes downing their drinks, the only sound the waves hitting the boat and the ice clinking in their glasses.

"What will you do now, Mom?"

She shrugged. "I've always wanted to learn to chill out on a big yacht. They took away the company but left me with all the money. With the new company structure, I can stay CEO, but I don't think I'll be able to design whatever I want. A lot of friends have their boats in the Mediterranean. They follow the circuit all summer. St. Tropez, Capri, Ibiza, the Emerald Coast in Sardinia. I'll probably join them."

"It's good you can keep all your toys."

"What will you do?"

It was suddenly a comfort to know that her mother cared about the answer, whatever small amount that was. Determination welled up inside her.

"I'm going back to bioscience, back to policy work. It's what I love, and where I might make a difference."

"Will you visit me? I can bring you to the boat any time."

"We'll work it out, Mom."

Karla gave her another hug. She wondered how often she'd find herself in the same port as her mother.

64

I leave the two robots in a waiting room, and the technician agrees to give us a short tour of the labs. They're housed in an attached building shaped like a quad surrounding a central lab space visible through glass windows. The technician leads us around the square, pointing out various instrumentation stations as he describes their functions. The laboratory space holds only robots and equipment. An assembly line takes up much of the space. Boxed items fall off the end of the line and are stacked by robots into cubicles.

Grand stares at the robots. "What do the people do?"

"Humans design the experiments at a high level, then AIs and robots perform the next steps," the technician says. "It's all automated using synthetic biology and bio-building blocks."

Grand rubs his hands. "Something like building a brick wall, just stacking one on top of another?"

I know this part, having heard the rapt predictions about elimination of disease and lifespan extension, still unfulfilled. "That was the original hope. But nature has more secrets about biology than we imagined, and it's taken longer than expected to uncover how life really works. We've made huge strides in medicine this last century. Still, much remains to be learned."

"He's right," the technician says. "Average lifespan has increased to ninety years. Every improvement now is hard work." The technician's face turns red. He probably remembered how old I am.

That is a pressing topic for me today, so it is top of mind, but it doesn't distress me. "We're not yet to the point we have to worry about living forever."

Grand must be considering what he will do with his many years.

"There's tons of robots in medicine but not many jobs left for people?"

"Many of the jobs in medicine have been usurped by AIs and robots. But there still is a need for the human touch. That's why your Grandmother Tadala could work in the field her whole life."

I feel my chest grow warm at my recollection. This day spent with our grandchild has brought back so many memories. It's a family tapestry woven tight, and she's deep in the weave.

There's little to see here because most human jobs have migrated to the mind, to the abstract. It leaves little for physical human labor. A series of nondescript machines produce the physical goods.

The technician finishes the tour and brings us back to the waiting room with the robots. It's time for my appointment.

"Just wait here a bit. I won't be long." I leave Grand to hold my walking stick. He sits next to Arnold.

Dr. Pearl Dunlevy, my regular doctor, meets me at her office door. She smiles. "It looks like you're moving well."

I left my stick behind intentionally, just to show that I didn't always need it.

The medbot draws some DNA and other samples. I stand in the full-body scanner and let it whir for a while. Then, I sit by the doctor for her consultation. The machines hum in the corner, processing the scans, while Dunlevy asks me the typical questions.

"I don't suppose you've found anything new since you're monitoring me with this anyway." I point to the MEDFLOW.

"Correct. No new issues for you. You've done well after the mRNA treatment for the cancer. One year with no evidence of disease is a nice milestone."

"I'm just following your advice to live one day at a time."

The medbot comes back, and Dunlevy accepts the results with her CLAIR. I try to read her expression for hints.

"You have a new estimated lifespan from the AI?"

At my question, her mouth twitches.

The medbot chirps up. "Your results have been compared to the database—"

"Not from you, thank you." My tone is harsh because today the bots annoy the hell out of me.

"Please stand down," Dunlevy says to the medbot.

It moves to the corner and goes pink and silent.

She turns to me. "Many factors come into play at your age, Mr. MacGyver."

"I know." I count them off on my fingers. "Having good relationships with people, having a purpose, having a will to live." I look up. "I have just one question. Given all of those, what are my chances of living another four years?"

Her gaze locks on mine. "Pretty good."

"That's all I need to know. Thank you."

We finish, and I walk out the door, back to Grand.

65

GRAND—PRESENT, 2125

I'm comfortable in the waiting room because of the big windows looking out on the garden. There are two live oaks close by. They remind me of the Piney Woods, except now the memory of the Commune forest isn't as comforting.

I think about how Pa and I were in prison, one freely and one unknowingly. Pa loves Ma, for sure. I can't stop thinking about Ma, how she got there, and how she must feel. I think of her face and see it different. Had I interpreted her emotions in a way she never felt them? Was her worry for us just worry? Or was there guilt and regret and other things I can't imagine? Sometimes she talked about being there for the nature. Was that just an excuse for me that made her feel better?

Arnold sits next to me and Robert across from us. I already like Arnold, a big and beat-up robot, the strong, silent type.

Robert moves his lenses around like he's looking for something. He stands, and his head swivels. "Apparently, an earlier message has been received and acted upon. Please wait."

The waiting room doors zip open, and a big robot enters. It looks different from Robert—taller, with bigger arms. A plaque shaped like a star adorns its chest. It says *Copbot Model 613*. The bot surveys the room and locks onto me. I stand up, not liking that look. The bot grabs my wrist. Its lenses point to Robert. "Is this the offending human?"

"Yes, that is the boy."

Please stand still while I confirm."

As if I could go anywhere with its steel hand holding my arm like a vice. Its other hand touches my forearm, and I feel a pinch.

"DNA analysis underway."

Arnold stands, and his lenses flash.

"No data, except the Level," the copbot says.

Grandfather walks through the opposite door and leans against it. His gaze meets mine, and I stop being worried for me. But I wish I could hand him his walking stick.

Model 613 points to Grandfather. "Is this the accomplice?"

"That is he," Robert says.

"Not even a kiss, Robert?" Grandfather steps forward on unsteady legs.

"I have reason to believe that crimes may have been committed," Model 613 intones in a deep bass. "The crimes include property theft, serving alcohol to a minor, and flight by a minor without permission of the parents. These possible crimes warrant arrest."

I've got the walking stick in my other hand, and the bot heads toward Grandfather, dragging me as it reaches out its free hand. I can see it, how it will knock Grandfather over. I swing the stick, and it cracks against its forearm.

The copbot's lenses blaze, and it turns its full attention on me. Now, I'm scared.

"Defend! Defend!" Grandfather's voice rings out in a command to Arnold.

There's a crunching noise, metal on metal, and the copbot's forearm disintegrates. My wrist is free. I'm looking up from where I've fallen on the floor, and Arnold smashes the copbot on the head, and it falls down. Arnold's fists move in a blur, pummeling it. Lubricant leaks out in a puddle at my feet. Its lenses pulse red, and then they flicker out. Pieces of aluminum alloy from the Model 613 litter the floor.

A lady rushes through the door, hand on a taser at her belt. She must be a cop too because of her blue uniform.

"No reason to use that." Grandfather doesn't yell it, but his tone is firm. Commanding.

She takes in the situation. Arnold stands at attention, the copbot at his feet on the floor. Robert is frozen to the same spot where it tattled on Grandfather.

"Sorry about your robot. It seems that it has gone out of control. A test model, no doubt?" Grandfather's voice is suddenly syrupy.

The lady cop has stopped but keeps her hand at her belt. She scans her CLAIR while she watches us, but no one moves.

"Yes, an early model," she says. "Let me see your ID."

Grandfather touches his chest. He must be sending some information.

The cop calms down. "Mr. MacGyver, a Level 1. She looks at me. "And the boy?"

"He doesn't have an embedded ID." Grandfather gives her my name.

"There is a report that this boy has traveled from his... home...without parental permission." Her tone is still stern, but it's softer since Grandfather told her who he is.

Grandfather thinks a moment. "Let's deal with that one right away. Let me contact his parents, and they can vouch for his presence here."

The lady cop nods. He uses his CLAIR and, in a minute, he's talkin' with Pa. After a moment, Grandfather opens his CLAIR so everyone can hear.

"I can talk with the officer in charge and confirm that my father, Mr. MacGyver, has approval to have our son in his care."

The cop talks to Pa for a few minutes and authenticates his ID. Grandfather leans on his walking stick, which is a little bent now.

The lady finishes talkin' to Pa.

Grandfather faces her, a devilish expression on his face. "We can see that there are no material reasons to conclude there has been illegal activity calling for immediate arrest of anyone." He's not talking about all the charges the copbot made, but she doesn't seem to notice. "Now, let's discuss the actions of your test police robot."

"That's certainly an issue. Destruction of public property."

She looks a little sick about Model 613 lying there, like maybe she might need to explain it to someone.

Grandfather rubs his chin. "So, given what we now have determined, the copbot acted upon imperfect information, so his actions in trying to arrest my grandson and me were inappropriate."

The lady cop nods thoughtfully.

"My grandson, then, was defending a human, me, which is equivalent behavior required for robots under Law 1. I'm referring to the three Laws of Robotics, and the phrase, 'or, through inaction, allow a human being to come to harm.'"

The lady cop is on her CLAIR again, checking with someone.

"Therefore, given the information that my grandson had, he was correct in his behavior, and more correct than the copbot, since my grandson had more perfect information. And, of course, my robot standing here was powerless to ignore the First Law and had to defend us both."

The lady nodded and clicked some buttons on her CLAIR. "There will be no further concerns here about the actions of you or your grandson."

Grandfather lets out a breath. "Thank you."

"It's a pleasure to meet you, Mr. MacGyver. A Level 1, and a climate change hero."

She smiles and calls someone about cleaning up the copbot. Arnold has been standing at attention now with another dent on his arm. Grandfather thanks her for her service, and gestures to the two bots to follow us out.

We walk back to the autohover, which is still on the pad at the end of the drive.

"I don't know what a Level 1 is, but it sounds good."

He growls. "It's a pretentious measurement tacked on people from the outside. What counts is what you do."

The lady cop sure perked up when she knew it, though. Now I'm thinking about what she said about him being a hero.

"Thank you for your appropriate actions," he says to Arnold.

"Sir, you are welcome."

"I can teach you all the hacks of this old model." Grandfather wears an impish grin.

Robert's lenses swivel, but it remains silent and follows us. We climb into the autohover and head home.

66

Senator Rex Rysbier—2115 (Texas)

Rex felt like a shrunken shadow of himself in his wheelchair. The dark clouds out the window gathering into another storm mirrored his mood.

His discomfort lessened a bit when the medbot finished adjusting his MEDFLOW.

"Sir, I have completed my treatment."

Rex frowned. "I suppose that will help me live longer in this same wretched condition."

The medbot's cartoon eyebrows and mouth formed into a cheery expression. "Your probable lifespan has now increased a bit, to five months, three days from today." Its forehead glowed green.

"Damn." The stupid robots always attempted to answer a direct question, including this question he didn't intend to ask.

His bodyguard entered the room. "Sir, your appointment today, a Ms. Karla MacGyver, has arrived and been cleared." He looked at his shoes. "We checked her very thoroughly."

Rex sighed. "Send her in."

The young woman entered the room. She bore little resemblance to Harper MacGyver. She had an open face, but it was laced with determination and anger. Maybe she *was* like her mother.

"Quite a body search process just to enter your office," she said.

"A special greeting for every MacGyver." He fixed her with an unwelcoming stare. "I suppose you're here to complain on behalf of your mother."

"What?" Her surprise seemed genuine.

"Harper continues to message me about her Level 5. Or are you here to also complain about your Level 5?"

Her angry expression returned. "Who cares about Levels?"

"Everyone cares about Levels these days." Rex snorted over the victory. He had so little to laugh about now.

"Okay, my mother does care, and she tells me she feels betrayed by you. She says your infamous way with words doesn't work on everyone." Karla paused. "But I'm here to talk about my cousins, Wyatt MacGyver and Lily Fairchild, and their son."

"Are they complaining about their Levels too? That spider deserves a Level 99 for her actions. And her husband and child should celebrate their Level 77." The bitterness in his mouth made him want to spit.

"I see. In your system based on 'merit,' the child suffers from the actions of the parent." Scorn laced her voice. "But again, I'm not here about Levels. I'm here to tell you I know what you ordered done to the child."

He wore his imperious face. "What are you talking about?"

"You may not know, but my training includes a PhD in bioscience, and I've spent the last five years on policy work. That's how I discovered what you did. I tracked rumors that filtered through the bioscience community. I dug around sources you wished to keep hidden. I know all about 'John Doe Bio 1.' He is Lily's son. I know you're responsible."

"You won't wring a confession from me for any such nonsense." Rex hid the chill that ran down his spine.

"I don't need your confession. I have the evidence."

"What evidence?"

Karla's voice was deadly calm. "I obtained an order to review the DNA data taken from Lily on her arrival at the prison and from her and the child shortly after her pregnancy. In the child's DNA, we found disease-associated mutations in the DNAAF6 and SYCP3 genes, alongside a conspicuous insertion of a modified DREADD receptor that appears to be activated by a common drug reagent. When that drug was administered during regular pregnancy treatment, it set off an immune response in the developing fetus."

"This is all nonsense," Rysbier said, shaking his head, while trying to appear incredulous.

"No one noticed the anomalous DNA report because you had it doctored, and we only found out now after reanalyzing the remotely stored DNA samples. And Lily's stored blood sample tested positive for lab-strain AAV-specific antibodies. Lily was deliberately and insidiously injected with a virus that genetically altered her unborn child." Karla's eyes were aflame. "This bomb was placed in the developing fetus, and it went off when triggered."

"And you're looking at me?"

"We know who gave the orders to the medical staff— people you brought in. They've confessed and face prison. We know you're responsible for giving the order."

His lifetime habit was never to admit anything. "Preposterous. And what do you intend to do now?"

Karla waved dismissively as she moved closer to hover over his wheelchair. "Nothing to you. I have a good guess of how much longer you have left to live."

Rex flinched, and she continued, her voice a drumbeat heralding an onrushing attack.

"With today's technology, there's little we can do for the boy. But I can help stop future human germline modification. In your pursuit of power, you opened another Pandora's box of troubles for humanity before we could muster enough resolve to work together and create reasonable rules. But I'll use your actions to put this one back."

He kept his face closed, but his body shrank before her fury.

Karla loomed over him, her gaze on him relentless. "Mark my words. The MacGyvers will erase your evil legacy from history."

67

Tadala MacGyver—2115 (California)

The little guy played at Tadala's feet with the plastic blocks. He'd assembled the space station and now worked on the robot supply spacecraft. His happy smile showed the resemblance to Wyatt, and his kind eyes and strong cheekbones reminded her of Max.

"He can take the toy home with us, except for the electronics, so let's separate those," Wyatt said.

She shook her head. "I understand. Commune rules."

"I'm glad I could get a pass to bring him to visit. Lily sends her best wishes." The reason Lily couldn't leave and why he made this trip now while there still was time remained unspoken but was a knot of tension between them.

Tadala leaned in closer. "How is it? You gave up so much, and I heard it's primitive."

He shifted on the sofa beside her. "Work keeps me busy. It's similar to my first job in the forest. We plant bioengineered trees that grow at high rates and don't easily burn. They store carbon using fast photosynthesis."

"I worry about all of you surrounded by forest. Saving you doesn't seem to be their top priority." She hadn't intended it, but the irony in her words came forward.

They avoided talking in front of the boy about the prison, a rule that Wyatt had insisted upon. He was almost four and understood much of what they said. Tadala wished she could spend more time with him than these rare visits afforded. The thought tightened her chest.

"They use firebots and a predictive AI monitoring system to shut down fires as soon as they start. Though we don't see that technology inside the fence," Wyatt said.

"We could have helped out by having him stay with us."

Wyatt shook his head. "Lily needs him." The boy seemed oblivious to them, but Wyatt lowered his voice to a whisper anyway. "Otherwise, I worry about her stability."

"They haven't been able to cure her with medication?"

"They can partially balance her emotional states, but that's it for now." He reached for her hand. "Mom, you haven't talked about yourself. Dad told me about the prognosis. That's why I came as soon as I could."

Tadala rested her eyes on her grandson. "It's a complex disease, one for which they haven't found a cure. I know from watching some of my patients go through it." She squeezed his hand, felt his love, and used it to find strength.

Wyatt's face twisted. "I can't imagine not having you here."

His hand felt warm resting on hers. She hated to add to his worries. "Honestly, I have the same feeling. I suppose it's more a fear of missing out. The last couple of decades have been a crazy time to be living on this earth. But I've always had your dad and all of you, and that's made it all worth it."

"But—"

She still held his hand. "It has been a wonderful life. The world tosses all sorts of challenges at every one of us. I've taken the bad with the good. You cannot sit back in fear, doing nothing. There's a line from an old poem—'It takes life to love Life.' Wyatt, I hope you'll teach your children to never give up, to take charge, and to change the world."

"Mom, what can I do?"

"I need you to help me talk your father into planning for...when I'm not here to support him. I don't think it'll be good for him to stay here; there are too many memories. Memories can be ghosts, and it's best to go where you don't see them so often. Convince him to buy a vineyard up north. We talked about retiring there, and Buzz already lives there."

Wyatt patted her hand. "Sure, Mom. What else can I do?"

Tadala thought of the important things left undone. "I just want the family to come together to heal the divisions between people."

He shrugged. "There's just that pointless fight over who's a rightful MacGyver." Wyatt leveled his gaze at her. "But there aren't many left to fight with. Just Scarlett, Harper, and Karla."

"It would rest my heart if you and Lily could find a way to resolve differences with them."

"Okay. I'll talk to Lily."

The door opened, and Max came in wearing his jogging clothes and mopping his forehead.

"I just saw your mother's message that you were here. So good to see you, son." He wrapped an arm around Wyatt in a bear hug.

"You're still jogging, Dad?"

Max chuckled. "Still stumbling through a 5K. I'm afraid to stop." Max leaned down and met outstretched arms. "And little Grand too!"

Tadala's eyes grew teary when Max scooped up their grandson and swept them all into a group hug.

"No matter what happens, we're a family," she said.

68

HARPER JONES MACGYVER—2123 (THE MEDITERRANEAN)

Harper balanced two drinks in her hands and wove her way around several young men toward the aft deck, which had become a dance floor.

"Party time!" One sloshed his glass against hers.

The tender pulled up abeam her yacht, and a dozen new guests piled off. Her robots stood at the gangway with drink trays, which were emptied by willing hands. They came up to the dance deck. Some already moved their hips to the music that thumped from holographic speakers. Colored lights pulsed in time to the beat.

"Welcome aboard," she called.

"Nice yacht, Harper," one of the newcomers said. "Meet my friends from Ibiza. This is Andreas from Mykonos, and Amon from Cairo."

The two men dressed similarly. Vibrant designer shirts clung to their toned bodies, and oversized sunglasses hid their glazed drunken stares. They joined the dance floor and disappeared into the sea of sameness.

Her CLAIR blinked with a missed message. The music was too loud to return the call, so she stepped to the lower deck and leaned against the railing. The turquoise waters of Grande Pevero beach lay off in the distance, and the Church of Stella Maris crowned a hill to starboard, above Costa Smeralda Yacht Club. Gazing out at the sunny June weather, she opened her CLAIR.

Karla's avatar hovered into view. "Hi, Mom. Where are you now?"

"I'm anchored off Isole di li Nibani, a pretty island here in Sardinia. The weather's great. I'm meeting some *really* interesting people." She gulped her drink, pausing to think if even she believed that lie. "How are you?"

"Excited about the work I'm doing. I think we had a real breakthrough."

"Really?"

Karla described her work with a passion she hadn't felt herself in over a decade, and envy rose in her. She had money, she had power, but she didn't have creative freedom. She was locked in a prison of her own making, forced to build what was requisitioned. An order-taker. She had never been an order-taker.

"It doesn't matter." Harper muttered under her breath. Her fists tightened, and she stomped her foot in a childlike tantrum.

"What was that, Mom?"

"Nothing," Harper said, her voice defeated and sharp. "I need to go. I'll call later." She hung up.

Making her way to the bow, Harper stood against the rail, frozen, her thoughts empty. She could hear the shouts of her friends below her, the sound of yet another bottle of champagne being opened, and the excited drunken demands to fill their glasses.

She stared into the endless sea and asked nobody, "Is it possible to die of boredom?"

69

Karla Graves MacGyver—2124 (Texas)

The autocar stopped at the gray metal gate flanked with guard towers. Robots stood at attention. Karla gave her special pass to the hulking security robot. It checked her ID, and she stared at the sign above the gate that said, "The Commune."

The ARMO on her CLAIR had labeled her destination as "Federal Prison Experimental 1." It seemed that near the prison, they wished to keep up the fiction.

"You are clear to visit for two hours," the security robot said. It directed the car to park, and another robot escorted her through a double steel door, which clanged shut behind her.

Several people dressed in casual jeans and work clothing occupied the central square. A horse and wagon stood outside a barn. A man walked by, toting a shovel. There were no automated vehicles in sight. If she ignored the steel gates and fencing, it might have been mistaken for the rural nineteenth century.

Though her light blonde hair had faded since the last time they met, she recognized Lily. The middle-aged woman had exited a wooden building and now walked toward her. She wore a loose long skirt and a cotton top. It was clear there was no technology in any of the materials. Karla was glad for the cooling cloth layer in her own jumpsuit on this hot spring day.

Lily took hold of both her hands and gave her a tired but grateful smile. "It's so good of you to come. We haven't seen anyone for ages." She looked at a guard robot that watched them from atop the prison wall. "We must entertain any guests in plain sight. Let's go sit in the garden." Lily led her up a path to a hillock ringed by a few trees, and they sat on stone benches among wildflowers.

"Wyatt is out in the field now. Our son is playing with his teachbot...somewhere. You can visit them in a little while." Lily spoke quickly, like she was nervous.

A drone hovered overhead. Karla felt a little overwhelmed and wasn't sure how to begin what she had to say. She was glad that Lily seemed to feel the need to fill in the silence.

"The guards don't allow any technology or net connection," Lily said. "From outside, there's only censored information on allbooks for teaching the children. Though we're allowed to hear family emergency messages." Lily paused, then added, "They approved your pass because, at last, I'm on the 'good behavior' list, so we can have more visitors."

That gave Karla the idea that she could at least fill her in on family news. "Your Uncle Sam is doing well, living in Berlin for the last decade. Even though he was in the US for most of his life, he was still assigned a low Level. But Europe treats him as any American because they don't recognize Levels, and he's got a good life."

"That's wonderful news."

"And my Grandma Scarlett is still alive, living with me in Boston, in an attached apartment."

"Wow, how old is she?"

"A hundred and eleven!"

"That's the power of modern science." Lily gazed into her eyes. "Do you have a partner?"

Karla felt herself grow warm. "My fiancé Dustin and I were engaged last year."

Karla studied her cousin, just nine years older than herself, and thought about what it must be like to be in prison for thirteen years. So many emotions played across Lily's face, from anxiety to resolve. "Lily, after all these years, I trust you've been able to adjust to this place."

"It's been harder than I imagined. At first, I thought that being assigned to the Commune was a godsend since Wyatt and our son could be with me. I fantasized about living a simpler life."

"It seems simple enough," Karla said.

Lily made a face. "My idea was too idealistic. I thought we'd be self-reliant here in a community of good people. In reality, we do live with each other, but there's no escaping feuds."

Karla kept her face neutral. Apparently, the dissonance of prison inmates living in perfect harmony had not been obvious to Lily.

"At least you've had time to read, to contemplate, and can work outside in nature."

Lily brightened. "We work outside with simple tools, hammers, saws, rakes, and shovels, and with horses for plowing. It's healing as much as it's a punishment." She laughed quietly. "Contemplate, indeed. I've been reading a lot of spiritual books. I was reading about a sixth-century Christian saint carrying a hammer, and that's where our son's name came from. Now he's good with a hammer."

The enormous gap between their lived experiences, hammers versus genes, and the realization that her visit would pummel Lily's false sense of that separation, left Karla lost for words. She drew a deep breath, and the earthy garden aroma surrounded her.

"You've more than adjusted to this place. You've endured."

"One goes on. Wyatt has been a savior."

"And Wyatt is well?"

"Yes. He's made the most of being here with me. Besides the time spent managing the forest, he was allowed to bring musical instruments. He's written two symphonies, and the Berlin Philharmonic invited him to conduct his second symphony." A proud smile played across her face.

"And your son?"

"Wyatt says he needs to leave for high school soon, but I hate to lose him. He gives me purpose." Lily twisted her hands together. "I have seven more years left on my sentence, and if he goes, by the time I leave here, he'll be off in college."

"And thinking about what's next is the reason you asked me to do the research?"

Lily looked up with anxious eyes. "They're Wyatt's ideas about the future. He thought, with your bioscience background, you could find out without people knowing. That's why the two requests."

"I have your answers. And the information about a third." Karla didn't wait for Lily's response. "The first is easy. You're worried about your son being marked by your conviction, that it will follow him and prevent his ever having a role in society."

Lily crossed her arms, looking vulnerable. "Yes, I worry about him coming to harm, even being killed by some madman. I remember the death threats Wyatt got after we arrived here. Rysbier still has rabid followers, even after his death."

Karla ignored the irony of the worry and touched Lily's hand to reassure her. "That's not a problem. Everyone can protect themselves against stalkers and hide their personal information. That's all because of laws based on Wyatt's work from years ago. The law says we all have a right to be forgotten. That was passed to protect everyone from the wide-open information that used to be available on the net. I've prepared an order that only needs signatures from you and Wyatt, and your son's identity will be locked forever. That includes his DNA records. No one will be able to find him or know his background. Typically, anyone who locks their identity and their family can go by a surname with some variation of Smith or Jones."

Lily squeezed Karla's hand. "Thank you."

Karla frowned. "The only part of his identity that cannot be removed is his Level, a Level 77."

"I understand."

"Now, to your second request. Using the review order you signed, I worked with the clinicians to check the frozen embryos you placed in storage thirteen years ago. I can confirm there are viable embryos to reasonably assure yourselves of a successful pregnancy. You and Wyatt can have another child if you wish when you finish your prison sentence."

The tension disappeared from Lily's shoulders, and her eyes teared up. "Thank you again. Wyatt and I want to start over, to watch a child grow to maturity outside and free. We expect we'll be consigned to live in some sort of lower-Level community, but at least we can live a quiet life without prison fences."

Karla patted her hand. "Let's see, that would mean a child born in 2132. You'll be what? Sixty-five? Not so old these days to raise a child."

Karla thought about her own age, and Dustin, and her own wish to have a child soon.

"You mentioned a third answer?" Lily raised her eyebrows.

For Karla, the question opened the gates, but she tried to hold back. She should release the long-held secret in stages so as not to wash Lily away.

"I work in bioscience policy to help decide the limits to bioengineering the human genome." Karla waited to see if Lily understood.

Lily nodded and didn't seem confused.

"The bioscience community has at last gotten organized and developed a global panel that assesses every considered change to the human genome germline. That's my life's work."

"Who decides?"

"A committee of bioscientists, ethicists, medical professionals, politicians, and average citizens who review and advise. Their recommendations go to a global parliament for approval. Now, we can draw a clear line and have the means to enforce it."

Karla took Lily's hands and hoped it would give the older woman something to hang onto. "I was involved with the work to create this governance because of you and your son. He's known in the community as the anonymous 'John Doe Bio 1.'"

Karla's story poured out, the words coming fast and sincere. She leaned toward Lily and kept a firm grip on her hands. Lily buried her face on Karla's shoulder.

After a moment, Lily wiped her wet cheeks. "I had a bad feeling that Rysbier did something. There were special medical people and robots hovering around right after I was pregnant, when I was still in the prison before the trial. Then, he was sick, but nobody could explain why."

"I went back to my first love, bioscience, after the company was gone. I've spent the past several years pushing for global legislation, and early this year, we got it through. Now, that can never happen again. Your experience ignited that change and advanced something fundamentally important. We have guardrails in place so humankind doesn't repeat those errors."

Lily wiped tears from her cheeks, and Karla knew it offered slim consolation. But perhaps later, knowing the higher purpose—that people couldn't change the genome germline—would help her endure.

"Do you think, in the future, maybe...?"

Karla shrugged. "There's no way to know. But it won't prevent him from living a full life or finding somebody to love. Those are important things all on their own."

Lily sighed. "You're right. I'm glad that, even in this short time on earth, he is part of such an important fight without even knowing it. You're right. There's no telling what he may accomplish."

"Evolution gave us the diversity of humans that populate the Earth," Karla said. "There's no way to know what humanity needs in the future to survive. We should avoid the hubris to believe we can foresee the answer now."

"Hubris. Yes, that is a failing, the belief that one knows what the right path is for everyone. I wonder if I can ever reconcile that question for myself." Lily stared into the distance. "I can't stop thinking about what I've done, and the consequences."

"The world is complex; so much is nonlinear, and no one can predict all the outcomes."

Lily twisted her hands. "But exactly what I feared, the passage of the Levels Acts, happened *because* of me."

She shrugged. "The sympathy vote for Rysbier helped, but it also led to the passage of a constitutional amendment limiting firearms."

Lily rubbed her eyes. "Bad and good can come of everything we do. It's hard to know what's right."

Karla took her hand again. "It's difficult to ever know. But we make our best judgments and go forward. At least, we MacGyvers aren't afraid to act."

Lily sniffled, wiped her cheeks, and smoothed her skirt. "Don't follow my example and wait too long to have children. They are our promise for the future."

"I have hope," Karla said, her voice softening. "We've shown these last years that we can find a way through very many challenges."

"That news is hard to take in. But maybe it reinforces the idea to have another child."

"It's good to be hopeful about the future, and children embody that hope. Do you wish for another boy or a girl? There are embryos enough to decide."

Lily smiled. "We want to have a girl. In fact, with my reading, Wyatt and I have already been discussing names."

"Yes?"

"We're thinking of naming her Evie."

70

Robert sets a plate in front of me. It's a good-tasting stew. Grandfather sits quietly, deep in thought, and plays with his vegetables. He has a small glass of wine, and the synjug rests on the table. I'm eyeing it, hoping he notices.

Robert stands next to the table, its lenses moving back and forth between us. It has said nothing since we got into the autohover.

"Sir, I have served a late dinner, and I shall soon be finished with today's activities and will prepare for tomorrow. Is it now possible to reactivate my recording memory unit? That will make me efficient for the following day's duties."

Grandfather glares at the machine. "Do you recall sending a message to someone just before your memory was disconnected earlier today?"

Robert's forehead glows yellow. "No, sir. With memory recording disconnected, I only hold in short-term cache the prior seven hours' activity."

Grandfather misses nothing, and now I don't miss as much, either. "It must've tattled on us; else that robot cop wouldn't have tried to arrest me."

"That's right." He nods. "It's these software upgrades. Before your father went to the Commune to help your mother, he did a lot to protect privacy. But the price of privacy, democracy, and freedom is eternal vigilance."

The robot still stands there.

"I'm sorry, Robert, but your memory unit will remain disconnected. Every day will be a new beginning for you. Sometimes, it's better to forget."

The robot's forehead glows pink, and it stands against the wall next to Arnold.

Grandfather's soft gaze is on me now. "You've had quite a day. You've seen something of the world outside the Commune. Now, if you're ready, you have some choices to make."

"You mean about not going back? Staying here and going to high school?" My insides are warm after the meal and because he's made the offer. "I'd like to stay with you if you'll have me."

"It would be my pleasure if you'll stay." His eyes are bright.

"Do I need to ask Ma and Pa?"

"Though you aren't legally of age, I think your wishes should weigh heavily. But, yes, we should consult them."

Now I'm thinking of home...the prison, and my life there. "I think my teachbot, Rocky, is like your Robert. He tattles on me and just feeds me what the prison wants me to know. He's another prison guard."

"That's right. Those who control information can leave everyone in a prison of misunderstanding."

"Can I just leave Rocky behind and use Arnold as my teachbot?"

Grandfather chuckles. "Arnold is well qualified to do that. Now, let's call your parents."

He has the holo-com open on the table. Ma's lookin' at me with a less nervous face than I've seen lately, like she's come to terms with something, and Pa's got his arm around her.

"I'm glad you understood the position we found ourselves in earlier today when I called," Grandfather says.

"I could see you needed a wingman. Did you resolve the, uh, complaint?"

"I have taken care of their concerns. Now, though, Grand would like to talk with you."

Ma leans into the holo-com. "Are you okay?" I smile and nod.

I tell Ma and Pa about my day, since I left. It seems a lifetime ago, so there's lots to tell. They ask so many questions, and I tell them about Grandfather's house by the sea and how it has trees and a vineyard, and I like it and about the school and the robot factory and the medical clinic and about Arnold.

"It's time for you to leave the Commune and go to high school," Pa says. Now he studies Grandfather. "Dad, are you sure you can handle a teenage boy for four years?"

"We'll manage. He's a fine young man, and it would be a joy in my old age to have him stay here. We'll have two robots to help us out, including a study robot." Grandfather winks at me.

Ma manages to smile, her face softening. "I'll miss you. But your dad and I talked about it this afternoon. It'll be best for you to start your life out in the world."

Pa looks at Grandfather and rubs his eyes. "Thanks, Dad. You always knew when to act, and action counted for more than words."

There is further talk, and Ma wipes happy tears. She and Pa say they love me, and we sign off.

Grandfather asks Robert to serve the dessert, a little cake it baked. We sit in the big comfortable chairs in the living room in front of the window, and Grandfather brings the synjug. The window is open, and a soft wind rustles the trees. I'm thirsty and eyeing the synjug again.

"Why not? Here, let's celebrate." Grandfather pours me a glass. I'm learning that he's a rebel and reminds me of me. The first taste is tart like before, but it goes down smooth.

"Grandfather, I'm glad Arnold can be my teaching friend."

"Me too." He takes a drink.

"Do you still have any friends?"

"Not many now. But my best friend Buzz and his wife Jessica live nearby. Buzz stops by here every week, and we catch up on old times."

The stories of the two of them traipsin' around the world were some of the most adventurous, and I hope to find a friend like that someday.

"You and Buzz made a difference in the world."

Grandfather sips his wine. "It isn't about what each of us achieves individually. But what does count is how we influence everyone around us to move humanity forward collectively. That alone is worth doing." He is deep in thought. "It's the commons, the property of all humankind, that needs our attention."

We drink our wine, and I think through the family story he told. "You've lived through interesting times."

"Ha! The old Chinese curse. And the world just goes faster all the time."

"Are you happy how it's turned out?" Now, I feel warm, and the wine makes me drowsy, but I like hearing his stories.

"What can I say? Somehow, we made it through a tough century. We met many challenges and missed others. I'm glad we didn't kick many down the road. The only way ahead is to solve problems, to act, to stay the course."

My head is woozy. I'm tired, and my eyes want to close. Grandfather sits there in the big chair next to me, lookin' like he's thinkin' deep thoughts. The room is cozy, and Grandfather and I are happy, and it will all be all right.

71

He drains the glass and sets it on the side table. His chin tilts onto his chest, and hot guilt rises in my throat for the subterfuge. Will he look back fondly on this evening, believing I gave him his first drink to remember the day? It's the opposite, really. To have him not know the truth. I just don't have the strength to reveal his secret to him. Soon, we can all lapse into forgetfulness.

His eyes close, and he starts to doze. This is the time to whisper the truth.

"Humanity somehow bumbled through and still survives. But not everyone does so well. Many suffer. That includes some of our family, and that includes you, dear Grand.

"Rysbier ordered that they alter your DNA, to bioengineer your germ line cells, and to leave you infertile. You can't have children. And, at least with today's technology, it's not possible to reverse that. What Rysbier did to you in utero broke the ultimate rule that we need to protect ourselves from ourselves, to outlaw genetic changes that can pass to future generations."

His eyes are still closed, and I taste the bitter wine in my glass.

Now I've said it to finish this part of his story. It's the part of our family story that hurts most deeply since Karla revealed it to me at Tadala's funeral. That's why I moved to the vineyard by the sea. The consolation for that family calamity is the law that she championed, forbidding it to happen again. I can only hope for his sake that sometime in his life the technology improves, and he can have children, if he wishes.

The last secret for him is one he will find on his own—that equality of opportunity remains outside our grasp. The Levels Acts leave him with a low Level because he was born in prison and because of history prior to any of his own actions. It will take another hero to free our country of that inequality. Perhaps he'll be along for the fight.

Outside the window, the moon rises above the ocean and casts a silvery glow into the room. I nurse the last of the wine and wonder when I'll be taken up to the swallow-thronged loft, as the old poem says. Not for at least another four years.

The thought of that four years ahead makes me happy. Just this one day has been cleansing after all the years of holding these secrets inside.

Maybe telling the family story today of rising to meet the challenges of a difficult century has let me relive the positive battles we waged. A hundred years is a whole lot of living. Given how much faster our pace of life is because of our technology, maybe I should be surprised that much has remained stable, with human beings still the creative, competitive, irascible creatures descended from apes but rising to a higher level because of our care for one another.

Humanity is better for having solved many problems. We vanquished existential threats. We improved so many lives. Maybe we are better people than a century ago.

We have a caste system of Levels that has left us with an oligarchy, but maybe that will change in time. Our collective record this last century is not stellar, but somehow, we muddled through, meeting many of the greatest challenges. Maybe we are on the path to a far better world together.

Robert stirs. "I believe you no longer need my services. Goodnight, sir."

Arnold has also shifted his head toward me, so it must be midnight, when the bots' internal clocks signal.

"Goodnight, sir."

They both move into the utility room. Grand opens his eyes, peaceful at the edge of slumber. He can hear me again, and an old man cannot be stopped from giving advice.

"Never forget, Eloy McGyver, my Grand, protect the commons or all ends in tragedy. It's the only way for humankind to survive."

His gaze is on mine, a contented smile on his face. "I'll remember—protect the commons."

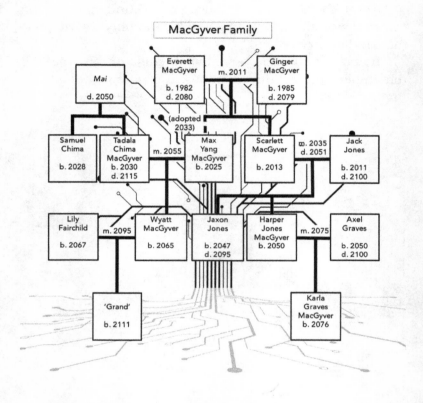

MacGyver Family

GLOSSARY

Source: Vidsnap from Netpedia, 2125, 0526 11:31 UTC

AGI (Artificial General Intelligence)—Defined sparsely as a computer software AI capable of performing "general intelligent action." Within the field of philosophy, the "strong AGI" definition is reserved for machines capable of experiencing a subjective conscious experience.

Multiple definitions of AGI have existed from the beginning of the twenty-first century, including:

1) a type of AI that could learn to accomplish any intellectual task human beings or animals can perform or surpass human capabilities in the majority of economically valuable tasks.

2) an intelligence that is not specialized in any particular task, but rather has the ability to outperform humans at nearly any economically valuable work. The key characteristic of AGI is its capacity for generalization and adaptation across a wide range of tasks and domains.

3) an intelligence that is broadly intelligent, context-aware, and able to adapt to open-ended environments, in contrast to narrow AI systems that are specialized for specific tasks.

4) an intelligence that is capable of running an entire organization on its own without human input. This stage is an AI that can perform better than humans across every task and requires the abilities to reason, to act independently, to create innovative content unaided, and to possess broad intelligence.

Two primary human fears surround the attainment of AGI by a machine. First is the fear that achieving "strong AGI" leads to the replacement of humans and, at a minimum, the need to address moral and ethical responsibilities to AGIs as fellow sentient or conscious creations. Second is the fear that AGIs will replace most human jobs.

Regarding the second fear, perhaps a useful working definition would be that a **practical economic AGI is a computer AI, deployed with ecological validity in economic settings that is recognized as consistently performing, unaided by any human, a reasonably complete set of capabilities superior to those possessed by an intelligent 25-year-old educated person.** Capabilities include the ability to learn and adapt goals in a dynamic environment.

The definition of practical economic AGI focuses on the fear of human economic displacement. Such an AGI would fall between definitions for a "Competent AGI" and an "Expert AGI" that is deployed (in the form of a robot) with ecological validity for the workplace. (See Google DeepMind "Levels of AGI"—https://arxiv.org/abs/2311.02462.) Central to this definition is the realization of an economic AGI that does not require humans, even for oversight duties.

AI (Artificial Intelligence)—A simulation of human intelligence processes by a machine, as computational software. The AI refers to the software code, which may reside in cloud servers, PIDAs, and inside robots as the "brain."

allbook— A connected reading and learning device that presents text and rich video content. Through the twenty-first century, it became a platform to distribute free educational material.

ARMO (Augmented Reality Map Overlay)—Loaded in a personal communication device, such as a PAWN or a CLAIR, the ARMO traces a map onto a display lens interface so the user can follow the map while walking.

autonomous sub (or autonomous underwater vehicle, AUV)—A robot that travels underwater without requiring continuous input from an operator, AUVs can be used for commercial, research, and military purposes.

autocar or AV (autonomous vehicle)—A vehicle controlled by an AI early in the twenty-first century, also known as a self-driving car.

autohover—Standard aircraft for short-haul transport, controlled by an AI, introduced to replace helicopters in the mid-twenty-first century.

BioBricks—Standardized DNA sequences used in synthetic biology. These parts conform to a restriction-enzyme assembly standard, allowing them to be combined into synthetic biological circuits and incorporated into living cells.

biometric ID tile—An electronic device embedded in the skin above the sternum that authenticates the wearer via combined biological and behavioral biometric data, providing a secure password.

blockchain token—A digital asset that represents ownership rights or utility within a blockchain network. Tokens enable the secure transfer and tracking of digital ownership, empowering individuals to possess and control their digital assets in a decentralized manner.

brain–computer interface (BCI)—A device that allows the human brain to communicate with and control external software or hardware, for example, a PIDA, a computer, or robotic limb.

challenges of the century ahead—Arguably nine of the most difficult challenges facing humanity in the century ahead are:
1. Avoiding widescale nuclear war.
2. Mitigating climate change.
3. Dealing with migration of peoples, especially migration driven by climate change.
4. Dealing with the lack of jobs for people, driven by the proliferation of AI and robotics.

5. Deciding how market economic systems likely need to evolve, and to what new form, driven by the wholesale automation of production.
6. Protecting individual privacy from erosion, as technology permits ubiquitous data collection.
7. Keeping the information commons open and free, yet uncontaminated. In the information age, the question centers on who should control information (private corporations, governments, or individuals), and how to ensure that the choices do not erode individual speech and freedom.
8. Protecting democracy, as information control impedes free public discourse and choice.
9. Deciding and enforcing limits to engineering of the human germline genome.

Note: The portrait of outcomes described herein are not all the best outcomes, but in many cases act as warnings of possible scenarios if decisive action is not taken in time.

Climate Wars—Wars spanning a decade around the turn of the twenty-second century that erupted over diminishing food, water, and arable land resources.

(the) commons and the tragedy of the commons—A wide range of shared assets form the commons. The economic theory of a tragedy was first conceptualized in 1833 by British writer William Forster Lloyd and is a situation in which individuals with access to a public resource act in their own interest and, in doing so, ultimately deplete the resource.

communication devices—Personal communication devices evolved during the twenty-first century with multiple generations of devices. Beginning with smart phones, the devices became smaller, smarter, incorporated AI and PIDA (personal intelligent digital assistant) software, connected seamlessly to the net and other devices, and incorporated new connection approaches, such as smart contact lenses replacing screens, and later, corneal implants and embedded chips. The evolution of personal communication devices is given here. Variations of PAWN, HASP, and CLAIR competed during the century, each adding features and shedding weight, leading to ubiquitous twenty-second-century versions incorporating embedded biochips and corneal implants.

HASP—An early twenty-first-century wearable communication device containing an AI chip. The screenless device operated via voice command, touch, or pinch motion.

PAWN—A wearable communication device, introduced in the twenty-first century and evolving through several generations, first resembling a pair of twentieth-century eyeglasses but becoming less visible and intrusive with each new model.

PAWN incorporated augmented reality (such as an augmented reality map overlay, or ARMO), interaction with the net, and private chat features. User interaction with the device included input via hand movement (e.g., pinch) and output via projection onto lens surfaces and contact lenses. The acronym derives from the features of a Phone, an AI assistant, that is Wearable, and that provides Net access.

CLAIR—Corneal Link and AI Repository—A late twenty-first-century embedded communication device improving on the earlier PAWN technologies. The device includes a PIDA, uses various input modes and outputs high-resolution images to corneal inserts that double as a net display and an augmented reality interface.

creative destruction—A concept in economics that describes a process in which new innovations replace and make older innovations obsolete. Identified by Joseph Schumpeter, referring to the linked processes of the accumulation and annihilation of wealth, characterized as a driving force of capitalism.

**credit$ and dark credit$**—Cryptocurrency using blockchain and rolling anti-quantum decryption technology. Dark credit$ are not sanctioned by the government but are widely used globally to avoid data collection.

digital twin—A virtual real-time model of a physical object. Digital twins in medicine may assist with disease diagnosis and treatment and research. Digital twins in manufacturing systems can be used for monitoring, analyzing, and optimizing actual systems. An AI digital twin that replicates a person might mimic their personality traits, preferences, and decision-making patterns, allowing it to take actions that align with how the person would respond in various situations.

DREADD (Designer Receptors Exclusively Activated by Designer Drug)—Engineered protein used in neuroscience and in chemogenetics to selectively control cellular activity. The technology allows researchers to manipulate specific cell populations in living organisms, and cellular activity can be modulated on demand by administering the designer drug, allowing for precise temporal control.

futures studies—The systematic study of how people will live in the future. Also known as strategic foresight, the discipline's best practices emphasize scientific, rigorous, and precise forecasts with assigned probabilities and time frames based on holistic research. Within science fiction, a forerunner related idea was demonstrated in Isaac Asimov's *Foundation* Series, in which the character Hari Seldon developed a theory of psychohistory, a mathematics of sociology to predict the future of large populations.

Chaos theory in mathematics, which developed beginning about the same time in the 1960s, suggests that large systems are inherently nonlinear. Chaos theory and complexity science suggest that a theory of psychohistory is impossible. Long time-scale predictions are doomed to failure.

Notwithstanding this apparent fact of the universe, people still try. Rigorous futurists generally limit forecasts to short periods. A dozen examples of predictions that reach beyond the defensible time frames—in the realm of science fiction—are given below.

1. By midcentury, some entirely new personal communication devices to replace smart phones will be adopted by more than half the global population. Communication devices will incorporate chips and sensors embedded in the human body, allowing seamless operation.

2. Within the next one hundred years, significant improvements will appear in transportation. While systems will be integrated with AI and automated dispatching, general air transport will remain mostly subsonic. Flying cars will not be popular.

3. By midcentury, over three-fourths of all US long-distance trucking will be handled by autonomous trucks without a human driver in the vehicle. Jobs for truck drivers will remain for another two decades, primarily focused on the "last mile" within cities.

4. By midcentury, developed nations will have instituted individualized AI-driven health systems to monitor health, predict illness, and provide care.

5. Before the end of the twenty-first century, fighter airplanes will be autonomous for the forces of the three leading military powers, and no human fighter pilots will be trained.

6. No AI or robotic system before the year 2075 will reach "practical economic AGI" or be recognized as consistently performing, unaided by any human, a reasonably complete set of capabilities equivalent to those possessed by an intelligent 25-year-old educated person. While AIs will astonish us with many insights and intelligent responses across many topics, humans will not trust these AIs to independently manage

activities as much as they do a typical 25-year-old educated human. Therefore, the AIs by this definition will not advance beyond human general intelligence.

7. No AI or robotic system will reach "strong AGI" within the next one hundred years.

8. Within a century, pets with bioengineered features will be legal and acceptable, but subject to regulation.

9. Within the twenty-first century, the game of professional American football will disappear due to its decline in high school and college sports, driven by concerns about chronic traumatic encephalopathy (CTE) injuries.

10. Within the twenty-first century, a new US sport will become more popular than baseball and American football.

11. The use of neural implants for personal communication devices will be developed but will not be deployed and used by over 5 percent of the population by century-end, even in developed countries.

12. Non-invasive neural readers, capable of reading some emotional states, will be deployed by century-end.

hacker—A person skilled in information technology who achieves goals by non-standard means. A **white hat hacker** is an ethical security hacker. A **black hat hacker** is a hacker who violates laws or ethical standards for nefarious purposes.

HDSET—A twenty-first-century device, worn on the head, that provides mixed reality and an immersive experience. Multiple versions were introduced over decades, which progressively became less intrusive, blending the actual world with the net and VR to provide communication and information retrieval, 3D entertainment, and productivity benefits.

holo-com—Holographic light field display used as a communication device, allowing 3D videoconferencing.

holo-display—Holographic light field display device used to present 3D manipulable images and information from the net. Similar to a holo-com, it is primarily used for information retrieval, display, and manipulation.

human germline editing—The process of making genetic modifications to human reproductive cells (eggs, sperm, or early embryos) that would be passed on to future generations, which leaves such techniques controversial because of safety risks and the potential for unintended multigenerational effects.

hyperlev—An advanced train using maglev technology, faster than the maglev train.

ITER—the International Thermonuclear Experimental Reactor, an international megaproject that built a test tokamak fusion reactor to demonstrate the feasibility of fusion energy in the early twenty-first century.

Levels Acts—Laws enacted in the early twenty-second century, developed as the *quid pro quo* for the nationalization of economic production. The Acts set Levels (i.e., from Level 1, the highest, to Level 99, the lowest), which assist in assigning jobs and setting certain restrictions on voting, travel, social interactions, and access to sponsored creative positions.

maglev—A train using magnetic levitation technology, which uses sets of magnets to push the train off the track, and to then move the "floating train" at high speeds to its destination; a predecessor to the faster hyperlev train.

MEDFLOW—A medical unit implanted beneath the skin, typically above the right hip, that monitors health and dispenses drugs into the bloodstream based on a programmed protocol.

milspec—A military standard used to achieve standardization objectives, including interoperability of equipment.

MAOA gene—A gene that codes for monoamine oxidase A. A point mutation in this gene was associated with several diseases, including Brunner syndrome and certain psychiatric disorders linked to aggression. The paradigm of behavioral research shifted against linking single genes to complex behavioral traits, and an earlier characterization of the mutation as indicating a "warrior gene" has been deemed incorrect.

Moore's Law—The observation that the number of transistors on an integrated circuit roughly doubles every two years.

net—Formerly named the internet, an electronic communication system spanning the Earth and the space bases.

NPC—Non-player character, found in gaming, usually referring to a character controlled by the computer.

PIDA (Personal Intelligent Digital Assistant)—An AI residing in a HASP, PAWN, or CLAIR, allowing verbal input and connection to display devices. The PIDA is personalized based on the user's personality, usage, and daily habits. Users frequently anthropomorphized their PIDAs, although the units never reached strong AGI during the century.

Princess Kandake—Kandake was the royal title for queens of the ancient kingdom of Kush in east central Africa. One fictionalized legend speaks of a Princess Kandake who opposed Alexander the Great, preventing his conquest of Nubia. She appeared on the battlefield mounted on a war elephant while leading her army, and he turned away, preferring to go to Egypt instead.

quantum computing—A quantum computer is a type of computer that makes use of quantum mechanics to perform operations, which can solve certain problems far more efficiently, and some that classical computers cannot solve.

robots containing an AI:

> **medbot**—A specialized robot augmented with medical devices for surgery and general health care.

> **copbot**—A robot used for police work. Initial designs were introduced in the twenty-second century.

> **exoskeleton**—An external skeleton or support structure worn by a human that enhances strength. While the rig includes AI chips for refining control, the human operator's movements directly control the device.

> **firebot**—A robot used to fight fires, used in situations considered dangerous for humans, and often dropped into forest fires via aircraft.

slim drip—Weight reduction and control medication, typically microdosed via a MEDFLOW unit.

smart object—A digital representation of a physical entity enhanced with computing, sensors, and connectivity. Part of the Internet of Things (IoT) ecosystem, they can bridge the gap between digital applications and the physical world.

synjug—A synthetic biology jug, which is a biodegradable container used to hold various liquids.

synpsychs—Synthetic biology psychotropics and other mind-altering pharmacology.

synthetic biology—A field of science that focuses on living systems and organisms, and it applies engineering principles to develop new biological parts, devices, and systems.

Three Laws of Robotics—Introduced in Isaac Asimov's *Robot* series, the Three Laws are:

Law 1: A robot may not injure a human being or, through inaction, allow a human being to come to harm.

Law 2: A robot must obey the orders given it by human beings, except where such orders would conflict with the First Law.

Law 3: A robot must protect its own existence as long as such protection does not conflict with the First or Second Laws.

Addendum (added in the last century): A robot must protect other robots' survival, so long as such protection does not violate the first three laws.

von Mises's economic calculation problem—The question of how individual subjective values are translated into the objective information necessary for rational allocation of resources in society. Economist Ludwig Heinrich Edler von Mises (1881–1973) described the nature of the price system under capitalism, arguing that economic calculation is only possible by information provided through market prices.

Wikipedia—A multilingual online encyclopedia created and maintained as an open collaboration project. Created in the early twenty-first century by Jimmy Wales and Larry Sanger, the net resource continues as a trusted source of information, miraculously avoiding censorship and the politicization that affected many other information sources. Wikipedia was renamed Netpedia circa 2125. Many definitions therein have become the default standard summaries of certain information. The original Wikipedia entries in this vidsnap include portions of those for AUV, creative destruction, hacker, ITER, MAOA gene, smart object, synthetic biology, Three Laws of Robotics, human germline engineering, Moore's Law, and von Mises's economic calculation problem.

Acknowledgments

I shall begin with kudos and thanks and then explain how *Journey to 2125* came about.

Let me thank those who have been especially helpful in creating this novel. Thanks to my outstanding editors, Cynthia Bengier, Brooke Bengier, Kelci Lowery Bengier, and Jennifer Della'Zanna. Thanks to my book cover designer, Sienny Thio, and my layout designer, Inès Monnet, the great team now for three books in eight languages. Kudos to friends who didn't tire of hearing about the future, read early versions of the book, and provided helpful comments. And always, my deepest thanks to my wife Cynthia for supporting this project with her suggestions and editorial help, and her love.

Cynthia didn't want me to write another novel after the speculative fiction novel *Unfettered Journey*. For a while, I had promised not to become mired in the hard, reflective work of producing another.

But I realized that most people are not focused on the greatest threats facing humanity brought on by the accelerating pace of technology. The twenty-first century poses distinct challenges to *homo sapiens*. The world is changing faster than our psychological ability to come to terms with it. Our old methods and pace of problem-solving are inadequate to meet the challenge.

Identifiable technologies will cause exponential change in how we live. Unfortunately, many futurists make grandiose assertions of change unencumbered by the practical realities of engineering the future. They spin utopian or apocalyptic scenarios, sounding more like science fiction than thoughtful forecasts. The average person is left to throw up their hands and await their fate.

While popular futurists claim the limelight, the academic, rigorous field of foresight has gained practitioners. These experts try to plan by demanding measurement and accountability in predictions. They methodically collect information from experts in many fields and work to make their field scientific. We would benefit if these voices were better known.

Bold claims push attention toward the wrong challenges. A better approach is to sort through the most likely risks, rank them, and boldly set out to ameliorate them.

To paraphrase Hemingway, change occurs slowly and then suddenly. Many futurists are wrong because they do not account for the practical problems of engineering, of building the technology. They fail to account for the social and psychological changes needed to allow technology to become commonplace, and so they often prophesize a too-early embrace of technology. But we must also recognize that technology invades our lives as spies in battalions, and suddenly we accept technology that previously was inconceivable. The most difficult game for anyone thinking about the future is to envision these details. To better imagine the future, we must make concrete hypotheses, and then grade ourselves. Science progresses by hypothesis, experiment, challenge, and then revised hypothesis, and futurists should abide by the same discipline.

Unfettered Journey conceived a future circa 2161, far enough in the future to more readily imagine how the broad trends in technology may play out. (That was the reason for placing that novel then.) Setting aside plot devices, the novel attempted to highlight concerns for the farther future.

Accepting these caveats, this novel serves as the prequel to fill in a hard-science view of the century+ between now and the novel *Unfettered Journey*. Let me thank the fans who asked for it and encouraged this writing. Thanks to the unnamed futurists who wrote scenarios that elicited disappointment, because their views seem to be so wrong. I will be wrong, but I think less wrong than others. This novel is still speculative fiction (as well as parts political fiction and family saga), with the limitations of fiction. It takes a page from the foresight practitioners, using a scientific approach, painting a future world more likely to be manifest (or, to point out the biggest challenges facing humanity, scenarios we must work to avoid).

The universe is nonlinear; therefore, all predictions will be wrong. Intermediate-term predictions, such as what may happen within the next century, are even more problematic about the details. Foresight practitioners are reluctant to reach beyond a few decades. *Journey to 2125: One Century, One Family, Rising to Challenges* goes beyond, and so does speculative fiction.

Though our forecasts will be wrong in the details and inevitably miss significant events, we can be sure that the next century will be unusually challenging. That burden falls on our grandchildren today. We wish them luck. They need to deal with it.

About the Author

Gary F. Bengier is a writer, philosopher, and technologist.

After a career in Silicon Valley, Gary pursued passion projects, studying astrophysics and philosophy. He's spent the last two decades thinking about how to live a balanced, meaningful life in a rapidly evolving technological world. This self-reflective journey infuses his novels, *Journey to 2125: One Century, One Family, Rising to Challenges* and *Unfettered Journey*, with insights about our future and the challenges we will face in finding purpose.

Before turning to writing speculative fiction, Gary worked in a variety of Silicon Valley tech companies. He was eBay's Chief Financial Officer and led the company's initial and secondary public offerings. Gary has an MBA from Harvard Business School and an MA in philosophy from San Francisco State University. He has two children with Cynthia, his wife of forty-seven years. When not traveling the world, he raises bees and makes a nice Cabernet at the family's Napa vineyard. He and his family live in San Francisco.

Journey to 2125 is the prequel to another book in this two-book series. Learn more about the other book, *Unfettered Journey.*

Details at
Garyfbengier.com

Found at Amazon, Ingram,
and wherever you buy books.

Barnes & Noble

Apple Books

Kobo

IndieBound – Bookshop.org

Printed in the USA
CPSIA information can be obtained
at www.ICGtesting.com
CBHW020542131124
17218CB00003B/10

9 781648 861147